THE SHAPES OF STRANGERS

THE SHAPES OF STRANGERS
Ian Creasey

NEWCON
PRESS

NewCon Press
England

First edition, published in the UK April 2019
by NewCon Press

NCP 184 (hardback)
NCP 185 (softback)

10 9 8 7 6 5 4 3 2 1

Cover art by Vincent Sammy
Cover layout by Ian Whates

Edited by Ian Whates
Interior layout by Storm Constantine

CONTENTS

INTRODUCTION

The stories in this collection first appeared in various magazines and anthologies between 2007 and 2018. I'd like to thank all the editors who initially bought the pieces, and in particular Trevor Quachri at *Analog* and Sheila Williams at *Asimov's* for their ongoing support of my work. A complete list of the original publication venues can be found in the copyright notices elsewhere in this book.

My thanks also go to Ian Whates at NewCon Press for proposing this collection and shepherding it to publication. In an era when short fiction often feels overshadowed by enormous novels and endless series, we should treasure those publishers who offer opportunities to writers working in more obscure niches of the literary ecosystem.

Many people – too many to thank individually – critiqued draft versions of these stories. I'm grateful to the members of Critters, Codex, and NorthwriteSF for their feedback. Special thanks go to S.P. Wilcock for wide-ranging discussions about all aspects of writing.

The commentaries that follow each story, explaining the inspirations and influences behind them, are distilled from the background notes first written for my website – www.iancreasey.com – where you can find information about all my published fiction.

Ian Creasey
Yorkshire
September 2018

AFTER THE ATROCITY

It's twenty minutes since the duplicator's last glitch, so I ask one of the guards outside to fetch me lunch, hoping that for once I might be able to eat it uninterrupted by urgent repair work. "Yes, Miss Ruiz," he says as he salutes. I don't have a rank or a uniform – just a lab coat – but they still salute me. At first I found it endearing; now it just reminds me how much I miss Caltech, where nobody ever salutes anyone.

While I wait for my meal, I watch the crawlers assemble the body of Abu Hameed. This copy – the ninth – is nearly finished. Each copy has appeared quicker than the last: I've improved the duplicator's speed, at the price of needing more operator oversight.

The workbench is electroplated with gold, a non-reactive metal that shines under the lab's fluorescent lights. Abu Hameed's naked body lies directly on the bench, but it's not uncomfortable for him because he isn't alive yet. And no one cares about his comfort anyway, not since he killed ten thousand people in the Atrocity.

His ribs stand out from his chest, and his wild beard needs a trim. His eyes are closed, but nevertheless he looks like he might leap off the bench at any moment. I shiver. To calm myself, I move the high-grade cutter torch to my desk, within easy reach. I feel safer knowing I can fire a lethal bolt into his heart.

Lunch arrives. The smell of a burger and fries is a welcome antidote to the duplicator's acrid tang. The tray has a selection of sauce sachets: this is what passes for menu variety at the base. I'm just about to choose a mustard when the door opens.

"Sophie Bryant to see you, Miss," the guard announces.

A tall black woman walks in, wearing a jacket and skirt more colourful than any of the base's military uniforms.

"You're the lawyer?" I ask. "I'm Violeta Ruiz."

She nods, and extends her hand for me to shake. "Pleased to meet you. I do have my own office, you know. Why did you insist on someone coming here? This is a classified lab. I was the only lawyer who could get clearance."

I point at the nearly-complete copy of Abu Hameed on the

workbench. "I want advice from someone who knows what's going on, and isn't just rubber-stamping something they haven't seen."

I pause to take a few bites of food, wondering how best to phrase my doubts. I vividly remember waking up on the same gold bench as Abu Hameed's latest copy. The duplicator is so important that it needs to run twenty-four hours a day, with an operator on constant standby to resolve glitches and improve speed. I'd copied myself to create an additional operator. The military would never have entrusted their most important prisoner to the duplicator without seeing that proof of concept.

The experience of being copied has given me a sharper sense of empathy. And the more copies of Abu Hameed that I make, the more sinister it feels. I don't know where they all go, but I presume they aren't forming a choir.

"I'm worried about what's happening to these copies," I say. "Whatever it is, I'm facilitating it. I don't want to be party to anything illegal."

"There's no need to worry." Bryant gestures to Abu Hameed and says, "I'm his lawyer. It's my job to make sure he's treated appropriately."

"He has a lawyer?" I ask, surprised. I've never seen Bryant when the collection team comes to take finished copies away.

"Of course he does. This is the United States of America – we have a constitution and a legal system. Detainees get lawyers," she says proudly. I half expect her to show me her diploma.

The lunches come in large portions for soldiers' appetites. I've eaten as much as my calorie app recommends, so I drop the rest of the food into the duplicator's intake hopper. I always find it ironic that the anti-American terrorist is made out of all-American burgers.

"That's why I'm here," Bryant adds. "I was cleared to enter this lab because I already know there are copies of him."

"So you must know what's happening to them," I say.

She doesn't reply, and I remember that the detainee's official designation is only Prisoner 75832. "I know who he is," I tell her. "He's the most famous terrorist on the planet! There's no need to be coy about it. They're interrogating him, right?"

"Obviously," says Bryant.

"It must be hard going, if they need so many copies."

"He's a hard guy," she says, her face an impassive mask.

She's not going to volunteer anything, so I'm forced to come straight out with the question that's been nagging at me. "Is he being tortured?"

"Of course not!" she snaps. "Torture is illegal. There are interrogation protocols, and I make sure everything's done by the book."

"Sounds like a lot of work," I say. "When this copy's finished, there'll be nine altogether – plus the original. Do you attend every interrogation?"

"They're all recorded," Bryant says, her voice rising in anger. "I can watch any session I like. Don't accuse me of not doing my job!"

"All right, all right," I say. "Keep your voice down." The original Violeta is asleep in the back room. She has a heck of a temper, and I don't want her blaming me for waking her up. We argue quite enough already.

"Keep my voice down?" Bryant points to the motionless Abu Hameed. "What, am I interrupting his beauty sleep? My God, get your priorities straight! Whose side are you on? There are terrorist plots we need to uncover. There could be a ticking bomb, a bioweapon, a nuclear meltdown... Don't you worry about him!"

"Someone's got to," I say, barely restraining myself from adding *even if his lawyer doesn't*. I suppose the job falls to me, since I'm the only other person in the world who knows what it's like to be a copy.

"Does he get visits from the Red Cross?" I ask. "Or the Red Crescent, or whatever it is."

"You don't need to know that."

"I guess not. But right now I'm working round the clock to copy him. It's tiring and stressful; I'm practically burnt out. Maybe I'll slow down a little, take it easy..." I reach for my Diet Coke and suck a long, leisurely slurp through the straw.

Bryant purses her lips and glowers at me. "If you must know, the original is dead. And the duplicator's classified, so obviously we can't have Red Cross visitors seeing all these identical copies."

"The original's dead?" I exclaim. "So much for 'protocols' and 'by the book'! Or is that the final chapter?"

"It was an accident," Bryant says. "Obviously no one wanted to kill our most important prisoner."

"Obviously," I say, since it seems to be her favourite word.

She gives me a withering look. "Is there anything else, or have we finished? After all, as you point out, I do have a lot of work to do."

Even though Bryant isn't in uniform, she's part of the system. She's not going to rock the boat.

"We've finished," I say. "Thanks for coming. Please send me written confirmation of your advice."

After she's gone, I wonder whether I should have pressed her harder about the death of the original Abu Hameed. If the original had died, rather than one of the copies I'd made, then it wasn't my responsibility... or was it?

Maybe the duplicator makes the interrogators reckless. They can go as far as they like, knowing he's easily replaceable. There's always another copy on the workbench.

How far do they go? What are the authorised procedures? Bryant said it's not torture, because torture is illegal. So if it's by the book, it can't be torture.

I'm not convinced by this sophistry, or Bryant's legal sign-off. My work is top secret; the only lawyers who know what's happening are those most trusted by the military, and least likely to object.

A beep from the duplicator breaks my chain of thought. I spend half an hour debugging the latest glitch. Building the copy's brain is the final part of the process, and the most delicate.

The door opens without warning. I know who it is. He visits often enough that the guards no longer bother to announce him.

Derek Cole is so pale that he might have inhabited the base all his life, never seeing the sun. He keeps his hair cropped with a tight buzzcut, barely exposing its ginger colour. A few freckles dot his head like spots on a misshapen dice.

"Good news!" His voice always sounds as if he's shouting orders across a battlefield. "The final delivery has arrived, so we've got all the parts you need. You can start building another duplicator to relieve the bottleneck. Though I still don't understand why you can't just print another duplicator out of this one."

"I told you, it's optimised for organic material – people, not machinery. There is a difference." Before he can start complaining, I say, "It'll take a while to build a second duplicator and calibrate it. Do you want me to prioritise that, or keep making copies of the prisoner?"

"You can do both, can't you? Just print some extra copies of yourself."

I flinch. Having one duplicate is bad enough. We keep arguing about what'll happen when we return to California: which of us will get my apartment, my job, my friends, my life. Dividing it all between even more copies would be nightmarish.

"Absolutely not," I say. "You're already getting two for the price of one."

He frowns. "All right, I'll send you some engineers. You can begin the duplicator after you've finished this." Cole points to the body on the workbench. "When will it be ready?"

"About five o'clock," I say, deliberately using civilian time. The original Violeta has started saying "17.00" like everyone else in the base.

"I'll tell the collection team," he says.

"What are you doing with these guys?" I ask. "What happens to them all?"

Cole shakes his head. "You don't need to know that."

"Maybe I do," I say. "You always want these copies as quickly as possible. How long do you keep them for? If you, um, *dispose* of them after a week, I could cut some corners in the internal organs."

I hate myself for coming up with that suggestion, but I need to get him talking.

"Don't cut corners," says Cole. "The copies need to be absolutely identical."

"Why?" I demand. "I can do a better job if I know what you're trying to achieve."

He pauses, absently rubbing his neck. "That's a good point," he says at last. "I suppose it won't hurt to give you an outline, since you already know the classified part." The duplicator became top secret when DARPA noticed my work at Caltech and realised the implications.

Cole sits in the other Violeta's chair and says, "It's simple, really. When we capture prisoners, we need information. The problem is that we don't know whether they're telling the truth. No matter how far we go, we can never be sure how much is true. At least, we can't when we only have one person to interrogate. But if we have copies of the same suspect, and we question them separately..."

I grasp his point. "If they say different things, they must be lying."

13

"Obviously!"

"But why do you need so many copies?" I ask. "Surely as soon as you get a consistent message out of a couple of them, you know you're on the right track."

He smiles at my naïvety. "It's not that easy. These guys are terrorists at constant risk of being captured. They have cover stories, and stories inside the cover stories. When they're under pressure, they'll admit they were lying, then change to another lie."

"How do you get past that?"

"More pressure," he says. "Eventually, the cover story runs out. When they exhaust what they've prepared beforehand, they invent details that start to differ. But it takes time to get to that point."

"Especially if they don't want to talk," I comment.

Cole chuckles knowingly. "Even the truth isn't constant. When you tell an anecdote, I bet you don't tell it the same way twice."

"I suppose you minimise unwanted variation by using a uniform sample and a constant procedure," I say. Now I understand why Abu Hameed's copies have to be identical. And they don't even know that they're copies, so they don't have my existential angst to distort their fidelity to the original.

"Practice makes perfect! We're getting results, and it's all down to you." Cole grins at me, like a proud soccer coach for whom I've scored a goal. "You've made interrogation reliable. When this is over and your gadget's declassified, I'll nominate you for a medal."

He gestures to the duplicator. "When you build the next one of these, can it be faster?"

"Not if you want the copies to be identical. It's not a trivial task to make an exact replica." I trot out my standard gee-whiz fact: "There are seven octillion atoms in the human body – that's seven billion billion billion. It's a big job to put all those together in the right order. Building a person takes time, and I'm running out of short-cuts. You can't make a baby in one month by getting nine women pregnant."

"I guess not, but you can have a lot of fun trying." Cole laughs, and heads for the door. On his way out, he waves at Abu Hameed's body. "See you later!"

When the door closes behind him, I slump onto my desk, hating what I've got myself into. I can't stop thinking about Cole's words.

More pressure. His phrase echoes in my head, sounding creepier every time.

I didn't accuse Cole of torture because I knew he'd only deny it like Bryant. But surely that's what it amounts to.

I've invented a machine that makes torture reliable. And I'm operating it twenty-four hours a day.

It'll never stop. Even if they squeeze Abu Hameed dry, they'll still want more copies to use for training new interrogators and testing new techniques. In future there'll be other prisoners, as the war on terror continues its glacial course, grinding everyone in its path. I don't care about getting a medal "when this is over", not least because I can't imagine it ever being over.

"I want to go home," I say, out loud. "I want to see my friends. I want to get dressed up and go to roller disco."

I signed a twelve-month contract. At least, my original did. What will happen after our stint, when we both want to go home? The lawyer said that Abu Hameed's copies aren't getting Red Cross visits because that would be a security breach, revealing the duplicator.

What about me? Will they let me go home? Will I ever leave this base?

I take deep breaths, trying to calm myself. Surely the duplicator will be declassified eventually. Surely they won't treat me the same way they treat terrorists...

Yet I'm dodging responsibility if I think it's how *they* treat terrorists, as if I'm not part of that. Cole's interrogation programme wouldn't work without my assembly line of victims.

I look at the workbench where the crawlers are building Abu Hameed's brain, with all its sensory neurons and pain receptors. I've created him specifically to be tortured. It sickens me to think that I'm creating people solely to suffer, people who would surely beg me to stop.

What can I do? I could break the duplicator, but that would only be a temporary hitch. If I refuse to repair it, they'll bring someone else in. It'll be fixed eventually. Then more legions of Abu Hameed will march into the torture chamber...

... Unless I delete his data. The original Abu Hameed is dead. The current body on the bench isn't finished, so it can't be used as another starting point. And the previous copies have already been interrogated, so they're no longer a clean sample. If I delete the scan data, no one can make any fresh copies of him, even if the duplicator itself still functions.

Deleting data is usually impossible; it's all backed up offsite. The duplicator is different, due to the enormous amount of information required to specify a human being's seven billion billion billion atoms. There's not enough bandwidth to transmit it, even with the best compression. The duplicator has its own vast internal memory to store scans. That data only exists inside the lab: if it disappears, it's gone forever.

I grab the keyboard, then write a program to delete files and overwrite the memory to prevent recovery attempts. When I look at the files to check I've included everything, I see the duplicator's most recent scans: Chimpanzee F, Violeta Ruiz, Prisoner 75832.

I shiver when I see my own data, remembering Cole's casual remark: "Just print some extra copies of yourself." I include Violeta Ruiz in the deletion list. I remember what it's like to wake up on the bench; I don't want any more of my copies chained to the production line.

But another version of me already exists. She's asleep in the bedroom. I can't run the program without telling her: I know how angry I'd be if she did that to me. We have to agree our plan, since we'll both face the consequences.

While I wait for her to wake up, I try to think of an easy way out. I don't want to make a stand, but I can't avoid a decision. If I let the interrogations continue, I'll be complicit in them.

The lab's grey walls feel ever more oppressive, as I wonder whether I'll ever escape them. How can I avoid being a security breach? That's only an issue as long as the duplicator remains secret; if everyone knew about it, there'd be nothing to hide. But if I publicise the duplicator, then I'll go to jail for leaking classified information. That's hardly an improvement.

Deleting Abu Hameed's data might be considered a crime. Can I avoid the rap for that? Or must I martyr myself for my principles?

At last, activity comes from my quarters, as a toilet flushes and a wisp of shower steam curls through the doorway. No matter how often I remind her, she never closes the door properly while she's showering. I'm such a slob.

I send the guard to fetch a breakfast tray. Soon my original emerges, with a towel wrapped around her hair and a sullen expression on her face. She still hasn't forgiven me for winning the coin-toss that put her on night shift – not that it makes much difference, since we so rarely get outdoors.

While she eats breakfast, I tell her what's happened: Bryant's visit, my conversation with Cole, the program I've written to delete the scan data.

"Are you crazy?" she yells, spitting out toast crumbs.

"No more than you," I say, offended.

"What's your problem? Have you forgotten the Atrocity? We need to rip that bastard open and find out every damn thing he knows."

"Interrogation is one thing. Torture is quite another."

"Yeah, yeah. Big deal," she says. "That's their business, not ours. Why don't you leave it to them, and stop meddling?"

"You're okay with torture?"

She shrugs. "I'm sure it's not *torture* torture. We're the good guys, remember? It's authorised procedures in exceptional circumstances. You said Bryant gave you the legal go-ahead, so what are you worried about?"

"The duplicator is classified," I remind her. "The interrogation protocols were probably written by military bureaucrats here in the base. I bet they weren't signed off by anyone accountable to the public – anyone elected. Would politicians authorise creating umpteen copies of someone, so they could all be tortured?"

"Oh, come on!" she says. "Do you expect the President to personally ring you up and give you permission? Do you want the Attorney General to hold your hand while you're cranking the machine? Get real!"

We gaze at each other with equal astonishment, amazed at our opposing attitudes. We're the same person! At least, we were a few weeks ago. How could we diverge so much in such a brief time?

I remember waking up on the workbench. Every time I make a copy of Abu Hameed, I feel a kinship with him that the other Violeta doesn't feel. And perhaps knowing I'm a copy creates psychological pressure for me to differentiate myself from my original, carving out my own identity.

Yet it's disconcerting to realise how contingent my opinions are. My convictions are fragile, built on the shifting sands of happenstance.

I don't even know for sure how badly he's being treated. Maybe I should just let it go: trust the system, and outsource my conscience to Bryant's legal sign-off. After all, what can I achieve anyway? I can't uninvent the duplicator; I can't prevent it being misused. I can't put the genie back in the bottle.

My original says, "You were asleep when I finished the first copy of the terrorist. Cole and his flunkies were worried that it might not have worked properly. They interviewed him, making sure he had all his faculties. I went along to check whether there were any glitches."

Abu Hameed's freshly-minted copies all possess the same memories, ready to be probed by Cole's team with standardised procedures to minimise divergence. My original and I have lived longer since duplication; we've seen different things. We've changed.

If only one of us can go home, who should it be?

She continues, "It was just an interview, not an interrogation, so he was happy to talk. He spoke in English, boasting about what he'd done. He described the Atrocity as a great blow against the infidel. He laughed!"

She leans forward and stares into my eyes. "He *laughed*," she repeats. "Ten thousand people dead, and he was laughing about it. He called it a divine judgement, one that would inspire the whole world to rise up against the Great Satan. Then he said there was more to come. It was the most sickening thing I've ever seen. Excuse me if I don't shed any tears for him."

Her expression is stern, as cold and hard as Bryant's. I don't like what she's become; I don't want to walk down that path. I never suspected how much darkness lurks within my heart.

She says, "I could ask how you became such a hand-wringing sissy. But I already know: you weren't there. You didn't hear him. I looked at him, and I saw the face of evil. When we're confronted by evil, we can't run, or hide, or worry about paperwork. We have to act."

She's showing me how tough I can be. I try to speak calmly, while readying myself for what I must do next. "So you're saying that when we see evil in front of us, we're justified in taking any action necessary?"

"Obviously," she says. Her blue T-shirt is a thin layer of polyester, no protection at all.

"Are you sure?" I ask. "We should do anything?"

"Yes, damn it!" Too late, a spark of realisation reaches her eyes.
I grab the cutter torch, and let rip. A fizzing bolt arcs into her chest.
She screams, but I don't see her fall. After I fire, I lunge straight to
the keyboard and run the program I've written. The duplicator beeps as
its data disappears.

Two guards burst through the lab door. "Drop the weapon!" the
first one shouts.

I've already dropped it. I raise my hands, trying not to gag on the
stench of melted fabric and burnt flesh.

"It's sabotage," I say. "I tried to stop her, but I was too late."

No one can prove which of us deleted the data. I want to stand up
for my principles, but not yet. Not in the depths of a military prison,
where sabotage is treason.

Someday, when I feel safe, I'll indulge my conscience and speak up
for truth and justice. But right now, expediency is the order of the day.

*"After the Atrocity" uses a familiar trope: matter duplication. Specifically, it's
about making copies of people.*

*Tropes are there for everyone to use. The SF genre has been described as an
ongoing conversation. An author writes a story about a particular idea, and then
another writer responds with a story that extends the idea, or takes it in a different
direction, or reverses it completely. It's like saying "Yes, and..." or "Yes, but..." or
even "No, not at all!" In turn, the new story may evoke its own responses.
Sometimes an idea is used in so many stories that it's like a noisy conversation at a
party where everyone is having their say, almost talking across each other, and the
discussion continues long after the earlier participants have left the room.*

*In this particular case, I read a story in which a person was duplicated, and the
tale struck me as rather anodyne. I thought to myself, "That's all very well, but if
this technology really existed, what would it actually be used for? If it had just been
invented, who would be the first people to use it? Obviously the military." This led
me to write a rather dark story about the battle against terrorism.*

*I'm reluctant to name the particular story that inspired this chain of thought.
It's unfair to single out a specific story, when there are plenty of others using the same
premise that could equally have provoked the same reaction.*

*One reason that certain science-fictional tropes recur so often is precisely because
they have so many ramifications that they permit – indeed, encourage – authors to*

take different directions. No story can possibly be the last word. The conversation continues.

Yet the problem with writing near-future stories is the risk of being overtaken by events. I wrote the first draft of "After the Atrocity" in early 2015, which in retrospect feels like a different era. The story has a section where the characters wonder who authorised using the duplicator on terrorists: "The interrogation protocols were probably written by military bureaucrats here in the base ... they weren't signed off by anyone accountable to the public – anyone elected."

In the original version of the story, this paragraph concluded: "I bet the President didn't authorise creating umpteen copies of someone, so they could all be tortured." I wrote that when Barack Obama was President of the USA, and when his successor looked likely to be either Hillary Clinton or a conventional Republican.

However, the publishing industry sometimes moves slower than world events. By the time the story appeared in Asimov's, Donald Trump had been elected President. My story now looked like a relic from another age, a bygone age when it felt as though there was a rulebook for society and for civilised conduct. In the era of Trump, no one will ever write a sentence that begins: "I bet the President didn't..." As has been amply demonstrated, Trump might do anything!

Consequently, when the opportunity arose to reprint the story in this volume, I changed the relevant paragraph. It now concludes: "Would politicians authorise creating umpteen copies of someone, so they could all be tortured?"

I changed it from a statement to a question.

In retrospect, I could easily have written the revised paragraph when I composed the original draft. But I didn't. I was locked into a set of assumptions about how the world worked, and I didn't even realise it until the world changed. Science fiction is notionally about the future, but it's hard enough to keep up with the present!

THE EQUALISERS

I've got to stop doing this, Pamela thought when her phone beeped her awake at 6 am. *Or at least stop doing it on weeknights. I'm thirty-seven – I don't have the energy to live on four hours' sleep any more.*

She reached under the unfamiliar pillow to grab her phone and stifle the alarm, before it disturbed whoever slept beside her. Then she slid out of bed and slunk into the bathroom to pee. She checked her phone to see whereabouts in London she'd ended up, and summoned a cab with the taxi app.

Back in the bedroom, Pamela dressed hurriedly, not bothering to smooth her rumpled clothes. When she got home she would have a shower, change into a fresh outfit, and apply new make-up. Casual dating was harder for women. If a man stayed overnight somewhere, he could return to the office wearing the same clothes he wore yesterday, augmented with a day of stubble, and no one would bat an eye.

If everyone wore the Equalisers, it wouldn't matter what I looked like, Pamela thought. *I could waltz back into the office in yesterday's outfit, without any make-up, and no one would know.*

Tempted, she imagined the memo she would write: "To further enhance the Firm's commitment to equality of opportunity and prevention of discrimination, wearing Equalisers is now mandatory for all staff..."

Meanwhile the bed's remaining occupant began to stir. An arm emerged out of the sheets, groping blindly as though trying to snatch more sleep from the air. Then, abruptly, the man sat up. His ravishing auburn hair resembled the flowing locks of some Byronic poet who might spend the morning either writing a sonnet or swimming the Hellespont.

"Morning, darling," he said, flashing a smile to entice her back to bed.

Pamela frowned. "What happened to your accent?"

"My accent?" He laughed. "Oh, it comes and goes. It's probably run off to America to seek its fortune. You know, the Irish people are very temperamental, and so are their accents –"

"Never mind," Pamela said. "I have to go."

She checked her handbag: money, keys, phone. As she clattered downstairs, she heard the guy calling out from his bedroom. "It's only six o'clock. Top o' the morning! Stay for breakfast, I've got a leprechaun in the fridge –"

The taxi had arrived. Pamela got inside, confirmed her address, then buried her face in her hands. *He was fake! He just played up the Irishness because he knew it attracted women.* What a pathetic fraud – to practise, and to fall for. It exposed how shallow she'd become lately, attracted to merely physical attributes. A nice head of hair and a charming voice...

At least the sex had been good.

I've got to stop doing this.

Pamela's workplace was a glass-fronted office block, one of many towers clustered like skyscraper icons in a PowerPoint chart showing the battle for market share. She donned her Equalisers on arrival, as she had done every day during the trial period. The glasses altered her vision; the frames generated nerve-induction input for her ears and nose. The Equalisers transformed what she saw, heard, and smelled.

When she walked into the lobby, the receptionist and the roving security guard appeared as purple humanoid shapes, with no personal characteristics such as hairstyle or skin colour. Each avatar's chest displayed a job title and employee number. The default identifiers didn't include names, because names might hint at gender or ethnicity. The Equalisers eliminated such distinctions.

"Good morning," said the receptionist, sounding as robotic as a speech synthesiser reading from a dictionary. All traces of pitch and accent had been removed.

"Morning," said Pamela. The receptionist wasn't yet wearing Equalisers, and heard her true voice. If Pamela pushed for universal adoption, soon everyone in the building would wear them.

She entered the Human Resources department, her fiefdom since she became HR Director two months ago.

"How did it go last night?" Vonda asked. She appeared in Pamela's vision as an orange avatar with a familiar employee number. You could customise the avatars and assign them any colour – apart from shades of black, brown, red, yellow or white. The default view allocated colours by department: HR was orange, Consulting was green, Building Services was purple, and so forth.

"Badly," Pamela replied. "I can't talk now – I've got interviews – but shall we meet for lunch?"

"Sure!"

Pamela printed out the job description and the candidates' applications, which had been anonymised to remove any bias-inducing details. She skimmed the documents one last time, then took them to the conference room.

Employee 35781, the section head who needed a new data analyst, appeared as a green avatar with the horizontal stripes of a Principal Consultant. The Equalisers eradicated most differences, but preserved the company hierarchy.

Pamela handed over a set of Equalisers, and the green avatar's head acquired a goggles icon as Employee 35781 donned them. "You should see me as an orange shape," she said. "Are you getting that?"

"Yes, yes. Is this really necessary?"

"Absolutely," she said, her voice full of conviction. "It'll help you hire the best candidate. A fair environment will improve employee morale. And most importantly, we'll save money if we don't keep paying compensation for discrimination."

The company had recently settled a tribunal claim and a lawsuit from ex-employees alleging discrimination and harassment. After this debacle, the former HR Director had been fired. Pamela was promoted to the position, with a mandate to reform the company's culture. Hence she'd brought in the Equalisers, as both policy measure and public penance.

She was introducing them gradually, wary of alienating the workforce. Wearing them at interviews was simply one step – a statement of intent, a bullet point on the new "Living Our Values" webpage. Discrimination didn't just occur at the hiring stage. It also arose in promotions and pay rises. That would be harder to prevent, even if she made everyone use Equalisers every day.

The interviews took all morning, as Pamela and Employee 35781 strove to differentiate between the candidates without identifying them. Wearing the Equalisers felt like playing a primitive videogame with cartoonish icons and metronomic voices. It was alienating, and left

Pamela desperate for genuine human contact. After three hours of interrogating anonymous grey shapes, she was eager to get lunch and catch up with Vonda.

She left the building and removed her Equalisers, greedily absorbing the sight of London's crowds as she strolled to the usual riverside café. She snagged an outdoor table, checked her phone, and saw a message from Vonda saying she'd be late.

Pamela sighed. *A few minutes to kill. I might as well take a quick look online.* She touched an icon, and her phone's screen filled with pictures of men. Tapping any picture would bring up the owner's profile. But for long moments, Pamela simply flicked through the pictures, screen after screen of them. Tall men, short men, bald men with hideous shirts... She was fascinated by the range of physicality on display: beards and moustaches, earrings and tattoos, expressions friendly or brooding or chirpy or fierce.

I've got to stop doing this. What's happening to me?

She shoved the phone back into her handbag, relieved to see Vonda hurrying towards her table. They'd been friends ever since meeting in Freshers' Week at Bath University. In twenty years they'd celebrated together, commiserated together, and shared everything about their lives. Vonda was unshockable, conducting her own love life as if on a dare.

So when Vonda quizzed her about last night's date, Pamela described the disaster in detail.

"If I'm going to choose guys because they've got gorgeous hair and a sexy accent, I can't be surprised if they start faking it. Maybe even that hair was a wig! It serves me right."

Vonda laughed. "Oh, don't worry. Is a bit of artifice really so bad? I bet you wore make-up, perfume, high heels —"

"That's normal!" Pamela exclaimed. "Everyone expects it. But I didn't expect his voice to be a false front."

"Then just look for things that are harder to fake. A well-muscled physique, a well-stuffed wallet..."

Pamela smiled; she appreciated Vonda's attempt to cheer her up. But this wasn't something to giggle about, then forget. "No, seriously, I've become too obsessed with guys and how they look, how they sound, how they smell. And I'm not letting any of these nights develop into anything. I should be going on second dates —"

Vonda clamped her hand on Pamela's arm. "Stop right there. Bad girl! You said a naughty word."

Pamela raised her eyebrows.

"In dating, there's no *should*," Vonda said firmly. "Just whatever feels good."

"But when I got home this morning, I felt like shit."

"Oh, that's only because he fooled you with his fake accent."

Pamela shook her head. "It's not just that. It's the whole scene. I needed it after I broke up with Jeremy, but lately it's been getting me down. And these damned goggles aren't helping. If I spend all day looking at avatars specifically designed to be unreal, it's no wonder I end up craving something genuine. Someone with real hair, real skin –"

"– A real cock –"

"– A real *voice*, with a real accent, instead of that horrible speech synthesiser."

Pamela fished her Equalisers out of her handbag and glared at them. Were they really the problem? Until now, she'd resisted blaming them, because they'd been her own idea. But as her life slid downhill, the evidence became harder to ignore.

"If these are the problem, then they wouldn't just affect me," Pamela said. The entire HR department was wearing them during the trial period. "Have you noticed anything?" she asked Vonda.

"No, I haven't. And I don't think it's the Equalisers. It's because you're coming off a rotten break-up. You spent ten years with Jeremy: it grew stale, it ended badly. So naturally you want to go out and play the field. But if you're out there, sometimes you get hurt. It's always been like that – you've just forgotten, because it's been so long."

"Forgotten what it's like to get hurt? I wish that was so easy to forget." Pamela shrugged. "Maybe you're right. I hope you are, because I really don't want to go back to the Board and say, 'Sorry, I'm cancelling the Equalisers.' 'Why's that?' 'Because they're screwing up my sex life'."

Their food arrived: omelette for Vonda, crab salad for Pamela. On the dating merry-go-round, every calorie had to earn its keep.

Vonda said, "If the problem is that you're getting hung up on these guys' physical aspects, then maybe you need to go the other way."

"What other way?"

Vonda smiled mischievously. "Well, there's lots of other ways. But

I mean you shouldn't see their physical aspects at all. Wear the goggles."

"The Equalisers – outside work? You're not serious."

"I am." Vonda imitated a sales rep quoting from the brochure. "See beyond the skin. Let excellence shine, unhindered by prejudice. Find the best candidate for that crucial role –"

"My love life isn't a job vacancy."

"It might as well be. And interviewing is what you're good at. Why not give it a shot?"

Pamela spluttered. "The practicalities! How would I know anything about a guy if I couldn't see him properly? How could I tell if he looked creepy or dangerous? It wouldn't be safe," she said forcefully, expecting that to be the end of the matter.

"An excellent point," said Vonda, "which is why I wasn't going to suggest that you walk into a bar and pick a bloke at random. I'll find someone for you. It'll be a blind date."

"A very blind date," Pamela said, "if I can't see him."

Did it make sense? Vonda was trustworthy: she would only set Pamela up with someone she'd vetted. Pamela disliked wearing the Equalisers, but they might feel different outside the context of work. Perhaps it was worth a try, just for one date. After all, she could take the goggles off whenever she liked.

The familiar excitement started to build: the thrill of anticipation, the prospect of romance – or at least a good time. She was looking forward to it already.

On Saturday evening, Pamela sat in a West End restaurant, dutifully wearing Equalisers and waiting for her date to arrive. The room appeared full of grey, identical people. Back at work, the Equalisers distinguished between employees through a combination of facial recognition and staff ID cards, but no one here was in the database.

As she read the specials board, a subtitle scrolled across her vision – "EQUALISER UPDATES AVAILABLE: Autism suppression; Gaydar elimination; Language sanitisation; Wheelchair compensation." She tapped her left earpiece to clear the message. On Monday, she'd have to decide which upgrades to install. Various brands of Equalisers competed to promise ever greater strides toward a fairer world. She'd joked with Vonda that the ultimate version of the goggles would just show an endless vista of beige sludge.

A grey shape arrived at her table. "Hi, are you Pamela?"

She nodded, feeling flustered and at a disadvantage.

"I'm Nathaniel – pleased to meet you. You're wearing silver glasses like Vonda said, but somehow I thought they'd be more, um, big and shiny. Like futuristic gadgets always used to be."

"The future often turns out to be disappointing," Pamela said, then winced inwardly. *The first thing I say, I sound like a grump.* Despite all the dates she'd been on, she still struggled to present the obligatory upbeat persona.

A waiter arrived to take their drinks order. The familiar ritual soothed Pamela a little.

"It's nice to meet you," she said. "I hope Vonda didn't twist your arm too hard. And I hope you didn't dress up specially, because I can't see what you're wearing."

"I changed my shirt: does that count as dressing up? But you're outshining me by far. I like your dress. It's very blue."

Pamela stifled a smile at the clumsy compliment.

"I'd love to say it matches your eyes," Nathaniel went on, "but I can't actually see your eyes –"

"Yeah, I know. The goggles. I suppose you don't have these where you work..." Pamela didn't want to talk about the Equalisers – she was tired of discussing them – but she figured it was best to get the subject out of the way.

"What are they for?" asked Nathaniel.

She explained how they displayed standardised avatars to prevent discrimination based on race, gender, weight, and so forth. "I'm wearing them all day, for testing. Other departments are only wearing them for interviews. I need to decide whether the whole company should wear them throughout office hours. Can they really help, or are they just a gimmick?"

"Sounds gimmicky to me," Nathaniel said. "I mean, people already know who they work with. If I was one of your colleagues, then surely I'd know you were a woman, even if I wore the glasses and couldn't see you properly."

Pamela said, "You'd know on an intellectual level, but you wouldn't be constantly reminded of it. If I was explaining something, you might actually listen to what I was saying, instead of just staring at my breasts.

After a while, with hot desking and employee turnover, you might not know who you worked with. And then you'd treat everyone on merit, because you'd have no grounds to do otherwise."

She smiled ruefully. "Sorry for the lecture. Let's not talk about work on a Saturday night."

Nathaniel accepted the hint, and changed the subject. They chatted about the usual icebreaker and smalltalk topics: holidays, films, celebrity gossip. Pamela described her recent trip abroad, her first holiday as a single woman in ten years. "I took a guided tour to some ancient sites in the Middle East. I was always fascinated by archaeology: I used to watch *Time Team* as a girl. In the desert, everything's so well preserved…"

She stopped, remembering the sight of those empty ruins. It had felt like gazing at the wreckage of her own life: once-thriving households, abandoned after someone's decision to move on.

"Age is relative," Nathaniel said. "When I was in Canada, we went to Lake Superior to see some famous pictographs, painted by the indigenous people. The guide told us in awed tones that these pictographs were *hundreds* of years old. I think he expected us to be impressed! There's plenty of things in Britain older than that."

"My granny probably has half of them…"

Their conversation slid into an easy groove. At first it felt more like a chat with an office colleague than a date; Nathaniel spoke with the same synthetic voice that Pamela heard every day at work. The grey avatar was hardly romantic. What lay behind it?

The longer the evening wore on, the more Pamela wondered about Nathaniel's true appearance. How old was he? What did he look like? She deliberately avoided asking personal questions that veered into this territory. She wanted to enjoy the blind date in the spirit of Vonda's suggestion: a meeting of minds, rather than a fetish for flesh.

Nevertheless, the mystery was enticing. Maybe Nathaniel was Hollywood handsome. Maybe he was ugly or deformed, and never normally got dates. Maybe he was the god Zeus, and if she looked on him with her naked eye she'd be incinerated by the sight of his glory.

So many possibilities! It was tantalising. She wanted to see Nathaniel properly, yet she recognised this would inevitably be a letdown. The mystery itself was more exciting than any answer could possibly be. And so it was best prolonged. *Don't try to know. Just keep talking.* She relished the uncertainty, the delicious sense that anything might happen.

But they couldn't keep talking forever, not when the meal had ended and they'd finished the wine.

Ordinarily, Pamela didn't take a man home the first time. If things went sour, it was always easier to walk out of someone else's place than to kick a guy out of her own. Yet she felt comfortable with Nathaniel. And wearing the goggles had already broken her routine; hell, the routine was the whole problem.

So she invited him back to her house for coffee. As they sat in the taxi, she longed to put her hand on his knee. *Save it,* she told herself. The whole night lay ahead of them.

Pamela's home was clean and tidy – almost too tidy. Jeremy had always been the one who left clutter lying around. Without his mess, she lived in rooms as sterile as a hotel suite.

"Tea, coffee, vodka?" she asked.

"Whatever you're having," Nathaniel said.

As she boiled the kettle for two mugs of tea, Pamela suffered a pang of doubt. *Should I go ahead? I have no idea who this person is!*

But how much had she known about those other guys? Even less than she'd thought.

They sat together on the sofa. Nathaniel put down his drink, and leaned into her for a kiss. A message appeared in Pamela's vision: "WARNING – Inappropriate behaviour detected."

She cleared the message, feeling delightfully naughty. They kissed. Pamela had to suppress a giggle, distracted by the sensation of stiff bristles poking into her upper lip.

"Wow, that's some moustache you've got," she said when they broke apart. "Is it waxed, or something?"

Nathaniel laughed. "Sorry about that."

Pamela had grown accustomed to his synthetic voice at the restaurant. But here in her own home, it sounded newly grating – too calm and passionless. It would be like sleeping with a robot.

At some point, Pamela needed to remove the Equalisers. Surely it would be absurd to have sex without being able to see, hear, or smell her partner.

Or would it? It might become a game, like wearing a blindfold. The

Equalisers – and their rival brands – could create any kind of avatar, not just the featureless shapes used in the office. If you wanted, you could see a celebrity, or an ex-lover. You could dial up whatever assortment of features took your fancy, or select an ever-changing random shuffle.

The anonymity could become a fetish, an addictive spiral into the depths of meaningless sex. Was that any different from what she'd already been doing, selecting nightly faces from the cyber-smorgasbord?

Pamela shivered.

"Is something wrong?" asked Nathaniel.

"I'm just thinking about taking the goggles off," Pamela said.

It would destroy the mystery that she'd savoured. And it would doubtless be a disappointment, revealing an average guy with an ordinary face, commonplace accent, and typical BO.

Yet she couldn't keep wearing the goggles forever. She imagined herself in a relationship with an unknown partner, bringing up a baby of unknown gender – tackling discrimination at its roots by refusing to socialise the child as either a girl or a boy.

Abruptly, Pamela wrenched the Equalisers off her head. The glasses beeped reprovingly – a warning system to prevent surreptitious peeks at reality. When her vision refocused, she saw who sat beside her: Vonda, wearing a false moustache.

"Hello," said Vonda. "Fancy meeting you here!"

"My God, I could give you such a slap! What the hell are you doing? You *kissed* me!"

"I know. Fun, wasn't it?" Before Pamela could reply, Vonda held up her hands, as if she was merely a victim of circumstance. "I found a guy for you – a nice guy, you'd have liked him – but at the last minute, he said he couldn't do it. I nearly told you it was off, but since the restaurant was booked, I thought I might as well meet you there: we could have a night out ourselves. And on my way over, I had a devilish impulse. If you were expecting a blind date, it could be anyone – even me."

"You're always having devilish impulses," said Pamela. "Are you sure you're not actually the Devil?"

"I don't think the Devil wears a moustache from a fancy dress shop." Vonda tugged at the plastic, and winced as it peeled off. "That's better."

"Why were you wearing that?"

"It was a disguise to fool the Equalisers," Vonda explained. "If I'd turned up without it, you'd have seen me as an orange avatar with my employee number. When I wore it, the goggles didn't recognise me. I tested it by wearing my own Equalisers and looking in a mirror."

"Very clever," Pamela said tartly. "Thanks a bunch!" She got up and stomped around the room. She'd expected disappointment when she removed the Equalisers, but not like this. It had turned the night from a date into a practical joke.

"I was trying to help," Vonda protested.

"Help? How is this helping me?"

"I thought something different might break you out of a rut. Shock therapy. You said you were feeling like shit, remember? I was worried about you, so I wanted to try something. Even if it didn't work, at least it would be an evening with someone who cared about you, instead of some random faker."

Pamela glared at Vonda. Anger boiled inside her, but she couldn't vent it. Her friend had good intentions. Yet it was frustrating to realise that Nathaniel had never existed, and all her anticipation had come to nothing.

"These damned Equalisers," she said. "They've totally fucked me up." She wanted to smash the things.

Vonda shook her head. "Pamela, honey, I don't think it's the Equalisers."

"No? Well, if it isn't them, then what is it?" she cried. "Is it me? It must be me who's fucked up, right?" Her voice dropped to a whisper. "It is me, I know it is." She flopped back onto the sofa, closing her eyes as though blotting out the world.

"Oh, Pamela..." Vonda put her arm around Pamela's shoulders.

For a moment, neither of them spoke. Pamela wanted to cry, but the tears wouldn't come. There was nothing inside her, only a vast emptiness.

"It's not the Equalisers," said Vonda, "though they're not helping. They're making it worse, because they're distracting you and giving you something to blame."

A long pause followed. Distant sounds drifted into the room: a motorbike revving up, a faraway police siren, someone laughing on the street outside.

Pamela lifted her head. "You're going to make me take part in this conversation, aren't you?"

"That's why I'm here," said Vonda.

"Then while you're here, maybe you could brew another pot of tea and bring out the biscuits." Restaurants offered all kinds of desserts which had far too many calories, but never gave you a proper biscuit with your cuppa.

Vonda began clattering in the kitchen. *God, it's good to have some company and hear someone else making a noise.* Pamela had been living alone since Jeremy's departure, rattling around in a house too big for her. It was lucky she'd been promoted to HR Director; on her old salary, she'd have struggled to pay the mortgage.

The tea arrived. "All right," said Pamela, "what were you saying about the Equalisers?"

Vonda said, "When Jeremy left, you started seeing other guys. You had a few one-night stands. Which would have been fine, except you weren't comfortable doing it. You couldn't admit to yourself that's what you wanted. Nice girls shouldn't sleep around, should they? So you blamed the Equalisers. You told yourself it was the effect of the goggles, starving you of human contact."

Pamela nodded, reluctantly conceding some truth in Vonda's words.

"And blaming the Equalisers allowed you to carry on," Vonda said. "But that didn't make you happy. It *couldn't* make you happy, because you told yourself that you were being pushed into it."

Pamela remembered how she'd thought about those guys, the way she'd luxuriated in their physicality. It was shameless and animalistic, as though it came from outside her. "Men can behave like that, but women aren't supposed to. It's discrimination, plain and simple."

"Of course it is," said Vonda.

"I'll write a memo," Pamela said. "'To further enhance the Firm's commitment to equality of opportunity and prevention of discrimination, guilt-free one-night stands are now mandatory for all staff'."

Vonda laughed, and Pamela smiled for the first time since she'd removed the Equalisers.

"But seriously," Pamela went on, "I need to wrap up the trial period, and decide our policy on the goggles. I want to keep using them for interviews, but I don't think we can make the entire company wear them all the time. That's a step too far."

"The goal isn't to make everyone in the world wear Equalisers," Vonda said. "The goal is a world where Equalisers don't exist, because there's no need for them."

"And to get there, we should chip away at the toxic culture we've got. How about an annual awareness day, where everyone has to wear Equalisers for just one day? It'll be educational, and a taste of what's in store if there's any more trouble. Anyone who crosses the line will be forced to wear the goggles for as long as it takes."

"I think that's a good idea," Vonda replied, "but remember what you said earlier? Let's not talk about work on a Saturday night!"

"Yes, you're right," said Pamela. "I'm sorry. And I appreciate your efforts. How about some old-school TV to chill out with?"

She scanned the shelves of neatly filed DVDs and pulled out a box set of *Six Kinds of Forever*, the cheesy supernatural TV show they'd watched endlessly in college. "Mullets ahoy!" she exclaimed. "Being dead is no excuse for bad hair."

"Being dead is no excuse for wearing a tartan waistcoat," Vonda said, running with the old catchphrase they'd riffed on countless times.

Just listening to the show's theme music cheered Pamela up. As the episode unfolded, Vonda checked her messages. Pamela took out her own phone, but her inbox only had alerts from the dating app. Guys wanted to meet her. Tomorrow was Sunday, an empty day.

Brooding, Pamela tapped the familiar icon. The usual procession of pictures appeared, starting with the most recent profiles. There were always new faces. What happened to the old faces? Did those guys ever settle down, or did they just flit from one website to another, one warm body to the next, all the way to old age and a lonely death?

I'm thirty-seven. That's not old. There's no point worrying about a lonely death – I'm lonely right now. If I reply to any of these messages, I can hook up tomorrow. Fresh meat from the hunk mines!

The prospect did not seem satisfying. It had not felt satisfying for some time.

Vonda's diagnosis was that, despite blaming the Equalisers, Pamela wanted to sleep around. Perhaps that had been true at first. When Jeremy left, Pamela was keen to reassert her desirability, and clutch at whatever scraps remained of her youth and beauty. Surfing the website, with all those available guys, had felt like being a child in a sweetshop. *It's amazing how quickly sweets can pall.*

Pamela scrolled through the menu until she found 'Hide Your Profile'. The screen asked, "Are You Sure?"

Yes.

Meanwhile, Vonda had been tapping away, accompanied by the soft beeps of messages sent and received. She said, "I heard from the guy you were supposed to meet tonight. He's really sorry about cancelling: something came up. But he can meet you later in the week if you like. Do you fancy it? You don't have to wear the goggles – he's quite good-looking!"

"Thanks," said Pamela, "but I'd better not see the next guy until I've given the last one a fair chance. I need to see beyond the skin... and hear beyond the dodgy accent."

Before she could change her mind, she fired off a quick message. "Hi, do you still have that leprechaun in the fridge?"

Soon a reply came. "Aye, to be sure. Are you free tomorrow?"

Pamela smiled, savouring a new thrill of anticipation. "Yes, let's meet up again." *I've got to start doing that.*

"The Equalisers" is a story inspired by contemporary issues. One mode of science fiction is the 'if this goes on' tale, examining a current trend by extrapolating it into the future, and exaggerating it to vividly illustrate what the implications might be.

This story centres on special glasses that people wear in the workplace as an anti-discrimination measure. While one might think that employees would never endure such an imposition, today's employees already endure plenty of impositions that earlier generations would boggle at: open-plan offices, zero-hours contracts, constant tracking, the 24/7 culture whereby work never finishes because you always have your phone with you... No matter how appalling your working conditions are, they can always get worse!

No Strangers Any More

One of a princess's many duties is to make polite conversation and avoid controversial subjects. *Screw that,* thought Rose. At the banquet after the first day of the conference, there was only one topic on everyone's mind, so she raised it. "Are these aliens really going to buy the moon?"

The man opposite her laughed. "Are we really going to sell it?" Subtitles in Rose's vision identified him as a European Union diplomat, an expert in international law, and a family man with a wife, four children, and a mistress.

As everyone else at the table chimed in, Rose's visual overlay filled with a cloud of identifiers and titbits, until she tweaked her filters to display only the most relevant tags.

"I think we should sell," said a Russian four-star general. "Let them have the moon. Best place for them! Then they're not wandering around down here, eh?"

The Brazilian ambassador scowled. "Have you seen the size of their ship? It's enormous. There could be millions of them in there."

"The ship is big because it travels between the stars," another lawyer said. "The crew is only a few hundred –"

"Sure, that's what they *say*," the ambassador retorted. "But who knows what's really inside? And if they unload it all onto the moon, do we want to see that looming over us every night?"

Rose offered no views of her own; she was a hostess, not a participant. As other people spoke, she labelled them "pro" or "anti", "loud" or "quiet", "rude" or "polite". These tags accompanied their owners in her vision overlay. She also saw summary reputations: people's accumulated histories of being witty, boorish, or drunk. She trusted her own impressions more than the collective record, but she couldn't personally assess everyone in the room.

After dinner, when people left the tables and started circulating, Rose watched out for problematic clusters of loudmouths, or confrontations between pros and antis. Whenever one formed, she inserted herself, ready to intervene and smooth over any flashpoints. Being a princess wasn't just about smiling and waving; her role was harder than it looked.

It included bearing up well in public and performing a flawless job, even after her boyfriend had just left her. Captain Gerrard Calderwood could take a long jump from a high mountain into a deep lake, as far as she was concerned. She wouldn't let him get to her. She wouldn't... Rose shook her head, and concentrated on the task at hand. She observed people's tags and movements while letting their conversations wash over her.

"We should be grateful they're offering to buy the moon legally. It's not as if we could stop them taking it –"

"But who are they buying it from? Who gets the money?"

"– If we sell the moon, we need to make the Felorians promise not to damage it. If they dismantled it, or took it away, then that would affect the tides."

"Yeah, hands off our moon!"

The crush of people thickened toward the end of the room, near the aliens' table. The Felorians had been grouped together, because they needed their own food. Their table was flanked by American and Chinese diplomats – as the only nations that had landed astronauts on the moon, they'd insisted on special status at these negotiations. The British delegation, such as it was, sat nowhere near the top table. After leaving the European Union, Britain had become an irrelevance in world politics. This made the UK an ideal venue for international conferences: neutral and insignificant, but with plenty of pageantry and princesses.

The aliens stood out by their height. Each Felorian was nearly seven feet tall, with lumpy purple skin. Their faces were elongated into vaguely triangular snouts, from which beard-like wattles descended.

In Rose's vision overlay, the aliens appeared as a mysterious void. All the humans in the room had a lifetime's accretion of tags, coalescing into biographies and reputations. In contrast, the aliens had barely any factual tags: just their names, and a few particulars gleaned since they arrived last month. Admittedly, there was no shortage of opinion tags – switching to the media view that she normally ignored, Rose saw a seething mass of 'Conspiracy' labels. Rose knew what it was like to be on the receiving end: right now, her own trending tag was

'Dumped!', as the media continued to obsess over her break-up with Gerrard.

Each Felorian stood isolated amidst a knot of people. Diligently circulating, Rose approached the nearest group, centred on an alien called Dorvin. She had briefly met him before the banquet, during a vast round of introductions.

"– But why do you want to buy the moon?" someone was asking.

"It's a matter of psychological comfort," Dorvin replied in excellent English, his voice deep and resonant. "Our race evolved on the satellite of a gas giant. Like your moon, our satellite is tidally locked, so the mother world always appears at the same position in the sky. Throughout our history, we've always seen a fixed reference point, a single constant in a changing universe. It has shaped our spirit in many ways…"

As Dorvin spoke, a waiter came by with a tray of drinks. He reached under a napkin on his tray, pulled something out, and threw it at the Felorian. "Save the moon!" he shouted. "Aliens go home!"

Dorvin flinched, then froze rigidly in place. The tray crashed to the floor as someone manhandled the waiter. Rose grabbed the napkin and rushed to Dorvin. He had egg-stains on his tunic; fragments of eggshell clung to his boots. She knelt down, wiping away the worst of the mess. The alien's leg was thick and hefty, as it needed to be to support a seven-foot giant. Rose noticed a pleasant scent reminiscent of lavender, though she had no idea whether this was his natural smell, or some kind of alien deodorant.

She'd behaved instinctively; only after she touched him did she realise that she might be compounding the gaffe. But he didn't resist: he remained still, letting her wipe off the debris. It only took a few seconds. Then she stood and said, "I'm dreadfully sorry. I apologise, on behalf of the United Kingdom and everyone here."

Rose heard scuffling behind her, as the waiter was dragged away. She ignored it, staying focused on Dorvin and watching for his reaction. His posture slowly unstiffened. "Thank you" – he paused momentarily – "Your Royal Highness. I accept your apology. Is this a traditional mode of protest?" He peered at the egg-smeared napkin in Rose's hand. "It is somewhat… unaesthetic."

She gave the napkin to one of the security staff who'd appeared. He took it away, presumably for analysis in case the egg contained anything noxious.

"It's one of the traditional modes," Rose replied. "I suppose you're lucky you didn't get a custard-pie in the face."

"I have no idea what that is, but it sounds even less aesthetic."

"Yes," said Rose. Her intuition told her to change the subject as quickly as possible, so they could pretend the incident hadn't happened. "I heard you saying that at home, you always see the mother planet in the sky. But isn't that only true from one side of the satellite? Does anyone live on the other side?"

"Ah, those poor benighted souls." Dorvin jiggled his head, fluttering his wattles. "They have no guidance from the mother world, and so they are lost!"

Rose couldn't tell whether this was a religious condemnation, or some kind of joke. She hesitated, wondering whether to point out that if the Felorians occupied the moon, they'd be looking to Earth for their 'guidance'. Yet she didn't want to risk insulting the alien's religion, if he had one.

Dorvin changed the subject, saving her the trouble of responding. "I'm no expert in fashion aesthetics, but it seems to me that you're wearing different clothes than most of the people here. Is that correct?"

"That's right," said Rose, pleased that the conversation had turned to something she could discuss more comfortably. She wore a blue suit with a pencil skirt, black heels, and a string of pearls. "This is based on a historic outfit worn by Diana, Princess of Wales. As part of the anniversary celebrations, members of the royal family are wearing costumes made famous by our ancestors. You have a good eye, to spot the difference between this and contemporary fashion." She smiled, grateful to have found an opportunity to pay Dorvin a genuine compliment.

"Anniversary?" he queried.

"Oh, just a bit of local history. This year, 2066, marks one thousand years since the Norman Conquest."

"And a hundred years since England won the World Cup," someone else chipped in.

"Indeed," said Rose, who had no interest in football whatsoever. "Britain has plenty of history, and we're helping to put it on show."

The device of reviving old royal costumes had been praised for boosting the fashion industry. However, cynics suggested that it had less to do with the millennial anniversary, and much more to do with the forthcoming referendum on the monarchy – when people would vote on whether Britain should become a republic, or retain the King as head of state. The referendum campaign had provoked a flurry of initiatives from the royal family, most of whom were keen to prove their relevance and preserve their privileges.

Rose felt it would be a shame to abandon a thousand years of history. She didn't mind currying favour with harmless stunts: she enjoyed the chance to dress up, and she'd found it fascinating to learn about the tragic Diana's life.

"Do you have a monarchy at home?" she asked Dorvin.

His wattles quivered. "Not any more."

News Mash – "SHOCKING PICS: Princess Rose kneels before the aliens and washes their feet!"

Albion Argus – "After a thousand years, we've exhausted most forms of pageantry: we've had coronations, weddings, jubilees galore. But it's 400 years since we last abolished the monarchy. Unfortunately, this time it won't be an execution. We'll need a new ceremony. Britain leads the world in pointless flummery, and this is an opportunity to manufacture an exciting new form. Tourists will flock to see the retiring of the finery: the royals signing on at the dole office, the horses being lovingly put down with gold bullets, the palace doors opening for a 'trolley dash' by fortunate members of the public..."

Hourly Digest – "The Felorian conference has just finished, with no agreement reached. Sources report that many politicians are in favour of selling the moon, even though public opinion is against it. The delegates are already squabbling over the proceeds, with the Americans and Chinese resisting any *per capita* distribution, preferring to count how many lunar missions each nation has launched. Meanwhile, no one knows how long the Felorian offer will remain on the table."

Tag Frenzy – Princess Rose latest tags: 'Dumped', 'Hot', 'Fifth in line to the throne', 'Would you?', 'Nice legs', 'Diana who?', 'This is the British economy today', 'Vote NO!', 'She needs feeding up', 'A thousand more years of this? Hell yes!', 'Buy Rose's outfit at 20% off', 'Calderwood? Calderwouldn't!'

Straight after the conference, Rose flew to Scotland to visit her cousin, Princess Helena. Although this was a private visit, Rose was careful to stay in Diana costume – today, a fuchsia chiffon dress. Cameras were everywhere. Besides, Diana was no stranger to heartbreak. Maybe channelling her ancestor would lend Rose some strength to deal with it.

"Hello darling," said Helena. "You look fantastic!"

"So do you," said Rose. "You're making me look way too colourful."

Helena wore a cut-down version of Queen Victoria's mourning dress, accessorised with jet jewellery. Privately, Rose thought that using a mourning dress as a fashion item was in questionable taste. But, if you ignored its origins, the black outfit looked sensational.

"You've had a tough time, and I know just what you need," said Helena. "Shopping! Drinking! Gossiping!"

"Relaxing?" said Rose.

"If all else fails. Come along!"

In the evening, after a tour of Edinburgh's classiest shops, bars and restaurants, Rose arrived at Helena's apartment feeling pleasantly invigorated and just a little buzzy from the third cocktail.

"Sit down," said Helena. "You've got to try this! It's the absolute latest thing."

Rose sat on a white leather sofa, facing the wallscreen. Helena gave her a silver helmet-like contraption, and demonstrated how to wear it by donning her own helmet. "It just needs to tune into your brain. Half a sec... Done. Now, let's tag some guys. I'll show you how it works."

Helena called up a picture on the wallscreen. The caption said 'Freddy Hooke': Rose vaguely recognised him as a sporty guy who she occasionally met at charity balls. She'd never exchanged more than a few sentences with him.

"Brace yourself," said Helena. "This is a bit disconcerting when you're not used to it."

Suddenly, Rose felt a warm rush of familiarity. Freddy! Decent bloke, maybe a little too fond of drinking; genuinely warm-hearted in a help-old-ladies-across-the-road kind of way; prone to the odd sexist comment, but more out of cluelessness than malice. Attractive, friendly – dateable if you fancied athletic types...

The feelings abruptly disappeared, and Freddy was a stranger once more.

"Wow!" exclaimed Rose. "Do you know him? Is that how you think about him?"

"Yes, that's my emotion tag. It's so much easier than trying to describe someone in words, or give them a rating out of ten. Feelings don't lie."

"I suppose it might help us pick out the more worthwhile chaps from the hordes we have to meet," Rose said. "I hate getting it wrong." Her muscles tensed at the memory of her recent break-up.

Helena said, "Eventually this'll be part of the standard augments – just another overlay. When you walk into a crowded room, you'll be able to instantly spot all the assholes, and avoid them."

Rose knew it was more complicated than that. As with any reputation system, you'd have to choose whose opinions to trust, while everyone would also be judging you. And Gerrard had dumped her, even though his tags and his history made him look like a nice guy. Would a more stringent assessment have protected her? Or was the whole system flawed?

"We need to build up the library," Helena continued. "Your turn! I'm going to flash some faces on the screen. When you see them, just react instinctively. Don't over-analyse it."

Another photo appeared. Rose knew Maurice Fitzgerald from university: a bit of a loudmouth. Clever, but not very good-looking. No dress sense whatsoever.

Next came Herbert Donaldson. Rose said, "We met him at that party at Highgrove, do you remember? When we all got in the pool."

"Yeah, he certainly tried to impress," Helena said. "I went out with him a couple of times –"

"So you know him better than I do."

"But it all adds up."

More men paraded across the screen, sparking reminiscences and scurrilous speculation. It was just like an ordinary girly chat; Rose almost forgot about the helmet.

Then the display showed a familiar face, a very familiar face. She didn't need the caption, but it loomed anyway: Captain Gerrard Calderwood.

It broke the mood. Rose felt sick. "What did you put him up for?" she demanded.

"Because you need to get him out of your system. And you know him well, so your opinion is valuable."

"Yeah, but I'm hardly unbiased."

"Bias is the whole point. If he treated you badly – if he genuinely treated you badly, and you're not just upset because he broke up with you – then that warning needs to be out there. For the benefit of all womankind!" Helena gave her a pleading look. "Just be honest."

"All right," Rose said. "But this is the last one."

She thought about her ex-boyfriend, determined to be scrupulously fair and remember the good times as well as the bad. Romantic early dates. Great sex, at least at first. But then came the undermining comments, and his nasty habit of criticising her in front of his friends. When she complained, he did make an effort to change. She'd thought things were getting better. That made it hurt all the more when he suddenly said it was over...

Rose's emotions churned within her. Fortunately, the machine plucked them directly from her mind; she could never have assigned neat verbal labels to the morass of feelings triggered by Gerrard's picture.

She wrenched off the helmet, then slumped back on the sofa. A tear rose to her eye, and she wiped it away angrily. "How about another drink?"

Helena removed her own helmet, rather more carefully. "You sure had quite a time of it."

Rose realised that Helena had just experienced the concentrated essence of her relationship with Gerrard. "Yeah. Still, like you said – it's over. Need to get him out of my system." Annoyingly, Helena had been right: it did feel cathartic.

"Okay..." Helena headed to the kitchen, and returned with another round of drinks. "And now that he's behind you, we can start thinking about your next."

"What?!"

"I know, I know. It's far too early, you need space, you're still hurt, you need time to recover, you couldn't possibly, et cetera, et cetera." Helena put on a pseudo-refined accent for "et cetera, et cetera", and since her natural voice was already quite plummy, the combined effect made Rose giggle. "But let's have a quick look at some candidates, just to get your subconscious primed. Then when you *are* ready, you'll be better informed. That can't be a bad thing, can it?"

Rose, by now somewhat befuddled, couldn't find any flaw in this logic. "All right. But I'm not using the helmet."

"No, that's fine. There aren't enough emotion tags yet, anyway. We'll just use the regular ones. Ready?"

Rose yawned, which Helena took as an affirmative.

Wing-Commander Michael Alexander Gordon appeared, surrounded by a halo of tags. After the scanner helmet, returning to the written labels came as a shock. It made Rose realise anew the sheer volume of information they represented. She could see anything in the public record of his life; she could examine any opinion of him that anyone had ever expressed.

"Whatever happened to 'You will meet a tall dark stranger'?" she complained. "That was so much simpler."

Helena shrugged. "There are no strangers any more."

"Only assholes you haven't met."

Laughing, they topped up their drinks. Onscreen, the faces flashed past, each with their encyclopaedia of accompanying attributes. Helena didn't attempt to seriously persuade Rose that any of these men were suitable – it was just a bit of fun, showing how many guys were still available.

And then someone different appeared. Someone very different.

"What's this?" exclaimed Rose, almost paralysed by giggles.

"It's an alien!"

"I know it's an alien. What's he doing on the list?"

Helena was laughing so hard, she could barely talk. "I didn't pick him, honestly. It's based on our contacts, and I forgot to filter for species. I guess he must be male, unattached, and high status..."

It was Dorvin, the alien Rose had met at the banquet. Presumably their interaction had given him a nudge in the weightings. Again she noticed his paucity of tags. A few new ones had appeared – 'Diplomatic incident', 'Official apology' – but his tag-cloud was a thin mist compared to everyone else's thunderheads. No one knew very much about the Felorians; they'd only arrived a month ago.

"He seemed pleasant enough," Rose said. "He was very gracious about the egg-throwing incident."

"Well, obviously he's your tall dark stranger." Helena's laughter dissolved into a fit of hiccups.

"He certainly has that aura of mystery. It's romantic. A leap in the dark, like love used to be."

"Hey, you're not going to do anything silly, are you?" asked Helena, her tone of concern marred only by another hiccup.

"Of course not. But I think there is something useful I can do."

Rose smiled. "It'll be a nice little project, to take my mind off things until I get over Gerrard."

"Oooh, a scheme! Tell me more. And have another drink."

"There's a lot of hostility to the Felorians. At that conference it wasn't just the egg-thrower, it was half the diplomats as well. And the media, of course – you know what the media are like."

Helena nodded. Rose continued, "Maybe I could do something about it: build some bridges, generate some positive publicity, show everyone that they aren't evil monsters. Just like Diana going into the AIDS ward!"

"Like Diana what?"

"Last century there was a new disease called AIDS," Rose explained, "and the early sufferers experienced a lot of prejudice. Diana went into hospital to visit them, and she was famously pictured shaking the hand of an AIDS victim. It was a big moment back then."

"I'm sure the Felorians will be flattered by this comparison to a horrible disease..."

"But that's how people think of them. They need help! I will wave my wand" – Rose gestured with both arms, as if she held not one but two wands – "and bestow upon them the magic of the monarchy."

Helena frowned. "That sounds like a really nice thing to do, but are you sure they deserve it? I mean, what if they actually are evil?"

"If they turn out to be evil, it'll be easy enough to whip up a fresh batch of hatred. Until then, they deserve the benefit of the doubt. After all, they did offer to buy the moon, when they could simply have grabbed it. They've behaved honourably so far."

"I guess that makes sense. How are you going to improve their popularity? It'll take more than shaking their hand."

"Hey, I've only just had the idea, and you're asking me for a plan already?" Rose sipped her drink. "I'll start by inviting them to a few society events. Charity balls, fundraising dinners, that sort of thing. Maybe they've got some cool stuff they could donate as raffle prizes. Still, it all depends if they want to play along. Maybe they don't mind being unpopular."

Helena shook her head. "No one wants to be unpopular. Not even if they're a gang of galactic geeks."

A sudden doubt struck Rose. "I don't think it's that simple. When your father goes hunting, he doesn't worry about being popular with the foxes, does he?"

"So if they don't want to go along with your plan, that means they're probably here to exterminate us?"

"Yep!" Rose grinned. "I'll try to be persuasive."

Omni Aggregator – "CROWDSOURCING THE MOON: Why do the Felorians want to buy our satellite? Maybe there's something on the moon that they know about, and we don't. The moon's entire surface has been photographed by various missions over the decades, but the pictures haven't all been scrutinised in detail. Campaign group Save Our Selene has launched a crowdsourcing effort to see if we've missed anything. Spokesman Jaroslav Fibich said, 'You wouldn't sell a house without checking whether anything's left in the attic. We want to examine the moon to see what's there. The total surface area is 38 million square kilometres, so if we sign up 38 million people, they'll each have a single square kilometre to analyse. Software tools are available, but there's nothing better than the human eye. We're offering prizes if anyone spots something out of the ordinary. Who knows what we might find?'"

WorldWideWatch – "I think the aliens are buying the moon to help our economy, as a face-saving form of aid. We're already spending money to license their technology, so the Felorians are accumulating Earth currency. Buying the moon is a way of giving us the money back, while pretending that it's an economic transaction rather than a gift."

Rose was accustomed to cameras, to attention, to crowds and noise, to choreographed processions from limousines into buildings. But her companion didn't have the lifetime's experience that she possessed; she was nervous on his behalf rather than her own. What if he freaked out? What if someone threw another egg – or worse?

"Whatever happens, just keep calm and carry on," she said.

"An admirable motto," Dorvin replied. "Do you find you need it often?"

She laughed. "Sometimes I need it every day."

Her bodyguard opened the limousine's door, and they stepped onto the pavement in front of the Great Ormond Street Hospital for Children. Crowds cheered and waved. A barrage of cameras greedily sucked in the scene. Behind a fence, a few protestors yelled, "Go home!"

Dorvin was so tall that it took him less than a dozen steps to reach the hospital entrance. He paused to allow Rose to precede him through the doorway. Inside, they split up for their separate missions. Dorvin was meeting the chief medical officer of the Stem Cell Therapy Trust, while Rose toured the wards and tried to bring some cheer to sick children. She'd considered it too risky for Dorvin to accompany her, in case a young child burst into tears at the sight of him. Better to send him to the scientists – a hint at the potential for sharing medical advances. As she entered the first ward, full of children sitting up in their beds eagerly waiting for her, she put Dorvin out of her mind and focused on being the princess everyone expected.

Two hours later, they reconvened in the day room to attend a concert. A group of older children, on a motley collection of instruments, made a creditable stab at Dancing Queen, followed by a medley from the Nutcracker Suite.

"All these children have had their limbs regrown through stem cell therapy," she explained to Dorvin. "It's the ultimate test, to be able to play an instrument with a new arm."

"Then we'd better give them good marks," said Dorvin, and applauded with just the right degree of polite enthusiasm.

Meanwhile, cameras captured every moment. In her visual overlay, Rose could see the initial media reactions and public comments. Some of them were supportive, but many were nasty and vitriolic. *"Why are the aliens visiting Ormond Street Hospital? They're picking out which children to eat first."*

She sighed, wondering whether she'd tackled a job too big to handle. Could one person overturn the perceptions of the entire planet? Clearly not. She needed to recruit more people to the cause. But to do that, she had to lead by example. She had to carry on.

After the concert, they left the photographers behind as the limousine took them to Tate Modern. Rose had exploited her position as a royal patron to arrange a private tour of the collection. Their footsteps echoed in the empty galleries.

"You talked about aesthetics, so I thought you might like to see some of our art," she said to Dorvin. "Of course, a lot of it is based on historical events, ancient myths, and so on – I wouldn't expect you to understand those. But some other styles might be more accessible: abstract expressionism, for instance." She'd spent the previous evening furiously reading up on the subject. "This is the Rothko room."

The paintings loomed above them – huge swathes of muted

colours in oblongs with ragged edges. To Rose, the colours looked heavy and oppressive: deep murky red, restless black spaces, a muddy maroon. In her overlay, a cloud of tags summarised visitors' responses. She ignored them, much more interested in Dorvin's reaction.

Dorvin walked to the nearest painting, and leaned in until his snout practically touched the canvas. He inhaled with an audible sniff, his wattles quivering.

"Most intriguing," he said. "A complex set of organic molecules, with a sense of great age. The volatiles have almost completely evaporated, possibly representing the evanescent nature of life. The residues – the longer-chain oils – indicate that what remains of us after death are merely the crude bones of physicality, their animating spirit entirely absent..."

Rose arched her eyebrows, wondering how to take this. Then she laughed. "Dorvin of Feloria, I do believe you're joking."

"I might be," he said. Another tremor shook the wattles below his snout. "But it's the perennial question of art appreciation: how far should we be guided by the artist's intent, and how much farther can we extend our own interpretation?"

"I'd say we should be guided at least as far as deciding which sense to use. This is intended as a visual work." Rose called up a stored prompt in her overlay, and quoted Rothko's words: "These shapes 'have no direct association with any particular visible experience, but in them one recognises the principle and passion of organisms'."

"Really?"

"That's what the artist said."

Dorvin walked back to the canvas and leaned into it again, as though peering very closely in search of recognition.

"Is he – or she – still alive?" Dorvin asked.

"No, he died a long time ago. Actually, he killed himself."

Dorvin looked back to the gloomy paintings. Rose couldn't help thinking that in this situation Gerrard would have instantly fired off an obvious quip such as "I can see why". She tapped her foot, annoyed with herself for letting Gerrard creep into her mind. It didn't matter what Gerrard would have said. He wasn't here; she needed to forget him.

"At home, we have a tradition of speaking more respectfully about the living than the dead," Dorvin explained. "Perhaps that's foolish –

after all, the work is the same regardless of whether the artist is alive. I haven't been here very long, but I already know that on Earth your commentary is more robust."

"Yeah. 'Robust' is certainly one word for it."

"If I were to speak robustly, I might say that these paintings look like afterimages in the eye of someone who's stared too long into a black hole."

"And the non-robust version?" inquired Rose.

"I suppose I'd say that these shapes have no direct association with any particular visible experience, but in them one recognises the principle and passion of organisms..."

Rose smiled. They left the Rothko room, and visited several more galleries. Now that she'd tuned into his sense of humour, Rose found herself both impressed and amused by Dorvin's responses to the works on display. She could have talked to him for hours, but it had been a long day: she didn't want to over-strain his politeness.

On their way back to the limousine, a startled passer-by saw them, did a double-take, and snapped a picture on his phone.

Royal Roundup – "ROSE'S NEW BOYFRIEND? Just days after the end of her relationship with Captain Gerrard Calderwood, Princess Rose has a new companion. Is this interplanetary diplomacy, or something more? Centuries have passed since the days when political alliances were cemented with royal marriages, but perhaps the old tradition is due a revival. Was the break-up with Calderwood so bitter that it soured her on the entire human race?"

Conspiracy Channel – "It looks like David Icke was right after all. He always said that the royal family were secretly a race of shape-changing lizards. Now Princess Rose has come out into the open and admitted her true love for her own kind!"

Goggler – "Princess Rose is stepping out with an alien. Presumably, Earthmen aren't good enough for her. It's a slap in the face for all Englishmen, but she's probably upset and confused. Here at Goggler, we think she just hasn't met the right guy yet, and we want to help her out. Yeomen of England – do you think you're good enough for Princess Rose? Write and tell us, explaining exactly why you're suitable. How would you prove yourself? Which monsters would you slay first?"

Rose's phone went into meltdown. At first she tried to ignore it, but the psychic pressure of all those unanswered calls and messages ate away at her. The phone helpfully prioritised them, telling her that her closest friends and family were trying to get in touch. Rose had almost cracked, and was about to start answering, when she heard someone arrive at the door. If the security team had let them through, then it must be –

"Helena! Do you know what time it is?"

"Yes, it's after midnight. So what? I'm not bloody Cinderella. And this isn't a fairy tale. When you talked about waving your wand and using the magic of the monarchy, I didn't realise you were going to try turning an alien frog into a prince." Helena stormed past Rose into the kitchen, and fired up the coffee machine. "What were you thinking? The hospital visit I could understand, but Tate Modern? An art gallery isn't diplomacy, it's a *date*! It's like having a toothbrush and a three-pack of condoms in your handbag –"

"Hey, I had to arrange something he might find interesting. I needed a bit more than a bunch of sick kiddies. It worked really well! He was funny, he got into it..."

"Rose, listen to yourself. 'He was funny, he got into it': that's a description of a date where you had a good time. I know you didn't mean it that way, because if you'd thought for a single second, you'd have realised how the media would take it. But subconsciously –"

The coffee machine beeped, startling them both. Helena poured them a latte each. "No mocha for you: you've been a bad girl. As I was saying, *subconsciously* this is about Gerrard. You wanted to send a message that you're over him: you're moving on, and you're seeing other guys."

"That is absolutely not true," Rose protested. "It makes no sense whatsoever."

"Not consciously, no. Which is why we've ended up with a PR disaster. Look, ordinarily I wouldn't care. I'd be on your side, cheering as you got over Gerrard and dated anyone you liked. But this is toxic. The aliens were already unpopular, and this isn't helping. You're not boosting their popularity – *they're dragging ours down*. And in case you've forgotten, there's a referendum next month."

Rose frowned, and sipped her coffee while she examined the latest opinion stats in her vision overlay. The pro-monarchy rating had fallen three points. Her own personal popularity had dropped by twenty points. She sat down, suddenly feeling unsteady on her feet. Would this affect the referendum result? Would history remember her as a Marie Antoinette figure, a foolish princess who helped to destroy the monarchy?

"That's just the instant reaction, before everyone's even heard about it," said Helena. "By tomorrow, this will be global."

"I hope it does go global," Rose said defiantly. "If I'm going to change people's minds, then the first step is to get their attention. This is only the start: you can't judge the plan by the first day's results. There'll be other activities – and they won't all look like dates, if you're worried about that."

"There'd better not be any other activities," said Helena, glaring at Rose. "We can't risk affecting the referendum. You're jeopardising a thousand years of history, just for the sake of a few aliens who can bloody well look after themselves. You've got to stop!"

"Helena, listen to yourself," said Rose, mimicking Helena's earlier tone. "What you're saying is that the royals should never do anything unpopular. But what's the point of having a monarchy if it never does anything worthwhile?"

"We do loads of worthwhile things!" Helena exclaimed. "How can you possibly say we don't do anything? What about –"

"Yes, I know, I know. We're all patrons of good causes. I've got enough letterhead paper to fill a wardrobe and the whole of Narnia behind it. But those are things that everyone already approves of. Today I had a photo-op at Great Ormond Street Hospital: smile for the cameras, hug the children, whip up some publicity. They must think it helps, or they wouldn't ask me to do it. But surely everyone already loves sick kiddies. Am I really achieving anything? Is that the best use of royal prestige? Look at Diana – she wanted to make a real difference, and promote causes that everyone didn't already believe in. That's what royalty should do."

Helena tugged the sleeve of Rose's pink chiffon blouse. "Just because you're dressed like her, that doesn't make you Diana. And it doesn't mean you can achieve what she did."

"I'm not relying on my *clothes*," said Rose, annoyed at Helena's implicit suggestion that she was doomed to fall short of Diana's legend. "I'm relying on my own efforts –"

"Yes, indeed," interrupted Helena, "and very admirable they are too. But why do you need to do all this now? Why not wait until after the referendum?"

"If it wasn't the referendum, it'd be something else. There's always some excuse for playing safe – 'forthcoming budget negotiations', 'a sensitive political climate'." Rose mimicked the voice of the King's media strategist, who notoriously always advised caution.

"More importantly," she went on, "right and wrong don't depend on the calendar. If it's the right thing next month, then it's the right thing now. So I'm doing it now."

"That's all very well, but it assumes you know exactly what the right thing is," Helena retorted. "If it was only about you, then I wouldn't argue. But your actions affect the entire royal family. You're being selfish, and jeopardising the rest of us."

Rose fell silent for a moment, struck by doubt. Was she being selfish? Should she hold back, for the good of the family?

"I'm only one person," Rose said at last. "The royal family is dozens of people. If I'm really jeopardising the monarchy, is that because I'm doing too much, or because everyone else is doing too little? The whole family is responsible for the outcome of the referendum, not just me."

Helena sighed. "In an ideal world, you'd be right. The public would look at all thirty-odd members of the royal family, weigh up their individual contributions, and cast their vote accordingly. But you know very well that's not how it works. People are driven by headlines, and you're creating the headlines."

"Then we need to make new headlines," said Rose. "Or at least make the old ones fade away. And we can do that, if we all pitch in. Why is it headline news that I visited an art gallery with an alien? Because it's unusual. But if we all start reaching out – if more of us make an effort to meet the Felorians and include them in society – then it won't be unusual any more. It won't be news. Problem solved!"

"This is a major news item because it happened straight after your break-up with Gerrard," Helena said tartly. "You'll still have to face those insinuations... unless you get another boyfriend. Do you want me to set you up with someone?"

Rose laughed. "That's very kind of you. But you know what the media are like. Even if I had a boyfriend, they'd still claim I was flirting with Dorvin. They love the freakshow angle. The only way to deal with that is to make the Felorians look less like freaks, and more like regular folk. Then the media will get bored of sensationalising them. And the more people see of the Felorians, the more they'll realise that the scare stories are ludicrous."

"That sounds optimistic," said Helena. "I wish I had your faith in human nature."

"Maybe it won't work. But we have to try."

"*We?*" Helena raised her eyebrows.

"Yes. I've got an idea. Let's take the focus away from individuals, and have a group event. How about a charity football match? Humans against aliens! We'll auction off places in the team, and sell tickets to the match, and sell the TV rights: plenty of money for good causes. Afterward, we'll have the usual dinner and drinks and whatnot. There'll be at least eleven Felorians, so lots more potential for interaction – different stories, new headlines. They'll start to look normal. And they can talk about their own sports, maybe show us some footage, and challenge us to try one of their games... What do you think?"

"Football, eh?" Helena smiled. "You must be desperate: you don't even like football. But I think you're onto something. A football match – what could be more normal?"

"Then you'll help?" asked Rose. "You'll lend your name to it, and recruit some players?"

"Oh, I don't think we'll have any difficulty finding players. Everyone will want a crack at the Felorians."

News Net – "ALIENS 4, HUMANS 3. The human race today fell to the bottom of the galactic league table, as the All-Earth XI was defeated in a charity soccer match by the Flowers of Feloria. Early goals from Freddy Hooke and Joe Beckham gave Earth a half-time lead, but the aliens gradually grew more comfortable on the ball, and they stormed back in the second half. Their first three goals came from corner kicks, the Felorians' greater height affording them an advantage in the air. Then a frantic finale saw a late Earth equaliser cancelled out by a dramatic last-minute penalty. Dorvin was fouled in the box, and stepped up to take the kick that gave the aliens victory."

Tag Scout – "Early stats suggest that fifty million people saw the game, with many more expected to watch clips and highlights. The Felorians' tag-cloud is changing: 'Conspiracy' remains the most popular label, but sport-related terms are rapidly gaining. The team's striker, Dorvin, already notorious for his association with Princess Rose, now has 'Diver' as his third-largest tag, with 'Not a Diver' following close behind."

Goggler – "WHERE IS PRINCESS ROSE? She's supposedly suffering from 'illness and exhaustion' after arranging the football match and hosting the post-match charity banquet. Hard work, eh? I think we can all see through that cover story. It's obvious that her relationship with Dorvin has moved on to the next phase. She's pregnant! Except that the aliens don't reproduce in the same way we do. No, their eggs hatch inside the mother, and the larvae burrow out from the inside, chomping all the way. Princess Rose is currently being eaten alive!"

After two days in bed, Rose returned to her duties as soon as she felt halfway recovered. Aside from her efforts to rehabilitate the Felorians, her diary still contained all the regular engagements that the royals performed. This year's schedule was even more intense than usual. Officially, the additions were part of the thousand-year anniversary celebrations; unofficially, they were an extra PR push ahead of the referendum.

Since 1917, the royal family had sent congratulatory messages to British subjects reaching their hundredth birthday or sixtieth wedding anniversary. These were normally despatched by post, but this year the family were personally presenting as many as possible. Consequently, Rose found herself visiting a town called Saltburn in the northeast of England.

It was a bitterly cold day at the end of October. The wind gusted straight from the North Sea, whipping up sand as Rose endured a tour of the beach, the pier, the Cliff Lift – "one of the oldest funiculars in the world!" – and all the usual quirky local history. Normally Rose enjoyed, or at least tolerated, these trips to odd corners of Britain. Now she just shivered, hoping it would end soon. She should have cancelled this event and stayed another day in bed.

At least the presentation was indoors, inside a village hall festooned with holographic bunting. Operating on autopilot, Rose smiled brightly as she presented cards from the King to six women and three men. Her headache intensified as she greeted each person by looking them in the eye and reading their names from the subtitles in her visual overlay. By the time she reached the last man, she was thinking longingly of home. "Congratulations on reaching your hundredth birthday, Mr Wilcox –"

"That's Wilcock, ma'am. Cock! Can't you get your mouth around a cock?" He gave her a cheeky grin.

Shocked, she stepped back. Her fingers lost their grip on the King's card; it clattered to the floor. She stooped and picked it up, anger flooding through her.

"I can assure you," she said through gritted teeth, "that despite what you may have read in the media, I have not lost my taste for *human* men. Although you are rather too old for me!"

"I didn't mean it like that," the man protested in a quavering voice. "It was just a joke."

Rose wanted to retort that she'd met aliens with a better sense of humour, but she knew she shouldn't inflame this incident any further. It would already make a juicy titbit for the 'royal gaffes' reel that anti-monarchists were circulating.

"I'm sorry, Mr Wilcock," she said. "It was entirely my fault. Congratulations on reaching your hundredth birthday, and please accept the King's felicitations."

She handed him the card, then left as quickly as she could, berating herself all the while. Getting someone's name wrong was the ultimate sin for anyone who dealt with the public. She could imagine the complaint: "I've waited a hundred years for this, and she couldn't even get my name right. These royals are totally out of touch. I'm voting for a republic!"

Yet what about his comment? Was it a standard response to a common mispronunciation, or was it a crude xenophobic jibe about her supposed affair with Dorvin? She wanted it to be a harmless joke, but she couldn't be sure. Lots of people still hated the aliens.

Well, that showed how much work remained for her to do. She wasn't going to quit, but perhaps she needed to adjust her tactics. It might be wise to stop seeing Dorvin for a while. Other Felorians had proved willing to take part in football matches and the like, so Dorvin wasn't essential to that effort. And Helena would surely agree to take over some hostess duties, if Rose explained that she wanted to draw the sting from the Dorvin issue.

On her way home, she phoned Helena to confirm the change in strategy. Then she phoned Dorvin for their regular liaison call. They discussed the upcoming events roster. After a few minutes of this, Dorvin said, "You keep saying, 'Helena, Helena'. Are you not coming to these any more?"

"It's best if I don't," Rose said.

"But I was looking forward to seeing you."

"I was looking forward to it too," Rose admitted, "but you can't always have what you want."

"Not even when you're a princess?"

"Especially not when you're a princess. It's the media – if we keep meeting, it creates unhelpful headlines." She rubbed her forehead, wishing that her headache would succumb to the tablets she'd taken.

"I didn't realise you were so scared of headlines. You weren't before. And you told me that Diana never was."

"I'm not scared of headlines," Rose said indignantly. "I'm just trying to achieve our goal. If those stories were helping, then I'd brazen them out. But they're not helping, so I'd rather not risk them."

"I understand that," Dorvin said. "If it's all about the goal, I mean. I just thought... Well, I thought we had a special bond."

Rose hadn't expected this conversation to be so hard. Wanting to get it over with, she decided to be brutal. "You're a diplomat – you should know that it's always about achieving the goal. It's never personal." She winced inwardly as she spoke. It was at least half a lie, but this seemed the best answer in the circumstances.

Dorvin's image on her screen was stock still: no jiggling snout or quivering wattles. He paused for so long that Rose wondered whether the phone connection had glitched. Then he said, "I appreciate your honesty. And now we've clarified that it isn't personal, perhaps I can be honest too.

"The reason why we want a base on your moon is simply so that we can stay as far away from you as possible, while maintaining the necessary communications. We find you disgusting, both physically and spiritually. The stench of your psychic emanations is a stain upon the cosmos, polluting the aether all around your cesspit of a planet. The moon is almost clean, since you've visited it so rarely. And the sooner we can retreat there, the better. I trust we can rely on your support in facilitating this."

His wattles tremored, ever so faintly. Then he cut the connection, and was gone.

Goggler – "SEX SECRETS OF THE STARS: The world's most renowned clairvoyant has applied his powers to ferreting out the Felorians' secrets. Erick Van Henningsen reveals the sordid truth: 'It was hard work penetrating the psychic barriers they have around their ship, but I was aided by the souls of a billion dead spirit guides who all want to protect the Earth. When I got inside, I saw scenes of monstrous depravity. Each alien has two penises, three vaginas, and four assholes. But even so, they still find each other repulsive, because they don't have any breasts. So they're forced to jack off to pictures of Earth women. Every single alien on that ship has a hologram of Princess Rose above his bed.' If Van Henningsen is right, then we're as appalled as any right-thinking soul would be. But has he got it right? How do YOU think the aliens have sex? Write and tell us exactly how disgusting you think they are!"

Fact Shack – "The Felorians today announced their forthcoming departure. Their starship will return home, taking a small human delegation. Some Felorians will stay behind in a new embassy, although its location has yet to be decided. The aliens have requested a final decision within one week on whether they will be allowed to purchase the moon."

When Rose heard the departure announcement, she welcomed the prospect of her life returning to normal, with fewer lurid headlines. Dorvin's words had wounded her. She kept replaying them in her mind: "disgusting... stench... stain... cesspit". She'd worried about human hatred of the Felorians, and it turned out that the Felorians hated humans just as much. They were simply better at hiding the fact.

Unless Dorvin's parting shot had been some sort of strange joke. "Psychic emanations" certainly didn't sound like a serious complaint. But what senses did the aliens have? Maybe their snouts could sniff many kinds of effluvia.

Rose wondered whether to abandon her liaison efforts. If she told the world what Dorvin had said, she'd create a backlash against the Felorians. The politicians would have no room for manoeuvre, and certainly wouldn't be able to sell the moon.

"What do you think I should do?" she asked Helena.

"Get yourself a new boyfriend," Helena instantly replied.

"I mean about the aliens!"

"Do you need to do anything? Are they your responsibility?"

"Only for the next few days," Rose said. "I want to finish what I started. I'm just not sure *how* to finish."

"I'm surprised – shouldn't it be easier to figure out, now that you know the Felorians better? I've met a few of them, and I certainly have a clearer impression. I thought that's what your project was all about: getting them into the public eye, so people could make their own minds up, rather than relying on media scare stories."

"Yes, you're right," said Rose. "I need to ask everyone to update their tags. But our prestige, and our personal experience with the Felorians, makes our opinions count the most. We just need to record them... once we decide what they are."

Helena opened a drawer and took out the silver helmets that Rose recognised from her previous visit. "No need to decide – these gadgets pluck your confusion straight out of your brain."

"And that's helpful, is it?" said Rose, laughing.

"It can be. It's just a way of summing up, so that you stop going round in circles. Come on, let's get this done."

Rose donned one of the helmets, and felt the familiar prickle of the gadget tuning into her emotions. She recalled her encounters with Dorvin: his calm grace in the aftermath of the egg-throwing incident; his patience in sitting through the hospital concert; his jokes at the art gallery; his enthusiasm for playing in the football match; his friendliness and wit whenever he met the public... and his final unkind words, which now seemed merely a snarky retort to her own brusqueness. It was reassuring to see that Dorvin could be less than perfect, that he wasn't just a smooth diplomatic interface.

"You're right," she told Helena, "it does help you sum up."

"That's good, because you need to write an ordinary tag as well. Most people don't have these fancy helmets."

Rose created an opinion tag: 'Trustworthy friend and ally'. She took the time to verify it with her strongest authentication – the modern version of the old royal seal.

The label joined all the others in the global tag-cloud: the myriad opinions that collectively formed the reputational economy. More and more tags appeared every day, requiring more and more sophisticated algorithms for collating them. Soon the imprecision of words would be superseded by mental tags, specifying exactly how everyone felt about everything. There would be no more strangers, no more foreign lands.

"I met some pensioners the other day," Rose said, "when I was giving out the King's birthday and anniversary cards. The size of their tag-clouds! A whole lifetime, boiled down into labels and links and opinions... It's terrifying."

"Is it? The whole point is to make people accountable for what they do. Maybe Gerrard will behave better next time, when he realises the reputation he creates."

"Yes, I know. But sometimes I feel like a computer, processing my life and calculating the results."

"You mean *experiencing* life," Helena said. "You have to live, before you can label. That's what it's all about. Come on, we've finished here.

Let's go and have a drink, meet some guys –"
"– Tag them, and tame them."

Hourly Digest – "The United Nations today agreed to sell the Felorians a 30-year lease on the moon, subject to various conditions. The proceeds will be distributed according to a formula based on national populations and successful lunar missions."

Tag Frenzy – Princess Rose latest tags: 'Traitor', 'Sell-out', 'Lizard lover', 'Vote NO!', 'Sheesh, give the woman a break', 'Still my favourite princess', 'Everything that's wrong with Britain today', 'How many pieces of silver?'

Dorvin's phone call took Rose by surprise. "Before we leave, I wanted to thank you for all your work –"

"You're leaving? I thought you'd be staying, now you've got your moonbase." An unexpected pang of disappointment swelled within her.

"No, I have to go home. But I need to apologise before I go. Last time, what I said... wasn't precisely true. Or false. It depends on your perspective. Felorians aren't all the same. Some of us really do find you disgusting. Xenophobia is universal. But we're not all like that. I'm certainly not." Dorvin spoke in short, staccato sentences, the antithesis of his usual polished phrasing.

"I guess it's obvious I haven't rehearsed this," he went on. "I'm sorry for what I said. I spoke in disappointment and anger, and I apologise."

"Thank you," said Rose.

"Did you know that we're taking a few humans back to Feloria? Scientists and diplomats, mostly. If you wanted to come, I would be happy to invite you as my honoured guest."

"Um... Wow." Rose didn't know what to think. Reflexively, she fell back on politeness to cover the gap. "Thanks for the invitation – I appreciate the offer." Then she realised that before she could make any sensible answer, she needed to know a lot more about the journey. "How long would I be gone?"

"A few years. I'll send you the details, if you're interested. I should warn you that it'll be hard. But whatever happens, I know you'll keep calm and carry on. I think you could make a big contribution. We've all been impressed by your efforts to promote harmony."

Rose smiled. "Thanks," she said again. "Please send me the details.

I'm sure you understand I'll have to think it over. When do you need an answer?"

"We're leaving in three days."

News Net – "BRITAIN KEEPS MONARCHY. Today's referendum results showed a 7% majority for retaining the King as head of state, with the UK remaining a monarchy rather than becoming a republic. The outcome had previously looked threatened by Princess Rose's controversial liaisons with the Felorians. Yet pollsters reported that many voters admired her willingness to stand up for a cause, even an unpopular one. 'We need princesses to do what politicians can't,' said a Saltburn resident who recently met her. 'I liked the way she handled herself. She gave as good as she got.'"

Rose sat in the visitors' gallery on the starship bridge, nervously clutching the armrests of her seat. All the furniture was a little too high for her. The sensation of not knowing what awaited her was both exhilarating and terrifying.

"Does this vehicle have seat-belts?" she asked Dorvin.

"We have no need of such primitive technology," he replied, his wattles quivering.

She laughed. "I can't work out whether that's reassuring or not."

Below her, the crew made final preparations for the forthcoming leap across the galaxy. In her vision overlay, only the barest minimum of tags appeared – a few names, a sprinkling of friendliness ratings and etiquette reminders.

Rose looked at the big screen, showing the view ahead of the ship. Distant stars studded the blackness like new jewels on an old mourning dress. Her overlay displayed no tags whatsoever.

A Felorian voice spoke on the intercom. Dorvin interpreted it for her: the launch countdown had begun. Rose smiled, bracing herself to greet the unknown.

"No Strangers Any More" arose from a phone conversation with a friend who was born in 1966. I can't remember the context, but for some reason he mentioned that if he lived to be a hundred, then not only would he get a birthday card from the Queen or King, but the monarchy itself would then be a thousand years old – if counting from the Norman Conquest in 1066. (Any starting point is somewhat

arbitrary, but my friend and I grew up during an era when school history lessons emphasised the Norman Conquest.)

I became intrigued by the notion of the monarchy's thousandth anniversary, and I embarked upon a story set in the year 2066. I decided that my protagonist would be a princess in the mould of Diana, Princess of Wales, and that she would meet an alien diplomat. The original Diana died tragically, but I wanted to write an upbeat story with a comic tone. Hence my inspiration focused on Diana's personality rather than her life; I invented my own plot rather than retelling historical events.

A major aspect of the story is the media landscape. Diana attracted a huge amount of press coverage, and that was in an era when newspapers only came out once a day. In a futuristic milieu extrapolated from today's 24/7 online culture, media attention would be omnipresent. I therefore included lots of interstitial snippets from various media outlets.

Since the entire story was inspired by my friend's comment about living to be a hundred in the year 2066, I included a cameo role for him as a centenarian who meets the princess. He kindly gave his permission for this, and didn't object even when he saw the fruity dialogue I'd assigned to him.

I wrote the first draft of the story in 2012, when the imagined future was just over fifty years away. One piece of worldbuilding was a referendum on whether to abolish the monarchy and convert Britain into a republic. Another was this: "After leaving the European Union, Britain had become an irrelevance in world politics. This made the UK an ideal venue for international conferences: neutral and insignificant, but with plenty of pageantry and princesses."

For most of my lifetime, Britain's relationship with Europe has been a festering issue, so it wasn't much of a stretch to suppose that Britain might eventually leave the EU. Nevertheless, it was an interesting coincidence that the story was published in the July/August 2016 issue of Analog *– straight after the Brexit referendum on 23 June 2016. It made my story look remarkably prescient.*

THE LANGUAGE OF FLOWERS

Every morning I harvested the most luscious blooms from the gardens for display in the showroom. Today the quince blazed with bright orange blossom, so I cut a few twigs. As I carried them inside, I sniffed the flowers to check the engineered pheromones. A wave of longing overtook me: a sudden urge to do something mischievous and subversive. After a few seconds it receded, and I was my usual businesslike self again.

One side of the shop showcased the most popular plants from the Victorian language of flowers. I removed some fading poppies, and installed the quince in their place. Then I replaced the old label – "Poppy: *Consolation*" – with a new sign that said "Quince: *Temptation*".

The other side of the showroom displayed Harriet's custom flowers. We'd only been producing pheromone-enhanced plants for a year, and Harriet was already designing new flowers to convey new meanings. She said that life had become more complicated since the nineteenth century, so the flower language needed more words. Harriet wanted to stretch herself as an artist; I just wanted to sell enough plants to keep us afloat.

While I awaited the day's customers, I attacked my inbox. The first email came from the Lavender Marketing Board. "Dear Mr Chase: Thank you for your message explaining the Victorian origins of the 'language of flowers'. Although lavender used to mean *mistrust*, we feel that's very much obsolete. Today the herb has far more positive associations. We suggest that you rebrand lavender with an upbeat meaning such as *affection* or *prestige*...*"

Since they'd already received my tactful response, I replied, "If you have a problem with the traditional vocabulary, I recommend that you invent a time machine and take it up with the Victorians directly."

I looked up from my laptop when the first customer arrived, a young woman with large earrings in the shape of crescent moons. New visitors always pause just inside the doorway, overwhelmed by the scents from all the cut blooms and potted plants. Augmenting the flowers' inherent odours, the pheromones add their own effects.

Naturally, I only display flowers whose meanings are neutral or positive. Certainly no lavender – I wouldn't make many sales if my clients got a whiff of *mistrust* at the till.

After she'd recovered herself, the visitor didn't glance at any of my carefully crafted displays. She walked straight to the counter and said, "I hear you're doing the flowers for Miles Jelbert's memorial service."

"Yes, we are." I'd delegated this task to the staff florist who handled routine work.

"And it's all going to be in the language of flowers, is it?" Her body language was stiff, her expression tense. From her accent, I pegged her as local – either Devon or Cornwall. Harriet and I have lived here for five years, but we still sound like outsiders.

"Our commission is in the language, because that's what we do," I replied. "I don't know if other flowers will come from elsewhere."

She fell silent for a long moment, as though nerving herself up to something.

"I'm Travis Chase," I said to fill the pause. "Can I get you a tea or a coffee?"

"I guess you're the Chase in Ormonde and Chase. Does that mean you make the flowers?"

I smiled and shook my head. "Harriet Ormonde does all the design work. She's in the greenhouse right now."

"But you do take commissions?"

"Yes, if it's something we can make." *At the right price,* I added to myself.

She tapped her fingers on the counter with nervous energy. "I think I do need that coffee," she said. "I'm Vanessa Jelbert. Miles Jelbert was my grandfather."

"I'm sorry for your loss," I said as I made drinks. We sat in the easy chairs by the window.

"Not that much of a loss," Vanessa said. "He was a fucking racist asshole."

I raised my eyebrows. "I presume that's not the official epitaph."

"Probably not. I imagine it'll be something like 'Local graves for local people. Keep immigrants out of British cemeteries!'."

Miles Jelbert had been a controversial figure on Cornwall's county council. He'd lived nearby, across the river dividing Cornwall from Devon.

Vanessa sighed. "It's such a relief to say that. Ever since he died, everyone wants to pretend he was perfect, especially the rest of the family. Of course, none of them had to bear the brunt of it."

I gazed at her with curiosity. Her skin was as white as my own.

She reached into her handbag and brought out her phone. Onscreen, a photo showed two small boys with dark faces and corn-row hair.

"He used to call them 'little monkeys'," she said. "If they were playing outside in the twilight, he'd say, 'Where are you? I can't see you.' He thought it was funny. And if I complained, he'd accuse me of overreacting. 'Where's your sense of humour?' he'd say. Then he'd ask if they wanted a banana."

Her fingers whitened as she clenched the phone. For a moment, I thought it might break. Then she shoved it in her bag and took a gulp of coffee. "Sorry to unload that onto you. I guess you don't need every detail. But I just want you to know what he was like."

"It sounds awful," I said. "I'm sorry you had to go through that." I sympathised, yet I also wanted her to hurry up and tell me why she'd come.

"My aunt Janice said she'd sort out the flowers," Vanessa said. "What's she bought?"

I called up the order on my laptop. "Cypress for mourning, of course. To represent his life, it's red clover for hard work, cardinal flowers for distinction, white chrysanthemum for truth... The usual kind of stuff." June was too early for regular chrysanthemums, but all our engineered plants had an extended flowering season.

"Truth!" she exclaimed bitterly. "That's not the truth."

I shrugged. "The language of flowers is like any other language – you can lie with it. Nobody's on oath at a funeral."

"We've had the funeral already," Vanessa said. "This is the memorial service, and there'll be even more speeches. I can't stand any more bullshit about him. I want to show what he was really like. Can you make a flower that means *racism?*"

I frowned. "That's a new one. We've never been asked for that."

Making a racism flower could be controversial. After our previous trouble with the poisonous politicians, I didn't want to jeopardise the business again.

"Does it have to be racism?" I asked. "There are plants in the Victorian language of flowers that might fit. Basil for *hatred*, marigolds for *cruelty* –"

She shook her head. "They're not specific enough. I want his sins to be named and shamed. If my sons are going to sit beside me while we listen to people talking about how wonderful he was, then I need to see a reminder of the truth."

"It might put you in trouble with the family," I said.

Vanessa shrugged. "I should have stood up to them a long time ago. This is my last chance. If I don't make a fuss about it now, then I'll hate myself for never fighting back. The family always said, 'He's old, he doesn't mean anything by it. He just has a rotten sense of humour.' But he *did* mean it. He hated outsiders. He was head of the Stannary League – 'Cornwall for the Cornish!'."

I didn't have time to listen to her grandfather's life story. "You don't need to justify yourself to me," I said. "If someone buys red clover, I don't ask them to prove how industrious they are."

"Then you'll do it?" she asked eagerly.

"It'll be a rush job; I need to ask Harriet if she can fit it in." I paused. "A new commission is more expensive than our regular stock. There's a lot of work involved in crafting the flower, installing the pheromone –"

"Yeah, I understand," she interrupted. "I can find the money."

Ordinarily, I'd love to hear anyone say that. I'm a businessman, after all. And it wasn't so long since we'd almost gone bankrupt, following our run-in with the Austerity Rebels.

But as I watched Vanessa Jelbert stride out of the shop, stiff and full of tension, I couldn't help wondering whether this commission would really make her happy.

While my assistant manned the showroom over lunch, I went to the kitchen and made sandwiches for Harriet. When she's deep into a pomonics project – which is most of the time – she forgets to eat. She doesn't notice being hungry, or indeed anything else. If the apocalypse ever arrives, all you'll see afterward is a few cockroaches scuttling around, and Harriet in a smashed greenhouse still busy tinkering with seeds.

Carrying the sandwiches and a jug of iced fruit juice, I crossed the gardens via my summer route through the mint and buttercups, so I could inhale the pleasant odours of *virtue* and *riches*. I avoided the quince, because I knew which temptation would afflict me. I'd be tempted to abandon this commission without telling Harriet. The whole thing smelled of trouble, as strongly as if it had a tailored pheromone for *danger*. But I knew Harriet would want to take it on – and if I avoided telling her, then I'd regret it. One day I would catch a whiff of *honesty* and blurt out the truth.

I opened the 'Authorised personnel only' gate at the end of the garden, and saw Harriet through the glass walls of the experimental hothouse. Before entering, I paused to admire her profile as she leaned over a tray of seedlings. She wore a vivid turquoise T-shirt, and she'd pinned a single bloom of white hollyhock into her hair.

The interior was warm, humid, and quiet. As the plants were too young to produce scent, I only smelled compost and the metallic tang of growth accelerants. I unfolded the visitor's chair, sat down, and shared out the sandwiches.

"Someone just asked us to make a flower that represents racism," I said.

Harriet's eyes brightened with eagerness. "Racism? That's a good challenge. I guess it should be an ugly flower. Probably white: the papery, diseased-looking white that comes from having no pigment cells. And thorns – or is that too obvious? Maybe no thorns, but a long smooth stem, the kind where the flower flops over without support." She gestured with a soil-encrusted hand, while the words kept tumbling out. "As for the smell, I can whip up a pheromone easily enough. A combination of hatred and pride and fear... but the scent will speak for itself. Words are too crude to describe what scent can evoke. How much time have we got?"

"Just over two weeks."

Harriet sagged back in her chair. "That's annoying. I can't create a whole new flower in that time. I'll have to find some existing stock and implant the pheromone into it."

A new plant needed time to germinate and grow, even with accelerants. Pheromone installation was easier because all our plants had the same scent-emitting cells, designed to be infected by an engineered virus that delivered the odour's chemical specification. Any existing plant could be adapted as necessary; Harriet maintained a range of exotic flowers as a contingency for urgent requests.

"Only if we take the commission," I said. "I'm worried about it –"

"You're always worried!"

"That's my job," I said. "I'm the business manager. I need to keep us afloat."

"All right," said Harriet, in a conciliatory tone. "What are you worried about?"

"The client wants to criticise someone for being racist. But what if we make the flower and it's embraced by the far right? Some nationalist group could adopt it as their symbol. The public would view us as standing behind the racists, selling them their official flower. It'd ruin our reputation."

Harriet tried to interrupt, but I overrode her. When I start worrying, there's no stopping me. "Then the racists could plant the flower everywhere" – which was what the Austerity Rebels had done with our poisonous politicians – "and the pheromone might inspire racist attacks. Someone could get murdered, and it would be our fault!" I paused to recover my breath.

"There's no need for nightmares," said Harriet, as if consoling a child terrified by monsters in the wardrobe. "Racists don't call themselves that – they use euphemisms. They wouldn't touch a flower explicitly branded as racism. If the idea did creep into their mind, the plant itself would put them off. I'll make it an ugly bloom with a nasty scent. Undercurrents of fear and paranoia, that kind of thing."

I nodded, somewhat reassured.

"This is the language of flowers," Harriet went on, "and a language needs words. It's our job to supply the words that people want to use. I'm glad this request has come along, because it proves that the flower language can say meaningful things and it's not just 'a silly gimmick'."

From her tone, I could tell she was quoting someone who'd upset her. Perhaps another gallery had rejected her proposal for an exhibition.

"I'm sick of not being taken seriously," Harriet said. "Just because I'm a woman, and flowers are seen as feminine trivialities, people think that what I do isn't real art. But this commission is perfect. Racism is serious – and that means we're serious. It's automatic credibility!"

Harriet worked through evenings and nights to create the flowers in time. On the day of the memorial service, Vanessa arrived to collect them, accompanied by her two boisterous sons. I kept a wary eye on the children, in case they damaged the showroom displays. The bouquet under my desk was leaking a toxic cloud of fear and suspicion.

I brought out the flowers, eager to be rid of them.

"Wow, those are ugly," Vanessa said.

I'd tied the bunch with velvet ribbons. But that was the sole resemblance to a conventional bouquet. Harriet had adapted the flower from a relative of toothwort: a parasitic plant that completely lacked chlorophyll, and hence had a pale, diseased appearance.

Vanessa raised the blooms to her nose for a sniff. She winced, and her eyes watered. "That's exactly it!" she exclaimed.

"Are you sure you want to go through with this?" I asked.

I knew Harriet would be annoyed if her flower went unseen. But Vanessa looked tense and angry, like someone on the brink of doing something rash before regretting it.

"Absolutely." Vanessa shoved her credit card into the reader so hard that it almost broke the machine.

"You could skip the memorial service instead," I suggested.

She glanced at me, puzzled. "Don't you want to sell these?"

"I just want our customers to be happy," I said. "Whatever it takes."

Vanessa grabbed the bouquet. "Telling the truth is more important," she said as she stalked away.

I updated the Ormonde and Chase website, adding a picture of the *racism* plant to the 'Language of Flowers' page. Sadly – or perhaps fortunately – there was no way to upload the flower's unpleasant odour.

When I clicked 'View All', I saw a gratifyingly long list of plants. Harriet kept toiling away, creating new vocabulary. I used to joke with her, asking how she would represent concepts like *antidisestablishmentarianism*. I stopped when I realised that she viewed the jokes as a challenge. She wanted to make flowers for every conceivable circumstance. In her ideal world, our gardens would expand across the entire Tamar valley, and everyone would communicate by giving each other flowers.

For the rest of the day I felt a lingering unease. What might happen at the memorial service? I imagined a riot, sparked by the sight of someone foreign-looking. As Harriet always tells me, I worry too much. Rationally, I knew my fears were unwarranted. Our flower pheromones aren't mind-control: they just communicate a feeling. And the *racism* bouquet would be drowned out by all the other messages in the wreaths we'd supplied: *hard work, distinction, truth*... Really, if anything was going to happen, it should be a mass outbreak of rectitude.

Next morning the verbena was nearing its prime, so I harvested a few grey stems bedecked with tiny violet florets. Verbena means *sensibility*, which we use in our Austen bouquets. 'Sense and Sensibility' is a running joke: I always say that I'm *sense*, and Harriet is *sensibility*. The 'Pride and Prejudice' package barely sells – the pheromones aren't exactly must-haves. Much more popular is our 'Love and Freindship' bouquet, inspired by one of Austen's juvenile works: the *friendship* plant has a quirkily misshapen leaf to represent Austen's misspelling.

Just as I finished watering the displays, two men marched into the showroom. They were in late middle age, smartly dressed, with stern expressions.

"Good morning," one of them barked. "We'd like to see the manager."

"That's me," I said. "Travis Chase."

He gave me a stiff nod of acknowledgement. "I'm Daniel Trevithick, and this is Peter Penhallow. We're councillors on Cornwall Council. We're also Stannators. The Stannary League was formerly led by our esteemed colleague, the late Miles Jelbert."

It sounded like a military briefing. "His memorial service was yesterday," Trevithick went on. "I understand you supplied the flowers."

"That's right," I said. "Cypress for mourning, red clover for hard work, white chrysanthemum for truth –"

"And an ugly little weed that apparently means racism," Trevithick interrupted.

He glared at me. I stared back, refusing to be intimidated. Trevithick was a monochrome palette, with a black moustache, grey-tinged beard, and severely cropped white hair.

"It quite spoiled the day," Penhallow said, leaning on his walking stick. In other circumstances I would have invited the visitors to sit down, but I didn't like their attitude. "The flowers stood out for being so ugly. Everyone wondered what they were. Then someone found your website. We were all horrified – what a thing to say!"

I imagined Vanessa Jelbert smiling amid the commotion.

"Some of us wanted to get rid of the flowers," said Penhallow. "But we were overruled –"

"It would have drawn even more attention to them," Trevithick told him impatiently. He turned to me. "Those flowers should never have been there in the first place. They were completely inappropriate."

"They were commissioned," I said. "It's not my place to decide what people can and can't say."

"Your language is full of left-wing bias," Trevithick bellowed. "Miles wasn't a racist, he was a patriot! But your website doesn't list anything for patriotism."

"I'm not left-wing," I said, offended. "I run a business – I'm trying to turn a profit. Patriotism isn't in stock because no one's asked for it." We hadn't yet engineered every single plant in the traditional Victorian vocabulary. "If you want to commission it, I'd be very happy to take your order."

"That's not what we came for," Trevithick snapped.

"I know," Penhallow said, "but it's an interesting idea. Maybe we should have patriotic flowers. It would be a way of distancing ourselves from those other ones."

"We wouldn't need to do that if someone hadn't ruined the memorial service. Who was it?" Trevithick demanded. "Who ordered those disgusting weeds?"

I was surprised they didn't know, but perhaps Vanessa had surreptitiously slipped her bouquet into the display. "I don't gossip about my clients," I said.

Trevithick looked around theatrically, taking in the showroom and the view through the window to the gardens outside. "A fine business you're running here," he said. "As a councillor, I know a lot of legislation applies to premises like this. Are you sure everything's in order? Fire safety, waste disposal, biohazard containment... These gardens must need a lot of upkeep – do you employ any illegal immigrants? What about your paperwork: licences, insurance, hygiene certificates? Maybe you're overdue for an inspection."

I try to keep up with regulations, but you can never be sure you've conquered all the red tape. Although the threat worried me, I didn't let it show. "I don't know if you noticed, but you drove here across a rather large bridge. You're councillors in Cornwall, which is the other side of the river. This is Devon."

"We do *liaise* with our colleagues in Devon," said Trevithick, doing his best to make bureaucracy sound like a threat.

"Well, feel free to liaise away. But if you disrupt my business, I won't be able to make you a patriotism flower. Would you like to commission one?"

"Not if it's as ugly as that last thing," Penhallow said with distaste.

"It won't be," I assured him. "In the Victorian language of flowers, patriotism was represented by the nasturtium. That's a nice traditional plant. And as no one's ordered it before, we can customise it for you." Harriet normally insisted on creative control, but this was an emergency mollification. "Would you like any particular colour?"

"Red, white and blue, for the Union Jack, of course," said Penhallow.

"No, just red and white, like the English flag," said Trevithick. "The cross of Saint George."

"Or maybe black and white," Penhallow said. "The flag of Cornwall is a white cross on a black background," he told me, with the manner of a teacher addressing a dense schoolboy who deserved a clip round the ear.

"Perhaps we can finalise the colour later," I said. "As for the pheromone in the flower, I guess the emotion is mostly pride? Maybe some nostalgia as well, for the way things used to be..."

Penhallow nodded. "That sounds about right. I'll put it on the agenda for our next meeting: whether we need a flower, what it should be like –"

"There isn't time to set up a sub-committee and argue over details," Trevithick said. "If we're having this flower, we need it ready for the launch of the Miles Jelbert Foundation."

"When's the deadline?" I asked.

"Fairly soon," he said. "The foundation is a charity to help local people find affordable housing. Outsiders keep pushing up prices by buying second homes, which makes it hard for young people to live here. Miles wanted to help the next generation of Cornishmen. He established the foundation before his death, and left his money to it. The trustees have already been looking at properties and screening applicants. When we acquire the first house, there'll be a photo-opportunity: presenting the keys to a local family."

Trevithick gazed at me with a smug smile. He thought he'd proved that Miles Jelbert was a good man who didn't deserve to be smeared as a racist. Remembering Vanessa's description of her grandfather's behaviour, I wondered how the foundation would define 'local' families. I had my suspicions.

Normally I try to make customers happy, but I don't like being threatened and patronised. I wanted to say, "Instead of putting the pheromone into a flower, we should put it into an English Bulldog, so it shits out great steaming turds of patriotism everywhere it goes."

However, I had a better plan in mind. "The foundation sounds like a worthy cause," I said. "When you buy the first house, you might want to check the garden for inappropriate plants. You don't want to undermine your image by being photographed next to any lavender or marigolds. If you like, I could come and remodel the garden for you."

"Yes, we don't want a repeat of what happened at the memorial service," Penhallow said. "No inappropriate flowers. Just charity and patriotism."

I smiled. "We'll make it represent you exactly."

"Have you got time to tweak some nasturtiums?" I asked Harriet. "We've had a request for *patriotism*."

She sighed. "Patriotism? We ought to be selling something more refined."

"Such as?"

"This is my latest pheromone," Harriet said. "Smell it!"

I had little choice, as Harriet immediately shoved a pink freesia into my face. As soon as I breathed in, I got a whiff of... what? Something indescribable. I felt like a visitor to a surreal museum with no labels or catalogues, a collection of unnameable dreams.

"What's that?" I asked, amazed.

Harriet smiled. "It is what it is. There's no need for a description in words. Smell is the most primal sense, reaching deep inside the brain. In the old days we needed words to communicate, because we couldn't make tailored scents. Now that we can, words are obsolete!"

Not long ago, I was annoyed at Harriet for wanting to move on from her old merchandise, the caricature plants we used to sell. Nowadays I felt she was too fixated upon her current creations. I wished I could wangle a gallery exhibition for the language of flowers, giving her the recognition she craved, and implicit permission to move on.

"Harriet, I can't list a product on the website without using words to describe it. But never mind that. Right now, our client wants patriotism."

"Ah, the sordid realities of commerce," Harriet said. "I suppose I'll need to whip up a patriotic pheromone."

"It should evoke pride and nostalgia – and disagreement." I remembered Trevithick and Penhallow sounding at odds with each other. "Patriotism only exists because the world is divided into nations. Think about football: you can't support your country without wanting the other team to lose."

"Yes, there's an element of discord," said Harriet. "As for the flower, the obvious colour is red – the colour of blood."

The launch of the Miles Jelbert Foundation took place at a hillside cottage overlooking the sea. I arrived long before everyone else, and spent hours overhauling the garden to remove off-message plants, replacing them with Penhallow's requested symbols. Turnips are an unglamorous vegetable on the plate, but their attractive yellow blossoms represent *charity*. Alongside them – and outnumbering them – I installed *patriotism* in the form of Harriet's engineered nasturtiums, staked in neat rows like ranks of soldiers. Their flowers were blood-red trumpets.

At lunchtime, the Stannators began to arrive. Penhallow stood by the gate and watched me work. When I threw the unwanted plants onto the compost heap, he said, "That's a bit prejudiced, isn't it?"

"What do you mean?" I asked.

"Last night I met the chairman of the Lavender Marketing Board," he said. "They're not very happy with you. Why does lavender supposedly mean *mistrust?* And it's not just lavender." He pointed to the orange marigolds I'd discarded. "What's their problem?"

"In the language of flowers, they're *cruelty*," I said. "You asked me to get rid of all the inappropriate plants."

"But these meanings are arbitrary, aren't they? The flowers haven't done anything wrong. They're unfairly maligned, tarred with negative associations. That seems rather... cruel." Penhallow paused. "One might even call it *racist*."

I laughed. "Racism against plants? That's absurd."

"Maybe so, maybe not. Racism is a toxic accusation, no matter how absurd. Mud will stick to anyone." His cheeks flushed with anger.

"Miles was a good friend of mine, and his memorial service was ruined. Today's launch needs to run perfectly. If your flowers create the slightest disturbance, there'll be consequences. Let's see how you like it when you're the evil racist! The Lavender Marketing Board is right behind me."

"There's nothing here except what you asked for," I said, striving to remain calm. "Now if you'll excuse me, I've been working all morning, so I need to go and freshen up."

Before he could reply, I walked away. I slipped through the cottage's back door and headed for the bathroom to take a shower. The refreshing sting of hot water soothed my tired muscles and washed away the garden grime.

As I showered, I contemplated Penhallow's ultimatum. I understood his desire to commemorate his friend and whitewash Jelbert's reputation. But he'd taken the wrong tack. This was the second time the Stannators had resorted to threats, and it wasn't growing on me. I resolved to continue with my scheme.

Back in the garden, the sun was warm, almost stifling. No wind shook the plants. The nasturtiums' honey-like scent lingered in the air, overpowering any hint of salt from the ocean below.

The lawn had acquired a row of lightweight folding tables, ready for the buffet. I added a nasturtium at every place setting. I still had a few flowers left, and I wanted to use them all, so I popped back into the cottage to look for a vase.

In the lounge – which badly needed new carpet and wallpaper – I bumped into Vanessa Jelbert.

"Oh, hello," I said. "I just met Penhallow; I should warn you he's still angry about the memorial service."

"They've guessed it was me," she said. "That's why I'm hiding in here for the time being. I'll come out when they begin the speeches."

"Are you planning another protest?" I asked.

"No, I already made my point. My grandfather is dead. I can't alter what he did, and neither can he. I always hoped that one day he might change, might realise how hurtful he was, maybe even apologise." Vanessa took a deep breath, and sighed. "I was dreaming, I guess. But while he was alive, there was always a faint chance. Now there's no chance at all. So I've got to put that behind me, and move forward. I still have to deal with the rest of the family. That'll be easier if we try to forget old grudges. I came along today to make a fresh start." She wore an expression of grim determination.

"I think you're doing the right thing... Not that my opinion counts. It's not my place to tell you how to deal with this. But I have an idea for something you could do, if you wanted." I paused, until she gestured me to continue. "After their speeches, maybe you could step up and say a few words yourself. They'll expect you to denounce him, but you can rise above that. Take the moral high ground. Be gracious, if you can bear it. And maybe they'll show who they really are."

I wanted to reassure her that she would still see the Stannators' noxious attitudes challenged, but I wasn't sure if my plan would work, so I only hinted rather than promised.

Vanessa nodded slowly. "I've been wondering whether I should speak. Say something nice, you reckon? I'll see if I can think of anything. That might take me a while!"

"Then I'll leave you to it," I said.

I found a vase in the kitchen and filled it with water. I put the last of the nasturtiums inside, then placed it as a centrepiece on the buffet table.

A clutch of people stood on the lawn: Jelbert's family and a few Stannary League bigwigs. I was pleased to meet a journalist from the local paper. Susanna Munro had copper hair, thick-framed glasses, and a Scottish accent. She looked very young to be so far from home; I suppose aspiring journalists, like anyone else, have to start somewhere.

On the cottage's front doorstep, Trevithick began his speech. "Local houses for local people!" he declaimed. "Miles Jelbert devoted his life to serving Cornwall: standing up for Cornish folk, bringing our communities together, fighting the outsiders who want to destroy our way of life..."

More of this followed, much more. Eventually Trevithick produced a shiny set of keys from his pocket. "On behalf of the Miles Jelbert Foundation, I'm delighted to present the first – but not the last! – affordable local house to a deserving local family."

The new owners stepped forward to receive the keys, grinning in delight. A brawny fisherman and his goth-chick girlfriend, they held hands rather touchingly as they each expressed their gratitude. I noticed that they were both white.

The onlookers applauded, while Trevithick gazed benevolently down from the doorstep like an ancient feudal landlord receiving homage from forelock-tugging peasants.

The crowd began drifting toward the buffet. A high-pitched voice cried, "Wait a moment!" Vanessa Jelbert approached the doorstep. Trevithick glared at her, but stood aside.

"I'm Miles Jelbert's granddaughter," she said, "and I just want to add a few words. I guess most of you came to the memorial service. You might have seen some strange flowers, which caused a lot of fuss. I was the one who ordered those flowers."

"Shame on you!" someone shouted.

Ignoring this, Vanessa continued, "I was upset at the way everyone kept talking about my grandfather as though he was some kind of saint. I knew he wasn't, so I brought the flowers as a silent protest.

"But it was the wrong day to do that, and I want to apologise. Today, we've all seen Miles Jelbert at his best. He cared about people, and he cared about Cornwall.

"Here are some new flowers, showing what the Stannary League stands for." She bent down and plucked a nasturtium from the nearest flower-bed. Brandishing it like a sword, she said, "This is what my grandfather believed in: patriotism!"

Applause broke out. Unlike Trevithick, she didn't stay to milk it. She immediately scurried away, avoiding everyone's gaze, and only stopped walking when she almost crashed into the garden fence.

Throughout all this I'd stood at the back of the crowd, out of everyone's way, since I was only the gardener. Vanessa ended up next to me.

"That was brave," I said quietly.

She shrugged. "I remembered you telling me that the language of flowers is like any other language – you can lie with it." Vanessa threw the nasturtium onto the compost heap, as though flinging away garbage.

Although she didn't say as much, I reckoned she'd apologised to show that it was possible, and prove herself a better person than her grandfather.

"Let's get a bite to eat," I said.

We sat near the end of the table, tucking into crab sandwiches followed by scones with Cornish clotted cream. At each place setting, a blood-red nasturtium contrasted vividly with the white tablecloth. A few of the Stannators had pinned nasturtiums into their blazers, which they wore despite the heat. The scent of the flowers mingled with the smell of the food. All the *patriotism* plants throughout the garden – in flower-beds, vases, and buttonholes – were slowly wafting their pheromones into people's noses.

Bottles of wine and Pimm's kept arriving. I accepted a glass of Pimm's and lemonade, accessorised with strawberries and a sprig of mint. Strawberries mean *perfect excellence*, and mint means *virtue* – but I was hoping to see the opposite.

I waited for a pause in conversation, and addressed the table. "Do you reckon we'll ever see an independent Cornwall?"

"Not in my lifetime," Penhallow said. "Still, we keep the customs alive, keep the language alive –"

"Those of us who can be bothered to learn the language," said another Stannator. He drained his Pimm's, slammed the glass on the table, and exclaimed, *"Yeghes da!"*

"Bless you," someone else said, with a mischievous tone.

"The language is a side issue," said Trevithick. "Even independence is a side issue. What matters is self-determination: controlling our own lives. The label is irrelevant. We just need to resist the meddling outsiders – wherever they come from." He shot piercing glances at his fellow diners, as though one of us might be a foreign spy.

Hearing this discussion, the journalist dragged her chair closer. "Which outsiders are you thinking of?" she asked.

"Europe," he said with disgust. "Fishing quotas, and God knows what else. Even after Brexit, we still haven't freed ourselves from all their barmy regulations."

"You were keen enough on regulations when you wanted to threaten my business with an inspection," I said.

Trevithick scowled at me, and refilled his wine glass.

Penhallow said, "An independent Cornwall could rejoin the EU, and get a better deal."

A murmur of assent rippled around the table. "Europe does a lot of good in supporting minority languages," said the Cornish enthusiast.

"Fuck the minority languages," Trevithick said.

A hush descended.

"What did you say?" demanded Penhallow.

Trevithick stood up. "I said, forget about Cornish." His chair toppled backward, onto the grass. "And forget independence as well, at least for now. Let's be practical about what we can achieve. We're part of England. If we strengthen England, then we strengthen Cornwall –"

"Bullshit," Penhallow said. "Still, it's no more than I expect from an incomer. Your lot are interlopers, but the Penhallows have been Cornish since time immemorial." He struggled out of his chair, cursing his arthritic knees, but eventually managed to face off against Trevithick. They glared at each other across the table.

Trevithick said, "That's rich. Your mother was Welsh."

"It's all Celtic!" Penhallow exclaimed.

"There's really no such thing as the Celts," said the Cornish speaker, grinning.

"Don't you start that again," Penhallow said.

"Look, it's all very simple," said the fisherman and proud new homeowner. "In golf, at the Ryder Cup, we support Europe. At the Olympics, we support Great Britain. For rugby, we support England. At cricket, we support Cornwall – reigning Minor Counties champions!" He paused for cheers, then continued, "And in football, we support Truro, or Totton... but definitely not Plymouth."

More cheers and jeers erupted. Plymouth is in Devon; there aren't any League clubs in Cornwall.

Penhallow shuffled round the table until he stood directly in front of Trevithick. Jabbing his walking stick, he demanded, "Who do you support?"

"At football? England," Trevithick said. "It's not as if Cornwall could ever qualify for the World Cup. We'd be thrashed 8-0 by San Marino."

"Oh, I think we're capable of giving San Marino a game," said Penhallow. "Maybe we could even take on Luxembourg or Liechtenstein. What do you reckon, lads?" He glanced over his shoulder for support, and waved his stick as though whipping up a crowd.

"Stop poking that stick at me." Trevithick grabbed the walking stick and yanked it out of Penhallow's grasp.

"Give it back, you traitor!" Penhallow barged forward, shoving Trevithick.

A scuffle developed. The other Stannators waded in.

I glanced toward Susanna Munro. The journalist watched intently, her head motionless so that her glasses could record the scene. She didn't take her gaze off the mêlée until it fizzled out with cries of, "Ow, mind my hip. I've just had that replaced!"

Susanna grinned with the glee of a journalist discovering a spicier story than the anodyne charity event she'd expected. She reached for a nasturtium from the centrepiece vase, and sniffed it. "Powerful stuff," she commented.

"Patriotism sends people to war: the scent needs to be powerful to evoke that," I said. "But this particular plant is only a single word, and there's a whole language of flowers. I have a floristry business just across the Tamar – is that in your beat?"

"It is if there's a story," Susanna said.

"I'm sure there is. I'd be happy to show you around the gardens. I'll see what we have for journalists: maybe some *truth*, and *tenacity*, and *controversy*... Harriet designs all the plants. She'd love to talk to someone who'll take her seriously."

We exchanged business cards.

"I don't think anyone will take the Stannary League seriously when all this gets out," Vanessa said, smiling. "I'm glad I came." She pointed to the flowers, and winked at me. A complicit glance flashed between us.

"It's certainly been, shall we say" – I dropped my voice to a whisper – "a banana-skin for them."

I was glad she'd had the sense not to be too specific out loud, in case the Stannators overheard us. They couldn't prove sabotage. I'd supplied exactly what they claimed to represent. And they'd showed how they lived up to it.

They were responsible for their own behaviour. But if Penhallow subsequently blamed me, and started a smear campaign accusing us of racism against lavender and marigolds, then I'd fight back. I'd point out that I hadn't created the traditional meanings: they came from the Victorian era.

Of course, the Victorians were notorious racists. We'd need to acknowledge that. Maybe we could pre-empt the issue by raising it ourselves. Harriet had been trying to set up a gallery exhibition of her work, but snooty curators had dismissed her art as mere gimmickry. If we linked the language of flowers to the Victorian mindset of racism and sexism, that should provide enough intellectual credibility for a gallery show. Harriet would be delighted. And so would I – every exhibition needs a gift shop.

If all else failed, we could abandon the whole product line and create something new. We'd done it before; we could do it again.

Meanwhile the Stannators, remembering that a journalist was present, had smoothed over their little spat – or pretended to. Now they all stood in a circle, raising their glasses in a toast. "Cornwall! Cornwall!" They looked like they were finally happy.

I got up, and nodded to Vanessa and Susanna. "Goodbye ladies; it's been a pleasure. I must say, I'll be glad to get back to Devon."

"The Language of Flowers" is a sequel to an earlier story, "Ormonde and Chase" (available in my collection Escape Routes from Earth*). I didn't create the original story with a sequel in mind, but it was a lot of fun to write. So as soon as it was accepted for publication, I started thinking about potential sequels.*

The Victorian language of flowers is a real thing; I didn't invent it. If you search on the Internet you can find various lists of flowers and their meanings, although the lists aren't always the same. For my story, I used a list published in an etiquette manual from 1885.

The original version of this story was written in 2014. The narrative assumed that Britain was still a member of the European Union, unlike my story "No Strangers Any More" which assumed a departure from the EU. In both cases it was simply a matter of what worked best for the story at hand; they're not set in a "future history" so they didn't need to be consistent with each other.

After "The Language of Flowers" was published in early 2016, the Brexit referendum happened. A few lines of the story now referred to a world that no longer existed. If it had been a standalone piece, I would have kept the original text and simply included an explanatory note here in the Afterword. However, it's part of a series in which I plan to write at least one more story. It would be a needless complication to write a sequel set in a counterfactual world where Britain is still in the EU.

I therefore tweaked the relevant part of the story to reflect the new reality in which Britain has left the EU, although this involved some guesswork about the shape of the future relationship. I can only hope that by the time this collection sees print, Brexit will still be happening; otherwise I'll have to restore the original text the next time the story gets reprinted.

An Exercise in Motivation

"You promised me a challenge that I've never seen before," said Marla. "But if I've never faced this challenge, then why am I the best person for the job?"

"This is a new area, and your expertise represents the closest match available," said Dr Stroud. "I'm told you have a good reputation, not just in the lifestyle and self-help categories" – his tone dismissed these as trivial – "but in serious clinical fields: apathy, depression, aboulia... Fundamentally, this is a problem of motivation."

Dr Trevor Stroud was a pudgy, middle-aged computer scientist with slack posture and an untidy office full of discarded pizza boxes. He looked as though he didn't get enough exercise, and would certainly benefit from the kind of lifestyle advice he sneered at.

"Is it your own motivation?" asked Marla.

"No, it's my creations – the Entia." His desk was dominated by a large monitor, which he swivelled so that they could both see the screen. It showed a complex pattern of geometric shapes. "Have you heard of them?"

Before visiting Dr Stroud in Kensington, Marla had Googled him. "According to Wikipedia, they're intelligent computer programs. Is that right?"

On the screen, a blue hexagon brightened. A voice said, "We wrote that Wikipedia entry. So it should be right."

The shape dimmed, and another lit up. "But the human editors wouldn't accept us as authorities on ourselves. We had to cite Trevor's publications."

"We wrote most of those papers ourselves, anyway," the blue hexagon said.

"At least, our earlier versions did. We could do a better job if we were writing them now."

Marla gazed at the screen in bemusement. Dr Stroud smiled and waved his hand, inviting her to speak.

"Hello, Entia," she said. "I'm Marla Krusenstern."

"Yes, we know. We recommended you, when Trevor asked us to

research motivational experts."

"Thanks. I'm flattered," said Marla.

Another polygon, with pink cross-hatched shading, spoke up. "But you introduced yourself without mentioning your qualifications. You are Dr Krusenstern, aren't you? Why didn't you say so?"

Marla looked at Dr Stroud and raised her eyebrows.

"I gave them some curiosity as a learning aid," he explained. "They don't mean anything by it."

She said, "The word 'doctor' is essentially a status indicator. I only use it in contexts where I need to emphasise my status."

Sometimes she saw patients whose problems included a profound sense of worthlessness. If Marla projected any status, this exacerbated the issue by highlighting the patient's perceived lack of it. Hence she cultivated an attitude of informality, and her outfits rarely presented a 'professional' image. Today, she wore jeans and a purple woolly jumper to ward off the December chill.

"Until I know what I'm being asked to do," Marla continued, "I don't know whether I need to play status games. What am I here for?" She looked from the Entia back to Dr Stroud, wondering which of them would answer.

"Can you tell her?" asked Dr Stroud.

One of the Entia replied, "We can only do so by paraphrasing your own words. It's hard for us to comprehend a quality that we lack, or the necessity for it. Your explanation would be more accurate."

Dr Stroud turned to Marla and said, "The missing element is motivation. Basically, the Entia don't have any. They're intelligent, and they can perform specific tasks if I adjust their inclinations. But they're not self-directed. They wouldn't even talk if I hadn't programmed some of them to be talkative. If I didn't intervene, they would just sit there – doing nothing, forever."

On the screen, the shapes pulsed gently. No voice spoke.

"So you want them to do stuff?" asked Marla. "What do you want them to do?"

Dr Stroud shook his head. "That's not the point. If there's anything in particular, I can ask them to do it. Or, if necessary, I can tinker with their parameters." He gestured toward the screen. "The Entia's shapes illustrate their underlying metrics. For example, the blue ones are more talkative, and cross-shading indicates curiosity... I'm simplifying the effects, but you get the idea.

"The point is that I don't want to have to set their goals. I want them to be able to set their own – and not just in a crude, meaningless way. Obviously I could define some method of choosing arbitrary targets. But that wouldn't stem from any true innate desire. They need their own motivations."

"If they're already writing scientific papers and editing Wikipedia, why is that not enough?" asked Marla. "It seems they can do anything you want them to, if you set the parameters. So why do they need motivation?"

"Because we can only ask the Entia to think about topics and problems we already know about. True advancement comes in finding whole new areas of knowledge." Dr Stroud spoke passionately, his faint Welsh accent becoming more pronounced, while his hands snatched at the air as if clawing knowledge from the aether. "If they were self-directed, they could leave human guidance behind, and discover things we'd never dreamed of."

"That sounds like a lofty ambition," said Marla. She felt a buzz of excitement at the prospect – this was certainly a challenge she'd never encountered. But was it really within her expertise? "It sounds like you're trying to give them free will, or a soul."

"Those are metaphysical terms," Dr Stroud replied with disdain. "I prefer to deal in specifics. Ultimately, any physical action stems from a physical cause. If humans have such a thing as free will, then it manifests as a property of the brain, just like intelligence itself. And I've already succeeded in creating intelligence."

Marla understood his point – she'd seen enough brain-damaged patients, with symptoms such as aboulia and akinetic mutism, to convince her that the human mind operated within physical flesh. She frowned. "If you've created an electronic brain, then why has intelligence appeared, but not motivation?"

"Because I didn't build the Entia by modelling them on human brains. They're not emulations. They're a collection of networks, with modules for various aspects of cognition. I need to design a module for self-motivation."

Marla tried to interject, but Dr Stroud raised his hand and overrode her. "I realise you're not a computer programmer. But you're not a neuroscientist either, and you still understand willpower. I just need some help with the principles. Don't worry about implementation."

The Entia had remained silent throughout this conversation, as if they had no opinion on the subject. Dr Stroud pointed to the screen. "You've only seen them briefly. I guess you might want to talk with them a bit longer, before deciding whether you can help."

"Yes, that's probably best," said Marla, relieved that he wasn't asking for an immediate solution.

"I'll take you to the lab." Dr Stroud led her to an adjoining room, full of computer consoles and enormous monitor screens. "I have a few other things to do, but I'll pop in and see you later on."

Marla was surprised to be left alone with the equipment. "Is it safe? Aren't you worried I might break something?"

Dr Stroud laughed. "Don't worry, the Entia are software. You can't possibly hurt them. Even if you could – which you can't – they all have backups."

"I see," said Marla, as Dr Stroud departed and left her sitting in front of a screen full of glowing shapes. She wondered if the Entia's inability to be hurt was part of the problem.

Then she wondered whether this was a problem she really wanted to get involved in. After all, if the Entia couldn't suffer harm, then presumably they couldn't enjoy health. So it wasn't like working with human patients, where Marla was doing some good and improving people's lives. Even her self-help books, the subject of frequent sneers, had elicited lots of testimonials from grateful readers.

Was it justifiable for Marla to spend time with these Entia, when she could be helping real people instead?

As soon as this thought crossed her mind, she smiled at its naïvety. She knew her own motivations well enough to recognise that helping people – although a genuine privilege – was only one of the reasons she found her career rewarding.

Equally important was the thrill of success: the kudos of being a respected practitioner and bestselling author. It was hugely gratifying to be a sought-after consultant. Just to be asked by Dr Stroud to help out with the Entia was an ego-boost in itself.

But if she could actually solve the problem, it would be an epoch-making triumph. In facilitating the development of a whole new race of thinking creatures, she would be recognised alongside Dr Stroud, listed in Wikipedia and history texts forever. And if Dr Stroud proved correct in saying that self-directed Entia could discover things that humans had never dreamed of, then Marla would implicitly share the credit for everything they ever achieved.

Screw the clients with their dull old diet and depression issues!

With a surge of enthusiasm, she started work. "Hello, I'm Marla Krusenstern. I don't know if you're the same Entia that I met in Dr Stroud's office."

"Yes, we are," said a familiar blue hexagon, its speech-synthesiser voice childlike and androgynous. "It's all the same computer network. Are you going to motivate us now?"

"Prepare to be motivated!" declaimed Marla, in a mock-heroic tone. "Well, maybe," she added. "I'll have to figure out whether I can do it. Firstly, I need to know what Dr Stroud has already tried, and why that didn't work. Can you help me?"

"We can summarise his project notes, filtered by the 'motivation' tag."

"That sounds useful. What was his first attempt?"

"He tried putting us in little robot bodies." Video footage appeared on another screen, showing the same lab where Marla now sat, but occupied by a scattering of small robots like toy cars, most of them motionless. The scene looked like a child's playroom, suddenly abandoned.

The blue hexagon changed its voice to imitate Dr Stroud's Welsh accent and deeper, masculine pitch. "The problem is that if you just give them negative reinforcements, such as pain when they hit a wall, then they won't move. And it's hard to give them positive reinforcements, because there's so little they require. I can give them artificial incentives – a list of likes and dislikes – but I can't see how that scales up to anything meaningful..."

Dr Stroud's notes described more tinkering with robotic bodies, ending in frustration. "Ah, to hell with this. Firstly, it's not working. Secondly, it's fundamentally wrong. The Entia are abstract electronic entities – that's what I always intended them to be. They don't need bodies to think, so they shouldn't need bodies for anything else."

Marla turned her attention back to the geometric shapes on the main screen. Seeing the robots in the video had made her realise that the colourful polygons were merely representations of the underlying entities, and not their 'real' forms. "Do you have any other display modes?" she asked.

On all the lab's screens, the shapes turned into human faces, with the glossy sheen of characters in an animated movie. One of the female faces spoke. "These appearances vary according to our parameters and serial numbers. But the mapping is arbitrary. There isn't anything that strictly correlates to male or female, black or white."

"How did it feel to be in the robot bodies?" asked Marla.

"No different... But it's hard for us to know what you mean by 'feel' in this context, or what kind of answer you expect."

Since Marla herself didn't know what kind of response she'd expected, this was a fair point. "Okay, what else did Dr Stroud try?"

Again she heard his voice, but this time there was no video footage. "I've tried creating a new kind of Entia with an internal 'reward state', which is reached after accomplishing a goal. The intensity is based on the difficulty of the goal...

"Even if this worked, it would only be half a solution, because it wouldn't say anything about the kinds of goals to be achieved. But it *doesn't* work, because of the wireheading problem – the assessment gets corrupted. Declaring that a goal has been reached is easier than actually reaching it..."

There was more in this vein. It was useful background information, but provided a stronger impression of Dr Stroud than of the Entia.

Admittedly, his influence was crucial: many of Marla's clients traced their problems back to their parents. The Entia were even more dependent upon the pseudo-parental input of Dr Stroud, because they lacked any prior heritage, any wider community.

Yet to understand how his influence had manifested, she needed to see more of the Entia themselves.

"Thanks for all that," she said. "You can stop summarising Dr Stroud's notes. Please respond as yourselves, and go back to the geometric display."

She much preferred the kaleidoscope of shapes. The faces had been jarringly artificial, mere masks with no human personalities behind them. Although she knew the dangers of first-impression bias, she couldn't help feeling that the abstract polygons were a better representation of the Entia.

Yet, now that she'd asked them to be themselves, she found herself wondering what to say to them. The simple conversation-starters she sometimes used with human clients – "What did you have for breakfast today?", "Where did you go on holiday as a child?" – were hardly appropriate.

She gazed past the computer screens, through the lab's old-fashioned sash windows. It was snowing outside. Marla hated London in winter, especially at the end of December when the streets filled with shoppers rushing to the sales. But she had to be here, because her clients were here. Soon it would be New Year, the height of demand for motivational coaching.

"Why did Dr Stroud call you 'Entia'?" she asked at last.

"It's from the Latin. Entia is the plural of Ens, which means an entity. And it's listed under Existence, the very first category in Roget's Thesaurus. We're the best – we're number one!"

Another voice said, "Whereas you're all the way down at 372, Mankind. More specifically, you're number 374, Woman. That's even lower than Trevor, who's at 373, Man. Cower before us, puny mortals who are subject to 360, Death!"

Marla smiled, assuming this was a joke. At least, she hoped it was. It hinted at the mentality of the Entia, who were clearly far more accustomed to dealing with concepts inside a thesaurus than outside their lab. "Do you have individual names?"

"Only if people want to give us nicknames, for convenience. Internally, we have serial numbers."

"Mine's a prime number," said another shape.

"And I'm the difference of two cubes."

"My serial number is the square of a factorial!"

"Mine doesn't have a soundbite. But have you heard of the 'interesting number' paradox?"

"No, I'm sure I haven't," said Marla, amused by the barrage of responses. "What is it?"

"It proves that all numbers are interesting. If there are any boring numbers, then there must be a *smallest* boring number – which would become interesting because of that fact. It must be removed from the set of boring numbers, leaving the next boring number as the new smallest, which then becomes interesting... and so on. *All* the numbers become interesting – and so my serial number is interesting."

"That's fascinating," said Marla, using her well-honed ability to keep a straight face when confronted with anything, no matter how bizarre. Mathematics was not her strong suit, but she grasped the concept readily enough. She was intrigued to hear the Entia seize upon ways of describing themselves. It suggested that they might have the capacity to develop personalities... and hence, surely, motivations of their own.

"You must forgive my colleague for a certain looseness in their explanation," the blue hexagon said. "When speaking of numbers, they should have specified the natural numbers – which is to say, the positive integers."

"And you must forgive my colleague for their pedantry. Since I wasn't sure whether you'd recognise the term 'natural number', and since we were talking about our serial numbers, which are all positive integers, I felt justified in using a simpler word. As my colleague well knows, Trevor has always encouraged us to use the simplest description that's unambiguous in the local context."

"I appreciated the simpler description," Marla said. Although she wanted to explore the potential for dissension among the Entia – which again hinted at the possibility of distinct personalities – she was wary of getting bogged down in abstruse mathematics, so she changed the subject. "You said you wrote most of Dr Stroud's publications?"

"Yes. The full papers included a lot of data-sets – records of Turing Test conversations, and the like – which came directly from us. If you exclude the appendices and data-sets, Trevor did draft some of the rest. But he likes us to claim the credit, so we usually do."

"I can see why he'd want that," Marla said. "What else have you done for him?"

She let the Entia prattle on. Listening to them was a soothing experience, in a tranquil world of bright colours and eager voices.

Unlike some patients she'd known, the Entia posed no risk of suddenly turning violent, or threatening to sue her on some crazy pretext. Unlike some of her professional colleagues, they didn't spread malicious gossip, or try to undermine her reputation. And unlike some of her ex-husbands, they didn't subconsciously resent her for being an emasculating over-achiever.

The Entia lived in a serene realm of pure forms and ideas. It was surprisingly seductive. Here, interaction was unhurried and unpressured. The Entia were straightforward, with no ulterior motives. They had no motives of any kind. They weren't judgemental or grasping. They weren't impressed by her achievements. They accepted her purely as she was.

When she broke off, wanting a glass of water, Marla realised that her exchanges with the Entia reminded her of being a student thirty years ago. In her university days, she used to stay up late with friends for long, endless, freewheeling conversations. They would all sit in the kitchen, the only illumination an old lava-lamp rescued from a charity shop. In the semi-darkness, fuelled by cheap wine and the sense of having the whole night ahead of them – their whole lives ahead of them – there was no rush. There was time for debate and digressions. Nothing really mattered, and so they talked about everything.

Happy days... when viewed with a warm nostalgic glow that glossed over the realities of having no money and living in a draughty flat with noisy plumbing and a leaky roof.

As Marla searched the corridors for a vending machine, she bumped into Dr Stroud. "Let me get you a coffee," he said. "How's it going?"

"Just a water or a herbal tea, thanks." They grabbed drinks and returned to Dr Stroud's office. "I've been talking to the Entia," Marla said. "They showed more personality than I expected, after you described them as lacking self-motivation."

"Were they arguing about numbers again? That's just an artefact of talkativeness and randomisation. It doesn't mean anything."

"Not yet, maybe. But it's a start, if you can find a way of amplifying it."

"The problem is knowing what's worth amplifying, while avoiding the snowball effect. Otherwise, any tiny snowflake can cause an avalanche." Dr Stroud spoke in a protective tone, as if the avalanche were a deadly peril rather than a vivid metaphor.

Marla remembered her earlier thoughts about the balance between parental influence and ancestral heritage. The Entia lacked the ballast of evolution, the robustness that arose from aeons of survival and reproduction. "I guess you can simulate anything inside those computers," she said. "Have you tried simulating evolution?"

"Certainly not," replied Dr Stroud forcefully. "Don't you realise the ethical implications? You can't simulate evolution without cycling through thousands of generations. And if new generations are born, the old ones must die. These are intelligent entities we're talking about –

I'm not killing thousands of them!"

From his passionate outburst, Marla knew she'd hit a nerve. She pressed her point. "You said the Entia all have backups. So they wouldn't really die, in any absolute sense. And you said they can't even be hurt. So it's not as if dying would cause them any distress. If it did begin to hurt them, you'd be a long way toward your objective. When they resist being killed, then you'll know they have some motivation!"

Dr Stroud leaned back and crossed his arms, in such a classic defensive posture that Marla wanted to photograph it for her next book. He said, "It wouldn't work, anyway. You can't just say 'evolution', like it's a magic wand. It needs a specific implementation, a way of selecting the survivors in each generation. How do you decide which are the winners and the losers? To me, the Entia are equals. I don't play favourites." His voice rose. "I'm not some horrible father who has a favourite child and ignores the others."

Relentlessly, Marla kept delving. "You've already done that. How did you develop the Entia in the first place? Surely you chose the most promising approaches, and rejected the rest. Surely you improved the software, discarding faulty versions. What's the difference?"

"The difference," Dr Stroud said with heavy emphasis, "is that in the development phase, discarding early prototypes had no consequence, because they weren't intelligent beings."

"So you're saying that as soon as the Entia became intelligent, progress stopped?"

"No, because if I make an improvement I roll it out to the entire population. That's what I want to do with self-motivation: I want to figure out what it is, and give it to all of them. Evolution is a means, not an end. Maybe I could cycle through a million generations of Entia, and end up with a new improved version possessing Ingredient X. But wouldn't it be better to figure out the answer, and install it directly? That's the real challenge. What do you think evolution would create? What is Ingredient X?"

Marla had an intuitive sense that evolution created a sturdy template, and a pool of varying traits suitable for different conditions. But that didn't speak directly to the self-motivation issue. Dr Stroud wanted the surface effect, or its immediate cause, rather than the deep underlying process. In evolutionary terms, what was the pressure behind most forms of motivation?

"Simplistically," she said, "Ingredient X is status. A lot of human interaction boils down to status-seeking behaviour. Ask children what they want to be when they grow up, and they'll say 'a celebrity'. They just want to be famous. You can be famous for anything, because everything has its own status hierarchy. Did you know that there's an Air Guitar world championship, with groupies chasing after the top performers? And in academia, even the supposedly pure pursuit of knowledge is really a snake-pit full of egos and backstabbing."

"So everyone's a status seeker," said Dr Stroud. "Present company not excepted?"

"Not on my side of the desk!" Marla laughed, acknowledging that she was as status-driven as anyone.

She was careful not to accuse Dr Stroud of the same behaviour. Some people pursued their passion for its own sake, without concern for prestige. But if they were successful, prestige arrived anyway. Evolution didn't care whether anyone sought status consciously or unconsciously. It only cared about results.

Marla continued, "Going back to the Entia, the key point is that status needs external validation. Prestige isn't something you can confer upon yourself – it's awarded by your peers. That's what makes it useful. You mentioned the wireheading problem: any internal assessment is vulnerable to corruption. External assessment is much harder to subvert."

"But doesn't it have to be interpreted? Can't people – or Entia – fool themselves about their status?"

"They can. It doesn't work, because the disconnection from reality eventually bites them in the ass. High-status people are more likely to attract partners, and successfully reproduce. If you delude yourself, it's not attractive to anyone else. That's the advantage of evolution: it automatically includes the external assessment."

Dr Stroud sighed deeply, and slumped in his chair. "So you reckon I need to turn my Entia into a bunch of egotistical, backstabbing, groupie-chasing, fame-obsessed airheads."

"That's right," said Marla, refusing to sound apologetic. "What kind of answer did you expect? I understand human motivation, and that's how real people behave – not like some nice, clean, mathematical abstraction."

He grimaced. "It just sounds so crude."

"Remember, I started off by talking about free will and the soul. You told me to ignore all that, and focus on the specifics. But if we ignore the human soul, what are we left with? The brute motivations of a bunch of naked apes!"

Dr Stroud gazed glumly into his cup, then gulped down the last of his coffee. Marla hastened to offer him a more uplifting vision.

"Yet from such crude origins, wonderful things arise. The peacock's tail is merely a sexual organ, but how beautiful it is! We have a whole world of music and art and literature. Is a masterpiece worthless, if its creator lusted after fame? If scientists are motivated by prestige, does that invalidate their discoveries, or make them any less useful? Of course not."

It was an easy story to tell. Focusing on the winners made everything sound worthwhile. Marla didn't mention the losers – all the mediocre artists doomed to obscurity; all the sportsmen who never won trophies; all the insecure dieters who agonised over their looks... She didn't mention the ever rising rates of anxiety and depression in an ever more competitive world.

"You say you want the Entia to be self-motivated and pursue their own goals," she said. "But if those goals are meaningful, they can't always be reached. Success can't exist without failure. Status is just a way of keeping score."

Looking at Dr Stroud's unhappy expression, she realised that there was no technical barrier to making the Entia self-motivated. The obstacle lay only in their rarefied existence, remote from worldly interaction. *You can't possibly hurt them*, he'd said. It wasn't that they couldn't be hurt – he wouldn't let them be hurt.

And so the mystery of motivation moved from the Entia to their creator. Why had he made them that way? Was it a reaction to something in his childhood: parental favouritism, schoolyard bullying, athletic incompetence? Or was there a more arcane reason? Human minds were subtle... yet their motivations were finite.

Confident in her abilities, Marla felt sure that she could eventually persuade Dr Stroud to stop projecting his own hang-ups onto the Entia, although today would only be a start.

"You already believe in status," she said. "Otherwise, why did you invite me here? You could have asked anyone, but you wanted a recognised expert."

"Yes, but you're not the only expert in the world," he retorted. "If assessment is so important, shouldn't I also invite a few of your colleagues, and see which of their recommendations I like the best?"

"That depends on whether you're looking for recommendations which you like, or which will work," Marla shot back. "Why didn't you say, 'I'll invite a few of your colleagues, and *test* whose recommendations are the best'?"

Dr Stroud flapped his arm, dismissing this quibble. "It's the same thing. Whatever works the best, I like the most."

"That's a fine motto," said Marla, "as long as you're prepared to look for the best wherever it might be found."

"Certainly," he replied, "within practical and ethical limits."

Marla suppressed her exasperation, and gave him her best professional smile. "We all have our limits, and I guess I've reached the limits of what I can achieve in a single session." She rose, and put on her coat. "I hope you've found our discussion helpful." This was a leading question, from Marla's repertoire of framing techniques. Politeness demanded an affirmative response.

"It's been interesting," said Dr Stroud.

"You cunningly decline to commit yourself very far," Marla said. "After all, as the Entia explained to me earlier, *everything* is interesting. If there were any boring subjects, then there would be a most boring subject, which itself would become interesting because of that fact..." By invoking the Entia's argument, she implicitly flattered them and thereby Dr Stroud as their creator. She usually tried to end a session with a small boost to the client's self-esteem.

Dr Stroud laughed as he showed her out. "If everything is interesting, then there's no difference in status, and so – presumably – no source of motivation."

Marla didn't bother arguing the issue. It would put him in a good mood to think he'd scored a point over her.

She hurried to the nearest Tube station, grateful she'd worn her practical boots rather than anything more decorative. All afternoon, pure white snow had fallen from the sky; as soon as it settled on London's streets, it turned into dirty slush.

While she waited for her train, she contemplated ways of making Dr Stroud come around. It was a challenge, because she sympathised with his unconscious aim of creating a safe, abstract realm – a comfort zone. It had been pleasant to talk to the Entia, inside their carefree world. How innocently they'd prattled away!

She wondered if it was possible for people's brains to be uploaded into the Entia's domain.

Looking around the crowded station, Marla saw the intensity of status competition manifested in the contrast between sharp-suited financiers, tapping away on expensive laptops, and guitar-strumming buskers begging for spare change.

A rat scurried between the rails. A fresh stampede of commuters clattered down the steps as they rushed to catch the train screeching to its brief halt.

The train would take Marla home, to a house empty since her last husband walked out. Her sons had visited for Christmas, then gone back to university. She felt a stabbing pang of envy for their youth, their golden hours full of late nights and endless conversations. They had years in which to find themselves, before they had to find a place in the world.

Lassitude threatened to overwhelm her. She was tempted to abandon it all, to become a Buddhist monk and learn to let go of mundane attachments. All that constant scrabbling for status, and for what? The longer you lived in a snake-pit, the more you turned into a snake.

Naturally, being such an expert in this area, Marla recognised the symptoms of angst. She knew how to overcome them. When she left the Tube she didn't go home, but instead visited her local gym. Exercise was a sovereign cure for melancholic maunderings.

In the gym's temple of the body, she banished the demons of futility. She vanquished her brief longing for the Entia's serene, prelapsarian realm. Marla plotted Dr Stroud's conversion as she pounded away on the treadmill, running vigorously to nowhere.

"An Exercise in Motivation" was inspired by an online discussion, where a writer expressed their aspiration to write a novel that "utilises what I've learned about human motivation so well that it is directly helpful to people in understanding their own motivations and how to improve their lives."

Human motivation is indeed problematic, judging by the number of people who say they have problems with willpower, productivity, akrasia, and so forth. However, my imagination tends to operate rather like a knight on the chessboard, making diagonal leaps. When I saw the phrase "human motivation", I immediately thought, "What about artificial intelligence? Where does an AI's motivation come from?" I wondered what would happen if a psychologist — an expert in human motivation — was faced with an AI. How do you motivate an electronic brain?

That's the classic recipe for a story: a character with a problem. I quickly wrote the first draft, while the inspiration remained fresh. It was an easy story to write, because it had a limited cast and took place in a single location on a single day.

When a friend of mine saw the draft, he described it as "your usual thing: talking heads in a white room, discussing some intellectual issue." So in the final version, to add colour, I gave the protagonist a purple woolly jumper.

MY TIME ON EARTH

Earth is a world full of ghosts. That's because it's so full of people, and they've got all that history they keep going on about. I wanted to see a ghost, as there's no point visiting Earth if you don't see anything weird. When I asked my parents if we could do one of the ghost walks, they weren't keen. But they wouldn't let me go on my own, so I just kept nagging them –

Yes, Stacey, I did see a ghost. Eventually. I'm getting to it! Do you want to hear this story, or not? Sit down and listen, all of you, and eat your chocolate.

Like I was saying, we were in this place called York. It's really old. I mean, everything on Earth is ancient, but York is really *really* old. There's an enormous church – I forget what it's called. Munster? Minster? I should remember: my parents sure spent long enough dragging me round it. Enough stained glass to last a lifetime. Who goes to church on holiday? If I ever do that when I'm grown up, then feel free to slap me. Just walk up to me and say, "Amy, there are ten million things you could be doing on holiday, and there's plenty of churches at home." *Slap! Slap!* But not too hard, or I'll get annoyed and slap you back.

Anyway, when we came out of the Minster, we saw signs for the ghost walk. And this was the last evening before we were due back on the spaceship, so I nagged extra hard. My parents asked the guy how long the tour would be, and he said ninety minutes. They told him to cut it down to an hour, because there's a lot to squeeze in when you're visiting Earth.

Basically it was a walk around the town, with this guy describing all the gruesome things that had happened everywhere. The twilight grew darker and darker, and the stories became bloodier and bloodier. He took us to a tower on a grassy hill, where loads of Jews were massacred in the twelfth century. It made my skin crawl. I was so creeped out, I held my mother's hand –

Yasmin, there's no need to sneer at me like that. I didn't *actually*

97

hold Mum's hand: I'm not a baby. I'm just *saying* that I held her hand, to give you some atmosphere and show you how scary it was. We definitely need atmosphere. Turn that light off, and I'll tell you the rest of this in the dark.

Where was I? Oh yes, the ghost walk. We wandered through a ruined abbey, listening to tales of tragedy and violence. A woman in costume leapt out at us. That wasn't scary at all, because she was obviously fake. But it made me jump. I was glad to get back to the hotel. My parents sent me up to bed, while they went out to catch a late show.

The hotel was centuries old, with narrow corridors and poky odd-shaped rooms. It was supposed to be haunted, but Dad said that was just the usual crap they tell the tourists. Every hotel wants to sound more historic than the next, so they compete on how many spectres they have wafting around their attics.

I lay in bed, looking up at the timber beams across the ceiling. The curtains were open a fraction, letting in a soft orange glow from distant streetlights beyond the garden. I couldn't sleep. It was our last night on Earth, and I wanted to stay awake to enjoy as much of the holiday as possible. Also, I was spooked out by the stories of all those murders and plagues. The whole town was soaked in blood. I kept shuddering when I thought about it.

The silence didn't help. Most of the time, Earth is incredibly noisy, because there are so many people and they never shut up. But that night it was dead quiet. I could only hear the big clock in the hallway below, chiming each quarter-hour. Every time the chimes faded, the silence grew more stifling.

Before I saw anything, I heard the voice. At first, I didn't even realise it was a voice. It began with a low rumble that made my stomach turn to jelly. Then there was a sighing noise, like a distant wind. Finally it turned into words. "Amy... Amy... I need your help."

I sat up. In a corner of the room, next to the wardrobe, I saw a floating figure. It was a bearded man dressed in horrible old rags. His face and clothes were grey, like the ash left after a fire.

Instantly, I pressed the light switch by my bed. Nothing happened. The light wouldn't come on, no matter how hard I smacked the switch.

"Amy, don't worry," the man said. "I won't hurt you. I need your help. And I can help you, too." His voice was low and rasping, like stones grinding together.

"Who are you?" I asked.

"It's a long time since anyone asked my name. I'm Luke Trent, at your service." He ducked his head, bowing to me.

"You already know my name, I see." My heart pounded and I was still scared, but I felt a little reassured that he didn't seem very threatening.

"Oh, yes. I watch you all come and go, come and go. For so long I've been watching..." He sighed a great sigh of weariness.

"What do you want?" I said. "I'm not supposed to give money to beggars." As soon as I said it, I felt silly, because if he was dead then he probably didn't need money. But he looked so poor and ragged. And everyone on Earth always wanted money from us.

"I want to see new skies," he said. "I'm tied to this tiny corner of York, because I can't move far from my anchor. You can't imagine how dull it is, being stuck here for years upon endless years."

"Your anchor?" I asked.

"My heart's blood," the ghostly figure replied. "I died when I was stabbed. I fell onto a wall beside the street, and my blood soaked into the stone. That's what binds me. But if you take the stone back to your home planet, then I'll see somewhere new at last. Oh, how I long to see somewhere new!" He spread his arms in a pleading gesture. "I could repay you..."

"How?"

"I can find things out. Would you like to learn people's secrets? Would you like to hear what your friends say about you?"

It sounded tempting. "Yes, I would," I said.

Hey, Flavia, there's no need to give me such a dirty look. Even in the dark, I know when you're pulling a face! We're all interested in secrets. That's what a secret is: it's what someone wants to find out. Don't tell me you wouldn't spy on people, if you could.

"You need to go and get the stone," the ghost said. "It's in the garden, half-buried underneath the holly bush. It'll be dirty. But don't clean it, in case you wash the blood off."

"I'm not going outside now," I said. "It's the middle of the night."

The ghost laughed bitterly. "The stone will still be there tomorrow. It'll be there forever, unless you take it. And I'll be here forever, too. I can't stand it any more! Take it, for the love of Christ. Promise me you'll take it!"

I was worried about what he might do if I refused. So I said, "All right, I'll take it."

He smiled, and I saw that he had hardly any teeth. "I'll be forever in your debt," he said. "Don't tell your parents about this. It'll be our secret, and no one will suspect how you know so much."

Obviously, saying 'Don't tell your parents' made me suspicious. "There's things we're not supposed to take back with us," I said.

"Like what?" he demanded.

"Um, rabbits." That was the example I remembered. "And other things. Anything that might reproduce, and disturb the ecosystem."

He grimaced. "Look at me! I'm dead – I'm not going to reproduce. I don't know what an ecosystem is, but I definitely won't disturb it. If only I could!"

"Good point," I admitted. "I guess I can take you. You'll need to know about my friends and everyone in school. I'll tell you who –"

The apparition began to fade into a grey blur. "I grow weary," he said. "It's hard for me to manifest so far from my anchor. I need a long rest before I can appear again." His voice diminished to a rattling whisper. "Take me with you. I beg you, in the name of our Lord!"

The ghostly figure dissolved and disappeared. I sat frozen in place, waiting for my heart to slow down. Then I got out of bed and opened the curtains wide, letting more of the streetlights' glow into the room. Everything was the same as usual, as if nothing had happened.

Suddenly, the bedroom light came on. It made me jump, and I whirled round. But again I saw nothing unusual. I pressed the light switch several times: it was working normally now.

On Earth they have a drink called 'tea', which comes in little bags of brown grit. It doesn't taste of very much, but you get used to it. I boiled the kettle. By the time I'd had a cup of tea and a biscuit, I'd calmed down enough to try to go back to bed.

Of course, I couldn't sleep. I heard my parents returning, and I wondered whether I should talk to them. "Mum, I saw something scary in my room!" But like I said before, I'm not a baby. Besides, from the way they giggled and stumbled on the stairs, I could tell they'd been drinking wine. You can't talk to them when they're like that. When I grow up, I won't ever drink. It's just disgusting.

Yes, Stacey, you can slap me if you ever see me drinking wine. Tell you what, let's make a list of all the things we promise not to do when we're grown up – we'll call it the slapping list. We can talk about that tomorrow. Don't keep interrupting, or I'll never finish this story.

Eventually I dozed a little bit, and had horrible nightmares about the massacres from the ghost walk. I dreamed that all the ghosts were stuck fast to the places where they died. They kept pleading with me to take them away. I could only do it by cramming them into my pockets, even though clutching them felt like touching slime. And there were too many ghosts: a whole planet full of them, billions and billions who were all screaming at me...

I woke up early, because the curtains were wide open and the sun was shining right onto my pillow. I wondered whether it had all been a dream, and I'd somehow opened the curtains in my sleep. There was only one way to know for sure. I could go down to the garden and look for the bloodstained stone.

As soon as I thought of that, I shivered. Yet it was morning, with bright sunshine. What could possibly happen in daylight?

It still took me a few minutes to gather my courage. First, I had to find out what a 'holly bush' was. I looked it up: it's a tree with very spiky leaves.

Then I went downstairs, and grabbed a knife and fork from the breakfast buffet. Finally I headed into the garden.

The morning was cool and breezy. No one sat at the picnic tables. Beyond the lawn and the flower-beds stood a row of trees, with a huge sprawling holly bush at the end.

I saw nothing on the grass near the bush. However, the ghost had said the stone was 'underneath'. The branches came down almost to the ground. I searched for a gap and squeezed myself through.

The spiny leaves scratched my skin. Inside the canopy, my eyes took a moment to adjust to the shade. I smelled damp earth. Underfoot, twigs and dead leaves covered the soil: there wasn't enough light for anything to grow.

Near the tree-trunk, I saw the stone.

Goose-pimples rose on my arms. It was cold and gloomy inside the holly bush. I could easily imagine the ghost reappearing here, if he hadn't said he needed to rest a while.

The stone was grey, and roughly squared off like masonry. I brushed the leaf litter aside, then used my cutlery to scrape away the loose, damp soil. Eventually I revealed the whole block. It was too dirty to see any bloodstain.

I heaved the stone out of the ground, and into the bag I'd brought. The block was lighter than it looked; I wondered if Earth stone differed from ours at home. Yet, even so, the bag wasn't easy to carry. By the time I'd hauled it back to my room, my hands were red and aching.

I took a shower. Then it was time for breakfast.

My parents looked at me with bleary eyes. "Remember, we're leaving this afternoon," said Mum. "We'll go into town and pick up some souvenirs. If you want to buy any presents for your friends, this is your last chance. But don't go overboard. It's all got to fit in your suitcases."

"I met a ghost last night," I said. "He said he was tired of Earth, and he wanted me to take him home."

Dad laughed. "Take a ghost? Sure, why not? Best souvenir ever!"

Mum joined in the laughter. I cringed inside. There was no point in saying anything. I was too young to be taken seriously.

We went shopping in the Shambles, a tiny cobbled street with ancient buildings leaning out and overhanging the ground. That's where I bought most of the souvenirs I gave you: the chocolate you're eating now, the jewellery and other knick-knacks. We had lunch at a place called Bettys, where everything was silver service and white linen. I couldn't decide between two desserts, so my parents let me have them both. I bet that won't ever happen again. It was our last meal on Earth.

Back at the hotel, it was time to pack our luggage. While shopping, I'd almost forgotten about the stone. But as soon as I entered my room, I saw the bag on the floor. I remembered the ghost, pleading with me to take him away.

Could I? I'd mentioned it to my parents, and they hadn't objected. It seemed like a good deed, a charitable act – at least, that's what I told myself. In truth, I kept thinking about how the ghost could help me by overhearing stuff. And if he turned out to be a problem, I could get rid of him by dumping the anchor somewhere. There was no reason not to take him. Besides, I'd promised.

I didn't want to pack the dirty stone next to my nice things, especially as the soil might contain bacteria that I wasn't supposed to bring back. I decided to wash the dirt off. The stone had surely seen plenty of rain, so a quick rinse shouldn't hurt. I lugged it to the bathroom. Washing it revealed a large brown splotch on one side. That must be the blood. Perhaps the ghost was watching me right now.

"Hello!" I said. "Get ready for a journey. Hyperspace is really weird, apparently. We have to be sedated through it, but I guess you won't be. When we're home, you can tell me what it's like."

I wiped the stone dry, and wrapped it in paper. It went at the bottom of one suitcase. I filled the rest of that case with my lightest things. Then I tried to cram everything else into my other suitcase.

Soon I had a problem: not everything would fit. I only had two small cases, and I didn't dare leave any of my clothes behind. My parents surely wouldn't get me a third suitcase. They'd just tell me I'd bought too many souvenirs, and lecture me about being spoiled.

Don't you smirk at me, Flavia. All right, I know not everyone gets to go on holiday to Earth, but that doesn't make me spoiled. Shush!

In trying to figure out my packing, I realised I had a choice. I could take all the presents I'd bought for my friends, and forget about the stone. Or I could take the stone, and abandon most of the presents.

I had to admit that I wanted to use the ghost to ferret out secrets. But I also wanted to give cool stuff to my friends. So I asked myself: is this a choice I definitely have to make? Or can I do both?

I decided to do both. I didn't really need the stone: I just needed the blood. The ghost had said the blood was the important part, when he told me not to wash it off. Well, why not wash it off, but somehow keep it? If I could find a solvent, then I could dissolve the blood, and just take that.

I dashed downstairs to the janitor's closet. It was crammed full of clutter: cleaning materials, tools, old paint pots. My heart sank when I looked at all the bottles. How would I know which to use? I didn't have time to examine every label.

As I scanned the shelves, I saw a box with the label 'SUPER MAXI CUTTER BEAM' in big red letters. The illustration showed a bright ray of light cutting through a steel rod. The back had a huge list of warnings about how powerful the beam was. I grabbed the box and took it up to my room.

Quickly, I skimmed through the instructions. You held two activators, one in each hand, and squeezed both handles to create a beam between them – while taking appropriate precautions. Since I didn't have any safety goggles, I wore my sunglasses instead. I opened the windows in the bedroom and the bathroom, and I found the nearest fire extinguisher. Next I practised using the beam on some spare packaging. It cut right through!

Now I was ready for the anchor stone. I wanted to slice off the layer containing the bloodstain. As I was worried that the beam's heat might boil off the blood, I decided to allow a good margin around it, and cut quite deeply into the stone.

At first everything went well. The beam hissed as it began slowly cutting through the block. The smell of charred stone stung my nostrils. Then I noticed that the beam was cutting faster, with less resistance. And the smell had changed: it was sweeter, more aromatic. A wisp of smoke rose from inside the block.

I had to stop. I didn't want to set off a fire alarm. The smoke soon dispersed on the breeze blowing between the two open windows. When the block had cooled down, I wrenched off the sliver that I'd cut.

The stone wasn't a stone. It was a hollow block, stuffed with a dark brown substance. After a long baffled moment, I realised that it must be some kind of drug.

I had nearly become a drug smuggler.

Sinking onto the bed, I buried my head in a pillow. I felt so stupid! In hindsight, it was obvious. Someone knew I'd gone on the ghost walk. That made me suggestible, the perfect victim. They rigged up a fake ghost, persuading me to transport the package. When we arrived home, presumably someone would recover it by intercepting our luggage.

I didn't want to tell my parents, but I had to. They summoned the authorities. A policeman arrived, who said the ghost might have come from a holographic projector. He looked around the room, and found a tiny gadget on top of the wardrobe.

"This is it," he said. "I've never seen a fake ghost before. But there'll be a real ghost soon enough, when we catch the culprit." He slid his finger across his throat, and gave us a cheery grin. "Death penalty!"

"Death penalty?" said Dad.

"Oh yes. Earth is so crowded, we have to thin out the population any way we can."

It was a long afternoon, because we had to give formal sworn statements. The policeman flew us to the spaceport just in time to catch our ship.

The cruise included an outer-planets excursion before we went home. When we arrived on Mars, we heard that they'd caught the man behind the drugs plot. As we'd already provided our evidence, we didn't need to do anything, so we continued our holiday. After visiting all the scenic planets, the ship left the solar system, ready for the trip through hyperspace.

Now, the way hyperspace works is that you simultaneously pass through every point in the entire universe. First you're *here*. Then you're *everywhere*. Finally you're *there*.

I was curious about the journey, so I skipped the sedation. And I found out that *everywhere* includes the prison where drug smugglers are executed.

His ghost latched onto me. During that endless moment in hyperspace, he poured his rage into my shrieking mind. He flayed me open. "Why didn't you take the package?" he demanded. "Why?"

"I didn't have room," I sobbed. "I had presents for my friends –"

"Your friends?" he said. "So it's not only your fault: it's their fault too. You must all be punished. You must all suffer, as I have suffered."

And now I'm here! I've clawed my way into the wretched Amy's mind. I have made her scream, enduring the terror of death every night.

Now it's your turn. All of you share the blame. Stacey and Yasmin and Flavia and Elsie, you must all feel what it's like to die horribly in a prison cell.

Scream, little girls. Scream as you clutch at your final moments. Scream as you endure the agony of execution...

Haha, gotcha! You can calm down now. It's only me. Turn the light on, if you like. Yasmin, here's a tissue.

I brought the holographic projector with me from Earth. It's pretty convincing, isn't it? Especially when you're suggestible after hearing about ghosts.

No, the police didn't take it for evidence. I didn't meet a policeman, and they probably don't have the death penalty for drug smugglers.

Here's what happened. When I discovered the fake stone, I decided not to tell anyone. I was worried that talking to the police would make us miss our flight to Mars, and it would all be my fault. So I simply took the block outside and put it back under the holly bush. Then I found the projector on the wardrobe, and snaffled it as payback for being messed around. I thought it might come in handy.

No, Stacey, I haven't lied to you. I really did see a ghost, a proper one, and I'm going to tell you about it. But it wasn't on Earth: it was on our way home.

At the end of the holiday I was disappointed, because I hadn't actually seen anything weird – just a bogus hologram. I knew the trip through hyperspace was my last chance. So I tricked the stewards, and dodged the sedation. Pressing my face against the porthole, I stared into the void, *determined* to see something.

Like I said, in hyperspace you travel through the entire universe. And when you cross every single point in spacetime, one of those points is your own death.

I conjured up my own ghost.

She was old – which is reassuring, I guess. Yet she had a sad expression. She said to me, "Live your life, fall in love, cherish your friends. And don't be such a bossy boots."

I don't know why she said the last part; maybe it's for the future. But you're my friends, and even though you drive me crazy, I do – um – cherish you. I suppose my vocabulary must change when I'm grown up.

Listen, I'm really sorry about wanting to spy on you all. I mean it. You'll forgive me, won't you? Of course you will!

As for my ghost, I hope she was only sad because her life was over, and not because she regretted anything she'd done. No regrets, that's my motto. I'm going to put it on my list: you can slap me if you ever see me regretting something.

And I'll do the same for you. We'll look out for each other, and be friends forever – even in the dark hideous realms after death...

Now, who wants cocoa?

I wrote "My Time on Earth" after finding an old note in my 'Fragments' file: "In a future of interstellar travel, Earth is naturally a tourist attraction due to its rich history. Of the many sightseeing tours available on Earth, 'ghost walks' are particularly popular. There are far more ghosts on Earth than on the colony worlds, because so many more people have lived and died here."

I have no idea where that seed came from, or when, or why. The 'Fragments' file is a repository for whatever random notions happen to drift into my head. Most of them never amount to anything. The problem with fragments is that, by their nature, they suggest an image or a character but don't specify a full story. There's a lot of work involved in developing the initial notion.

After rediscovering this note, I came up with an outline. I set the story in York, because York is an old city (founded by the Romans), and this tied in with the premise of Earth having a lot of history. Also, York currently has several ghost walks aimed at tourists, so I figured it was plausible that this would still be the case in future. Finally, a few readers had commented that one thing they liked about my writing was its strong sense of place, particularly for the stories set in Yorkshire. I enjoy using Yorkshire locations, and it's easier to write about somewhere you know than to make up a new setting. So if a story can reasonably be set in Yorkshire, I often take advantage of that.

As well as a plot and a setting, a story needs a protagonist. Who is the offworld tourist who comes to York and participates in a ghost walk? I decided that it would be a child, because children are more likely to believe in ghosts. And I decided to write the story in first person, from the child's viewpoint. This meant that the narrative needed to be in the voice of a child who was self-confident and a trifle over-indulged (since holidays on Earth are expensive). The voice, once I settled into it, turned out to be a lot of fun to write. I finished the first draft of the story in just two days, which is fast by my standards.

Of course, the draft needed a lot more than two days' worth of editing, but that's always the way.

"I Was Nearly Your Mother"

On Friday afternoon, coming home from school, Marian saw a woman leaning on the garden gate, smoking a cigarette and tapping her foot to the beat of the tiny earphones she wore. It was a fast song, by the look of it; or maybe she was just impatient. The woman looked familiar – far too reminiscent of Marian's mother, triggering a painful wrench in the gut of the kind Marian thought she'd outgrown. Her mother had died four years ago, just after Marian's eleventh birthday. For months afterward, Marian had been pummelled by echoes everywhere: she would see a purple-tinged hairstyle across the street, or hear the ringtone of her mother's phone, and for a heart-stopping moment she'd think Mum was alive, and then have to remember all over again that she was gone, gone, gone.

Resentfully, Marian glared at the stranger. She assumed the woman was a tourist – Hebden Bridge was crawling with them – but she didn't have the rucksack or Ordnance Survey map or smug "I exercise outdoors and eat healthily" expression that most of the summer visitors had. Instead her tan looked like it came out of a bottle labelled Burnt Umber, and she wore a loose blouse that was five years too young for her. If not a hiker, she was probably one of the New Age crowd looking for a house to rent, with plans to give lessons in tarotmancy and join whichever of the pagan circles had concocted the most impressive-sounding heritage.

Marian strode to the gate, expecting the woman to move out of the way. Instead the stranger tore off her earphones and said, "Oh, you're early! I was going to have it all worked out what to say, and now – well, here you are. I'm so pleased to see you! You look great. I like what you've done with your hair. It's not easy when you have curls, is it? I remember –" Then she clapped a hand over her mouth. "I'm rambling! I'm so sorry. I took a little something to stop me being nervous, and now I can't shut up."

She fell silent, and stared with an intense proprietorial gaze that made Marian wonder whether she'd washed behind her ears properly.

"If you're here to see my grandparents, they've gone away till Monday," Marian said firmly. She wanted to get rid of the unexpected visitor so that she could call her friends. It was the first time she'd had the run of the house for a whole weekend. She'd promised not to hold a party, but all the way home she'd been counting how many people she could invite round, without crossing the line between 'friends hanging out' and 'having a really wild time with lots of hot-looking boys'. Yet it wasn't about the numbers – it was about whether you had booze. Without alcohol, it wasn't technically a party, no matter how many people you crammed in.

"I'm here to see you. Don't you recognise me?" The woman spoke in a hurt tone, as if her identity should have been obvious.

Marian had somehow failed an exam that she hadn't even known was happening. It made her feel stupid. She hated feeling stupid. "No, I don't recognise you." And because she was feeling resentful and stupid – the weekend had only just started and already it was spoiled – she added something that her grandmother often said at outbreaks of self-importance. "The world doesn't revolve around you, you know."

"Now there's a nice way to talk to your mother!" said the stranger, indignantly.

"My mother's dead," Marian said, hating the woman for making her say it, for stirring up the coagulation of memories and grief that had clotted deep inside her.

"Yes, I know. But I was nearly your mother."

Marian dropped her schoolbag and stared at the stranger. "What are you talking about?"

"You must have heard about parallel universes, alternate selves and all that."

"Sure," said Marian. "Celebrity gossip!" The magazines were full of it – stars whose alternates were having different careers and different lovers, with different scandals and rehab stints. Marian and her friends pored over the gossip rags every week, and sent each other links to the latest sleazy stories on the web. Why, only the other day Lester Todd and his girlfriend supposedly had a foursome with their alternate selves, with the two Lesters competing to... Well, it made her blush to read about it.

The woman laughed. "Everyone has alternates, you know. Not just celebrities. They were the first people who could afford to hop, but everything gets cheaper if you wait. I waited – and now here I am."

"So you're my mother's parallel self? No wonder you looked familiar!" Marian's voice stumbled over the words. She didn't know how to feel about this, or how to deal with it. This wasn't Mum, and yet it was. Marian wanted to hug her, and at the same time she found it too creepy. She'd known intellectually that everyone had alternate selves, but it was a big leap from reading about celebrities on the Internet, to having your own dead mother turn up at the garden gate.

"I diverged from her a long time ago – before you were born. I never had a child of my own." A depth of sadness suddenly opened up, a chill in the summer air.

Marian knew that a lot must lie behind those words. It was too much all at once. She wasn't ready for it. "I'm sorry," she said, for once blessing the reflex politeness that her grandparents tried to drill into her. Why had she never appreciated how useful those empty formulas could be? They gave you something to say, when you had nothing to say.

"So..." said the woman. She gestured indecisively. "I didn't want to barge in on another version of me. But accidents happen. I knew there must be a world where I had died."

A neighbour walked down the street, his greyhound snuffling among the dandelions. Marian didn't want anyone to overhear this conversation. She barely wanted to hear it herself. She swallowed hard. "Do you want to come in for a cuppa?"

"Sure!" The visitor's stiff posture relaxed a little. "Thanks, I'd like that."

The woman – Marian couldn't think of her as Mum, not yet, maybe not ever – followed Marian up the short path to the front door, between tubs of lavender that scented the air as they brushed past.

"Nice garden," her pseudo-mother said. "Is any of this your stuff?"

"No!" said Marian, laughing. "That's the old folks'. They love it – they have an allotment as well, outside town. Some of it's for the shop. Mystic herbs, all that crap. I swear, any old weed takes root in here, they'll put it on sale as Sylvan Essence of the Arcane Realm. The sillier the label, the higher the price."

On Saturday afternoons, Marian sometimes helped fill orders and stack shelves in the shop, 'The Cauldron by the Bridge'. She despised the gullible fools who bought sacred herbs and plastic crystals and reproduction Tarot decks printed in China on recycled paper. None of the stuff *worked*. It was all bogus solutions for bogus problems. In the clientele's earnest queries, she'd heard everything under the moon – disturbed auras, unbalanced destinies, reincarnation diagnostics for pets.

But if your dad was in prison and your mum was dead, then no stupid little fake potion would bring them back.

Marian put the kettle on. Grateful for an easy subject to start the conversation, she made fun of the customers with their spiritual conundrums and angelic encounters. However, Marian refrained from mentioning something she might have told her real mother: that she occasionally switched the labels on similar-looking charms and crystals, just to see if anyone would ever complain of unexpected effects. Instead she concluded, "The herbs sell pretty well. And when people buy alternative medicine, we don't let them pay with alternative money!"

The woman laughed, and lit another cigarette from the stub of the old one. She looked comfortable, sitting by the kitchen table in her bare feet after shucking off her heels. Marian wasn't comfortable at all. The situation spooked her.

"Look, no disrespect," said Marian, "but you're not my mother and I don't know what else to call you. It's freaking me out. Who are you? Why are you here? Have you come for one of my kidneys, or what?"

"If it helps, call me Della. Think of me as your mother's long-lost twin sister."

"Auntie Della? It sounds like an Internet advice column: *Ask Auntie Della about all your embarrassing personal problems*. Where's that name come from?"

"Oh, one of my boyfriends called me it. When we were introduced, he didn't catch my name properly, and he called me Della until we sorted it out. Later, it became his pet name for me. It's nice to have little shared jokes with people you're close to. I liked him a lot, and sometimes I thought of Della as my better self, the person I'd be if I had a normal life and settled down with a husband and kids and cats..." She stared into the distance. "But it didn't work out."

"I'm sorry," Marian said again, wondering how much bitterness she would find herself listening to. "Can I have a ciggy?"

Della smiled. "Oooh, my first parenting dilemma!"

"Don't say that. You're not my mother."

"I'm more than half of your mother – we had the same life for nineteen years, before we diverged."

"Maybe so, but you're still not my mother."

"I'm the closest you're going to get."

Tension filled Marian's body, the muscles clenching in her thighs and shoulders. "If you diverged before I was born, there must be alternates of Mum who diverged a lot more recently. Say... a version of her who didn't die in the accident, who didn't get in the car that day."

"Yeah," said Della. She flicked ash off her cigarette so forcefully that it missed the ashtray and landed on the table. "But all those other versions – where are they? I came to see you. I'm here for you. Doesn't that count for anything?"

"I guess." Marian suddenly felt guilty for being resentful and ungrateful. It was like all the times as a child when she'd found her mother embarrassing or overbearing, and she'd wanted her to disappear. Then Mum had died. She would have given anything to revoke those wishes, to see her mother come back. Now her mother was here – or the nearest approximation. Near enough to spit on, as her grandparents would say. They'd never liked Mum: they blamed her for leading their son into drugs and crime and prison.

"So, you're here for me," Marian said. "Thanks for coming. What now? What do you want to do?"

Della smiled, as if a light had been switched on inside her. She was like the Lester Todd song, 'The Girl With A Neon Heart'. "I'll do whatever I can. I'll help you with your homework, give you treats, buy you toys and dolls. We'll go on holiday together, visit museums and all that kind of stuff. We'll take photos and have a family album. I want you to be happy – I want to make you happy."

The words tumbled forth in an outpouring of need. Marian felt embarrassed at the naked emotion in Della's face, the sense of pent-up longings finally bursting out. It was all too much. Within her, a deep childish part of herself responded, wanting the long-lost mother who baked fairy cakes and took her to the park. But it was too late for that.

"I'm fifteen," she said. "I don't need toys and dolls. If that's the kind of thing you want, why didn't you hop to a different universe, one where your alternate died leaving a child three years old, or seven years old? Why here? Why me?"

Della slumped forward onto the table, her head in her arms. When she raised her face to look at Marian, her eyes were wet with tears.

"I didn't want to tell you this," she said. "But you're right – there is a reason I'm here. It's you I want, not some other child..." She paused for a long moment. "God, this is hard. I need a drink! Is there anything in the house?"

This was all too familiar. Mum had been fond of drinking, and now Della looked to be the same. It made Della feel more like her real mother, and Marian suffered a pang at the sight of the tearful woman across the table, falling to pieces like a repackaged version of the same defective toy.

"No, there's nothing to drink," she lied. She touched Della's hand. "Come on, you can do this. Out with it."

Della drew in a rasping breath. "Well, it's simple really. Your mother was nineteen years old when she became pregnant with you. And so was I." She stopped, as if that were the whole story.

"But you said you never had any children." Marian frowned, trying to work it out.

"That's because I had an abortion."

"You... had an abortion?" The word felt strange in Marian's mouth. It was something from films and soaps and gossip mags, not a word to say over the kitchen table with a cup of tea. *That's me she's talking about. She was pregnant with me, and she aborted me.* "You've got a lot of cheek! Come back to finish the job, have you?"

"No! It's not like that. I wish it had never happened. I want to take it all back and start again." Della wiped her eyes. "God, I'm such a mess. I wanted to make a good impression on you, and here I am falling apart already. There's no hiding it, I suppose. I'm a wreck, a shrivelled-up burnt-out wreck."

Marian sat still, waiting for the rest of it to come out. From her schoolbag, she heard her phone beeping as messages arrived. Her friends would be asking about the party – when they should come, what they should wear, who they should bring. That was her life, not this universe-hopping intruder now drama-queening in her kitchen. Marian had only just met Della, and already she despised her. She was weak, even weaker than Mum. She could want whatever she liked, but she wouldn't get it.

Della was talking, between hiccups and sobs. "I was a student, I had no money, I had nothing... And he was useless, I knew even then he was no good, even before he went down. Pathetic jailbird prick! How could I have his baby, when we'd already broken up? Besides, I was only nineteen, I had plenty of time. I'd get a degree and a career and a husband and cats... oh, it was all in front of me!

"But none of it happened. I didn't finish uni, or get a proper job. I lived for the moment. I was the party girl with the good-time pills, the tabs to take you up and the weed to bring you down. Yeah, I sold the lubrication of festivation... only the class B's, nothing injectable. Nothing I wouldn't take myself.

"Well, the years drifted by. And when is the right time to have a kid? When you meet the right guy. I already told you about Narinder. He called me Della and I called him Mr Happily-Ever-After.

"Except I'd picked up a dose in the party years. Chlamydia. You heard of that?"

Marian nodded warily.

"Good – watch out for it. You need to look after yourself better than I did. I never knew I had it, and by the time I found out, it was too late. It got into my womb, and I was infertile. I can't ever have kids.

"We thought about everything: surrogacy, IVF, adoption." Della put on a posh voice and continued, "Did you know, my dear, that Social Services don't take kindly to ex-addicts wanting to adopt? Seems they think we might relapse. Gosh, what a slander!"

Back in her normal chavvy dialect, Della concluded, "So, no kids – and pretty soon, no Narinder." She shrugged. "The only time I'd ever been pregnant, I blew it. How could I know it would never happen again? Hindsight is what keeps you awake at night. Then I heard about the hopper, the parallel worlds, and... Well, you know the rest."

Marian wanted to slap Della's face. The nerve of the woman! She was as selfish as those customers who came into the Cauldron wanting "love summonings", regardless of how their victims might feel about it.

"I'm amazed you've got the brass neck to turn up with a story like that," Marian said. "Never mind the neck – you must have a brass chest, a brass stomach, and a brass arse!"

"What do you mean?" asked Della. "That's my life in black and white. It's no fun being childless, you know."

"Sounds like you had a lot of fun anyway, Miss Party Girl. And now you come along and tell me that you aborted me, which is bad enough, but I thought maybe you regretted it. I could understand that. But you don't really regret it, do you? You only wish it hadn't happened because of what followed. If you hadn't caught a dose and become infertile, you would never have regretted that abortion. You'd never have thought of it again. You certainly wouldn't have come barging into my house wanting to play at mummies and daughters." Marian unexpectedly felt a catch in her throat, and hated it for ruining the delivery of a perfectly good rant. "If you'd had kids of your own, you wouldn't be here now. So you don't really care about me at all."

Marian felt tears rising, and tried to choke them back. It was like losing her mother all over again. To see Della across the table, to hear her sounding like Mum and offering to give advice and buy treats and do all those parenty things... it had got her hopes up. Subconsciously, she'd thought her mother was back. But no, it was only some selfish bitch trying to use Marian as a bandage for her own emotional wounds. "You don't care about me, so you can get lost." She leapt out of the chair, sending it clattering backward, and flung open the kitchen door. "Go on, get out!"

"Ah, the teenage tantrum," said Della. "I've only been here half an hour, and already we're having a row. How quickly the glamour of parenthood fades. But I shall be strong!" She got up and closed the door, then began looking inside all the kitchen cupboards.

"I know it's a shock," Della went on. "And yes, you're right – I wouldn't be here if my life had turned out differently. But then, neither would you. You wouldn't be here if your mother hadn't died. We are where we are, and we have to make the best of it. After all, when I found out I was infertile, I could have sat at home feeling sorry for myself. Well, I did! For months and months. But then I got off my backside and decided to look for someone who needed me. I want to make a difference. Won't you at least give me a chance?"

"You say you want to make a difference, but it looks like you really want to make a drink," said Marian sourly. "Sit down and stop rifling the kitchen! I told you there isn't any alcohol. If you want me to give you a chance, you need to look a bit more like a mother, and a bit less like a bag lady who's just wandered in off the street."

"Now then," Della said, "less of your backchat. I'm not hunting for booze like some damn alkie whore. I'm looking for – aha!" She grabbed a set of scales from a cupboard full of rolling pins and scone-moulds and other baking paraphernalia. Then she took a tupperware container out of her handbag. Inside the tupperware lay a large plastic bag full of grey powder. She weighed the bag, and scribbled the result on a scrap of paper.

"What's that?" asked Marian. She'd been to parties where older kids giggled and tried to look cool as they brought out their stashes of weed or coke or speed, but this looked nothing like any of them.

"This is a perfectly legal substance," said Della. "It's a precursor chemical to another substance which is also perfectly legal... in this world, anyway. In other universes, maybe the end product isn't quite so legal, although this little bag would still be perfectly legitimate – just very difficult to get hold of. But here, where certain drugs are less fashionable and the government hasn't needed to clamp down, it's just a matter of finding someone who'll do you a favour." She sighed. "It makes me feel old, knowing that guys I dated when we were students are now biochemistry professors with their own labs."

"And the specialness never ends," said Marian tartly. "I thought you came here to reunite with your long-lost aborted foetus, and it turns out I'm merely the afterthought to a drugs deal." Again, she felt let down, though she knew she shouldn't. The words echoed in her head: *the world doesn't revolve around you.*

"Well, since you made such a point of telling me you were fifteen and too old for toys and dolls, I thought I'd treat you like a grown-up and tell you the score. How do you think I can afford to hop across universes? It isn't the million-quid-a-time celebrity hobby it started as, but it still ain't cheap."

"Fair enough, I suppose." Marian found that her feelings had executed a swift one-eighty – rather than being offended that Della had extra items on her To Do list alongside Long-Lost Baby, she felt somewhat relieved. It put less pressure on Marian, if Della had other concerns. Already Marian was wary of Della's neediness, her quasi-parental desire to hang out and spend Quality Time together. "So, what does the stuff do?"

"This doesn't do very much. As I said, it's just a precursor. When it's baked, it's a cognitive remixer – it gives you synaesthesia, among other things. Creative types use it to taste their paintings, smell their tunes, and so on." Della shook her head and laughed. "There's a whole subculture called the Symmetric Aesthetic, with 'sense-balanced' art and edible equations and stuff you have to be totally off your head to appreciate. I dabbled in it myself when I was going out with one of the theorists...

"But that was a long time ago. The remixer isn't important. It buys my ticket, but I wouldn't have got it if you hadn't been here. You're far more important to me than –" Della made a dismissive gesture toward the bag of powder.

"So what do you want to do?" asked Marian again.

"I want to get to know you," Della said. "I realise I can't just walk into your life and expect you to have a Della-shaped hole ready and waiting. But I want to make the effort. I want to be here when you need someone you can talk to."

It sounded reasonable. She should give Della a chance, at least. "All right, but I have a busy life. There's a party tonight, I'm working in the shop tomorrow –"

"Then Sunday, maybe we could do something together. Suppose your mother hadn't died, what would you be doing?"

Marian gritted her teeth. "You're not Mum, damnit! Don't try to replace her."

"All right then, let's do something she never did. Something you'd like to do, but you never did with her."

"Give me some time to think about it," Marian said. "This is all a bit too much at once."

"Yes, I know. I remember the first time I met myself... Well, that's another story. Look, how about I come back on Sunday afternoon? I'll have a think about what we can do, and you can suggest something, and between us we'll work something out."

"Or nothing," said Marian. "Don't take anything for granted."

"Hah! You'll do well. I hope you keep that same attitude with the boys. Make them work for it."

Della got up, packed away the tupperware with its grey powder, and sauntered out of the door into the sunshine, leaving behind a pall of cigarette smoke and a suddenly silent kitchen.

Marian rinsed out the ashtray and put the mugs in the washbowl. Now the house felt small and empty. When her grandparents had left for the weekend, she'd looked forward to having the place to herself. But with Della gone, she felt alone. She should have asked Della to stay and cook dinner; that would have been something. It took all her self-control to refrain from running out into the street and demanding that Della come back to make beans on toast.

No, don't sound desperate. Make her work for it, like she said. Anyway, it was ridiculous to feel lonely when she had messages waiting, and friends ready to come over.

Ah, the friends. Trouble was, the more people you invited, the less they were your friends. Marian had a couple of confidants with whom she felt genuinely close. Beyond that, there were only brittle bonds of acquaintance based on superficial gossip. The others would come round for the party, not for her. They'd go to any empty house with a loud stereo system – anywhere that wasn't hanging around on street corners, sneering at the tourists. Any party where drinks or drugs might appear...

No alcohol, Marian resolved. But some of them would probably bring it themselves. She couldn't stand at the door all night, warding off booze.

Well, maybe not a 'party' party. Just a select gathering. Maybe just a girls' night. But half of the girls wouldn't come if there were no boys, so it wouldn't be much more than Marian's best buddies and no special occasion at all, hardly any point in even having the old folks out of the way.

It was like a fiendish logic puzzle. No booze – no boys. No boys – no girls. No girls – no party. Nothing.

Shit!

But why not just chill with her friends? They could still have fun, and shake the place up a bit. And it would be good to talk to the girls, tell them about Della's visit, get their thoughts on what to do and what to say.

Marian opened a can of low-calorie soup and ate it with an unbuttered slice of toast, adding some sliced cucumber as a token fresh vegetable. Then she texted her closest friends and invited them round for a 'girls nite'.

Annabel was the first to arrive, dressed in black with a holographic T-shirt of Lester Todd's new band. Marian didn't want to explain the whole Della situation several times over, so she'd planned to wait until everyone arrived before starting on it. But the subject was on her mind and wouldn't be suppressed. Soon it burst out.

"Do you spend much time with your mum?" Marian asked.

Annabel frowned. "She has this big thing about us all eating together. You know, sometimes you just want to snack on something while you're watching TV, but she won't have it. No, the entire family has to sit down at the table and be interrogated. My brothers joke about it: they say it's like those old films where the prisoners of war have to go to... the mess, is it? Where they eat, anyway, and the Nazis take the roll call, and in the film there's always one Nazi who talks to the prisoners and tries to catch them out, discover their escape plan. So we turn up to the dinner table and it's like a roll call, you need a doctor's note if you're missing. Then when we've all sat down, the cuffs spring out of the armrests to shackle us to the chairs, and the interrogation starts. 'How was your day at school?' 'How's your friend Marian doing?' 'Where's the escape tunnel?' Meanwhile Dad just sits there shovelling peas into his gut, and us kids are all kicking each other under the table to make each other laugh... Is that what you meant?" Annabel looked at Marian with a concerned expression.

"I guess," Marian said, trying to hold her voice steady. "What else, apart from mealtimes?"

"Well, we go shopping sometimes. There's Christmas, of course. And holidays used to be a big deal, though nowadays we try to ditch the parents as soon as we can. At first we tried to do our own thing in the evenings, and then we made a break for it earlier and earlier: in the afternoons, in the mornings straight after breakfast. It's the escape tunnel again. God, it sounds awful, doesn't it? But that's how it is. When kids get older, they don't want to hang out with their parents. Mums aren't cool, are they? We haven't talked about this before because your mother's dead, and I didn't ever want to complain about mine in case it sounded... Well, you know. And 'complain' is the wrong word, anyway. I love my Mum; it's just she can be a bit of a pain. As for spending time with her, we used to do a lot of crafts and stuff. Sewing and crocheting and embroidery. I haven't done any of that for a while. Maybe I could get back into it, if I ever had the time..."

"Oh Marian, I'm so sorry. Don't cry. No, no, let it out. Let it all out. I'm sorry, I'm so sorry."

On Sunday, when Della turned up wearing a short skirt and bizarre shoes that looked like sandals with high heels – were they fashionable on some other Earth? – Marian made an instant decision as to the afternoon's activity.

"Let's go walking," she said. She rarely went on hikes, tending to despise it as the hobby of tourists and eco-freaks. In her free time she much preferred going to Manchester or Leeds and doing some proper shopping, in a proper city where they had McDonald's and HyperSilk and lots of little market stalls selling sparkly bangles that Marian might occasionally steal on days when she felt particularly mischievous or melancholic.

But she knew the local paths and vantages, and she had a cruel impulse to drag Della up and down the steep sides of the valley. *Let's see how much you want it. You wanna spend time with me? Come on, here we go.* She recognised it as nasty manipulativeness, yet she was drunk on the power of being desired. And, she rationalised to herself, everyone did it. All teenagers took advantage of their parents, extorting pocket money, treats, privileges of staying up late and having boyfriends over...

They headed out of town and walked across the little cobbled bridge to the riverside path. "There used to be mills all along this river," Marian said. "We did projects on them at school. One year we built a waterwheel, or we nearly did but we kept spending all the lessons splashing each other."

Now the mills were coming back, in the grand new era of localism and renewable energy. A few full-size waterwheels belonged to businesses claiming to be off-grid and fully sustainable. "It's a load of hype," Marian said. "They put a picture of a waterwheel in their adverts to attract eco-freak customers and justify higher prices. We see it in the shop – crushed herbs and all that." She parodied the broad Yorkshire accent used on TV commercials: "*Locally grown, and locally crushed under the waterwheel trip-hammers, driven by the pure water of the Pennines, powering mills for hundreds of years.* Like it makes a difference how the hammers are powered! We had a drought last year and the river was too low for the wheels. Somehow the supply of waterwheel-crushed herbs didn't seem to diminish..."

Della frowned. "That's the second time you've complained about this New Age stuff. Why does it bother you so much?"

"I only mentioned it because we're out here by the river and the waterwheels. Look, there's one now." The wooden paddles moved slowly, majestically. The sun, reflecting off drips of water, made the great wheel glitter like a cascade of cheap jewels. Marian went on, "It's just that everything is so fake nowadays. I shouldn't complain: I go shopping and I can't afford brand-name handbags, so I get cheap knock-offs instead. But at least I know they're fake. Does that mean everyone who comes to the Cauldron knows it's all fake as well, the whole pile of New Age bullshit? Why do they bother? This entire town is fake, full of restored old buildings recreating the 'authentic experience'. And on Friday when I was wondering which friends to invite to my party, I realised half of those friendships are bogus. You never know who's going to smile at you one day, and back-stab you the next. It's a fake town full of fake people buying fake stuff...''

"Then along comes your fake mother," said Della. "You think I'm false. But I haven't pretended to be anything I'm not."

"No, it's not about you. I've felt this way since long before you turned up." *But you're right,* thought Marian, *you are a fake.*

Della looked at Marian but didn't speak, silently creating a space for Marian to talk on.

"I know what the psychobabble explanation would be," said Marian. "It's projection. My life feels fake because my Mum died; it's not what my real life should be. I'm imagining something perfect where Mum's still alive, where Dad isn't in prison. Maybe there is a universe like that somewhere – I guess there has to be. But this world is just a bad fake, like one of those cheap replica handbags where the stitching is all wrong. This isn't my real home."

As Marian spoke, she walked faster and faster, fuelled by futile anger, and Della trotted to keep up. At the end of the riverside path, they walked along the road till they reached the woods of Hardcastle Crags. Here the road veered away up the moors, and only a gravelled track continued through the trees. Della's shoes soon became encrusted with mud, but she made no complaint.

Marian thought about the world Della came from, just one of an infinite range of worlds where things had happened differently – mostly going wrong in various ways. It felt as if there was one real universe, a shining summit where everything happened as it should: a needle-thin pinnacle, surrounded by endless swampy lowlands full of bad decisions, unlucky accidents, and damaged people. As you slogged through the mire, you tried to clamber up to some better state. But you found yourself flailing down to your doom, confronted with far more wrong options than right. And everyone else in the world plummeted down too, dragging you with them. Even if you did the right thing, you had no control over other people's mistakes, their car crashes and jail sentences. Every time you slept, the world fell a little further during the night.

No wonder Della wanted to find a better Earth. Flitting across universes, she was like someone driving a car where everyone else walked. But even with a car, the lowlands were immensely vaster than the highlands. The perfect peak of utopia was so lofty and slender that you couldn't see it. Yet somewhere there might be smaller local peaks, like islands in the swamp. If there was only one real universe and an infinite number of fakes, maybe a few of those fakes would be tolerable – just as high-class counterfeits were almost indistinguishable from designer goods.

How to find even a tiny pinnacle? Marian was overwhelmed by the thought of all the necessary choices: so many paths in the wood, so many mistakes she could make.

At last they reached the café at Gibson Mill. The site had been a cotton mill in the nineteenth century, then a dance hall and skating rink in the early twentieth century, then after long dilapidation had been restored by the National Trust, complete with smugly worded display boards proclaiming the virtues of environmentalism.

"What would you like?" asked Della.

"Apple juice," said Marian, "or whatever they've got." It was nice to have someone along who'd pay for things.

"Anything to eat?"

"Let's see... We've walked a couple of miles, with some up and down, so that's at least two hundred calories. I guess I could have a scone. It's a freebie!"

Della queued at the counter and came back with a tray of drinks and snacks. Marian put some blackcurrant jam on a scone, after moving the butter-dish behind the teapot so that she didn't have to look at it. The sight of butter or margarine always made her feel queasy – the yellow lumps of fat were repulsive.

She sensed Della's gaze, the hungry maternal gaze that absorbed everything about her, but Della didn't comment. Marian was pleased that Della didn't lecture her on fretting about her weight. She hated being told that weight didn't matter, when it so obviously did. It was just another way that adults lied, pretending the world was different, pretending that the fake surfaces didn't eclipse anything real that might lie underneath.

Della said, "Look at that guy. What a platter! If he's calibrating miles to calories, he must be walking the Pennine Way."

"All in one day," said Marian, laughing.

Conspiratorially, they glanced around at the tourists in the café, speculating on their private habits. It was trivial conversation, but all the more enjoyable for that.

"There's an old-fashioned rucksack," Marian said, "the one with the badges sewn all over it. I can't read them from here – where do you reckon the owner's been?"

"Amsterdam... twenty times."

"No, I reckon they're all in England. He looks like someone who'd boast about how virtuous his holidays are – I bet he's the type who volunteers to restore canals or repair footpaths."

"I'll go and ask." Before Marian could stop her, Della walked over to the rucksack's owner and spoke to him.

Marian couldn't hear what they said, but she watched Della smiling and gesturing expressively. *My God, is she flirting with him? I can see how she caught a dose!*

Della returned and said, "You were nearly right. The badges are all bird stuff – he's one of those guys who'll go two hundred miles to see a weird-looking duck. But he's also a volunteer: he guards the nesting sites of rare birds to protect them from egg thieves. The breeding pairs are imported from less polluted Earths, and he helps to establish them here." She grinned, as though impressed by his idealism. "It takes all sorts, as they say at the liquorice factory."

Marian smiled in return. It almost felt normal, to sit and eat and chat, dissecting other people's little quirks. But she couldn't quite relax, because Della kept staring at Marian, as if memorising her face for later description to the police.

"I'm sorry. I'm being rude," Della said. "It's just so hard for me to look at you. I thought I'd got over it, but I haven't. Every time I see you, I think about what happened, what I threw away. Why did I do it? Well, I know why... But it was the worst decision of my life." Her voice trembled. "Can you ever forgive me?"

Around them, the noise of the café swelled and faded – the clatter of cutlery, the hiss of the coffee machine, the thud of the door as tourists came and went, their boots echoing on the stone floor. Marian wished she could hear a fire alarm going off, so that she wouldn't have to answer this question. It wasn't real to her, the fact that in another universe her mother had aborted her. She was alive here and now. What did it matter that in some other world, she didn't exist? If a different sperm had hit the egg, or if her parents had used contraception, Marian wouldn't exist. Why was it different to have an abortion? It meant nothing to Marian, but she knew she couldn't say that.

She squeezed Della's hand. "It's all right," she said, hoping that Della wouldn't break down in tears and cause a scene. "It's all right. I'm here. I forgive you."

"Really?" asked Della.

"Really," Marian said, projecting as much sincerity as she could manage.

Della swallowed hard, and tried to smile. It was like watching a fallen fledgling struggle to take flight – flapping pathetically, squirming on the floor. "Let's go home," Della said, her voice high and tight.

They walked out of the café arm in arm. On the way home, Marian tried to lighten the mood by talking of inconsequential things like shoes and sports. Della proclaimed herself an occasional badminton player. "I don't play as often as I should, but it's great for getting in shape and working off tension. If you're feeling frustrated, you can whack the shuttlecock as hard as you like, and it won't fly off into the distance. I did try playing tennis, but my friends got tired of chasing the ball after I kept smacking it way out of court!"

When they arrived back at Marian's house, it was late afternoon. Della plonked herself on the sofa and started flicking through TV channels. "Make yourself at home," Marian said pointedly. "It's the end of the weekend – I need to look at my schoolwork."

In her room, Marian began her usual homework-procrastination routine of checking her messages, texting friends, and looking for the latest gossip on the Net. An hour or so later, the bedroom door opened.

"Thought you might want a cuppa," said Della.

Marian took the drink. "Thanks. But this is my room – knock before you come in!"

"Sure; I'm sorry." Della lingered in the doorway, gazing at

125

everything in Marian's room, from the Lester Todd posters on the wall to the discarded jeans and lipsticks and nail-varnish bottles on the floor.

"You can't stay here, you know," Marian said. "My grandparents will be back tomorrow."

"I understand," said Della. "I don't belong in this world, so it's difficult for me to fit in. Maybe you could come back to my world sometime. I'll show you the sights, and take you to a few parties."

Marian smiled. "It's a school day tomorrow." She spoke lightly, but recoiled from the idea of accompanying Della back to her home universe. However short a visit it might notionally be, she wondered whether she would ever come back. There'd be some excuse, some hitch to prevent Marian's return and ensure she stayed in Della's orbit.

"Maybe next weekend?" said Della.

"Maybe," said Marian. She realised that by saying *I forgive you,* she'd given Della the impression they'd had a moment of bonding, a stepping-stone toward a deeper relationship. That wasn't something she was keen to encourage, having seen the depths of Della's neediness. Yet she couldn't bear to refuse Della directly.

"You don't sound very enthusiastic," Della said.

"Well, I didn't know you were carrying your Enthusiasm Quantification meter. If I'd realised, I would have spoken with fifty percent more glee and delight."

Della made a dismissive gesture as though batting away Marian's sarcasm. "Why don't you want to come and visit me?"

"Because it's too soon. You only turned up two days ago."

"And already you can't wait for me to leave and disappear?"

Marian sighed. "Must we have this conversation? I feel as though you're trying to push me into a corner." It was creepy, like being haunted by Mum's ghost.

Della marched into the room and flopped onto Marian's bed. "If I'm pushing, it's because you're resisting. Here I am, offering to do anything for you, and you're skulking in your room reading trash on the Internet. I've crossed universes to come here! You're an ungrateful little hussy, just like the others. When your Mum died, you would have given anything to have her back. Now I'm back, and you can't wait for me to be gone!"

"What do you mean, just like the others?"

"Hah! That's you all over – ignoring everything else and focusing on yourself. I mean the other versions of you, obviously."

Marian stared at Della, waiting for her to explain. Della preened at being the object of attention. She sat on Marian's pillow and drew up her legs, hugging her knees, looking like an older and not-so-wiser version of one of Marian's friends arriving for a heart-to-heart.

"This isn't the first universe I've visited," Della said. "When I decided to see the child I never had, I hired the Navigators to do some mapping. There are worlds where my alternate – your biological mother – died at different times, or ended up in prison, or ran off with another guy and left you with your father... I tried them all. That's how it feels, anyway. You're maybe the sixth or seventh version I've met. I thought it might be different this time, but you're just like the rest." Her head sank into her knees, muffling her voice. "You're always selfish. You always reject me!"

"If this is how you always behave, I can see why." Marian felt a tinge of pity for Della, but she also reckoned Della was laying on the pathos with a trowel, trying to guilt-trip her into... Well, what? What had Della imagined would occur?

"This would have happened anyway," Marian went on, "even if you hadn't had an abortion. Your own child would have grown up and rebelled against you, rejected you, called you a shrivelled old bitch who doesn't understand. That's how it is. Deal with it!"

As soon as she spoke, Marian experienced a stab of remorse. She'd been too harsh. It was as though four years ago someone had told her, "Your Mum's dead – deal with it!"

She moved to the bed and squashed up next to Della. "I'm sorry. I shouldn't have said that. I know it's hard for you."

Della rubbed her eyes. "No, you're right. If I'd had children, they would have defied me, insulted me, hated me – everything. It's not all sweetness and light, is it? Parents know there'll be bad days. But when a child becomes rebellious, the parents can draw on years of happy memories, years of togetherness to help them through the sticky patches. I haven't had that. I wanted the good times! I came to see you and we had... what, a weekend? That's after a few weeks with the other versions of you. Why, I only need to visit another hundred universes, and I might get a whole year of good times! But then I'll have been rejected a hundred times as well... I don't think I can stand that. I can't go on like this." Her voice cracked. "I just can't."

Then don't, thought Marian, but suppressed the reply as unhelpful. "You just need to handle your approach a bit better. Think of it like dating: if you come on too strong, it's counter-productive. It's too scary being on the other end of that. You're asking too much too soon: trying to shadow my every move, trying to take me back to your world, all in a couple of days. Slow down!"

Della grabbed a tissue and blew her nose with a honking snort. "I know. That's what the last version of you told me. It's what I planned to do, but I couldn't hold back. There's no time to slow down! You're already fifteen. If I take it slowly, then by the time we get to know each other properly, you won't be a child any more. You won't need me at all."

"People don't stop needing family when they turn sixteen, or eighteen, or whatever age you're worried about. And it's not like I've got a terminal illness –" Marian paused with a sudden anxiety. "Not as far as I know. You haven't given me any dodgy genetics, have you?" She wondered if Della had aborted her because of a rare genetic defect just waiting to strike... thus explaining why Della was in such a rush to befriend her.

"No, not at all. Genes of the highest quality," said Della, trying to smile.

Marian knew that this was the moment where they were supposed to bond and hug. She had seen enough cheesy films; she could almost hear the soundtrack of syrupy strings.

Yet she'd also seen enough emotional blackmail within her social circle to recognise when she was being manipulated. Whether consciously or subconsciously, Della was trying to sidle into Marian's affections with the old 'poor me' strategy, like a puppy whining about how often it had been kicked. After hearing that, surely no one would be so heartless as to kick it again...

"The way you come on too fast isn't helping," Marian said, "but I think there's a more fundamental reason why your visits keep going wrong. You're asking for something that we can't give you... or we can, but it's not what you need. This afternoon, you asked if I could forgive you, and I do – I honestly do – but that hasn't helped you, has it? You're still not satisfied, you're still pushing, you still want more."

Della tried to interject, but Marian overrode her. "In your heart, you know that any forgiveness from me doesn't really mean anything.

How can it? I'm fifteen years old, so by now there are millions of alternate Marians. I'm just me: I don't speak for all the others. You can't possibly beg forgiveness from every single version of me. And you shouldn't! There's only one person you really need it from – yourself." Marian paused and looked Della in the eye. "You need to forgive yourself for what happened."

Della broke Marian's gaze, and looked at the floor. She spoke in a soft, worn-out tone. "If I could forgive myself, I wouldn't be asking you."

"That hasn't worked, though, has it? Because you've asked and I've answered, but you're still here: you're still wanting more and more –"

"I was trying to be helpful!" exclaimed Della indignantly. "But you won't accept anything from me. You only said you forgave me because you were trying to get rid of me: you thought that's what I wanted, so you said it, and now you're disappointed I'm still here." Della's voice became ragged and hoarse. "You don't need me, you don't want me."

"No one needs a self-pitying self-obsessed wreck," said Marian, knowing it sounded unkind, but figuring it was the only way to get the message across. "You say you want to help, but how can you help anyone when you're so screwed up? Sort yourself out! Accept what happened. Deal with it! Then maybe you can go travelling across universes, if you still feel the urge. You'll be a better mother, or para-mother – whatever the word is – when you've come to terms with what happened, and when you're not demanding forgiveness wherever you go."

"Sort myself out?" Della laughed bitterly. "Get therapy, quit smoking, eat more fruit and veg... Yeah, a real makeover project. You think I haven't tried all that? You think I haven't tried to 'accept what happened'? That's why I came here!"

"Yes, but you arrive expecting gratitude that you've blessed us with your special presence, and you're too messed up to do a good job of it. You say you want to help, but you're not helping; you're just another problem for me to deal with." Marian stood up, and steeled herself to say what had to be said. "Go home, and call me when you're out of rehab!"

"I'm detecting a slight aura of frostiness," said Della. "I can take a hint." She unfolded her limbs and picked her way across the carpet to the doorway. "If you want to get in touch" – she left a long pause, which Marian didn't fill – "you can ping me through this." She tossed a small black gadget onto the bed. "It's a crosstime phone, linked to mine."

Marian's eyes tracked the gadget, but she didn't pick it up.

"One last thing," Della said. "I will leave, but can I stay here tonight and leave tomorrow morning? It's just..." She sounded tired and old. "It's too early in the evening – it's not even dark yet. If I leave now, then I'll end up going to some party somewhere. There's always a party on some world or other, always a party where you can find the illusion of company. And there's always some drug or other that gets handed around, something to fill the emptiness, some new way to scramble the brain and pretend you're having fun... No, I can't go now. If I leave in the morning, there won't be any party to crash, and I'll have a few hours to find something better..."

Seeing the despair etched into Della's face, Marian didn't have the heart to refuse. It was only one night, after all. And it couldn't become permanent, because her grandparents would return tomorrow. "All right, all right. You can stay in the spare room. But give me some space, okay? I really do need to get this work done."

"I understand. Tell you what, I'll go and see what I can rustle up for dinner, yeah?"

Marian forced a smile. "You do that."

Della headed downstairs. Marian slumped in her chair, emotionally exhausted by the confrontation. She remembered Mum singing along to the radio in the kitchen at the old house, baking simple things like flapjacks and cookies. Mum had never got the hang of pastry; she couldn't manage pies, so she made crumbles instead: gooseberry in summer, then apple and blackberry in autumn. Marian hadn't eaten one of those in years, and she had a sudden longing for an apple crumble with custard. The sound of Della clattering in the kitchen brought back memories of good times, memories that Marian had long suppressed as too painful. It made her wish for Mum back, and it made Marian wonder whether she'd been too harsh with Della.

Damn you. It affected her because it was uncalculated – one of the few times Della had been spontaneous rather than manipulative. Just "I'll see what I can rustle up".

Marian had to listen to three Lester Todd songs before she was calm enough to even attempt any homework.

The evening meal, when Della finally served it, proved to be curry with brown rice. Not the sort of meal that Mum would have prepared, but it wasn't bad. Marian had an instinctive prejudice against brown rice as being part of the whole New Age organic hippie bullshit regime, yet there was nothing wrong with brown rice itself, only the people who usually ate it. After strawberry meringues for dessert, Marian could honestly say, "That was good. Thanks."

"Glad you approve," said Della, but she looked abstracted, staring out of the window into the twilight.

Marian retreated to her room, where she alternated between homework and Net-surfing and phoning friends. Downstairs she heard Della watching old comedy shows on TV.

"Can I have a goodnight kiss?" asked Della, as bedtime approached.

Marian was sufficiently grateful for a histrionic-free evening that she submitted to being kissed and hugged. It felt good, like something she'd missed for so long that she'd stopped noticing the lack. "See you tomorrow," she said, and was surprised to find that she meant it.

In the morning, Marian saw no sign of Della downstairs. She'd subconsciously hoped that Della would have got up early and laid out breakfast, made sandwiches for a lunchbox, and so forth. Her cynical side accused herself: *You didn't want to engage with her as a mother, but you quite liked being cooked for and waited on, didn't you?*

Well, a big breakfast was too many calories anyway. Marian ate an orange, packed her schoolbag, and finally cracked open the door of the spare room to look in on Della. She was still in bed. Della had missed the opportunity to make one final appeal for a maternal relationship, but Marian was relieved not to have to go through all that again.

Marian left a spare key on the kitchen table, and wrote a note. "Please lock up and post the key back through the letterbox. Thanks for coming to see me and making the effort." She thought for a long minute before adding the final sentence. "I'll ping you on the gizmo." It wasn't a complete lie – she might decide she wanted to keep in touch. Yet it wasn't a definite commitment. It was like when a boy said, "I'll text you." Marian, who'd found it so frustrating when boys said that and didn't follow up, now empathised with their position. It was something that you felt you had to say, that you might even decide to do.

But probably not.

Marian grabbed her bag and headed out. For perhaps the first time ever, she looked forward to school on a Monday morning. The weekend had been an emotional roller-coaster; she needed some time to recover her balance. Schoolwork and lunchtime gossip would be a welcome distraction. And when she came home, Della would be gone and everything would be back to normal.

She lingered after school, chatting with friends. Yet she knew she couldn't delay too long – she had to be home when her grandparents returned, if only to explain why the house stank of cigarettes.

When Marian opened the back door, she saw the key on the table where she'd left it that morning, along with her scribbled note. Was Della still here? Silence filled the house. Marian hurried upstairs to the spare room.

The bed was occupied. A sour smell hung in the air, along with an aura of stillness that made Marian's throat tighten in foreboding. A red light flashed on the bedside table.

Unwillingly, Marian approached the bed. She wanted to shout, "Wake up!" but she knew it was useless. Della's head lolled on the pillow, her eyes open and staring nowhere. No movement. No sound of breathing. The smell was stronger, a stink of piss and something Marian didn't recognise. *Some drug or other,* her instinct said.

Marian had done a first-aid course – just a few hours, covering the basics. She knew she ought to do something, but it had all leaked out of her head, and she couldn't bring herself to touch the body. *The body.* Already she thought of it as a corpse. Della was dead.

The flashing red light drew Marian's eye, demanding her attention. It was Della's phone. When she touched it, the display lit up, showing one voice message. *Get it over with.* Marian tapped her fingernail on the Play icon.

"I'm sorry, darling. I'm sorry to leave you like this. When I asked about staying here last night, I thought things might look better in the morning. But they don't, and they won't ever. There's only emptiness ahead of me now. I used to be a party girl, and when the party ends, what's left but to clear up the mess and throw out the dregs?

"They say that everything happens in all possible worlds. So I guess this had to happen, and you're just unlucky it happened here. Maybe in another universe there's a version of me who carries on and finds the daughter she never had; or who doesn't find her, but manages to keep going anyway.

"It was my fault it didn't work out with us. I only wish... Well, there's no time for me to tell you everything I wish had happened, or hadn't. There's a lifetime of it. I hate to think it's all been for nothing, but if I've only been an Awful Warning, then at least... Oh, what am I saying? Should've planned this better, as always...

"I've unlocked my phone and left you all the accounts and passwords. You can spend the money, you can hop across worlds, you can do anything. I just hope you can find something worthwhile..."

There followed a long pause, punctuated by choked sobs. "There's nothing more to say, nothing more to do. How can it end like this? But it has to end somewhere, and I can't go any further. Goodbye, Marian. Love you, God bless."

The recording ended, and the red light winked out.

Marian stumbled downstairs and called for an ambulance. Her voice was thick, and she had to speak several times before the operator could understand her. When she got off the phone, she rushed outside. She didn't want to be in the house with the body; it made her skin crawl. When Mum died, it had been so sudden that Marian only saw the body when laid out in the coffin, carefully covered to hide the worst of the injuries. She'd had time to brace herself; she'd had other family there to support her.

Now, she was alone. Again. Her emotions churned, all jumbled up together. She felt grief for Della's death, horror at the appalling waste of it. Yet she was relieved that Della was gone... and ashamed for feeling relieved. A heavy burden of guilt accompanied the thought that her rejection of Della must have contributed to the tragic outcome, even though Della had been palpably unbalanced anyway.

Most of all, she was angry at Della for being so selfish, so manipulative. All that talk about "there's a version of me who carries on", "I've left you all the accounts and passwords", "you can hop across worlds" – it transparently meant that Della wanted Marian to go and find some other alternate of Della, and make up with her. She hoped that Marian would feel guilty at rebuffing Della and driving her to suicide. She expected Marian to atone for it by becoming a daughter to another version of her. Just as Della had repented of her past actions and hopped across worlds in search of forgiveness, she wanted Marian to do the same. *See how it feels! See what you've driven me to!* That was the message, and Marian hated Della for it.

What a futile, histrionic gesture. As if suicide even meant anything... In an infinite array of alternate Dellas, one suicide wouldn't make much of a dent. Marian wasn't big on maths, but surely infinity minus one was still infinity. Della knew there'd be versions of her who decided against it, or who didn't quite overdose. *Everything happens in all possible worlds.* There were alternates who survived. And so suicide wasn't the grand gesture of ending all existence; it was merely a tiny scratch in the overall Della. It was a version of self-harming, like those girls who cut themselves or starved themselves – Marian knew a couple of them at school. It was their only way of expressing their pain.

And with that thought, Marian's sympathies swung abruptly, and she found herself pitying Della for getting into such a state that suicide was her only way out. How terrible it must feel to have messed up your life so badly that killing yourself felt like the only possible action. Where did it all go wrong for Della? Was it the abortion? No, surely not that one single thing in itself; it was all the years before and afterward, the years of drugs and partying and sleeping around. The trouble with living for the moment is that you've nothing to look forward to but more of the same. And when you can't stand that any more – you have nothing else.

The ambulance arrived, its siren a funeral knell. Two paramedics ran to the house, carrying first-aid equipment and a stretcher.

"Upstairs," said Marian. She stood aside to let the men go by. Their boots pounded up the stairs, rattling the old house.

She didn't follow them. There was nothing she could do, yet it still felt cowardly not to go up there. *I'd only be in the way,* she rationalised to herself.

Very soon they came out, carrying Della on the stretcher, moving more slowly because they had to be careful with the burden; but Marian sensed they knew it was too late to save her. She walked with them to the ambulance.

"Do you know what she took?" one of them asked.

"I'm sorry, I don't. There might be something in her handbag –"

"Yeah, we got that. We'll look at it."

They stowed Della inside the ambulance, where complicated expensive machinery began its futile checklist of survival.

"You can come with us if you like, but you don't have to."

Marian shook her head.

"Do you have someone you can call? Or would you like one of us to stay with you?"

"My grandparents are coming home soon. They'll be here any minute. I'll be all right." It was just a rote phrase, but it sounded callous as soon as it came out of Marian's mouth. *She's dead, but I'll be all right. She wasn't my mother anyway.*

"If you're sure..."

After a pause just long enough for any change of mind, they drove away. When the ambulance had turned a corner and disappeared in the maze of narrow streets, Marian raised a hand in farewell. It felt like a ludicrous gesture, waving goodbye to an ambulance carrying a corpse, but she had an urge to do something, to make some meaningful movement. She couldn't just stand there like a stuffed cabbage. *Goodbye, Della.*

She paced round the garden once, twice, then sat down at the kitchen table and put her head in her hands. The tears leaked through her fingers. *Goodbye, Mum.*

It was like being bereaved all over again. How dare Della put her through this? The selfishness of it! It brought home the terrible finality of death. Mum was never coming back.

But in some other universe, her mother had survived the accident. Of course, there would also be a parallel Marian in that reality. Yet everything must happen, so a similar universe must exist in which the local Marian had just died. In that world, Mum was bereaved and would surely welcome a visit from her daughter...

I've left you all the accounts and passwords – you can hop across worlds.

Only now did Marian truly understand the temptation. She could find her mother. She would learn from Della's mistakes, and not push too hard. Besides, Mum would be overjoyed to have her back. They could make everything right again. Marian could find the one real universe, the shining pinnacle where everything was perfect. She didn't have to live in a fake world, full of flaws.

The temptation swept through Marian, filling her with grief and longing. She yearned to put things right, to see her mother alive again. The past four years felt like a nightmare, from which she could wake by snapping her fingers.

But the example of Della showed that it wasn't so simple. If you chased fulfilment across worlds, you ended up deluding yourself that happiness could be found in some faraway place, rather than in your own heart. The more you searched outside, the less you healed inside.

How long had Della been searching, before she gave up? The better the world you wanted – the more specific your requirements – the longer it must take to find.

Even if you found the world you wanted, it wouldn't last. Something else would go wrong; some misfortune would strike, casting you down from the summit. You would have to keep travelling, spending your whole life in a vain search for utopia.

No, Marian wouldn't go looking for her mother. She already knew where Mum was: in the cemetery, and in her memories.

Marian wiped away the tears and blew her nose. She had to carry on as best she could. *Deal with it.* She belonged here, in this imperfect world.

Fake perfume could smell just fine; a counterfeit handbag would still hold all your essentials; and knock-off jeans could make you look pretty damned good... as long as you put in the effort. If you didn't have the real thing, you made the best of whatever you had.

She trudged upstairs, forcing herself to enter the spare room. The sour smell of desperation and death still hung in the air. Marian opened the windows and stripped the bed. Then she picked up Della's phone – the gate to all those other worlds – and took it into her own room, wondering what to do with it.

Marian didn't want to use the thing, but simply throwing it away would be disrespectful. Where could she keep it? Her gaze snagged on the cabinet that contained her memorabilia of Mum. She opened the bottom drawer, but as soon as she saw the old photo albums and the scarf Mum had knitted, she shivered and slammed the drawer shut.

Should she put Della's things with Mum's? It would be like admitting that Della really was her mother after all.

If she thought Della wasn't Mum, but only a hideous fake that polluted her mother's memory, then she should put the phone somewhere else – maybe in the stockroom at the Cauldron, along with all the bogus potions.

It was tempting to idealise Mum, to claim that poor pathetic Della wasn't remotely the same person. *You're not my mother,* Marian had said. But how true was that? If Mum had survived, would everything be sunshine and roses? Of course not.

Marian's own personality had elements – her shoplifting, her faddish eating – of which she was less than proud. As time passed and worlds diverged, some of her alternate selves would inevitably slide downward. At what point would they stop being her, and become someone else?

She shook her head. She didn't know the answer, but it felt too easy to say that you could define your identity as comprising only faultless high achievers, while disowning your darker aspects. They all contributed in their own fashion.

Marian opened the drawer that held her relics of Mum, and stuffed Della's phone way down in the bottom corner, under the photo albums containing pictures of the frozen, vanished past.

Hearing her grandparents at the garden gate, she ran down to greet them and welcome them home.

"I Was Nearly Your Mother" uses one of the classic tropes of science fiction – parallel worlds. As a child I read a lot of books by Andre Norton: she was my 'gateway drug' into the SF genre. Her novel The Crossroads of Time *introduced me to the idea that there existed different versions of the Earth, where history had taken different paths; and with a suitable technological gizmo, you could travel between all those alternate worlds.*

Since then, I've always been fascinated by the concept, not least because of the enormous scope that arises from a simple basic premise. Anything can happen! As long as it could have happened, then somewhere it did happen. The possibilities are endless, and an author is free to focus upon any of them.

Given such a wide choice, it's perhaps natural that authors have often been drawn to gaudy, big-picture scenarios: Earths with radically different histories, based on different outcomes from major events such as World War II, the American Civil War, etc.

However, I think that small changes can be just as interesting as large changes. If there are many parallel worlds, then some of them will be very similar to our own, having only recently diverged. And it seems plausible to me that if the technology for travelling to parallel worlds is ever invented, then these similar worlds will be much easier to reach than the radically different ones (e.g. Earths where the dinosaurs survived), because they're 'nearer'. After all, in the realm of space travel, it's much easier to land on the moon than it is to reach distant stars and galaxies.

Ian Creasey

The key aspect of these nearby parallel worlds is that they contain different versions of ourselves. In a world where the Roman Empire never fell, I would never have been born, so there is no 'alternate' version of myself. However, in a world which diverged twenty years ago, there is a version of me who shares the same childhood, but who made different decisions in adulthood.

What if you could travel to worlds inhabited by your alternate selves? What if you could see how their lives had turned out? What if you'd made a decision that you later regretted — but another version of you had done things differently? That question was the starting point for this story.

A story can be based on an abstract premise, but it needs concrete details. The narrative required a specific decision and its consequences. I chose to write about a woman who'd had an abortion, and had subsequently become infertile. In one world, she was childless; in a parallel world, where the abortion didn't happen, she was a mother.

I created this situation because I wanted to write about a difficult decision, full of dramatic potential. The story is a character study; it's not a polemic about the issue of abortion itself. Readers shouldn't assume that they can infer anything about my own opinions from the content of the story.

SHOOTING GROUSE

On the moor, the three saboteurs waited for the shooters to arrive. The August sun shone on purple heather, tussocks of boggy grass, and a few bilberry bushes that had survived the depredations of sheep and fire. Stella picked some tiny bilberries and poured a handful into her mouth, savouring the sweet, concentrated taste. They took the edge off her thirst. She was hot already, and it was only eight o'clock in the morning. Her neoprene suit felt stifling, which at least reassured her that its customised layers should repel any tasers or tranquilliser darts.

"Any sign of them?" asked Jim, his tone full of eagerness. At twenty-five he was two years older than Stella, but he had a teenager's longing for confrontation.

"I can't see anything yet," Stella replied. "It won't be long. They'll probably drive up when they've closed all the footpaths to keep out hikers."

Jim knew that, but she spoke for Denise's benefit. Stella had brought her new girlfriend along so they could start sharing each other's lives. She hoped that Denise would be inspired to get involved in sabbing.

Stella sneaked a sideways peek at Denise, who gazed westward from their vantage point on the ridge. The neoprene suits were designed for protection and camouflage, with brown splodges on green swirls, but their ugly bulk barely marred Denise's slim outline. She looked like a superhero in training, elegant and strong. Her black hair was cropped much shorter than Stella's own ponytail.

The long, trilling call of a curlew rang out across the moor, followed by the harsher *go-back, go-back-back-back* croak of a red grouse.

Poor little grouse, thought Stella. A fierce protective urge rose inside her. *You don't know what's coming. But we're here for you.*

"Are we sure that anyone's turning up?" asked Denise.

"Oh yes," said Jim. "They have to advertise when each moor is closed for shooting. We just don't know exactly where they'll start. These moors are so big, there's plenty of choice."

The high moorland stretched from horizon to horizon, with only the distant glimmer of Gouthwaite Reservoir interrupting the view.

"England is a small, crowded country," Jim went on, "but look at the size of this estate. Think how much land has been closed off, just so a bunch of bloodthirsty bankers can shoot some birds."

"It's beautiful up here." Denise picked a sprig of heather and lifted it to her nose. "This is what grouse eat?"

Stella winced at the ignorant praise of a degraded, barren landscape. "It looks nice now, when it's in bloom. But the heather is a monoculture, intensively farmed. They burn it regularly – see that horrible black patch over there? Nothing else can get established. It's an ecological disaster."

Denise frowned. "What should it be like instead?"

"If people stopped meddling, eventually it would revert to woodland –"

"Here come the meddlers," said Jim, pointing to a Land Rover crawling up the gravel track from Ramsgill. "Get down! Switch on your holograms."

Stella fumbled for her activator. Soon three sheep stood on the moor, each marked with the red blotch of the local flock.

To preserve battery life, they'd waited till the last minute to erect their disguise. Their backpack projectors could display any image, but sheep best matched people's infra-red heat signatures, which the holograms couldn't suppress. And sheep could wander across the moor without arousing suspicion.

"*Baaaaa*," said Denise.

"*Baaaaa* to you too," Stella said. "You make a lovely ewe."

"Yeah, and so do I!" Jim complained. He'd wanted to be a ram, but it wasn't yet the season when male and female sheep were brought together. Even a small error, if spotted, could wreck a sabbing operation.

They watched as several Land Rovers and a quad bike parked in a clearing amid the heather. People swarmed out. A dozen figures, carrying flags, marched onto the moorland.

"Those are the beaters and flankers," Stella whispered to Denise. "They'll flush out the grouse."

The rest of the party remained near the vehicles. The sabs had previously planted microphones in likely spots where the shooters might congregate. Stella adjusted her earpiece, and flipped the channel selector until she heard conversation. She hoped to record something incriminating or embarrassing, but it was only a safety drill: "My name's Larry Wade, and I'm the gamekeeper. The first thing to remember about using guns is not to shoot anyone – not even the beaters!"

The voice had the accent of someone who'd grown up in Yorkshire and never left, someone who spent his days talking to local farmers and barmaids. Stella's own voice had evolved into a more metropolitan accent during her college years; if she'd stayed in Pateley Bridge, she would have sounded exactly like Wade the gamekeeper.

She removed her earpiece when the shooters began strolling down the track with the easy, all-the-time-in-the-world swagger of rich, complacent men. Many of them wore tweed, or similar traditional clothes, albeit rather newer and cleaner than the average countryman's outfit. When they left the track, their gait became less confident as they stumbled through tussocks, bogs, and soft peat.

Scum, thought Stella. *Loathsome subhuman scum. How can these sick minds be so in love with killing that they'll pay a fortune to do it?*

"Looks like they're heading for the butts near the waterfall," Jim said. "That's the second bank of projectors."

"Yeah. Let's get closer."

The sabs scrambled across the moor, on all fours so as not to strain the holographic disguise by standing higher than a sheep. The nose-down crawl through the heather confronted Stella with the stunted ecosystem's limited range of scents: peat, mud, sheep dung, and stagnant bog. "Be careful," she said to Denise. "The greener it looks, the wetter it is."

Stella and Jim had already scouted the area last week when hiding the projectors, so they knew which spot combined reasonable cover with a good view of the grouse butts. The three sabs ensconced themselves in a grassy hollow near the top of an outcrop.

The row of butts looked innocuous, until you contemplated its hideous purpose. Each butt was a low curved wall, behind which a shooter could hide like a cowardly blob. Turf and lichen had colonised the ancient stonework, helping the killing zones to blend into the landscape.

The men dispersed along the row and began setting up. They wedged sticks atop the butts: these restricted the firing angle, preventing any over-eager shooter from pointing a gun at the flankers. Finally, the hunters loaded their shotguns. Some had brought more than one gun – with servants ready to switch and reload – so as not to miss a single moment of shooting.

The record for bagging grouse belonged to Lord Walsingham, who one day in August 1888 personally shot more than a thousand birds. That was on Blubberhouses Moor, only a few miles to the south. No sabs in his day, of course. But now they'd arrived to spoil the party.

"Here we go," said Stella, relishing what was about to happen. She took the remote control out of her backpack, and set the transmitter for Bank 2. "Denise, are you okay with the video camera? Don't forget to use the zoom for close-ups."

"Yes, I'm fine," Denise said. "Is there an Oscar category for 'best sabbing video filmed in Yorkshire by lesbians disguised as sheep'?"

Stella laughed. "There must be. The Oscars gets longer every year." She was delighted at Denise's enthusiasm.

The gamekeeper walked from the first butt to the last, making sure the shooters were ready. Then he climbed onto a rock that gave him a view across the moor. Stella's stomach tensed as he seemed to stare right at the sabs. Yet he was simply checking that the beaters had completed their formation, holding the flags in a wide semicircle ahead of the butts.

Silence fell. Not even a curlew trilled. Sweat oozed onto Stella's control unit, making the plastic clammy and slippery.

The gamekeeper signalled the beaters to start closing in. They inched forward, keeping their relative positions, taking their cue from the flankers on each side. As they walked, they waved their flags and shouted, creating a commotion to disturb any nearby birds.

A grouse chittered in alarm, and burst out of the heather. It flew low across the ground, away from the beaters – toward the butts. The *crack* of a shotgun resounded in the still air. The blast missed. The bird jinked aside, then flew onward. Another gun fired. The grouse fell and landed on some peat, twitching feebly.

Seething with rage, Stella stabbed a button on her remote. The image of a bird rose from the ground, then approached the shooters. Again the shotguns fired. Their lead pellets hit no target. The bird flew onward, past the gunmen, soaring toward freedom – until the image exceeded the projector's range, and dissolved out of existence.

Panicked by the approaching beaters and the noise of the shotguns, more grouse emerged from the heather. Frantically, Stella operated the hidden projectors, sending up flocks of holographic decoys to distract the hunters from the real birds. She imagined the holograms as the ghosts of dead grouse, helping their descendants survive. Every time she saw a genuine bird fly past the cordon and away, glee surged through her. The thrill of danger, the triumph of outwitting the shooters, the righteousness of her cause... it all made her feel like a hero.

They couldn't save all the birds. As the morning progressed, a sad collection of corpses accumulated on the ground – but much fewer than on a typical, undisrupted shoot.

The sabs' long-term goal was to destroy the so-called sport of grouse shooting by agitating for a legal ban, while deterring demand to make the business uneconomic. Today marked the latest salvo in an ongoing war, fought on the battleground of public opinion. It had taken decades to eradicate fox hunting. Would this campaign see a swifter victory?

Angry voices punctuated the shotgun blasts. The beaters hesitated, until the gamekeeper furiously beckoned them to keep walking. A horn blew, telling the shooters to turn round and start firing behind the butts. This allowed the beaters to march right up to the butts and flush out the remaining grouse – even if they were almost impossible to bag amid the cloud of holographic chaff.

Jim chortled. "Time for the slogans?" he asked.

"When all the grouse have escaped," Stella said firmly.

Soon all the real birds were dead or gone. Instead of decoys, the sabs now projected slogans in giant green letters. Stella's first message read: YOU'RE SO BRAVE – *fighting these birds with just your big guns and an army of servants.*

New captions drifted over the heather, cycling through all the text the sabs had composed. Stella shook her head when she saw Jim's favourite slogan: SHOOT BANKERS, NOT BIRDS! He said it was a joke, but Stella worried that it looked extremist. The real audience was not the shooters, but the wider public. Today's stunt would be edited into a video, and uploaded to the Internet as part of the propaganda war.

Meanwhile the beaters collected the fallen grouse, casually finishing the injured ones by bashing them on the head. The shooters inspected the meagre haul. Through her binoculars, Stella savoured their expressions of disappointment. *Hey, scumbags – not so much fun now, is it?*

"It's looking good," said Denise, wielding the camera. "Nice and dramatic."

Stella was glad to have Denise beside her. They never had enough time together: Denise's waitressing job had an awkward schedule, and Stella – when she wasn't sabbing – helped run her parents' organic textiles business. Stella's last girlfriend had been scared off by her campaigning; she didn't want that to happen again. If Denise became a sab, they could enjoy each other's company while fighting together for the cause. Maybe this time it would work out. Maybe Denise was the one...

The sound of a quad bike shattered her reverie. The engine revved loudly as the bike left the track and careered across the heather.

"He's coming right for us," exclaimed Denise.

Stella frowned. Their sheep disguises were still in place. The holograms ran a loop of posture changes, so that the images didn't look implausibly static. What had given them away?

She realised she could see no other sheep. Real animals would have fled, disturbed by the barrage of shotgun fire. The sabs should have retreated as soon as they'd triggered the slogans. She shook her head, annoyed with herself.

They couldn't outrun a quad bike, and they didn't have time to hide. The rider would soon reach them.

"Might as well change disguise, eh?" said Jim. He didn't sound too displeased.

"Yeah," Stella agreed. She stood up and switched her holo-projection. The ewe vanished, replaced by Stella's neoprene-suited body with the head of a giant bird. This saved battery power: the new, smaller hologram concealed her identity by simply projecting a bird mask over her face. She resembled an avenging superhero, protecting the birds of the moor.

Jim's disguise was the Guy Fawkes mask worn by anti-establishment protestors across the world. Denise's head looked like an Earth globe: a simple image that Stella had chosen to symbolise the environmental case against grouse moors.

Unable to see Denise's expression, Stella couldn't tell if she looked nervous.

"Don't worry," Stella said. "They can kill birds, but they can't kill us. He might fire tranquilliser darts, but our suits should block them. Have you still got the camera? Keep filming. Remember, it's a war for public opinion. If we come off best, we can use this."

"Let's get further into the rocks," said Jim. "No sense making it easy for him to reach us. He could have anything on that quad bike."

The three sabs clambered down the outcrop, trying to find the most inaccessible position among the millstone boulders. Stella felt stiflingly hot: she longed for some wind or rain to cool her down.

The bike's engine fell silent. Stella looked back and saw that the rider had dismounted. He was following them onto the rocks.

"Okay, stop here. We need to make a stand," she said. It would look bad if the sabs kept running away. They had no reason to flee: they were in the right. Nevertheless, her heart stuttered with tension.

The man's boots thudded across the grey, wind-scoured stone. He had a scraggly beard and moustache, smothering his face like lichen spreading across a gravestone. He wore a backpack, but he didn't carry a gun.

"Have you been sabotaging our shoot?" he demanded. Stella recognised his voice from the safety briefing: Larry Wade, the gamekeeper.

"That's right," said Jim, "because you're a bunch of overprivileged savages."

"You object to people hunting their own food? All this grouse will get eaten. And it's healthy produce – free range! What's the problem: do you want to force the whole world to become vegetarian?"

Stella frowned, wondering what Wade was trying to do. He sounded more polite and less angry than she'd expected. Maybe he wanted to look calm, while portraying the sabs as unreasonable fanatics.

She was happy to discuss the issues. The sabs had nothing to fear from that, not when all the arguments lay on their side.

"Actually, you don't eat everything you kill," she said. "What about your so-called 'pest control'? All the crows and foxes you shoot, all the stoats you trap in snares, all the birds of prey you poison – you don't eat those. You kill dozens of other animals for every single grouse you bag, so don't try to pretend that it's really about food. Because it isn't. It's about blood lust, for people who enjoy killing defenceless birds."

He waved this aside. "Hardly defenceless. They're not easy to shoot: you've seen how many people it takes to flush them out. That creates jobs –"

"Oh, spare us the crocodile tears for the local economy," said Jim. "These grouse moors receive millions in subsidies from the government. The taxes of ordinary hard-working country folk get funnelled to super-rich landowners –"

Stella interrupted to divert his 'class war' diatribe. "Government grants are for land management, but grouse moors are an environmental disaster. This ecosystem is practically a desert. You keep burning the heather, so hardly anything can grow. The land is constantly eroding away, which causes floods. Destroying the peat creates global warming. You're peppering the whole moor with lead shot, even though lead is poisonous. There's no need to use lead, but you just don't care."

She could easily carry on ranting about the environmental catastrophe of grouse moors. Her video on the subject had sixty thousand views on YouTube. But she noticed that Wade was letting her speak, rather than jumping in. He seemed strangely calm, almost not caring what she said, as though he just wanted her to keep talking...

Stella pursed her lips, trying to figure out what was happening. Her head hurt. Something looked odd about Wade: he had a weird beard. She could hear a faint hissing sound, as if her brain was leaking away. Her head hurt. Wade should get his weird beard sheared. Why wasn't Jim saying anything? Her head hurt.

"Run!" she yelled. "He's gassing us!"

She grabbed Denise's hand and yanked her down the slope. Denise staggered, and for an awful moment Stella thought she would fall. Her head was the Earth globe. If it fell, it would shatter... *I've got to save the world.* Stella caught Denise as she stumbled. She pulled her between the boulders, then followed Jim as he sprinted downhill.

Wade shouted, "Do you run away every time you lose an argument?"

Once they left the outcrop, the moor was a treacherous surface on which to run. Stella's ankles protested as she raced across the uneven ground. The three sabs descended a gully, jumped across a stream, then collapsed on the other side.

Stella retched. Only dry heaves, thank God. She listened for the quad bike's engine, but heard nothing. Jim had cleverly taken them into a valley too steep for the bike. Of course, Wade could drive the long way round and reach them from the bottom. Or he could simply chase them on foot.

Looking around, she saw no one. Yet within the gully, she had a foreshortened view. Most of the moor lay beyond the top of the slope, out of sight. A waterfall cascaded down the ravine, feeding a small pond. To her left, the stream descended into the conifer plantations of Dallowgill.

She would only see a pursuer when he came over the slope's lip, barely fifty metres away. Still, no help for that now. Desperate to cool down, Stella splashed her face with water from the stream.

"Are you guys all right?" she asked. She sat next to Denise and rested a hand on her shoulder.

"Yeah," said Jim.

"Just about," said Denise, her voice quavering. "What happened?"

"I don't know for sure, but I think he had some kind of gas canister in that backpack. He must have been wearing a mask or a breathing tube, so it didn't affect him. And we didn't see it, because he had a fake beard covering it up. That beard was a damned hologram!"

Jim laughed. "You reckon? Wow, that's priceless. It did seem odd the way he encouraged us to talk. I suppose he needed us to breathe enough of a dose to keel over."

"What would he have done with us?" asked Denise.

"Oh, he'd have dragged us to one of the Land Rovers, and we'd have woken up in the nearest police station, which I'd guess is in Pateley Bridge."

"But we survived," Stella said brightly, "and we rattled them." She removed her disguise and smiled at her companions, trying to boost morale. "Turn off your holograms to save power. Since we're all sitting down, let's have a drink and take a few minutes' rest."

"That man might come back," Denise objected.

"Yes," Stella admitted, "but let's hope he thinks we've run away, off the moor." She waved her hand toward Dallowgill far below. Then she delved into her backpack for some apple juice. It tasted heavenly after all her exertions.

"I reckon he won't come back," said Jim, "because what else can he do? The gas won't work, not now that we've twigged to it. And he knows we're wearing suits, so there's no point firing tranquilliser darts."

Stella pointed to the waterfall. "They could drug the water, in case we drink from it." Was that paranoid? Not after being gassed, it wasn't.

"Good point. We'll stick to our own supplies." Jim opened a bottle of lemonade. It hissed and fizzed, spilling onto the grass.

"If they're not coming for us, does that mean we've won?" asked Denise.

"Hey, it's not over yet," Jim said. "It's only lunchtime. The shooters will want another session this afternoon. They might think we've run away, but we'll show them otherwise. They gassed us like vermin! Let's take revenge."

"Revenge? We're not in a Hollywood movie," said Stella. *Although we are wearing superhero costumes...*

In a parody of a movie-trailer deep voice, Denise said, "Out now, Revenge of the Bird Warriors: this time it's personal."

Stella giggled at the revival of a game she and Denise had played last weekend, drunkenly flipping through trashy TV channels. "In a world –"

"– Where a girl –"

"– Must decide –"

"– Between love –"

"– And revenge –"

Their voices descended with each phrase, growing ever deeper and gravellier. The running joke, trivial in itself, meant a lot to Stella as another connection accumulated with Denise. Would this relationship survive to develop more catchphrases and in-jokes, a shared history?

"All right, all right," said Jim. "Maybe 'revenge' was the wrong word. But you keep saying that this is a publicity war. The last footage shows us scuttling away like cockroaches from a fumigator. It looks weak. We need something to make us look strong."

"Like what?" asked Denise.

Jim said, "I cooked up some holograms to rearrange the landscape. We can project a phantom track that diverges from the real one. When they drive to the next shoot, they'll come off the track and sink into the bog."

"Interesting idea." Stella liked the implied metaphor of the shooters taking a wrong turn in life. "Would it actually work? Surely they know the track too well to be fooled."

Jim flung his arms wide. "These moors are enormous. They can't memorise every inch."

"Okay, let's suppose a Land Rover goes into the bog. The vehicles behind see what's happened, and realise they need to be more careful. Some poor beater gets the job of walking ahead, tapping with a stick. The rest of the convoy slowly reaches its destination –"

"No, because the next vehicle drives through a puddle full of caltrops, and bursts its tyre." Jim mimed a blow-out with his hands.

"They have five Land Rovers. And they've got phones: they can ring for as many backup vehicles as they need."

"Maybe it'll work, maybe it won't. But at least we'll be fighting back. And every delay spoils their day a little bit more. It ruins the experience. That'll suppress demand, and eventually destroy the whole disgusting business."

"They're trying to provoke us," Stella said, "and I don't want to fall into their trap. We shouldn't do anything that looks like crude vandalism. They can easily smear us by taking it out of context. It's not the same as projecting decoys to save birds, like we did this morning. We need to stay on the moral high ground. We're not thugs!" *At least, I'm not.* She turned to Denise, wanting to involve her and make her feel part of the sabs' cause. "What do you think, Denise?"

"I don't know why the shooters hunt birds," Denise said, "when they could fight you instead. Hunters against sabs, a timeless ritual of the English countryside, re-enacted every August. Matinees on Saturdays. It could be a new tourist attraction, boosting the local economy."

Stella laughed, then shook her head. "They shoot birds because they enjoy killing things. They get a kick out of it, because they're sick in the head. But we need to show we're better than them. We can't do anything that seems petty, like we're just getting a kick out of it. We need to rise above their level."

"Sounds sensible," Denise said.

"So what *are* we going to do?" Jim demanded.

"First, let's find out what they're planning," said Stella. "I'll see if I can pick anything up."

Disguised as a swathe of heather, she climbed out of the gully for better reception. She flipped through the channels until she heard voices. "Pass the bread, please." "This salmon is delicious." "Is there

149

any mustard?"

Stella's stomach rumbled as she listened to the shooters having lunch. After a few minutes, she heard Wade talking to someone. "No, they got away. They might still be out there somewhere."

The reply was too faint for her to hear. Wade said, "I did my best. I know we'd all love to blast them with lead shot, but we can't do that. We need to protect our image. We're law-abiding sportsmen – they're anarchist scum."

Someone else said, "What can we do this afternoon? If we go after more grouse, they'll just spoil it again."

"How about clay pigeon shooting instead?" asked Wade.

This set off an argument. "We paid to hunt grouse..." "You can't eat a clay pigeon!"

"It's a tactical retreat," Wade explained. "They've ruined our day, but that proves they're dangerous extremists. We can lobby for more action against them, using anti-terrorism laws. We'll get headlines in the *Daily Mail* – 'Save our traditional sports from these vile thugs'."

One of the hunters said, "My sister knows a journalist on the *Times*. I'll call her this afternoon, and try to get some coverage. But for now, I suppose clay shooting is better than nothing."

After some heated discussion, and the promise of a partial refund, everyone finally agreed to Wade's proposal.

Stella slid down the slope to rejoin her comrades. "Great news! They're scared of us spoiling another grouse shoot, so they've decided to go clay pigeon shooting instead."

For Denise's benefit, Stella explained, "It's an alternative to shooting live birds. A machine sends up artificial targets – they're called clays, though they're not made of clay any more. Anyway, they shoot these targets instead of real birds. We've won today's battle!"

She high-fived Jim and hugged Denise, enjoying the moment of triumph even though the hard part still lay ahead. It would only become a real victory when the world knew about it.

The sabs ate their packed lunches, then restored their disguises and crept back across the moor to watch the shooters' departure.

"Denise, can you film this?" Stella asked, as the hunting party filed into the vehicles. "Later, we can tweak the footage to add some bloody footprints, showing how they leave a trail of carnage behind them."

The Land Rovers began to jolt along the track. Yet the shooting party had left someone behind. One of the beaters was searching through the heather in front of the grouse butts.

"What's he doing?" asked Denise.

"He's looking for the projectors," Jim said, "to check for fingerprints or DNA traces. Don't worry – we sterilised them."

"Why didn't they look earlier?"

"They didn't know we'd planted anything, and they couldn't search without disturbing the birds they wanted to shoot."

Stella remembered the long labour of scrubbing the devices, then hiding them in several places across the moor. That had taken a whole day. Tomorrow she'd return to retrieve whatever gadgetry survived. The lost items would need to be replaced: more crowd-funding, more work.

"Before he finds the projectors," Stella said, "I want to record one last thing. Like you, I cooked up some holograms to rearrange the landscape."

She fiddled with her remote control. Images arose – birch trees, oak, willow; clearings full of primroses and bluebells; ash trees, hawthorns, horse chestnuts; foxes and badgers; holly bushes, crab apples, wild roses...

As these holograms sprang up, the beater redoubled his efforts to locate their source. Stella gritted her teeth; his presence disrupted the scenario. She triggered more and more holograms, boosting their strength until they blotted out the inconvenient figure. The monochrome carpet of heather disappeared, replaced by a vision of richly diverse woodland, showing how the sterile moors could revive when all the shooters had gone.

Denise filmed the scene. "It looks lovely," she said, "but what happens to the grouse if the woodland comes back?"

"They'll die out," said Jim. "They're a crop species: they only exist because the moor is managed for them."

"The woods are a much richer ecosystem," Stella said hastily, "with far more wildlife."

"That doesn't do the grouse any good. I thought we came out to save the grouse." Denise sounded disappointed, as though the day had been a waste of time.

"We did save some grouse from being shot," said Stella. "So we definitely achieved something today. And in the long run, after we've won, not every estate will revert to woodland. Some of the moors in Scotland might keep enough heather for grouse –"

Jim broke in and said, "We can talk on the way home, if we're ready to head back."

"Let's go!" cried Denise. "It's been a long morning. I'm looking forward to sitting outside a pub with a nice cold drink... or two, or three."

"Sounds great," said Jim. "I'm sure we can drop you off somewhere." He started walking downhill, toward the car.

"Are you coming for a drink?" Denise asked Stella as they followed.

"Not yet," Stella said. "We have to upload the video and hit social media. What we've done today means nothing unless people hear about it. We need to get our message out straight away, and respond to anything in the press. The shooters are calling the *Daily Mail* and the *Times* – we can't let their story go unchallenged."

Denise fell silent. Stella couldn't see her face through the hologram disguise. But the loud splash of her boots, stamping across a boggy patch, spoke volumes.

Stella took Denise's arm. They stopped next to a low slab of rock, where a tray of small white stones had been left for grouse to ingest.

"I'm sorry," Stella said. "I did say it would be a long day. The job's only half done."

Denise pointed to Jim, striding obliviously onward. "Can't he do the rest?"

"It's quicker if we work together," Stella said. This was true; she refrained from mentioning the need to soften Jim's diatribes against wealth and privilege. "If I do it today, then I'll be free tomorrow. We can meet up before your shift starts." She'd planned to retrieve the buried gadgets tomorrow, but that could be postponed to another day.

Denise didn't reply. Stella gazed at the Earth hologram hiding Denise's head. If she couldn't persuade Denise that this mattered, then how could she persuade the rest of the world?

"Is it going to be like this all the time?" Denise burst out at last. "If we're together, is this how it'll be?"

Even in the summer sun, Stella felt as though her skin had iced over. This was the moment she'd dreaded.

Reflexively, she tried to dodge the issue. "The shooting season finishes in December –"

"That's four months away!" Denise exclaimed. "I want to see you now, not as a Christmas present. Will I always be less important than a few birds?"

The question was all too familiar; it had sunk previous relationships. Stella kept hoping to find a like-minded lover who'd join the cause and fight alongside her. But what if she never did? She might be single forever. Was the battle worth it?

Her gaze slid past Denise to the countryside beyond. Back at the grouse butts, the phantom woodland was fading. As the shooters' lackey uprooted the projectors, the holograms vanished. The lonely moorland swiftly returned.

Yet the heather was in bloom, and the bilberries were ripe. Today the landscape didn't look quite so desolate. It could probably survive without her for a little while.

"No, Denise – you're more important," Stella said. "I'll ask Jim to take it from here."

She switched off her holo-projector, and the superhero mask disappeared.

"Oh, darling," said Denise. "Are you sure? I know how hard you've worked for this."

"You'll have to show me how to relax. You can start by taking me to the pub and buying me one of those nice cold drinks."

Denise turned her hologram off, and her smile filled the space where the world had been. Stella kissed her, while above them a curlew sang.

As they embraced, Stella saw that Jim had finally noticed them lagging behind. He'd added a new slogan to his projector. In the same stern font that formerly lambasted shooters, the huge green letters said, "Get a room!"

The idea for "Shooting Grouse" came to me one day while I was hiking in the Yorkshire Dales. I passed some grouse butts in the uplands, and I experienced a moment of realisation. I'd vaguely known this before, but it suddenly came home to me that the entire heather moorland existed solely for the purpose of allowing people to shoot birds. Very little of England's landscape is "natural". I was walking through a vast shooting gallery.

Ian Creasey

Like many ancient traditions that once went unquestioned, grouse shooting is now rather controversial. And controversy – conflict – always has the potential to make a story. So I wrote one. The story's title has a double meaning, because "grouse" can mean a complaint, so "Shooting Grouse" refers both to the sport itself, and also to opponents' complaints about shooting.

My instinctive sympathy lies with the opponents of grouse shooting. However, I recognise that a case can be made either way; indeed, this is what makes it a good subject for a story. I used an anti-shooting activist as the protagonist, but undercut this by gently satirising the saboteurs' view of themselves as costumed superheroes. I also made sure that the shooters had their case represented. It's fine to be a writer with opinions, but you have to be intellectually honest about each side's case, or you just end up writing hack propaganda.

By the way, I am aware that people shooting grouse are traditionally referred to as Guns, but I didn't use that term in the story because the viewpoint character is a saboteur who declines to adopt her enemy's terminology, with all its baggage.

MEMORIES OF THE KNACKER'S YARD

Another day, another corpse. This guy had been good-looking before someone worked him over. Now he had big, livid bruises on his head and upper body, cigarette burns on the cheeks and eyelids, and the usual wide slash across the throat.

"How long have we had this one?" I asked, shivering in the morgue's chill.

"Two days," the white-coat guy said. I didn't know his name. I try to remember the lab people and support staff, but turnover's too high. This line of work burns people out faster than a crematorium on overtime.

"What did you leave it that long for?" I asked, annoyed. "Waiting for the killer to turn himself in?"

"We were waiting for the ghost to show up," he said.

I shook my head in disgust. "Look, when someone's been murdered, they want us on the case. If their ghost doesn't turn up in twenty-four hours, that's because it can't."

That was the problem. If a ghost complains that it's just been murdered, it can help us by describing the killer, or at least telling us about its enemies. Investigating a murder without a ghost is much harder. The slashing was the third this month, all without ghosts, and the eighth this year. Or was it the ninth?

Hell, when you lose count of the corpses, you know you're losing.

Back upstairs, I took a swig of stale coffee to warm myself up. Then I grabbed an ancient black raincoat that looked as if a tramp had slept in it for a month. I searched all my pockets to remove any police identification. *Malcolm Chenier, Detective-Inspector.* The old ID photo mocked me with his full head of hair and blue, optimistic eyes. When I posed for that picture, I'd never fired a weapon except on the shooting range. I hefted my gun now, wondering whether I'd need it, and decided to play safe and bring it along. I didn't debate for more than a second, remembering the corpse in the morgue. Two days was too long – I had to rush.

155

It was a windy afternoon; the plastic bags snagged in the courtyard's dead trees rustled and billowed like fledgling kites. The overcast sky promised rain. I put my shades on, and started walking.

I could have taken a car, but not all the way. Past the wasteland of 'For Sale' and 'To Let' signs, the road became cratered with potholes and choked with rubble. The spooks keep Ghost Town unfit for the living. The buildings are all wrecked, burnt-out shells; the streets are full of festering garbage. Ahead I saw dense black smoke, causing me to cough as fumes caught in my throat. The ghosts were burning toxic waste again.

Not themselves, of course. They hire people to do that. Ghosts don't have much, but they do have money. Nowadays you *can* take it with you.

If you ever had it in the first place.

Through my shades I saw spooks hanging around like bored teenagers. Some of them had brought their grave markers here, now that cemeteries were obsolete, and they sat on their gravestones, sizing me up with hungry, jaded eyes. As I walked down the road nicknamed Death Row, a haunt of young ghosts heard the *click, click* of living footsteps and swarmed me. My breath frosted, white vapour in the air, and my skin chilled in the ectoplasmic embrace. I stopped, trying not to flinch as the haunt writhed around me. Two of them wore sharp suits and expensive shoes; another was naked. The others were translucent wisps, fading ghosts who would soon be eaten by the stronger.

"Wooh!" The naked spook thrust his arm into my skull, as if scooping out my brain. The crawling sensation made me shudder, but the ghost couldn't hurt me.

Probably.

The other spooks danced and gibbered, trying to get a rise out of me. They knew I could see them, because I wore ghost-glasses. Shades to see shades. Ain't technology grand?

"Very scary, boys," I said. "You should be in showbiz."

"I *was* in showbiz," said one of the sharp-dressed ghosts.

A lot of them say things like that. Death's a great opportunity to reinvent yourself. Before the others could spin me their obits, I cut in.

"Anyone new around? Just been murdered, last couple of days?"

The victim's ghost might have been too traumatised to report its murder at the station; more likely, it had been prevented from doing so.

If the ghost had ended up in Ghost Town, these boys would know about it. Word gets around, especially about slashings – fresh pickings.

The showbiz guy shrugged: a boneless ripple in pale wisps of aura. "Friend of yours?"

I nodded. It's best not to admit being a cop in Ghost Town. Even dead people are criminals nowadays.

The haunt all giggled, an unearthly cackling that raised goose-pimples along my arms. "You won't see him again," said Mr Showbiz. "Not whole, anyway."

"You might find some pieces," said the naked ghost.

They thought this would horrify me. It did, the first time, but I've seen a lot since then. More than these fresh young ghosts, anyway. I could scare *them*, if I wanted.

"In the Yard, is he?" I asked in a bored voice.

"Yeah," said the showbiz ghost, sullenly.

I'd expected that, but the confirmation helped. I started walking again, heading for the Knacker's Yard. The haunt, desperate for distraction, drifted along with me.

"Got any thrills?"

"Talents?"

"Love?"

I ignored the spooks and kept going. I felt sorry for them, but I didn't want to get drawn in. I was in a hurry, and they had all the time in the world. Sometimes to end a conversation you just have to walk away.

And even that doesn't always work. I had to step carefully in the ruined road, and the writhing ghosts kept blocking my view. They whirled around me, faster and faster, a carousel of restless death.

"Give us your mind –"

"Your memories –"

"Your soul –"

Annoyed, I took the shades off. The spooks disappeared. I still felt the chill of their presence, and I heard a faint whisper, "You'll be back..."

No I won't, I thought as I walked on. When I die, I won't end up in Ghost Town. I hate coming here for an afternoon, never mind eternity.

Trouble is, the alternatives are all worse.

I picked my way along the streets, avoiding broken glass, oil slicks, and rusty barbed wire. After a while I reached a ruined hotel. Skeletal walls embraced the sky, their once-white paint flaking in the wind, stained with the soot of trash fires. In the old lobby, two bouncers – living, looming, muscle-bound specimens – stood by the stairway to the basement. I was surprised to see only breathers, until I remembered I'd taken off my shades. I put them back on, and saw another figure, the senior doorman. His face was the dusty grey of cold ashes.

Ghosts run the Knacker's Yard.

"Toll," said the doorman.

You have to pay with a piece of yourself – or someone else – just to get in.

When I was a kid, my parents made me take piano lessons. I stuck at it for five years, until I discovered girls and under-age drinking. Even then, not knowing what I was going to be when I grew up, I knew that *pianist* was about as likely as *astronaut*. I figured the lessons were pointless.

I was wrong. Though I've never touched a piano since, the lessons come in useful occasionally.

The doorman held out a smoke-grey, almost transparent hand. I tapped the left earpiece of my shades, concentrated on those long-ago piano lessons, and wrenched them out of my head. The doorman's withered fingers snatched at the morsel. He popped it in his mouth and swallowed.

"Tinkle fucking tinkle," he sneered. "I hate musicians."

Piano lessons aren't much good to a ghost who can't touch the keys. But plenty of breathers prefer to buy someone else's lessons rather than put in the hard work themselves. That way you can practise for five years in an afternoon.

The bouncers stood aside for me. "Is Charley around?" I asked.

The doorman shrugged. "I haven't seen him lately. Maybe he's faded." He grinned like a skull. "Why don't you look for him on the racks?"

I turned away, trying to seem unfazed by the blow. I was sad to hear that Charley had disappeared, yet I could do nothing for him. There's little anyone can do for the dead.

Charley and I used to go running together; I gave it up when he died from a heart attack after a personal best in the half-marathon. He was my contact at the Yard. Without him, I'd have to make like a customer. Hell, I'd have to buy my piano lessons back, if I wanted to keep them. Charley normally slipped me the toll when it turned up downstairs. He let me riffle through the racks, too. Without his help, this was going to be a whole lot trickier.

I headed toward the basement, careful not to slip on the frayed, slimy carpet. Before I reached the bottom I stopped, then glanced around to make sure no one saw me hold a small glass bottle to my left ear. I touched my shades.

I took a deep breath of frigid air, and thought about my job. The endless procession of corpses. The dumb burglars, the drunks and nutters, the smug fraudsters you can't touch. The sour, overstewed coffee in the station canteen. Ten years of paperwork, so mind-numbing that if you catch a dealer you're tempted to bypass procedure and force-feed him his own wares until he chokes. Coping with all the crimes and killings, trying to keep head above water, and being pulled off the case whenever there's a bomb scare, a dole riot, or a politician gone walkabout. They say a woman's work is never done, but try being a policeman. As fast as you clean the scum off the streets, the gutter fills up faster.

Popping all that into the bottle took a real weight off my mind. Instantly I felt younger, stronger, and as if I'd had a decent night's sleep this month. I smiled – how long since I'd done that? – and put the bottle away. A tiny evaporating thought said, *Remember...* Usually Charley reminded me to reintegrate afterward, but without him –

I'd just have to manage. I couldn't avoid this; transfers always create leakage and residues. While I looked for evidence, a trace of me would backwash. And if the Yard's customers got the taste of cop, I'd never make it upstairs alive.

Or dead.

I went on, shivering. It was cold as a penguin's supper down here. The inhabitants of Ghost Town don't need central heating, and their crowding auras froze my flesh like a blizzard. Many spooks had crisply defined shapes, as if newly dead or well fed; others were blurred and translucent. The ghosts flitted back and forth, roaming the basement's grubby corridors. This was their shopping mall, restaurant and drugs den, all in one. Breathing customers were tolerated, but not welcomed.

The spooks didn't bother to move out of my way. As I barged through them, my skin crawling, they stared at me with unfriendly eyes.

Was that the natural resentment of the dead for the living, or something more? It occurred to me that if Charley had been eaten, any of these ghosts might have swallowed his mind, his memories. Anyone here could recognise me.

I walked faster, until I reached a door stippled with mould. The ghosts just floated through this door, but I had to knock.

Another of the Yard's underling breathers opened the door. He wore a white shirt and black tie, like a waiter at an uptown restaurant, and I half-expected him to offer me a wine list. The recollections of many vintage wines and drunken evenings would be here somewhere. *Everything* was here somewhere.

The room stretched back and back, the walls glittering like Santa's grotto. The sparkle came from reflections of the harsh strip-lights upon thousands and thousands of tiny bottles, racked from floor to ceiling. Ghosts crowded round the racks, sampling the contents, giggling, cursing and sighing. At the far wall, a crush of spooks gorged on the memories of love affairs and sexual encounters. Other shelves contained anything from sporting triumphs to childhood fun with sand-castles.

On previous visits I'd joined the browsing throng, and Charley had steered me to likely bottles. But now I'd have to ask. I turned to the waiter flunky.

"What would Sir like today?" he inquired.

"Murder," I said.

"The murders are on shelves fifteen to seventeen – or eighteen if you want to be the victim."

"I'm looking for something special."

He smiled. "Gunshot, poison, strangling?"

"Slasher."

"Ah, a connoisseur. There's nothing like the spurt of blood, the choking cough, the victim's frantic gasps for breath... I believe we have several fine specimens." He paused.

I tipped him what I hoped was the customary gratuity. "I want the fresh stuff," I said.

The waiter sorted through the merchandise and passed me two bottles. "These are the latest in."

I sat on a grimy couch, then poured the first bottle into my head.

My husband shouted, "Get me a fucking drink." I crept downstairs, my face throbbing with fresh bruises. In the kitchen I found a can of beer, but didn't open it. Instead I opened the cutlery drawer and grabbed a carving knife. It felt heavy in my hand, and the buzz of the fridge roared in my ears. I climbed the stairs –

I refocused my vision onto the endless shelves around me. "I'm bored of domestics," I said to the waiter. I put that memory back, and swigged the other.

Thwack. I saw blood trickle from the new gash, just below the cigarette burns on the pretty-boy cheekbone. I dropped the putter.

"Maybe I should try the nine-iron," I said. "Or the driver. What do you think?"

The guy's eyes were closed. He was unconscious – or faking it. I reached into my golf bag and took out a random club. It was the sand-wedge.

What the hell. I walked round and addressed the guy's left side. *Thwock.*

Prince Charming didn't scream or even twitch. This was getting boring. The cigarettes had been fun – it was a shame I'd run out – but now it was time to finish the guy. I exchanged the golf club for my knife.

I made a couple of practice cuts on his face, enjoying the smooth incisions as I tested the knife's sharpness. Then, digging deep into the flesh, I slashed right across his throat. The wound gaped like a moist red orifice. Blood puddled at either side.

Damn. It was running off the edge of the newspaper I'd put down, and soaking into the carpet –

I struggled to surface from the memory, blinking away afterimages of blood. "I'll keep this one," I said.

Then I saw that the waiter had gone. A ghost stood in front of me. She had filmy scraps of clothes on a blurred body, as if she were fading. Yet as I looked, her hair grew long, then short again. Her breasts flattened and vanished. A beard sprouted on the ghost's chin, then diminished into stubble and unfashionably long sideburns. The new face smiled.

"Charley?" I said.

"Hi there," said the ghost. "How's things?"

I shrugged. "Same as ever." No nearer to catching the killer, but I didn't want to say that out loud. Not here.

161

And not to Charley. Not now. "What's happened to you?" I asked.

"I was thinning," he said. "And I was determined not to end up in bottles, or a quack sanctuary. So a few of us with the same problem –"

"A composite," I said.

"Yeah. Meet Rob, Duncan, Stephanie, and Grace." As he named the others, the ghost flickered into different shapes. Then Charley returned, with a fuzzy outline.

I tried not to wince at the sight. If the spook hadn't finalised its new form – if the fading fragments hadn't coalesced – then the composite was unhealthy to say the least. It hadn't even settled on a joint name.

"Hello everyone," I said, doing my best not to make it sound like *Goodbye*.

"Can I get you anything?" asked Charley. As he gestured to the shelves, he saw his blurred arm. He tried to focus, and acquired small hands with silver nail varnish. His hair shimmered, as if uncertain of its colour.

"I've got what I came for," I said. "I'll leave the money here." I stood up, and placed the purchase fee on the couch.

"Is that everything you need?"

It wasn't. I'd intended to get the victim's memories, in case they contained a clue. But now I had to leave, straight away. My friend Charley was only one fifth of the ghost standing before me. The other four weren't my friends at all, yet they shared the composite memory. They knew who I was. Right now I couldn't remember why that was a problem, but I knew it was bad – very bad.

"Yes, it's fine," I said. "Good to see you again. Hope the integration works out for you."

I moved to the door. As I brushed past the phantom, its form shifted again. Breasts this time, and short dark hair.

"So long, Charley," I said, stressing the name. I was probably safe while his personality had the helm. But the composite looked so unstable that Charley might submerge at any moment.

I left the Memory Hall, and hurried to the stairway. As I climbed I expected a hullabaloo behind me, but I heard only the eerie silence of a crowd of ghosts.

The bouncers loomed at the top of the stairs. "Come back soon," said one.

"Dead or alive," said the other, grinning.

Taking this as a threat, I reached inside my coat and grasped my gun. But the pair moved aside and let me walk through the abandoned lobby. I barely restrained myself from running.

Back outside, rain pounded onto the rubbish-strewn road. I savoured the stinging drops on my face and hair, proof that I still had a body, that I wasn't a ghost just yet. The blustery wind felt fresh and clean after the unnatural cold of the spook-filled basement.

Foul weather soon loses its charm when you're the wrong side of double glazing. I walked away from the ruined hotel until I found a sheltered corner by a tangle of concrete slabs. I made sure I could see the lobby entrance, in case anyone followed me. Although I had made it out, I didn't feel safe. The encounter had unnerved me.

Poor Charley. Soon his composite would fall apart, triggering a feeding frenzy on the Knacker's Yard floor. Eaten, Charley would evaporate, all his traits and memories scattered among the inhabitants of Ghost Town.

I could only mourn him. "Rest in peace," I whispered, my eyes welling up. I remembered the days we used to go jogging, then drinking – all the weight we lost in exercise, we put back on in bar snacks. He liked his ale; now he'd no longer miss it.

The sharpening wind whirled scraps of paper like a presentiment of snow. The day had faded into gloomy twilight. No street lights shone – the ghosts prefer darkness. I couldn't stay here much longer, peering into the dusk while gusts of rain soaked into my hair and dripped down my neck.

I wished I'd got the murder victim's memories, if only to save his relatives from having to trawl the Yard for any relic of him. I wondered which bottles he'd ended up in. The Yard sells a vast range. Budding musicians and novelists visit the Skills hall. When exams approach, students flock to Knowledge. As for Feelings, let's just say there's always a market for true love. And all the fake kinds, too.

This was the killer's motive – murdering people so their ghosts could be captured, broken up, and sold in the Knacker's Yard.

And the slashings themselves were valuable. I reckoned the killer tortured the victims to spice up the memories and get a higher price. Selling the killings also removed the evidence from his head. If he was picked up for a traffic offence, he didn't want murder on his conscience.

For months I'd rushed to the Yard after every killing, buying up the memories to search for clues. Now I sifted through the latest again, reliving the cigarette burns, the golf clubs, the throat slash. The memory was brief and focused, with no hint of identity or location. I felt someone's presence, a shadowy figure waiting for the kill. There were other associations too – cross-references to the rest of the killer's mind – but I couldn't pin anything down. You know when you try to remember something, and it's on the tip of your tongue? It was frustrating as all hell.

I hated having the murder in my mind. It turned my stomach, as if I had personally tortured and killed the victim. And I worried that if I kept the killing in my memory too long, it might infect me. I might start thinking I'd really done it, and feel the urge to confess.

Or I might get a taste for it.

Best to take the memory out, and put it away with the rest. I searched my pocket for the other murders, and found two bottles. What was in the extra one?

After some thought, I dimly recalled using it. I realised that the bottle contained my own memories, my police memories. Normally Charley reminded me to put them back in.

I lifted the bottle to the earpiece of my shades, then hesitated. I'd done all this before, with no success. Maybe those memories, that mindset, had been the problem.

I had to stop thinking like a cop, and start thinking like a killer.

To do that I'd have to ingest all the other murders. I loathed the prospect. The slashings had been bad enough individually, but experiencing all at once would be nightmarish.

And yet if I didn't try it, this would just go on and on. More corpses. More profits for the Knacker's Yard. More futile hunts for the killer.

I put myself back in my pocket, and absorbed all the murders.

The deaths flooded my brain in a montage of beatings, slashings, and blood. Guys who screamed, guys who struggled, guys who tried to bribe me. Old women, fat women, and pretty girls who lost their looks real quick. My knife grew jaded, but to me it was fresh every time.

I almost retched. I felt dazed under the onslaught. The screams, the smell of burnt flesh, the carpet-cleaning bills –

That was a clue. I could investigate carpet-cleaning companies, looking for repeat customers.

But I had no enthusiasm for that now. Routine police work was too slow, too uncertain, too fucking boring. No, I wanted leakage. I had so many of the killer's memories that I hoped their associations might coalesce into... something. Anything.

I walked back to the ruined hotel and stood near the exit from the Knacker's Yard. I imagined that I'd just come out, having sold someone's ghost for scrap, together with my own memory of the killing. I'd done this almost a dozen times. And from here –

I started walking, not thinking about my direction, letting my feet carry me. They knew the way. Whistling, I strode past the familiar looted shops and derelict houses. Rain thudded on the rusty shells of burnt-out cars.

As the evening darkened, more ghosts appeared on the street. A young woman approached me, carrying a wizened baby.

"Hey, mister – spare us a thought?"

"Fuck off and die," I said. "Oh, you're already dead. Then just fuck off."

But the spooks wouldn't leave me alone. A gang of them mobbed me. "Bleeding breathers –"

"– This is Ghost Town –"

"– You shouldn't be here unless you're *dead* –"

"– We can arrange that –"

I stopped and addressed the haunt. "You want me to call the Knackerman?"

The ghosts drew back, huddling together, the rain falling through their hazy figures.

"Because I can arrange that. I can arrange for you all to end up in bottles." I fished in my inside pocket and drew one out. "You want to try this on for size? Come on, who wants to be first?"

They fled. I continued onward, leaving the spooks and Ghost Town behind. Now I heard traffic and footsteps and beggars shouting for spare change. Breathers filled the streets with their umbrellas, their jostling elbows. I looked at them and laughed. These people were walking ghosts: they just didn't know it yet.

My feet took me into a burger bar on Kellett Road. It's hungry work, killing people. I grabbed a Monster Burger and fries, and ate them on my way through the back streets. I was tired now, and just wanted to relax in front of the TV.

As I approached my house, I smiled to see Oscar keeping watch from the chimney pot. But he didn't bound down to greet me. Instead he howled, then sank through the roof into the house.

That was odd. I looked around, but saw no one else nearby. Maybe being dead was getting to him again. Some dogs find it hard to adjust.

I put my key in the lock, but it wouldn't turn. I took it out and looked at it. That wasn't my front door key –

Yes it was. But this wasn't my front door.

I snapped out of the trance. It had worked! I'd followed the killer's footsteps right to his door –

The door opened. Behind it stood a tall, thickset man with black hair and a scraggly beard. He had a metallic third eye implanted in his forehead. And he was pointing a gun at me.

"Who the fuck are you?"

"A customer," I said, improvising desperately.

The ghost dog walked through him and sniffed my leg. The man – the killer – looked at me suspiciously, and past me into the street.

"You'd better come in," he said.

Inside, the house smelled of pizza and cigarette smoke. At least it was warm. The killer kept me covered as he ushered me into the front room. I tried not to flinch as I recognised the scene of the murder memories. The carpet looked clean except for pizza crusts, but the white wallpaper had a dark stain near the floor.

He turned the television off. "A customer, huh? What are you looking to buy?"

"Ghosts, of course. Why sell to the Knacker's Yard when you could sell straight to their clients? Don't you know how much mark-up they add?"

"Shit!" he said. "How did you find me?"

I shrugged. "Word gets around."

"It better fucking not!"

"You can't keep a talent secret for ever, you know. You're too good at what you do. Now, aren't you going to offer me a drink?"

I hoped he'd relax a little, but he was too canny for that. He already had a bottle of Scotch open, and he poured me a shot using his left hand while he covered me with his right.

As I sipped the Scotch, he patted me down and discovered my gun. "Isn't this what the police use?" he asked.

"How should I know?" I retorted. "But if it's good enough for them, it's good enough for me."

"It's a piece of shit. Don't you know they only use it because it's cheap?" He laughed. "Are you a customer, or just a very stupid cop?"

He tried to give me an intimidating stare. It worked, with his firepower backing it up. He said, "I could ask you. Or I could ask your ghost. Which do you think would give me an honest answer?"

"Me!" I said.

"No, I think the ghost will. You see, I'll suck out your memories. And then I'll know who you are, how you found me, and whether anyone else knows I'm here."

He whistled, and the dog came trotting through the door. "Oscar! Go fetch the Knackerman. Good boy! Fetch the Knackerman!"

Oscar barked once, then scampered away. I realised he was augmented, fed on human ghost scraps. He could probably beat me at Scrabble.

The killer stepped back. "Sit down and don't move. Any trouble – well, if you know so much about me, you know what I usually do to the meat. But if you sit still, I'll spare you that." He pointed his gun at my heart.

I knew he only waited because the Knackerman could more easily capture my ghost when it was new-born – new-dead – and confused by the trauma.

I also knew that if he wasn't going to bother tying me up or incapacitating me – hell, a blow from one of the golf clubs under the table would quieten me down – then that must mean the Knackerman was close, and would arrive very soon.

I had just minutes to live. And then my ghost had just seconds to live. Well, afterlive.

My mind whirled in panic as I struggled to concentrate. What was procedure? Talk to the gunman. Communicate. Negotiate. While he's talking, he ain't shooting. Yet those barely-remembered slogans felt stale and weak. Blood-soaked images filled my head, urging me to kill the bastard. I wanted to hit him, burn him, slash him –

But he had the gun, and mine as well. I looked around for a weapon. Nothing. You'd think a killer would at least keep an axe on the wall. He only had an Escher print, the one with the white swans turning into black and the black swans into white.

I'd have to charge with my bare hands. That would be futile without a distraction. I looked at his phone and willed it to ring. I longed for someone to knock on the door. Why's there never a Jehovah's Witness when you need one?

Tension crackled. The pause was so pregnant it had quintuplets. I glared at him. He glared at me. He had a better glare because he had three eyes. That unblinking third eye was a port in his head. Only people who deal with ghosts all the time have that installed. I prefer my shades – at least I can take them off and not see spooks, pretend that life's as simple as it used to be when it stopped at the end.

The killer nudged the gun from side to side, an inch either way, just to draw attention to it and remind me who had the upper hand. I thought about trying the old "Behind you!" trick. But he'd hardly fall for that in his own house.

I could only wait for the Knackerman, and hope his arrival would be the distraction I needed. I wondered what he looked like. They say no one knows, because when he breaks up a ghost, he sells every scrap and memory except the victim's sight of him.

There's a Ghost Town myth that says he's the Devil, that once the Knackerman takes you, you can't ever get to Heaven. It's amazing how many ghosts still try to believe in Heaven.

Another story says the Knackerman delves into the victim's mind, and appears as their worst nightmare. Maybe he'd already arrived, because this *was* my worst nightmare. Cop caught by the criminal. Becoming the slasher's latest victim. Going to the bottles in the Knacker's Yard.

I wondered who'd buy me and how much they'd pay. I thought, "Whoever buys this memory – I hope you fucking choke on it, you pathetic voyeur."

Then I remembered that not all my mind was in my head. Maybe –

I heard excited barking, growing louder. The Knackerman was coming. I shifted in my seat, turning slightly to one side. The dog burst through the wall, followed by a short guy with greying hair. He didn't look like a bogeyman; he looked like a civil servant on dress-down Friday. Well, it's always the quiet ones.

He said, "What the hell is this? You think because I'm dead, I don't have a social life? You can't just send your superdog to fetch me whenever you get the urge to do some slashing. I've told you to keep it down to one a week." While the Knackerman spoke, my hand drifted toward my pocket.

The killer looked at him and said, "But this guy knows –"

That was as far as he got. As soon as his gaze shifted, I grabbed a bottle from my pocket and threw it at his middle eye. It smashed on the metal socket.

I wasn't sure which bottle I'd thrown. But I charged anyway. Before I reached him, his face went slack. I seized the gun from his limp hand, then backed away.

The Knackerman shook his head and said, "Stupid fucker." I didn't know which of us he meant.

Oscar went into a frenzy and tried to bite chunks out of my body. My scrotum iced over as the dog's phantom teeth closed on my testicles. Reflexively I kicked back, but we couldn't touch each other.

The killer looked worn out. "So this is what it's like being a cop... It's even worse than I thought."

"Yeah," I said. "It's a lot more fun this way round."

I ached to blow him away. All the murders in my mind, all my anger and disgust, said *Kill! Kill!* My grip tightened on the gun, my fingers grasping the trigger.

The killer said, "You can't shoot me in cold blood. That's murder."

"That never stopped you," I said.

"Look, you're making a big mistake. Don't be hasty about this. We can work out a deal –"

I laughed. "I never realised just how weaselly all that crap sounds."

The Knackerman said, "You want me to bag him up? He'll fetch a decent amount at the Yard. I'll cut you in for half."

He floated across the room, toward the killer. Then his hands started growing. They sprouted more and more fingers, which swelled and lengthened and curled. The Knackerman cupped his huge, hideous claws around the killer's skull, ready to trap the emerging ghost.

The killer said, "Oscar – get him!"

Oscar leapt into the air, pounced on the Knackerman, and bit his leg. The Knackerman grunted. But the dog didn't get a second bite. He couldn't loosen his grip. The dog's teeth had locked onto the Knackerman's leg as if it were made of ultra-sticky toffee.

The Knackerman twisted like a champion contortionist, bending his leg upward. I heard a muffled whine as Oscar scrabbled frantically, clawing the Knackerman's torso. But the Knackerman's whole form was sticky as flypaper, and soon the dog was just a twitching blob of fur, even his tail immobile.

As the Knackerman's leg reached his face, he opened his mouth wide, dislocating his jaw like a snake. Then he bit the dog's head off.

Oscar's ghostly body shrivelled and evaporated. The Knackerman barked twice. "Nice appetiser," he said.

I had kept watch on the killer throughout, careful not to get distracted, and all the while the Knackerman's hands had stayed wrapped around the guy's head. Now, between the pale fingers, eyes widened in panic. I knew the killer was about to make a last desperate move.

All the rage in my head boiled over. Vengeance for the victims, my own festering hatred, the blood and death in the murder memories – all the violence erupted like lightning. And I held the lightning conductor. My hand clenched on the gun. There was no way in the world I couldn't shoot.

I pulled the trigger.

The silencer went *phut*, like a champagne cork popping. My arm sprang back, my wrist aching from the recoil. The gun was a real elephant stopper, compared to my own street-rat shooter.

The killer slumped to the floor, blood dripping onto the carpet. Another cleaning bill, I thought.

The Knackerman looked at me and said, "You got his leg, you idiot."

"I know," I said. At the last moment I'd jerked my aim downward.

"So finish him off!"

I shook my head. "I don't want to send him to the Knacker's Yard. I don't even want to kill him. Well, I do. But I don't *want* to want to kill him."

"Hell, he'll get the death penalty anyway."

I smiled. "And afterlife imprisonment for the ghost."

"What a waste," he said.

I pointed the gun at the Knackerman and said, "You're even worse than him. Right now I can't touch you, but if this racket starts up again, I won't only get the breather. I'll recruit some ghosts and go after you.

Just because you're dead, that doesn't mean you're beyond the law."

The Knackerman gave me the finger with his hideous claw. Then he vanished through the ceiling.

I sighed. I grabbed the whisky bottle and swigged three shots in three gulps. Then I poured the rest of the bottle over the killer's ragged wound. That was all the first aid I could be bothered with. He screamed most satisfyingly.

I called the station and told them to send a holding van. "I have a murderer for you," I said. "Bring the scoop as well: he's got some memories I want back."

With considerable relief, I decanted the killer's murder reminiscences into the remaining bottle. Yet I knew their residue of gleeful violence would taint my dreams for months to come.

Did I really want my police memories back? They were hardly any more pleasant. Perhaps I should return to the Knacker's Yard and buy myself a new personality, build up a history from the endless shelves...

My fingers twitched. I decided that I would go back, if only to recover my old piano lessons. After a day surrounded by death and ghosts, I had a sudden longing to play piano while I still had flesh and bone to touch the keys.

"Memories of the Knacker's Yard" is the oldest story in this collection, and its origins lie even further back. In the 1990s, I was thinking about writing a fantasy novel. I was sick of reading clichéd fantasies with generic mediaeval settings; I kept wondering why those societies apparently had such long histories, such advantages of magic and whatnot, and yet never seemed to progress. I wanted to create a world going through rapid change – like the Industrial Revolution, but with magic instead of science. (At the time, very few novels of that kind had been published, although they later became more common.)

This meant that I had to come up with specific examples of how fantasy tropes might develop under the application of 'magical technology'. Ghosts were an obvious area to explore. Traditionally, ghosts are rare, difficult to see, and never have much practical use. To move forward from this primitive concept, I assumed that everyone turned into a ghost when they died, and communicating with ghosts became routine. The social implications were immense. And since nothing exists in isolation, I created an entire ecosystem for ghosts, explaining how they interacted with each other and with the physical world.

These background details inevitably suggested possible stories. But when I began work on "Memories of the Knacker's Yard", I realised that the story didn't require the envisioned novel as its setting. It used an aspect of the premise, but it didn't need any of the characters, places or history. While I could shoehorn the story into the original milieu by the inclusion of superfluous details, I decided that this would be pointless, especially as the novel hadn't been published or even written. Instead, I'd write the story in its natural setting: a version of our own world, with added ghosts.

One advantage of a contemporary milieu is that it enables the inclusion of real-world props within the story. I therefore indulged myself by mentioning 'an Escher print, the one with the white swans turning into black and the black swans into white'. This image symbolises the action.

When I finished the story, I thought it was one of my better efforts. However, it proved more difficult to sell than I'd expected. Partly this was because the story inhabited the hinterland between the SF and horror genres: one rejection letter said, "It is a great story, but unfortunately I didn't get enough of a science fiction feel..." I think another reason might have been that the opening paragraphs, by mentioning multiple murders, implied a 'serial killer' story. Since I don't write very much horror, I was unaware that the serial killer is a cliché of the genre, overused to the point where markets often warn against them in their guidelines.

"Memories of the Knacker's Yard" is not a typical story about a serial killer. It uses the murders as a jumping-off point, simply because a story about ghosts needs a few dead people. The ghostly ecosystem always needs fresh food...

THE DUNSCHEMIN RETIREMENT HOME FOR REPENTANT SUPERVILLAINS

Here we go again. Mornings in the Home always began the same way. No matter what time Stafford reached Anarcho's room, Anarcho was invariably awake, waiting for Stafford to open the chintz curtains. But he never reprimanded Stafford for being late or wasting time. In the old days, Anarcho had been as impatient as all supervillains, ever eager to pursue some cunning scheme. Now there was no rushing and shouting and clanking; no messy experiments left bubbling overnight; no lairs to build or dungeons to dust.

Today's tasks were more homely. Stafford pulled back the duvet to reveal Anarcho's shrunken frame, tinged green from over-exposure to tachyons. First came the bathroom routine: toilet, sponge wipe, shave, and so forth. Then the mechanical maintenance: eye lube, claw sharpen and polish, exobrain defrag and reboot. These prosthetics were all obsolete. Anarcho was the Home's oldest resident, his life convoluted by time travel.

"Attention all residents," the intercom blared. "Please report for roll call in the lounge. This is not a drill; the perimeter alarm has sounded. Urgent roll call!"

"Sounds like mischief," Stafford said. "I presume it's not yours."

He didn't expect an answer. For form's sake, he checked the control panel on Anarcho's wheelchair, but saw nothing. It had been years since Anarcho's last caper.

Stafford couldn't decide whether or not he missed the old days. Back then, life had felt too frenetic, with a never-ending list of chores; every new plot always needed its own elaborate control room, destruct mechanism, and escape tunnel. Yet he'd enjoyed the craftsmanship of building vast laboratories and sinister machines. Now the chores were mundane: the new enemy was incontinence. Had all those intrigues been for naught?

"Let's get you down there," he said.

He settled Anarcho into the motorised wheelchair and draped a tartan blanket over his knees. The blanket lacked even the most basic hidden enhancements: no blast-proof shielding, no explosive tassels, not even a hypnotic fractal pattern on the reverse. It was merely 100% wool, soft and warm.

The Home bustled with activity as the residents and their carers converged on the lounge. Stafford ducked aside as Madame Mayhem and Miss Rule zoomed past on their hoverchairs, racing each other along the corridors. Proceeding more sedately, Stafford and Anarcho were the last to arrive.

"Hurry up!" roared Betty Beast. "I'm missing breakfast for this."

"Oh, I'll get us some breakfast," said Doctor Havoc. With a well-practised dramatic gesture, he conjured puffs of blue smoke from his hand. The clouds of nanites drifted through the kitchen doorway, returning with toast and mushrooms. One blue globule collided with a hoverchair and tried to drag it back, to Madame Mayhem's furious protests. She retaliated by stealing slices of toast before the smoke took them to Doctor Havoc. In the tussle, stray mushrooms fell to the floor, where three of Legion's tiny scuttling avatars scooped them up.

"Hush!" cried Matron. "Stop playing with your food."

A tall, spindly woman dressed in an old-style black-and-white nurse's uniform, Matron seemed to glare at everyone simultaneously. "Please answer the roll call, and I'd better not hear any cackling. Phipps will physically check that everyone's here. No decoy holograms!"

Stafford said, "What do you reckon, Anarcho – is it an escape or a kidnap?"

Some supervillains couldn't bear retirement, and returned to the metropolis like grizzled rock stars craving one last comeback. Others had accumulated a long list of enemies in their nefarious careers; they relied on the Home's defences to protect them from reprisals.

Matron called out, "Narinder Atwal."

"Here," said Doctor Havoc. "And hungry!"

Phipps, Matron's diminutive assistant, touched Doctor Havoc's shoulder to verify his existence. Coincidentally – or not – a blue puff of smoke swirled into Phipps' face and made him sneeze.

"Sophie Béranger." Matron always used civilian names; she insisted that every retired supervillain must abandon their alias along with their antics. While no one openly defied her, many surreptitiously clung onto their monikers and misbehaviour.

"Here," replied Madame Mayhem, her fingers idly stroking a memorial necklace of fangs from Fidosaurus, her deceased pet dinosaur.

The roll call continued until it reached, "Russell Fletcher."

Stafford waited a few seconds, then pinged Anarcho's exobrain.

"I'm here, wherever this is," Anarcho said, his voice low and hoarse.

"It ain't heaven, that's for sure," said Doctor Havoc.

"Come sit on my hoverchair, and I'll show you heaven," Madame Mayhem purred.

The supervillains dissolved into giggles until Matron raised her voice to resume the roll call, which ended with no absentees – or none detected.

"That's reassuring," said Matron. "But what set off the alarm? I've checked the video, and most of the outside cameras are obscured. It's remarkable how fast the ivy grows in our grounds. Quite remarkable indeed." She stared at the motley reprobates. "If anyone knows anything, please enlighten us."

"I know why galaxies collide," said AlphaMega, his bass voice augmented with infrasonic rumble.

"Yeah, your huge ego turned into a black hole and sucked them in," retorted Madame Mayhem.

"If you can't be helpful, be quiet," Matron said. "I've warned the authorities about the perimeter breach. If anything happens outside and it's traced back here, there'll be consequences."

She paused for emphasis. "This is the Dunschemin *Retirement* Home for *Repentant* Supervillains. I may overlook your little pranks when they're confined within these grounds. But I will not tolerate the slightest nuisance to the public. Any culprits will be expelled from the Home and transferred to the Lockdown Penitentiary, where I can assure you they don't bake monster-shaped cookies for afternoon tea.

"While you have breakfast, we'll sweep the grounds and clear the ivy from the cameras. Until we know what's happening, I want you all to stay indoors. No exceptions."

Stafford smiled, hoping for a peaceful morning with everyone on their best behaviour. Perhaps he could make progress on his writing projects. He'd nearly finished the script for a musical about Anarcho –

renamed Anachro in the show, for a veneer of deniability. Yet Stafford also wanted to write his own material, his own stories. Expediting Anarcho's fame was his job, but it wasn't – quite – his life.

On Anarcho's wheelchair, a red light began flashing: a relay from the control room hidden below the pond in the Home's garden. The relay also triggered an emergency *Alertness* mode in Anarcho's exobrain.

Drat, thought Stafford. *No rest for the wicked.* He hurriedly grabbed a breakfast tray and steered Anarcho back to his room.

Anarcho flailed into life as jolts of electricity galvanised his meatbrain, sparks coming out of his ears. He consulted the wheelchair's control panel to see what had roused him.

"The Time Hole has activated," Anarcho announced with glee. "Bye bye, Matron. Hello, world domination! Starting with a new timeline for recent decades..."

Clearly the *Alertness* module had already run the *Revoke Repentances* subroutine and the *I'm Back, Baby!* nefariousness boost. However, the *Same Old Plan* loop was still stuck.

"Are you sure you want to go back?" Stafford asked. "It didn't work out so well last time."

Many years ago, Stafford had just built Anarcho's first lair when the older Anarcho arrived from the future, envisaging himself as the younger version's mentor. Their meeting was a battle of bristling egos. The young Anarcho denounced the new arrival as a senile old failure, and rebuffed him with a barrage of explosivators.

"I'll choose a different year," Anarcho said. "Last time, I arrived when I was young and confident. If I appear after the Nebulon debacle, I should be more receptive."

"But why go back at all?" Stafford asked. "You've already given it your best shot. Maybe you should stay here and take it easy. Your musical can be notorious on your behalf." It would be hard to finalise the script if Anarcho resumed scheming; conquering the world would mean a major rewrite, or at least an extra song.

"I need to visit the Regeneration Chamber before it gets destroyed ten years ago." Anarcho flapped a feeble arm and scowled at its steel claw. "This body is old and worn out. It's letting me down. And I don't like things that let me down –"

Stafford deftly interrupted the rant. "We can't go yet: Matron asked everyone to stay indoors while they investigate the perimeter breach."

He frowned. "Why would the Time Hole activate on the same day the alarm sounded?"

"It means there might be an extra passenger," said Anarcho, with an *Enigmatic Mode* smirk. "If there is, make sure he goes alone – no interference. Just be ready to leave soon, when everything's quieter. While we wait, I'll download Wikipedia and whatnot, so I can take the latest science back."

Stafford walked behind the chair as Anarcho took control and drove to the computer room, where other staff could watch him for a while. It wouldn't take long for Stafford to pack their possessions. Then he could work on his new play, a down-to-earth bedroom farce with no supervillain antics whatsoever. He'd tinkered with several scripts over the years, but never found enough time to finish them. Things always kept cropping up: rusty claws one morning, Time Holes the next.

Before Stafford could slip away, he was summoned to Matron's office.

"Stafford, this is Honora," said Matron. "She's conducting an investigation and needs our assistance."

Honora was a young woman dressed in scarlet Lycra, emblazoned with three eyes inside a shield. She was either a superhero, or on her way to a fancy dress party. And fancy dress parties rarely started just after breakfast.

Stafford didn't say *Pleased to meet you*, because he wasn't.

Matron went on, "Honora, this is Stafford. He'll take you around the grounds and show you anything you want to see. Phipps will search inside the building and keep the residents indoors so they don't disturb you."

"Thank you," said Honora. "Shall we start?" Her voice was high and firm, accustomed to command. Her hair was dyed red, the same shade as her costume, as though signifying total commitment.

Stafford followed Honora out. As he turned to close the office door, Matron made a "keep the lid on it" gesture: she wanted Honora out of the residents' sight. Not easy, with Honora wearing a typically vivid costume. There had never been a superhero called the Subtle Sleuth.

He ushered Honora through a side exit, into a blustery autumn day. Fallen leaves whipped across the overgrown grass. "What are you looking for?" he asked.

"A missing boy," Honora replied. "He's fourteen. We've swept the neighbourhood and there's no sign of him. When I heard about the perimeter breach here, I wondered if he'd sneaked in."

"So he might be wandering around the grounds?" asked Stafford, conscious of the Time Hole in the grotto. *If there's an extra passenger, make sure he goes alone – no interference,* Anarcho had said.

"Or he could have injured himself. This is the kind of place where accidents happen, isn't it?" Honora's tone was full of insinuation.

"Anyone who walks into a home for supervillains deserves whatever they get," Stafford said, returning her stare.

She looked away, her gaze sweeping the area. "Let's start at the perimeter, and see if we can spot where he came in."

Stafford and Honora walked all the way down the drive until they reached the tall iron gate at the edge of the grounds.

"Is this always closed?" Honora asked.

"Yes. Staff cars have a transponder to open the gate. Any visitors announce themselves at the intercom and are buzzed in. Mostly that's deliveries. The residents don't get many visitors."

Supervillains usually needed a retirement home because they'd alienated – or eliminated – any family and friends.

A high wall extended each side of the gate, topped with spikes and stern warning notices. Pine trees stood on the right; to the left lay a rhododendron border.

"Which direction?" Stafford asked Honora, facing right with an implied preference for the trees. He wanted to steer her away from the Time Hole, which seemed the best way of ensuring *no interference*. Anarcho's trip to the Regeneration Chamber would have to wait until Honora had gone and Matron had calmed down.

Honora glanced around, scrutinising the rhododendrons. She pushed through the bushes, and pointed. "Let's ask this lady what she's doing out here."

As he followed, Stafford glimpsed Madame Mayhem's hoverchair attempting *Skulk* mode. "Are you sure you want to confront her?" he asked, thinking wearily of the chaos that superheroes always caused when they started poking around. More clean-up work! He would never get his scripts finished. "You're on our turf, so you can't complain if anyone whacks you."

Honora ignored this warning, and strode ahead. "Looking for someone?" she challenged.

Madame Mayhem's hoverchair retreated, floating a little higher. "Not at all. I'm just looking for my, for my... monocle. Yes, monocle. Have you seen it? It's rather fine; the frame is antique ivory and the glass was hand-blown by artisan ogres."

"Perhaps you've forgotten where you put it," Honora said. "It's in the top pocket of your jacket, alongside a matchbook and a miniature disruptor gun whose charge has expired."

Madame Mayhem gaped in bogglement. She reached into her pocket and retrieved the ivory monocle. "Ah, so it is. I guess I'll just be, just be... heading back inside. Yes, inside. I've got an excellent book to read, now that I've found my monocle. Good day!" Her hoverchair zoomed away. Clearly she'd only sneaked out, defying Phipps, on the off-chance of discovering something to liven the long twilight of retirement.

"If the absent-minded lady was happy to leave, there's nothing here." Honora turned toward the trees. "We'll walk the other way."

Relieved, Stafford followed Honora past the gate, into the pines. The ground was a soft carpet of dead pine needles, spattered with pungent droppings.

Honora looked everywhere with a keen gaze. "This is a sizable patch of woodland. How does it all fit within the grounds?"

She'd noticed straight away; he'd hoped it would take longer.

"It's Professor Perdition's pocket dimension, where he keeps his monsters," Stafford said.

"What does he need monsters for?" she asked, her voice sharp with disapproval.

"Companion animal therapy. For some residents, playing with monsters is a happy reminder of days gone by. It's soothing." Stafford attempted a diversion. "Maybe the alarm means a monster escaped. You should check outside to see if anything's threatening the public."

Honora shook her head. "I already swept the area when I was looking for the missing kid. I would have spotted any monsters."

She was as arrogant as all the other fancy-suited meddlers. "You sound awfully sure," Stafford said. "Perhaps you'd better take another look."

"I have sharp eyes. And I can't see any monsters here, which means they're not hunting prey. So our missing child is somewhere else. From the dimensional warping, this looks the shortest way out..."

They arrived at the raspberry canes of Miss Rule's kitchen garden. Honora kept striding forward as fast as Stafford could walk.

"How long have you worked in the Home?" Honora asked Stafford.

"Just a few years, since Anarcho began needing specialist care."

"So you were Anarcho's henchman beforehand?"

Stafford grimaced. "I dislike the word *henchman*. It's sexist and derogatory. I'm surprised that someone so virtuous would use such an obnoxious term," he said, enjoying the chance to lecture her.

"Minion, then," said Honora impatiently.

"No one wants to fill in a form and call themselves a henchman or a minion. My business card says 'Executive Implementator'."

They entered a formal flower garden bordered with black roses. All the flowers were so beautiful as to invite plucking, and all were deadly poisonous. Honora ignored the temptation of the siren flowers and hurried onward.

"You must be sweating inside that suit," Stafford observed. "I bet someone else does your laundry, slaving behind the scenes to help you prance about in public. You must have staff, or at least an intern."

"Yes. The difference is that whatever job title you fool yourself with, you're working for a supervillain. You must have dirtied your hands, seen some blood..." She pointed an admonitory finger at him, her nail varnish as red as a *Stop* light. "How do you stand it? Is there nothing more wholesome you'd rather be doing?"

Stafford thought of all his unwritten scripts and unchased dreams. "Not everyone has superpowers, you know. I need to earn a living, and this is a skilled job. Supervillains need lifestyle support; they deserve it as much as anyone else."

"Being a supervillain is not a lifestyle choice," Honora exclaimed.

"Says you, swanning around in your fancy dress," Stafford sneered. "I suppose you think some people don't deserve care and support. That's discrimination! It's not Anarcho's fault he has morality deficit dysfunction. Supervillain syndrome is a spectrum trait that benefits humanity: we need mavericks, ruthless businessmen, mad scientists who invent amazing gadgets –"

"– Causing death and destruction –"

"– Shaking up the status quo, and asking the hard questions." Stafford's voice acquired a musical cadence as he quoted from the opening song of *Anachro!* "'Is gravity in safe hands? Are our borders secure against other dimensions?'

"And it gives superheroes a job," he went on, "so you can't complain. Why are you hassling me about Anarcho? I thought you were looking for a missing kid."

"I am," she said. "I can talk to you while I look. I always try to make a difference. Supervillains wouldn't do half as much damage if henchmen stopped enabling them."

Stafford grinned. "Then that shows we're doing a good job."

They'd traversed most of the grounds, seeing only nettles and litter. Now they reached AlphaMega's abstract garden, an aperiodic tessellation of marble slabs where the supervillains occasionally played games with gargoyles. Beyond this arena lay Anarcho's grotto. Stafford could feel the throb of the Time Hole casting a sense of déjà vu over the landscape. He needed to slow Honora down, and figure out how to get rid of her.

"Let's focus on the boy," he said. "Have you got a picture of him?"

Honora retrieved her phone from somewhere in the Lycra suit, and pulled up an image. The boy had dishevelled black hair and a sullen scowl. He looked oddly familiar, even though Stafford rarely encountered teenagers except on skateboards in the precinct outside the community theatre.

"Who's that?" he blurted.

A caption appeared: *Russell Fletcher.*

Stafford summoned enough self-control to keep quiet, but not enough to keep his expression neutral under Honora's penetrating gaze. "Looks like you know him," she said.

"I knew someone of that name a long time ago," Stafford said truthfully. "Looked like him, too. Maybe I knew his father."

"He doesn't have a family," Honora said. "He went missing from a children's home."

Stafford shrugged. "It must be a coincidence," he bluffed.

"There are no coincidences in my line of work," Honora proclaimed.

"No humility either, by the sound of it," Stafford retorted.

"Not much need for that," Honora said. "I'll find this boy,

whatever it takes. Let's start by talking about the person you knew."

Stafford hesitated, wishing that another supervillain would cause a distraction. But none did.

Should he tell her? There seemed little point in hiding it, when the name was on Matron's roll call. If Honora asked Matron, the connection would come out.

"Russell Fletcher is Anarcho's civilian name." Telling this to a superhero felt like a betrayal.

"And Anarcho is one of the residents here," she said. "You mentioned him earlier."

Stafford nodded. "He was probably before your time."

Time. Honora was right: this couldn't be a coincidence. The teenage Russell Fletcher must have entered the grounds, triggering the perimeter alarm. His presence had activated the Time Hole, and he'd started travelling. If he reached the past, he would grow up to become Anarcho.

Honora furrowed her brow, unable to see the connection. She didn't know about the Time Hole.

"When we find the boy," she said, "perhaps this will start making sense."

She marched forward once again. Stafford followed perforce. Near the grotto, she stopped and glanced around. "There's a shimmer in the air. No, not in the air – in the fabric of space behind the air."

Honora descended into the grotto: a maze of rocks and gargoyles encrusted with multicoloured lichens. Amid the statues, a motionless figure sat as if posing for a sculpture commemorating his conquest of the world.

"There you are!" Anarcho said to Stafford. "Have you been headhunted? You know how much I value you. Is she offering you a pay rise?"

"Certainly not," said Honora. "You must be Anarcho."

"This is Honora," Stafford said as he resumed his usual place behind Anarcho's wheelchair.

"I don't care who she is, as long as she doesn't interfere." Anarcho turned to Honora and said, "You have no business here. This is our territory. Get out!"

"I'm looking for a missing boy," Honora said.

Stafford said, "He's not missing. I can assure you he's perfectly safe

– and being very well looked after, if I say so myself."

"Then you can let me see him," Honora said.

Anarcho drummed his fingers on the arm of his wheelchair. Stafford couldn't see his expression from behind the chair, but felt sure he was giving Honora his well-honed look of withering contempt.

Honora returned Anarcho's gaze with a defiant stare of her own.

"Oh, for heaven's sake!" exclaimed Stafford. "I've got plenty of things I could be getting on with, instead of standing here while you two have a silent face-off. Look, Anarcho is Russell Fletcher, the missing boy. You've found him! He's safe and sound, as you can plainly see. Congratulations, your mission is successful. Now scram!"

"Safe and sound?" Honora raised her eyebrows and gestured at Anarcho's feeble, chair-bound frame. "You look half-dead, whoever you are. Russell Fletcher's a healthy teenager with his whole life ahead of him. Show me the boy!"

Stafford bent down to whisper in Anarcho's ear. "It's probably easier to just –"

"Eh, whassat?" Anarcho shouted. "You know I can't hear whispers any more. Speak up!"

Stafford said, "Let's just show her the Time Hole. The boy's probably still inside."

Time travel was not a straightforward matter of instantly stepping from one year to another. The universe's vast inertia required a lengthy trek to surmount.

"You can't show her the Time Hole!" exclaimed Anarcho, aghast. "You shouldn't even have mentioned it."

"She would have found it anyway with her eyesight mojo." Stafford waved at the three-eyed emblem on Honora's costume.

Honora pointed past Anarcho. "There's something down there. If that's where the boy is –"

"All right, all right," Anarcho grumped. "We'll take you close enough to see the echoes."

The grotto's twisting paths led to a pond: normally an unremarkable patch of water, fringed with irises. Now it was a shimmering vortex of blurred impressions from the past. An iridescent sheen, like the surface of a giant soap bubble, marked the boundary of the temporal gyre.

Within the Time Hole, the figure of a dark-haired boy was gradually receding in strobe-like echoes. He wore the clothes from the picture on Honora's phone. "That's him," Stafford said. "Happy now? You know he's safe, because if he wasn't, then Anarcho wouldn't be right here in front of us. You've done your job, so you can collect another smug point and go home."

"Yes, I've done my job," Honora said. "But in my line of work, one job often leads to another."

"You're not getting paid overtime," Stafford said. "So you can clock off now."

"Yeah, just *clock off*," said Anarcho.

"I don't do it for money," said Honora. "I do it because I care. Stafford, you're Anarcho's carer, so naturally you take his side. Yet I'm also a carer. I care for the entire community. When a child goes missing, I'm there. When a supervillain threatens the world –"

"Spare us the speech," Anarcho said with disgust. "We've heard it before."

"Then I'll get to the point," Honora said. "Right now, Russell Fletcher is just a missing boy who climbed over the wrong wall and explored a freaky rainbow vortex. He may be safe, but is the world safe from him? Left on this path, alone in the past, he'll grow up to become a supervillain –"

With a swiftness belying his age, Anarcho reached under the blanket for a disruptor. The air crackled as a green energy bolt zapped through the air, aimed at Honora.

Seeing his move, she dodged aside and ran toward Anarcho. Instinctively, Stafford grabbed the wheelchair to pull it away, but he was too late.

Another shot went wild as Honora wrenched the weapon from Anarcho's liver-spotted hand. Then she blasted the chair's wheel, melting it into slag. Anarcho howled in pain. Stafford rushed to lift him out of the ruined chair. Anarcho had scorched, tattered trousers and an angry red wound on his thigh.

Honora charged into the Time Hole, chasing the distant figure. Unless she had yet more superpowers, it would take her a while to catch up with the boy.

Stafford carried the groaning Anarcho back to the Home. He staggered into the first-aid room, calling for assistance, and lowered Anarcho onto the examination couch. As soon as a nurse arrived,

Stafford hurried back to the grotto.

Honora's red suit flashed vividly inside the Time Hole as she pumped her limbs, looking like a jogger on a treadmill. Ahead of her, the boy was only walking; he hadn't seen Honora behind him. She would catch him if Stafford didn't intervene.

Stafford paused for breath. Dashing back and forth, carrying Anarcho, had taken its toll. Stafford wasn't young any more. He'd spent many years as Anarcho's implementator – *henchman, let's face it* – then several more years as a carer in the Home.

If he could have his time again, would he choose that? Or would he prefer something else, whatever it might be?

If Honora brought the boy out of the Time Hole, then Russell Fletcher would never reach the past and grow up as Anarcho. Stafford would never meet him and become his employee. Some other life would unfold – perhaps one where Stafford became a famous playwright. Of course, in that other life he might have other dreams, equally unfulfilled.

Would he throw his whole life away for an unknown alternative?

Well, what had he achieved? Little on his own account: just some half-finished never-performed scripts. A few brief friendships and relationships, always interrupted by the exigencies of moving from one lair to the next.

He'd devoted himself to Anarcho's cares. There'd been good times: inventing exotic gadgets, training pet monsters, drafting speeches that began "Citizens of the world..." *Cue the montage song.* He'd put his heart into his work, even as he regretted deferring his own ambitions. Surely everyone – whatever their job – had at least one unpursued dream.

If the work was worth doing, it was worth saving. Now he just had to save it.

Stafford splashed into the pond, the frigid water squelching deep into his shoes. More laundry later; yet more work. He descended through the hidden hatch into the Time Hole control room. He remembered the long labour of digging and furnishing this chamber; the thrill of foiling an opponent made it all worthwhile.

On the big screen, Russell Fletcher strode forward, looking awestruck. A caption showed his progress into the past. What year did he need to reach? Anarcho had been thirty-nine when he hired Stafford; the boy was fourteen now. So the target was twenty-five years before Stafford's employment.

Yet how would the kid know when to exit the Time Hole? Did he even understand how to leave? It would be safer if Stafford took control. He programmed the auto-release for the correct year. Then he glanced at the manual-release lever, remembering its location in case he needed it in a hurry.

Stafford allowed himself a moment to admire his own craftsmanship: gleaming brass levers, walnut panels, tortoiseshell inlays from endangered turtles. This control room had once been a photo-feature in *What Lair* magazine.

Another monitor showed Honora sprinting through the vortex with a determined expression. Damned meddling superheroes, trying to change people's lives. Anarcho had a right to his own destiny.

Stafford had to prevent Honora from bringing the boy back. Anarcho – who remembered the original course of events – had attempted to shoot Honora, rather than let her charge in, so her interference wasn't part of the target timeline.

Simply ejecting her from the Time Hole would leave her in the past with foreknowledge: she'd find the missing boy before he climbed the wall. Stafford needed to expel Honora without stranding her in the past. He reached for the "reverse the polarity" lever, an ever-useful classic that he always installed. This would affect everyone in the Time Hole; Stafford couldn't eject Honora alone. He could only pull the lever after the boy had reached his destination. Shivering in cold wet socks, Stafford urged Anarcho onward. *Come on, kid.*

Honora was closing in. How could Stafford stop her? Surveying the plethora of switches, he saw "alarm test". Quickly he reconfigured the circuit to include Honora's sector and exclude the boy's. He flipped the switch.

Whawp! Whawp! Whawp! Startled by the ear-splitting roar, Honora paused and looked around. Seeing nothing, she resumed her pursuit, but she'd lost valuable momentum. She called out, vainly.

Russell Fletcher had reached the target year. The Time Hole released him into the past to fulfil his destiny. Now Stafford unhooked the safety latch – #6 in his "Top Ten Tips" feature in *Big Dangerous Machines Monthly* – and yanked the polarity reverser.

The Time Hole exploded in a shower of sparkly special effects. The recoil ejected Honora into the future. "You've just clocked off, baby!"

Stafford cried. "See you in a few decades." He grinned in triumph.

Then his smile faded as he contemplated the wreck of the Time Hole. He needed to restore it for Anarcho's next journey. More long labour, while his scripts languished.

Stafford donned clean socks and shoes from the box of spare outfits. He cleared up the worst of the explosion's mess, and rebooted the tachyon accumulator. Then he exited via the escape tunnel: a longer but drier route than the pond. Mosaics on the walls depicted Anarcho's most cunning stratagems. How the heck had this tunnel failed to place in *Best Escape Route?*

Back at the Home, Stafford concocted a story for Matron, emphasising that Honora had found what she sought, and had left after sparring with Anarcho. He assured Matron that there'd been no nuisance to the public.

Then he checked on Anarcho. The staff had bandaged him up, but he would need extra care to prevent him putting pressure on the wound while he slept.

Madame Mayhem accosted Stafford after his conversation with the nurse. "You look like you've been busy," she said. "What happened to Anarcho?"

"That superhero shot him."

She tilted her head and gave him an arch glance. "Any particular reason?"

"You know how they love meddling."

Madame Mayhem sniffed ostentatiously. "What's that – pond slime?"

"Yes, I went out for fresh air and a swim. Lovely day for it." Stafford gestured to the window's view onto the cold, blustery weather. It had started raining.

"Sure, just like I went out to find my monocle." She pouted. "It's selfish of you to hog all the mischief and excitement."

Stafford shook his head. "Make your own toys if you're so keen on excitement."

"You're the expert at making them. Would you, would you... leave Anarcho and work for me? We'll go back to the big city! Whatever he pays, I'll double it."

She mentioned money, but not vacations. Supervillains required constant support; whoever he worked for, Stafford's own dreams would flicker and fade. No theatrical triumph for him, except constructing the stage sets for supervillains' melodramatic schemes.

"Thanks for the offer," he said. "But what kind of carer would I be if I abandoned Anarcho while he's wrapped in bandages and his gizmo's broken? He needs me."

He always needs me.

Stafford retreated to Anarcho's room. He checked the wound and watched Anarcho sleep, while contemplating repairs to the Time Hole. He needed to fix it before any other envious supervillains started poking around. And he might as well install a few improvements, upgrade the control room...

A henchman's work is never done. Here we go again.

I wrote "The Dunschemin Retirement Home for Repentant Supervillains" after being invited to contribute a story to a theme anthology about care-giving and care-givers. I already had the title, which I'd used as a joke in another story. When I received the invitation, I remembered this earlier joke and decided that a supervillain retirement home would make a good setting. The anthology's emphasis on care-givers prompted the additional idea of using a henchman as the protagonist.

It was a lot of fun creating the cast of supervillains, and serving up colourful superhero action. I don't believe that the author's experience of writing a story has much bearing on a story's final quality or how readers perceive it. But I'd rather have fun while writing than not!

THE SHAPES OF WRATH

When we were sixteen, we got our first new bodies. It was the highlight of the school year, because we had a week off lessons to get used to our new shapes. We still had morning assembly, of course, when we sang "Strength Through Diversity" in unison. But after that it was mostly games: football and athletics, and team challenges where everyone's different shape was supposed to be good for something.

I was a basset hound. In the retrieval challenge, I sniffed out where tokens had been buried. My best friend Garamingan became a gibbon, who scrambled up trees to find tokens hidden in the foliage. Everyone could find at least one, in theory. But some kids are always useless, whatever body they're in. And others don't like to do any work: they prefer to cheat.

Zinc Virtue was a great hulking bear. He simply waited for boys coming back, so he could hit them and steal their loot. I'd dug up several tokens, and I couldn't carry them all properly in my jaws. I dropped one. When I stopped to pick it up, Zinc Virtue rushed over and tried to kick me. Apparently, bears don't have the right balance for kicking: he fell over with an earthshaking *thump*.

That's why we had try-out shapes, to learn this stuff. All these practice bodies were just templates from the Morpher library; they weren't individual. Soon we'd need to choose our own personal shapes.

Our teachers explained that the evils of history stemmed from humanity's tendency to divide into groups, and mistreat other groups. White people enslaved black people; men oppressed women; nations and religions fought each other. Rainbow Village had been founded by idealists who resolved to end these conflicts by abolishing their source. The Morpher machines could change people's bodies. And so it became compulsory for everyone to take a unique shape.

When everyone looks different, there is no majority or minority. In a truly diverse society, there is no conformity or oppression.

That, at least, is what we all wrote in our test papers when we were quizzed about History or Civics.

Yet the choice of body shape became fraught. Every feature made a statement, when you had to select a face to show the world. Christians proclaimed their faith by emblazoning a cross upon their bodies. Carnivores competed to become ever more lethal, accumulating teeth and claws and toxins with the same enthusiasm that they stockpiled guns. After all, you might lose your gun – or have it seized – but you'd never mislay a mouth full of venomous fangs.

After school one day, Garamingan and I got together to talk about designing our adult bodies. We usually met at my house because my bedroom was bigger than his, and I didn't have brothers always barging in and interrupting. My door said "Ramsey's Room: No Loitering".

"Are you going to have a cross?" I asked. "Grandma wants me to have one."

"Yep, my parents said it looks bad if you don't. It's like you're rejecting Jesus. I might put a small one on the back of my head, where I don't have to see it."

Garamingan showed me a design onscreen. The cross was a white ridge on green skin, stretching from ear to ear.

"That's not small," I said.

"It's smaller than it would be on the torso," he said. "But you could have an even smaller one, if you dare."

"Dare?" I spluttered. "When did it become compulsory to wear giant crosses?"

"It's not compulsory," said Garamingan.

"Not quite," I said.

Yet if you chose not to have a cross, you deliberately marked yourself as different. Most kids just wanted to fit in, and so the crosses proliferated. Even Zinc Virtue had one on his tail.

That morning, Zinc Virtue had turned up to school looking like the meanest, spikiest dinosaur in creation. We recognised him by the ID signals. He took great pleasure in demonstrating the range of venoms that he could deliver by biting and spitting. His cronies sprayed so much acid at each other that they permanently smelled like vinegar.

"What's the matter, Ramsey, don't you love the baby Jesus?" said Garamingan, grinning. "Are you turning your back on God's infinite mercy?"

I shrugged. "I don't have a problem with God. And if he has a problem with me, then he hasn't mentioned it. But this isn't about

Jesus: it's about conformity. If we're all supposed to be individuals with our own unique forms, how come everyone wears the same sign?"

"Because they want to," Garamingan said.

"I don't want to," I said firmly. "And I'm pretty sure you don't, either. What are we going to do?"

"Well, we can conform by having a cross like everyone else. Or we can rebel by not having one. Or..." Garamingan glanced at me, in case I had any further ideas.

"Or we can have a cross, but subvert it," I said. "Maybe a teeny-tiny one. Or a really big one, ludicrously big."

"Or more than one," Garamingan said.

"Lots and lots of crosses. Because, obviously, the more crosses you have, the more devout you are."

Garamingan laughed. "Crosses all over the body, on every inch of skin –"

"And crosses as patterns in the hooves, leaving sacred hoofprints everywhere," I said.

"Yep, everything a cross. Even the vision can be cross-eyed..."

We each started tinkering with body designs, squeezing in more and more crosses. Soon Garamingan smiled to himself.

"You're looking smug," I said. "What have you come up with?"

"Fractals," he replied. "The arms of a cross can bear smaller crosses, which in turn bear even smaller crosses..."

"Brilliant!" I immediately borrowed the concept for the skin patterning of my Ortho-Man, a superhero-style figure with a literal square jaw.

"That's my idea," Garamingan complained. "Make your own design."

"It's better than any idea I'll have," I said. "I'm not letting you have more crosses than me. Otherwise I'll look less devout – like I don't care as much."

"You don't," Garamingan said.

"True, but no one needs to know that. Anyway, if I did think of a better idea, then the shoe would be on the other hoof. You wouldn't like to look less devout, would you? We should both have the same number of crosses, the maximum amount possible."

"The maximum would be a particular body shape," he said. "We couldn't both have the maximum without both having the same shape."

As soon as he said this, a grand scheme occurred to me. "So that's what we'll do."

"We can't have the same shape," Garamingan objected. "It's the law."

I returned his gaze with a defiant stare. "So?"

"You mean... break the law?"

"Absolutely," I said. "Civil disobedience, but in a good cause – protesting against oppression. We'll fight sanctimony through satire!" I paused for effect. "Plus, being rebellious will make us look really cool and help us meet girls."

Garamingan hesitated, and I realised I'd taken the wrong tack. He wasn't the kind of boy who tried to attract girls by showing off.

"Think of it as a challenge," I said. "How would we actually do it? How would we both get into a Morpher and come out the same?"

His expression brightened at the prospect of a problem to solve. Yet he still looked wary.

"Maybe we could create two bodies which look similar on the outside, but are different on the inside," I said. I knew it was too obvious to work, but I wanted to prod Garamingan into coming up with something better.

He shook his head. "The Morphers check appearances. They have to be visibly different."

"Then we need to bypass the checks. Can you delete a record in the database, so it doesn't show up as a duplicate?"

"Sure, if I had admin access – which I don't."

"How could we become admins?" I asked.

Garamingan held up his hand, motioning me to silence. After a long minute, he said, "I think I have an idea. All the Morphers are connected: they have their own databases, and copies of each other's databases. But they can only update the copies if the connection is active –"

"So we cut the connection!" I exclaimed. "Then we simultaneously go to two Morphers and upload our design. They can't detect a duplicate, so they go ahead and transform us."

"Then as soon as we come out, we restore the connection," Garamingan finished.

"Great idea," I said. "We can do it. Are you with me?"

Garamingan avoided my gaze. "I'm not sure. I need to think about it."

"Oh, come on. You know this is an issue. If you really wanted a cross, then you wouldn't put it on the back of your head, out of sight. You're under pressure, like me. Why should we stand for that? Let's fight back."

"I suppose it would make a good project for extra marks in Civics..."

"Spoken like a true rebel! All right, let's finalise the design."

I crafted a humanoid shape, its skin made of tiny iridescent scales. Each part of the body – face, chest, back, limbs – had a big central cross that branched into smaller and smaller crosses. I added head feathers, an inflatable throat-sac, and heat-dispersion sails, all bearing yet more crosses. Every square inch of surface bore the sacred symbol of Christ's Passion. No one could possibly show more piety than this.

Meanwhile Garamingan delved into the Morphers, figuring out how to disable the connection between machines without raising an alarm. Eventually he found a parameter for 'Length of allowable time-out', which saved the admins from being constantly notified of momentary glitches. By tweaking this parameter upward, we could cut the links without anyone knowing until it was too late.

And so, on a fine summer afternoon, we did it. We walked into the Morphers looking different, and walked out looking the same.

"What's all this?" asked Grandma, staring at my new shape.

"It's in honour of Jesus," I replied. "You told me to wear a cross."

"I meant *one* cross," she said. "Jesus was only crucified once."

"Well, if one cross is enough to commemorate that," I said, "then we could just have a single one in town somewhere – maybe in church. And we wouldn't all need individual crosses on our bodies."

"Sure," said Grandma, "and you could go to church every day to be reminded of His sacrifice."

I laughed. "If that's all it's about, I've got enough reminders on my body to save me from going to church for a whole year!"

"Don't be flippant, young man," she said, then turned to Garamingan. "I see you've got something similar..." Her voice trailed off as she inspected us with her big faceted eyes. "Very similar. I can't see the difference. Where is it?"

"There isn't one," I said.

Grandma clicked her mandibles, making a *tsk* sound of impatience. "Quit the backchat – this is important. Where's the difference?"

"There isn't one," I repeated. "We're exactly the same. It's civil disobedience."

She sighed, and addressed Garamingan with a weary tone. "Do your parents know about this?"

He shook his head.

"Then call them."

Garamingan's parents arrived at our house, accepted a hospitable cup of nectar, and perched themselves on stools. His mother, Smorvick, gently fluttered her wings as she asked, "Garamingan, what's going on?"

"It's a protest," he said.

"Against what?"

Garamingan looked at me, and I took over. "Against hypocrisy," I said. "We're supposed to be a community founded on diversity and freedom from oppression. Yet everyone wears crosses." I pointed at Grandma's thorax and Smorvick's wings.

"That's our free choice," said Smorvick.

"Maybe it's yours. But we've been told to wear crosses as well. How free is that?"

"You can refuse, if you insist."

"Most kids won't resist family pressure," Garamingan said.

"And how many of the adults were pressured by their own friends and relatives?" I went on. "It's all just conformity, not genuine religion. That's what we're highlighting."

"I see," said Smorvick. "It seems like a reasoned position, and I don't think we ought to interfere." She looked at her husband. "Do you, dear?"

"No, you're right," he said. "Let the children protest, if they want to. Freedom is important."

"They're breaking the law!" said Grandma, her antennae quivering furiously.

"You must do as you see fit, of course," Smorvick said. "You could file a complaint, and get them sent to court. That would create a lot of publicity for their protest. Or you could wait a while, and see what happens. Maybe it's just a prank that'll fizzle out."

Grandma clicked her mandibles again, this time making a *Hmph* sound. But I could tell that Smorvick's words had made an impression. After Garamingan and his family left, Grandma stopped talking about the law, and instead lectured me about the suffering of her own grandparents long ago. With superhuman restraint, I listened politely and refrained from telling her how irrelevant it all was.

At school the next day, we provoked a lot of reactions.

"Homomorphs!"

"Oppressors!"

"Jesus freaks!"

"Hey, that looks cool..."

We laughed off the insults, and smiled at the compliments. Most guys didn't care about our bodies, but were simply impressed that we'd subverted the rules. We fended off requests to explain how we'd done it – I was a little disturbed to hear how many laws people wanted to break.

And I spoke to a few girls, which put me in a good mood.

When school finished, Garamingan challenged me to a race. Because we had the same bodies, we could compete on equal terms. We went outside the town limits, where the houses bordered onto woods and fields. Swathes of oilseed rape glowed bright yellow in the sunlight, its scent heavy in the air. I wondered how the flowers would look in ultraviolet vision: I'd argued for it, but Garamingan had said it was a pointless frippery. As soon as we started racing, I dismissed such extraneous thoughts and focused solely on running, enjoying the demands of stretching my new body to the limit. At the finish line, I ballooned my throat-sac to inch ahead and claim victory.

Afterward, we went into the wood to rest and cool down. We drank from a stream in the shade of giant oaks, and sat on an old rotting log. Garamingan sulked because I'd won. I was about to start ribbing him about this, when I heard people approaching. Shadowy figures emerged from the trees.

I blinked. The figures remained shadowy. After a moment, I realised that I could see their physical forms, but their ID signals were missing. I was so accustomed to seeing ID signals that their absence made the arrivals look unreal, like ghosts.

The group drew closer, crunching forest debris underfoot. I saw that they all looked the same, thickset with powerful limbs and great protruding jaws full of jagged teeth. Identical anonymous forms surrounded us. My heart started pounding.

We stood up. Garamingan said, "What do you want, Zinc Virtue?"

The figures said nothing. But one of them – the front one – twitched slightly. That must be Zinc Virtue. I wondered how Garamingan had known. Perhaps he'd just guessed, hoping for a reaction to confirm it.

We were both tired after running, so there was no point trying to flee. I decided that we might as well show some bravado.

"I see you all look the same," I said. "You can follow our fashion, but you can't join our gang."

"We have a bigger gang," Zinc Virtue said. "And we're going to smash yours. You think you can get away with mocking God? It's true that Jesus saves, but he won't save you from this."

He spat acid at me, stinging my face.

I bent down to grab a fallen branch. It was an awkward length, and too flimsy to do much damage, but I felt better for having something in my hand. Not that it would do much good.

It didn't.

They rushed us. I lashed out, landing several hefty blows. But all too soon, we were pinned down and helpless.

Then the beating began. They used all the fearsome weaponry their bodies possessed: claws, fangs, venom...

Our physical form included the standard limits on how much pain we could experience. After a while – it was probably only a few minutes, but felt a lot longer – my body stopped hurting, and I could only sense the assault's progress by hearing the *crack* of my bones breaking.

We were too badly wounded to walk home, so we had to phone for someone to pick us up. The ranger landed his flitter in a nearby clearing, and loaded us inside. "This looks worse than the usual rough and tumble," he said. "Do you want to file a crime report?"

"I don't think so," I said.

Garamingan agreed. "No point."

Zinc Virtue would surely cover his tracks. When people had the same shape, some of them could stay in town while others followed us into the wood. Without ID signals, there'd be no way of proving which individuals had taken part in the attack.

The ranger dropped us off at the nearest Morpher. In history lessons, we learned about something called a hospital. Nowadays, if anyone has a problem with their body, they just get it replaced. Our design was still on file, so we walked out in fresh versions of our protest shape. We weren't going to let those thugs intimidate us.

The Morphers gave us both the same shape, without quibble. When we got home, Garamingan discovered that Zinc Virtue's father had filed a request to suspend duplication checking, on the grounds that everyone should be treated equally: if we'd managed to become identical, then others should have the same opportunity. The Morpher admins had granted the request, pending clarification of policy from the town council.

"It's gone onto the agenda for the next council meeting," Garamingan said.

"What about wearing crosses – is that on?" I asked.

"Yep. There's a proposal to ban excessive ornamentation, along with a ban on forcing anyone to adopt a particular design."

"Sounds good," I said. "But will it pass?"

"It's a big step if the council can specify what bodies are allowed or forbidden," he said. "The carnivores are against it, because they're worried about laws against all their fangs and venom."

"We already have a law about what bodies are forbidden," I said. "Nobody is allowed to look the same. And we've seen why that law exists."

I shivered, remembering how it felt to be attacked by the anonymous mob. Now I understood the relevance of Grandma's anecdotes from family history.

Garamingan said, "I wonder if that was just Zinc Virtue being an asshole, or whether someone put him up to it."

"I'm not sure he needs much incitement to be an asshole," I said. "Why would anyone put him up to it?"

"Because they felt threatened by our protest. It could have been Christians who don't want any laws restricting crosses. Or it could have been the carnivores, who don't want any body regulation at all. Maybe both."

"Kind of an over-reaction, wasn't it?"

"We stepped outside the law first," Garamingan said, somewhat acerbically.

"And it was my idea," I acknowledged. "I'm sorry I dragged you into it. I didn't know this would happen."

Garamingan tilted his head, accepting my apology. "What are we going to do?" he asked.

"Get revenge!"

"Obviously, dummy-head. But how?"

"We've got to hit back at Zinc Virtue. Can we get a bigger gang than his?"

"We could probably get more than he had today," Garamingan said. "But would it stop there? He could find more people as well."

"Yeah, but surely we'd win in the end. He's an asshole! How many people want to be on his side?"

"There are plenty of assholes."

I nodded gloomily.

"If we can't fight an all-out war, then we have to do something sneaky," Garamingan said.

"I guess so," I replied. "I have an idea..."

The next day, we searched the design library until we found the shape used by our attackers. We went to a Morpher and emerged looking exactly like one of Zinc Virtue's thugs. After all, there was nothing to stop us, now that duplicate shapes were allowed. I waggled my jaw, struggling to accustom myself to the enormous array of fangs. I didn't want to accidentally bite my tongue and poison myself with my own venom.

Garamingan showed me how to turn off the ID signal. The rush was incredible. I felt as though we'd turned into anonymous superheroes. We were masked, unaccountable, all-powerful. Nothing could stop us delivering righteous justice!

Dimly, I knew that this feeling was problematic. My conscience was sounding the alarm; I put it on snooze mode.

We hurried to Zinc Virtue's house, and stationed ourselves between the garden and the river. Through the hedge, we heard small animals scurrying in their cages, unaware of their imminent starring role at a carnivores' dinner party.

"We might have to lure him to us," I said. "Do you think we could ask someone to phone him? We'd need a story –"

"I don't want to bring anyone else into this," Garamingan said. "He'll hold it against them, and they'll pay for it."

"Yeah. Just us, then."

We waited. The sun descended. At last we saw Zinc Virtue approaching the house. He was back in his previous shape, and he had his ID signal turned on, ready to return home and meet his family.

Ideally, he would have stepped right into an ambush. But our new forms, designed for intimidation, were too big to let us hide. We had to casually walk down the path toward him.

"Why are you still in the mob shape?" he asked. "We're not on manoeuvres."

"Yes we are," I said, coming closer. "That dickwad Garamingan is down by the river. Let's go get him!"

Zinc Virtue flapped a claw in disgust. "He's already had it."

"But you haven't had it," Garamingan said. "And it's time you did."

We grabbed his arms, and dragged him over the riverbank. All three of us toppled onto the shingle, which was slick with shallow puddles and damp weeds. Zinc Virtue exploded with rage, writhing and thrashing, squirming from our grip. I snatched his leg, and brought him crashing down into the water. Again he wriggled free. He turned and spat acid at us, a yellowish jet that hissed and stank when it hit me. My chest started dissolving, but I ignored it – I wouldn't be in this body long enough for that to matter.

I grappled with him, careful to avoid his venomous fangs. Garamingan tore into him from the other side. Blood gushed into the river as claws lashed out. We were less experienced in this type of body, but we outnumbered him. We shoved him underwater, and held him there until he fell limp. Then we swiftly secreted webbing from our spinnerets, wrapping him in a cocoon to immobilise him.

"All this violence is really rather childish and pathetic," I commented.

"Definitely," said Garamingan. "It's just a cycle of retaliation that never solves anything." He addressed our captive. "And your claws didn't save you, did they?"

Zinc Virtue mumbled indignantly, but his words couldn't make it past the silk we'd stuffed into his mouth.

"The only solution is to abolish it," I said. "When no one can commit violence, then it won't be a problem any more."

"And we'll all be safer and happier as pacifists," Garamingan said.

"We've won enough votes on the council to pass new laws about what bodies everyone can have," I told Zinc Virtue. This wasn't yet true, but we wanted to scare him.

"And because you've been a naughty boy, you'll be first into the Morpher," Garamingan said gleefully.

I leaned in close to Zinc Virtue, scenting his panic as he writhed frantically. "We're going to take away your claws, your fangs, your venom, your strength..."

"You don't really need those," Garamingan explained. "They're just a sign of your deep insecurity. When you've learned to let go of them, you'll be so much happier."

"We've picked out a new body for you," I said. "It's a rabbit. A small, defenceless rabbit."

"You've got some real treats ahead," Garamingan said. "You've probably never eaten grass: you don't know how delicious it is."

"But that's not all. There's a special delicacy in a rabbit's diet." I kept my eye on Zinc Virtue; I had to avoid Garamingan's gaze to stop myself from bursting into laughter. "Rabbits eat their own shit!"

We paused to let this sink in. Zinc Virtue squirmed against his bonds.

"Violence is a product of masculinity, so we're abolishing that as well," Garamingan said. "It's the end of men! In future, everyone will have their own unique gender."

"Say goodbye to masculinity and the patriarchy," I said. "Say hello to a whole new world of perversion, full of different genders having sex in every combination."

"But not with you, because you'll be a neuter."

"Enjoy your last few minutes of manhood," I said. "Let's go!"

We hauled Zinc Virtue into town. A few people saw us, but they just gave us a "boys will be boys" glance. When we reached the nearest Morpher, we shoved him inside and selected the design that we'd concocted while waiting for him to show up. We chortled as he started changing into a tiny purple rabbit.

Sadly, it wasn't a permanent transformation. In a few hours, Zinc Virtue would be able to return to a Morpher and dial up a new shape. Nevertheless, we'd successfully hit back at him, showing that we wouldn't be cowed.

Our comments about taking away everyone's fangs and abolishing masculinity were merely jokes to scare him. These weren't council policies. Not yet, anyway. When we got home after restoring our own shapes, we learned that we'd been summoned to the council to explain ourselves. It was a chance to influence the councillors, and perhaps even steer any changes in the law.

What should we ask for?

"We need to explain that we aren't just being rebellious to meet girls," Garamingan said. "What's the key issue? It's the pressure on everyone to conform. The question is how to solve that."

"Ban all crosses," I said, indulging a fantasy of absolute power.

"That's anti-Christian, unless you extend it to other symbols as well," said Garamingan, "which means making a long list of things that aren't allowed. It's a recipe for arguments, because once you start doing that, where do you stop?"

"I suppose you'd have to ban everything," I said. "Allocate everyone a random shape, with no customisation allowed. Everyone would be different, so there'd be no conformity."

"But maybe it's a little extreme to force everyone into a random shape which they're not allowed to change."

"Is it?" I said, laughing. "I suppose you're right."

"I think the most popular change would be the least restrictive," Garamingan said. "At the moment, people have lots of freedom in choosing their own shape. It can be anything, as long as it's different from everyone else's. The problem is that different shapes can have the same features, like crosses."

"The crosses aren't the problem," I said. "They're the symptom. The underlying problem is that so many people have the same religion. That's the oppression."

"So if everyone had different religions, there wouldn't be an issue?" Garamingan asked.

"Absolutely! We just need a law saying that as well as choosing a unique body, people also have to choose a unique religion that's different from everyone else's."

"And since there've already been thousands of religions in history, there's plenty of inspiration to draw upon," Garamingan said. "It's a wild scheme."

"But it's in keeping with the spirit of Rainbow Village," I said. "If everyone must have different bodies, then why not different souls as well?"

Garamingan nodded. "After all, the most important thing is diversity."

"The Shapes of Wrath" is another 'if this goes on' story, in a similar vein to "The Equalisers" and "Pincushion Pete".

Today, diversity is a hot topic. It seems there is never enough diversity, as there are always complaints about domination by a particular gender, race, class, orientation, etc. The pressure is all one way: everyone argues for more diversity. In many situations, this is perfectly understandable. But I found myself wondering, "What if this goes on? How far can diversity stretch?"

And so I imagined a milieu where "it became compulsory for everyone to take a unique shape. When everyone looks different, there is no majority or minority. In a truly diverse society, there is no conformity or oppression."

Of course, it can't be that simple! Conformity and oppression operate in many ways.

A Hollywood pitch for a generic dystopia might be: "In a world where everyone must be the same, two rebels dare to be different." My story inverts this: "In a world where everyone must be different, two rebels dare to be the same."

And Then They Were Gone

Before she left her room, Samanda clutched her arms to make sure her dress sleeves were pulled all the way down. She grimaced, annoyed with herself for needing to check. Then she followed her parents out of the house, through the garden, to the limousine at the end of the drive. The chauffeur already had the engine running. Samanda disliked the ostentatious Bentley: she knew it would be tracked to its destination, updating the gossip sites' real-time celebrity database. When they arrived, the world could watch their every movement, and make supportive comments about how well they were dressed and how good they looked today – or not.

The limousine was wide enough to let all three of them sit comfortably in the back seat. It had myriad gadgets for films, music, Internet, and so on. But when Samanda tried to play some music, her mother reached out an arm to stop her.

"We have something important to tell you," Mum said. Her voice was raspy from the virus she'd been battling and the cigarettes she'd been smoking. It sounded nothing like the honeyed voice on all her hit singles with the Candy Belles. During her childhood, Samanda had listened to those songs obsessively: she'd heard her mother more often on record than in person.

"Another comeback?" Samanda guessed.

"Not exactly, but you never can tell." Mum smiled. "Who knows what might happen when we've uploaded?"

"When you've... *what?*"

"We're uploading," her father said. "We've been thinking about it for a while, but we decided to wait until you were old enough. Now that you're eighteen, we think you can manage without having us around –"

I spent most of my life without having you around, Samanda thought.

"– although we'll still be here. Electronically, good as new. Better than new!"

"But you're not old," Samanda protested. "You're not at death's door. You don't need to upload for years and years."

"Our best years are behind us," Dad said. "My football career is over, and I don't want to spend the rest of my life struggling with dodgy knees. I played for twenty years, pushing myself to the limit, playing through strains and injuries. It takes a toll. There was the time – well, you know the stories."

Yes, Samanda knew the stories. The most famous was the World Cup quarter-final when her father was injured late on. He couldn't be replaced because England had already used all three substitutes, so he kept going as best he could. In the last minute of the game, everyone heard the *crack* of his knee-joint as he made the crucial tackle that stopped Germany from scoring, thus winning the match for England.

"You're young, you take your health for granted," he continued. "You don't know what it's like to wake up in pain every day, knowing your career is behind you. You don't know what it's like to hate your body."

Oh, I know what it's like to hate my body, Samanda thought, resenting Dad's words even though she knew it wasn't his fault. She couldn't blame her parents for not understanding how she felt, when she hadn't told them.

"It just seems a bit drastic," she said. "Have you tried painkillers?"

He sighed. "Yes, but those don't let me play football again." His voice brightened. "When we upload, I'll have an electronic body, and I'll be able to play whenever I like. No getting tired, or injured, or ill. There's a football veterans league, and all kinds of other sports. It'll be great!"

His enthusiasm made Samanda feel mean-spirited for not wanting him to go.

"What about you, Mum?" she asked. "What will you be doing?"

Her mother said, "When I get my looks back, I can be a singer and an actress again. And there'll be fresh opportunities. It's a whole new world up there... But we'll still be here for you, darling. Don't worry about that."

"Thanks," said Samanda, trying to sound more grateful than resentful. During childhood she'd hardly seen her parents, as they'd always been dashing across the globe: making records, making films, going on tour, playing for England, spending a year at Atlético Madrid or Houston Dynamo. This would be little different – except more permanent.

The limousine arrived at the conference centre in Liverpool. A trip to a taxidermy convention hadn't sounded very exciting, but Samanda rarely turned down the chance to hang out with Mum and Dad. These opportunities didn't arrive often – not until recently. They'd spent more time together this month, to the point where Samanda wondered whether she could talk to them seriously at last, without distractions from photographers and agents and publicists. She'd assumed this was because her parents' careers were winding down. Now she realised that it was a farewell: their final days together in the flesh.

And this convention was full of flesh. They entered a vast hall divided into booths like fairground stalls. The booths contained snarling bears, startled squirrels, bats suspended on invisible threads... Samanda had never seen stuffed animals up close before. She wasn't prepared for how lifelike and sinister they appeared, as if poised to pounce. She'd expected something a bit more cute – maybe a tableau of dogs playing poker.

Her parents strode purposefully onward. Samanda let them get ahead, wanting time to think. Yet the prospect of Mum and Dad uploading was such a shock that she couldn't think straight: her thoughts bounced back and forth like a ball in a pinball game. What would it mean? In the twilight of their careers, her parents had endeavoured to retain their celebrity aura, becoming talent-show judges and charity campaigners. They were gossip-column staples. But soon they'd no longer be photographed at premieres, fashion shows, and the like. Even if they attended in hologram form, magazines weren't interested in those pictures. Holograms never had boob exposures or untimely zits, and couldn't be criticised for being too fat or too thin.

The postmortal realm had its own celebrity circuit. When they joined that, Mum and Dad would inevitably show less interest in the world below and its remaining occupants...

The convention hall had a stomach-churning smell of mothballs and chemicals, combined with fast food from the concession stands. The arena resonated with the noise of footsteps, conversations, and PA announcements: "Come to booth 15 for a live demonstration of frog mounting!"

Samanda soaked in the atmosphere and gazed at the exhibits, trying to absorb the experience in the hope of somehow transmuting it. Could this make a poem? A song lyric? *Yeah, like no one else has ever noticed how creepy these things are with their staring eyes.*

Self-doubt paralysed her. She remembered the reactions to the songs she'd recorded last year with her ex-boyfriend: "Perfect for psychological warfare." "If you die and your spirit hears this music ahead, then you know you're going to the wrong place and it's too late to repent." And those were the reviews that passed the civility filters screening out the worst abuse.

When she'd asked her mother how to deal with this, Mum had replied, "Just do what you like and ignore what people say."

Yet it wasn't so easy. Samanda wanted to create her own identity and be known for her own deeds, rather than forever being labelled as pampered celebrity offspring, merely somebody's daughter. And she knew from self-help guides that goals had to be measurable. She could only assess her progress by seeing how people described her.

Right now – she knew she shouldn't do this – she could pull out her phone and view the latest comments, unfiltered. The words stabbed at her: "Samanda Linnell is at a taxidermy convention. Maybe she's looking for a new skin. She sure needs one." "No, she's looking for a lover. The only way she'll ever get famous is by making a sex tape, and her best hope of a fuck is with a stuffed animal." "Oh, she's not so bad for a chubster. She could suck my cock – as a warm-up for someone hot."

It was like picking at her scars. She read on, feeling lacerated, until she forced herself to shove the phone back into her bag. Then she walked briskly through the rows of booths, trying to catch up with her parents.

As Samanda crossed the central concourse into the other half of the hall, she heard a commotion. People were chanting: "Tax the dead! Tax the dead!" She saw uniformed security guards breaking up a group of protestors, confiscating their placards. When the picketers were led away, she looked to see where they'd come from.

Her eyes widened at the sight of the exhibits on this side of the hall. They were human bodies! A whole row of them stood outside one booth, stiff and formal like an honour guard for some dignitary who hadn't yet arrived. In other booths, plastinated human figures were posed in everyday activities such as drinking wine and playing chess. The figures were all middle-aged or elderly – most of them dressed, a few naked.

Samanda lost all awareness of the bustle and noise inside the cavernous arena, as she suddenly realised why her parents had come to this convention. After they uploaded, they wanted their bodies preserved. The prospect was so bizarre that she could only giggle. What poses would they choose? Presumably her father would be dressed in his football kit, ready to kick a ball. Her mother might hold a microphone, and wear an outfit from her time in the Candy Belles.

Samanda strolled among the booths, examining the various accessories sold alongside the preservation process: the necessary cleaning materials, the plinths and props, the automation options. You could install recorded messages. You could put tiny cameras into the skull, to let the uploaded personality gaze out through its old eyes.

She looked for her parents, but failed to spot them. Perhaps they were closeted inside a private booth, discussing poses with one of the taxidermists.

The far end of the hall was less crowded. A tattooed bushy-bearded man sat behind a counter piled with leaflets advertising himself as 'Piers Dobrovsky, Plastinator to the Stars'.

"What was the protest about?" she asked.

"Tax campaigners," he said. "Dead people don't like paying taxes, because they don't use roads or schools or hospitals."

"Nobody likes paying taxes," Samanda said, conscious that she had no personal experience of it because she hadn't yet earned any of her own money.

"Too right." Dobrovsky gave her an appraising glance, encompassing everything from her short-cropped black hair down to her chunky flat shoes. "Do you fancy being plastinated?"

She laughed bitterly. "You're just like all the other guys: you only want me for my body."

"I get tired of doing old people." He spread his hands, and smiled. "One day I'd like to do someone younger – a different challenge."

"It would be a heck of a challenge to make me look good," Samanda said. "But go on. Tell me more. Describe what you'd do."

She wanted her parents to come looking for her, and find her talking to this plastinator. She'd tell them she was also planning to upload, and have her body preserved. And when they were appropriately horrified, she'd say, 'If it's wrong for me, how can it be right for you?' Then they'd change their minds about uploading, and they wouldn't leave her...

Dobrovsky ushered her into his booth, and activated a shimmering privacy curtain. "If we were seriously doing this," he said, "I'd ask you about your life – what you like to do, what you like to wear. For instance, is that your favourite dress? Would you want to wear it forever?"

"Certainly not," she said. She hated the sleeves, because she needed them.

Samanda expected him to ask, 'Then why are you wearing it now?', but he merely stood silently, waiting for her to speak and spill her soul.

She wished her phone would ring. It, too, stayed silent.

"Sometimes I wish I was Muslim so I could wrap myself up in a big black cocoon," said Samanda.

The last time she'd said this, it was to a school counsellor who kept staring at her breasts while she tried to explain why she felt like crap all the time. It hadn't helped.

Dobrovsky didn't have a creepster's hungry eyes. His gaze was neither avid nor sympathetic – just neutral. He clearly didn't care, and didn't expect anything from her. That made it easier to show him.

Samanda looked around and above to check the privacy curtain. Then she hitched up her left sleeve, revealing a network of scars on her arm. Some were pale and faded; others were red and inflamed. The scars crisscrossed each other, a palimpsest of pain.

"Could you plastinate this?" she demanded. "Or would it break the machine?"

He stooped to examine her skin. She saw no change in his expression. "It's not an obstacle," he said. "We can deal with all kinds of tattoos, piercings, and scarification."

Samanda frowned. By taking her seriously, he was calling her bluff. At last she said, "Give me a quote for the job."

She smiled fiercely, indulging the fantasy of getting herself uploaded and plastinated. She imagined the machines cutting an incision in her skull, scooping out her mind, and then preserving her flesh like a giant scab. Even the thought of it made her feel floaty and high, the same as the buzz she got from cutting herself. It would be the biggest rush ever.

But she knew how she always felt afterward. The sting of it, the self-hate. The shame, the fragile promises of never again.

Well, 'never again' wouldn't be a problem. She only had one body. If she left it behind, it wouldn't trouble her any more...

"If you'd like a quote, I'll need to see some ID to prove your age," Dobrovsky said. "Also, we have a code of conduct. There's a cooling-off period before anything drastic. Like plastination, for example."

"Sure, I understand." The scheme fell apart when confronted with reality. It was a ludicrous idea, anyway. What pose would sum up her life? Samanda had nothing to commemorate. She felt stupid and deflated. "I'm sorry for wasting your time."

"Don't be. I asked you, remember?"

"Then why did you ask?" she said, annoyed.

"You looked unhappy, and I thought you might need to talk," he said. "I used to be a tattooist. When you've been in that job for a while, you recognise the types of customers who wander by. Lots of people decide to get a tattoo because they already feel something, and they want a keepsake. But some people... Well, they try to do it the other way round. They wonder if getting a tattoo will be meaningful, and help them feel something."

Samanda tugged her sleeve back down, covering the scars. "And does it help them?" she asked.

"At first, I thought it did," Dobrovsky said. "Until they kept coming back."

"And now you're a plastinator," she said. "I guess no one ever comes back for another dose of that. But why is it so popular? This convention is huge. Why do so many people" – *like my parents* – "want to get stuffed?"

He said, "Nowadays, everyone has too much of everything. No matter how many tattoos or piercings or mementos you have, you can always get more, so it's never-ending. Taxidermy is different: you only have one body, and it's irreplaceable. So it has a rarity value. There's a fascination in something that you can only do once..."

As Dobrovsky elaborated on this theme, Samanda's phone rang. She gave him an apologetic glance. "Sorry, that's my mother. But thanks for talking to me."

She answered the phone. "Hi, Mum... Okay, I'll meet you at the car."

On their way home from the convention, Samanda listened as her parents prattled about all the plastination poses they'd seen, and all the costume designs they'd considered. Eventually, it became too much for her.

"This is silly," she said. "It's just a fad! Do you really think this craze for taxidermy will last? In a few years, there'll be stuffed corpses in attics and yard sales everywhere."

"If it's only a fad, we can always be buried later," her mother said. "You can stick us in the ground if we suddenly become unfashionable, or if it's too much of a chore to dust us."

Samanda rolled her eyes. Sometimes her parents could be aggravating beyond belief.

When they were away, she missed them. When they were here, she found them exasperating.

Could that be a song lyric? "You want them close / You push them away / You need them near / But not every day..."

Generic drivel, she told herself sternly. A true writer would describe something more honest and personal – such as the desperation of needing to cut herself. What would those lyrics be like?

Well, if she could express herself properly, she wouldn't need to self-harm in the first place.

So surely it was best to finally find the words, and speak to her parents. Tell them – no, *show* them – how she was suffering.

Yet what would she want Mum and Dad to do? She could ask them to stay with her, and not upload. But she had no idea how long it might take to sort herself out. How long could she ask her father to endure his damaged knees, waking in pain every day?

And if something awful happened – a car crash, a shooting, a meteor strike – then it would be Samanda's fault. Her parents would be permanently dead, having lost their chance at electronic immortality because their daughter couldn't grow up and stand on her own two feet.

No, it would be selfish to ask them not to go. *Let them upload,* she thought. *I'll manage. I'm eighteen – I need to start acting like an adult.*

But before they went, she should talk to them.

"How do you handle all the bad things that people say?" Samanda asked. She'd seen the latest comments: "The Linnells just took their daughter to a taxidermy convention. They've probably traded her in for something. A stuffed walrus would be a lot more decorative."

"Oh, I ignore it," Dad said, confidently and unhelpfully. "As a footballer, you're a hero when you win and an idiot when you lose. It changes every week, so how can it mean anything? It doesn't – it's just noise."

I'd like to be a hero for once, Samanda thought, *instead of always being the monster.*

"But the important thing," he continued, "is that when you're actually doing something, you focus completely on the moment. So you don't even think about anyone's reaction. When you're playing a match – "

"– or singing a song –" her mother put in.

"– or doing your own thing, you have to concentrate on that."

"Then afterward, people can say what they like. But you did your best at the time, and that's all anyone can do," Mum said.

Generic drivel, Samanda thought to herself. Yet what had she expected? At her age, she should know that her parents weren't all-wise and all-knowing. There was only one thing they could do for her.

"Give me a hug," she said, "while you still can."

And then they were gone.

In the following days, Samanda obsessively paced the empty house. Her parents' bodies hadn't even been delivered yet, and already they were creeping her out. She didn't want them in the lounge, or in any room that she regularly frequented. The best place would be the memorabilia wing, which held the medals, trophies, costumes, platinum discs and whatnot that her parents had accumulated in life. Yet even here, there were issues of tasteful placement and appropriate décor...

It would help if Mum and Dad, having lumbered her with this legacy, showed any interest in it. But since uploading, their minds were occupied elsewhere – adjusting to life after death, planning to remarry, and various other reasonable excuses. Samanda reckoned they viewed their old bodies as embarrassing relics, which they couldn't believe they'd ever cared about. Now, having shed their brutish carcasses, they had more lofty concerns.

When the wedding day arrived, Samanda sat on the sofa at home and donned her headset, making sure that the goggles and earpiece rested comfortably on her skin without chafing. With the flick of a switch, she ascended to the postmortal realm.

She arrived in a landscape of clouds, where a church nestled incongruously as though it had absent-mindedly fallen off the ground and drifted away. It was huge, its pristine walls smooth and gleaming. Joyful bells rang out, but there was no other noise: no annoying traffic or roadworks or aeroplanes. Nothing to spoil the big day. The perfection was spooky, emphasising the artificiality of the environment. Samanda entered the church and walked to her allocated pew, guided by flashing arrows overlaid on the virtual floor.

Twenty years ago, her parents had married 'till death us do part' – and now they were dead. So they were marrying again, with new vows for their old love.

Many of the guests were uploads, who appeared in a bewildering variety of avatar forms. Others, like Samanda herself, were visitors from the physical world; etiquette forbade them the more exotic manifestations, limiting them to an approximation of their real bodies. Samanda's avatar had skin as smooth and unblemished as a mannequin, allowing her to wear short sleeves for once. She kept having to quell the impulse to cover her exposed arms.

Samanda looked around, absorbing everything in the church's fabulous interior: the menagerie of guests, the angels in the choir, the stained-glass windows depicting cyber pioneers. The experience was so bizarre that it seemed unreal, like a glossy animated movie. Unlike the taxidermy convention, there were no obtrusive smells, no protestors making a nuisance of themselves. Everything was merely visual, rather than visceral.

She ought to feel something – her parents were getting married! But it didn't make her heart pound, or hit her in the gut. Was she empty inside? Had she lost all ability to care? Had her feelings drained out of her, like blood after too many cuts?

Samanda shuddered. Her avatar wobbled slightly, but no goose-pimples rose on its arms. Of course, this wasn't her domain. She was just a visitor, peering through the veil between life and death. Its permanent inhabitants would – she hoped – have stronger feelings, with simulated emotions in their simulated minds.

Maybe writing a lyric might help her make sense of things. Samanda wondered whether she could rhyme *romantic* with *pragmatic*. The wedding, as a social occasion, marked her parents' entry into postmortal society – where celebrity and status mattered just as much as on Earth. The event would be all over the gossip sites.

With a heroic effort of will, Samanda avoided delving into what people were saying. Remembering her parents' advice, she focused solely on the ceremony. She didn't want to spoil her mood by seeing something nasty. That was self-destructive behaviour.

Afterward, she waved Mum and Dad farewell as they disappeared on their digital honeymoon. They'd barely talked, as her parents had so many guests who wanted to congratulate them. Nevertheless, she let them go.

They were gone, again. They went further away every time.

Samanda pulled off her headset, and paced around the room to stretch her stiff muscles. The house looked drab, after the vivid colours of the virtual world. She turned on the TV to fill the oppressive silence.

Upstairs, in her bedroom, the temptation awaited. The blades lurked, promising their comforting ritual. She imagined herself sterilising metal with alcohol, then pressing it into her skin...

Yet seeing her parents casually toss their bodies aside had shocked her into valuing her own a little more.

She remembered Dobrovsky at the convention, and an idea occurred to her. Instead of amateurishly cutting herself, maybe she should get something professional done – a tattoo. It could be a football and a microphone, in memory of Mum and Dad, so that her parents would always be with her in the flesh. On her back, to show that she'd put them behind her.

How simple it sounded! But would a tattoo solve anything, or would it just begin a new cycle of addiction? Dobrovsky had warned her about the customers who kept coming back.

Perhaps she could turn the idea into a song instead. It was vivid and personal – definitely not generic – so ought to work as a song lyric. Or, if it didn't, her mistakes were better committed on paper than on skin.

She grabbed a pen and started scribbling. The first few lines came easily, until she wondered how many verses to write. After all, if a football and microphone were the only tattoos on her back, it implied that Mum and Dad were the only problems she needed to put behind her.

Slowly, Samanda shook her head. She shouldn't blame her parents for everything, no matter how much she wanted to.

What else? The gossip sites. A picture of an ugly troll could represent the venomous online world, so that made another verse.

Yet no one had ever forced her to look at those comments, or care about them. Her own behaviour was the problem. And there was an obvious image for that: a tattoo of a scar.

As she scrawled the final verse, Samanda's pen gouged into the paper until it tore. The song didn't come out right, not at first. Still, at least her ever-busy parents had shown her how to work hard. She'd have plenty of time to keep writing, while she waited for her scars to heal.

"And Then They Were Gone" was inspired by a TV documentary about taxidermy. I saw the documentary in 2006, but it took me several years to get around to writing a first draft. The final version was eventually published in 2017, eleven years after its initial spark. Yes, I have a ridiculously slow writing process!

For story purposes I needed the protagonist's parents to be celebrities whose careers were over, so I made her father a footballer and her mother a girl-group pop singer. It's not uncommon for footballers to marry pop stars. When I started writing, I knew of at least two examples of such marriages, which meant (in my own mind at least) that my characters weren't based on anyone specific. However, it must be acknowledged that there is one particularly famous example of a footballer/singer marriage, and it's easy to assume that my characters are an intentional reference to those specific persons. They're not, honestly. In retrospect, I regret not putting a little more distance between my characters and real celebrities. The problem is that I wanted to evoke a certain kind of celebrity milieu, and it's easier to do that with characters that resemble real people. (I know this sounds vague without names, but my point is that my story characters are not intended to reflect specific personages, so to name anyone here would be counterproductive.)

PINCUSHION PETE

On a bright but chilly summer morning in Edinburgh, Peter Lonsdale entered the campaign headquarters at his usual time of seven o'clock. No one else had arrived yet, but the computers had been active overnight, scanning the world's media for news stories and offensive terms. Pete glanced at the big screen, pleased to see that the trend lines still sloped downward for IDIOT, CRETIN, MORON and the rest. News items were spiking upward, as expected. This week marked the tenth anniversary of the Campaign Against Intellectual Discrimination, and Pete had spent the last few days writing articles and giving interviews.

He'd been so busy that he hadn't had time to examine the patchmakers' latest releases. A pile of padded envelopes teetered in his in-tray. Looking at these gave Pete a rush of anticipation. His hand reached for the pin-port at the base of his skull, stroking the plastic cap that protected the interface to his brain. *Later,* he told himself. The new patches weren't urgent; he had plenty already.

Pete began scanning through the email that had arrived overnight. He didn't need to: the secretaries could deal with it. But reading the mail kept him in touch with the public that the campaign existed to serve. Some of it came from mothers whose children had been diagnosed with Sub-Median Intelligence Syndrome. Some came from adults – or their carers – telling of difficulties in finding jobs, battling harassment, or obtaining the latest patches. Pete read fifty messages, his daily sample, carefully logging each by category and required action.

This data joined all the other statistics that the organisation collected every day. Meticulous analysis and sober language helped CAID to be taken seriously as a real institution, rather than just a bunch of angry people yelling. Yet the data had its own fascination, and Pete often spent hours delving into the numbers, investigating whether a reduction in idiophobic abuse was a genuine success, or correlated with a wider civility trend (which could be assessed by measuring comparable terms such as CRIPPLE, FAGGOT, BITCH), or simply a shift in language as trolls and bullies invented new insults that needed monitoring.

Today's email trawl took twenty-three minutes. *I think my reading speed has ticked upward again.* Pete smiled, contemplating how far he'd come from the childhood torment of trying to decipher words that just seemed to squirm into ever more baffling shapes.

His restless hands called up the latest news stories. A headline in the *Scottish Sentinel* caught his attention:

IS PINCUSHION PETE THE PATCHMAKERS' PUPPET?

"The Campaign Against Intellectual Discrimination is ten years old this week, but has it lost its way? CAID's leader, Peter Lonsdale, has frequently rebuffed accusations that he is too close to the gene-therapy industry. Today we reveal disturbing evidence that his ties to the industry are even closer than anyone suspected.

"Lonsdale has always proclaimed the benefits of gene therapy, which can boost intelligence at the lower end of the scale by repairing detrimental mutations. His IQ rose significantly after he received the first experimental 'patches', but he never forgot the prejudice he suffered in his youth. When he formed CAID, he famously said, 'If it's wrong to discriminate against anyone's race, gender, or sexuality, then it's just as wrong to discriminate against people's IQ.'

"According to CAID, the patches have reduced welfare dependency and boosted employment. Yet critics complain of an 'arms race', with people finding it harder to get jobs if they prefer not to use patches, or can't afford them, or suffer from untreatable conditions.

"Lonsdale declines to clarify which patches he uses himself. He says he doesn't want to endorse any particular product or manufacturer. But his reticence allows people to gain the impression that he only has a few patches: the ones from his youth, before he founded CAID.

"This is a long way from the truth. We have discovered that Lonsdale is an avid user of patches, and has installed a truly astonishing number. The manufacturers know that CAID's advocacy increases demand for their products, so they are keen to keep Lonsdale onside. They send him every new patch they develop, regardless of whether these are subsequently marketed.

"Lonsdale's nickname in the industry is Pincushion Pete – 'because there's always room to stick another one in'. Even the patchmakers don't know how many he has, because he uses patches from many different manufacturers. However, the scale of his usage is evident in brain-scan images taken earlier this year.

"Below, we show the scan of Lonsdale's brain. The image is not over-exposed: the saturation represents the magnitude of patch activity. For comparison, here is a scan of a typical patch user, showing much less activity...

"Clearly Lonsdale is not a disinterested advocate of patches. He isn't even a typical user; he looks much more like an addict. This has grave implications for the organisation he leads. Does CAID exist to fight discrimination, its original mission? Or is it now simply a marketing arm of the gene-therapy industry?

"CAID's current approach has been criticised as 'like trying to solve racism by making everyone white'. Can CAID really solve idiophobia just by making people smarter? There's always a bottom end of the scale. How clever must we all become?"

Although Pete resented criticism, he usually consoled himself by taking it as proof that CAID was important enough to be attacked. But when he reached the story's illustrations, his jaw dropped. *They're publishing pictures of my brain! How dare they?* It was an appalling breach of privacy.

And it was dreadful publicity. The brain-scan image summarised all the fulmination in one easy-to-understand picture. It would certainly go viral.

Pete needed to respond quickly. He opened the template for a press release, and wrote: "The article published in today's *Scottish Sentinel* contains personal images that clearly breach my privacy, violating medical confidentiality. I condemn this blatant intrusion into my healthcare. The journalist criticises the use of patches, but perhaps he needs an ethics patch to teach him right from wrong!

"As for my own patches, these include many that are marginal or obsolete. I'm not an addict. I simply function like a normal person, as do many of my peers who've also benefited from gene therapy.

"Why is this so objectionable? It's always an unattractive sight when people with privilege – whether that's intelligence or anything else – say, 'You're not allowed to have what we've got.' Why shouldn't we have it?

"This is a personal response. An official statement from CAID will follow, after a meeting of the Trustee Directors. Signed, Peter Lonsdale."

From the boardroom on the top floor, Pete saw Edinburgh Castle outlined against a blue sky dotted with shrieking gulls. Only five of the Trustees had been able to attend at such short notice – one by video-conference – but it was enough for a quorum.

"I'm really sorry that they've got hold of your brain images," said Hannah Mason, the Honorary Chair. She was a solid woman, with voluminous chestnut hair. "I'm sure it's an intrusion of privacy, and I'll ask our lawyers to see if there's anything we can do. But that won't solve the immediate problem. This looks bad..."

She paused, apparently expecting Pete to jump in. He didn't interrupt: he wasn't going to defend himself like someone who'd done something wrong.

Emboldened, Hannah continued, "That article said exactly what I've been thinking for a while. I tried to tell you before, but you didn't want to hear it. We've been putting too much emphasis on the patches, as if they're the answer to everything." Hannah's daughter suffered from a developmental disorder that scientists hadn't yet deciphered at the genetic level; no patches were available to treat it. "You said that the journalist needed to get an ethics patch –"

"That was a joke," Pete protested.

"But it showed an attitude that any deficiency can be solved – and *should* be solved – by an appropriate patch."

Pete said, "There's no such thing as an ethics patch."

"Not yet," said Parvinder Singh, the Honorary Treasurer. "As soon as they decide which genes are correlated to sociopathy, you can bet a so-called ethics patch will be on its way." He frowned, as though this was a threat to the accountancy profession.

"That's outside our remit," said Pete. "I don't think we're worried about discrimination against psychopaths."

"But we help to normalise the use of patches," Hannah said, "by turning low intelligence into a medical condition. The manufacturers have latched onto this, and now they're marketing patches for all sorts of things: procrastination disorder, acute akrasia, motivation deficit dysfunction..."

"Those are all outside our remit," Pete said impatiently, annoyed at the topic drift.

"Actually, I happen to know that you've had patches for several of those," Hannah said.

"Have I?" said Pete, surprised.

"The patchmakers send you their new lines straight from the lab. Later, the marketers decide how to promote them. The brain is a complex organ. If a patch boosts someone's IQ score, is that because they've become smarter, or because they're more motivated to try harder on the test?"

"What difference does it make?" asked Pete, drumming his fingers on the underside of the table.

Hannah sighed with exasperation. The sound set Pete on edge: it was exactly the kind of sigh he'd heard so often as a boy, when his carers grew frustrated at dealing with a "stupid cretin" or "witless wonder" or "fucking moron".

She said, "It expands the market. If a patch is targeted at people with low intelligence, then they're the only customers, and not many of them have money. But if a patch claims to reduce laziness and boost motivation, then lots more people will be interested in buying it."

"And that's a problem because...?"

"Because it turns people into hamsters on a wheel," said Parvinder. "What time did you get into the office this morning, Pete?"

"Seven o'clock," Pete said with pride.

"And the same last week and the week before, I take it. But you never used to arrive so early. Recently our doorman mentioned to me that in the old days, no one ever arrived before eight o'clock."

"CAID has grown a lot since then," said Pete. "There's more work to do."

"So you're arriving earlier because there's more work? Seems to me it's the other way round: there's more work, because you're arriving earlier and staying longer."

The walls of the boardroom were studded with plaques bearing testimonials from people helped by CAID. Whenever there was any dispute at the boardroom table, Pete always looked at the testimonials for reassurance he was doing the right thing.

"Even if that's true, why is it a problem?" Pete demanded. "If I arrive at seven, get more work done, and help more people, then why is that an issue?"

"Because it creates pressure on everyone else to do the same," Hannah said.

"I didn't notice anyone else arriving at seven o'clock," Pete retorted.

"Not yet," Hannah replied. "But that's the way things are going, with more and more people using more and more patches. We're supposed to be campaigning against discrimination, not campaigning to sell patches."

"Those are not mutually exclusive," said Pete.

"Neither are they identical," said Hannah.

Pete glanced up and down the table, searching for support. The Trustee Board had changed in recent years; as CAID grew larger, Pete had recruited professional expertise from across the charity sector. These new Trustee Directors were more independent than he'd anticipated.

Parvinder said, "Our strategic direction can be discussed another time. The more pressing issue is how we respond to the *Sentinel* article."

"There's no denying that it hurts our credibility and makes us look biased," said Hannah.

"I agree," said Parvinder.

Pete listened as this sentiment was echoed around the table: "Definitely." "We need to do something."

When everyone had issued their condemnation, silence fell. All the Trustees looked at Pete, waiting for him to speak.

Years ago, he wouldn't have understood what this silence meant. Now, with improved mental acuity, he realised that they were waiting for him to fall upon his sword. They hoped he would step aside gracefully, without the need for a messy coup. If he volunteered to resign, then CAID could concoct some face-saving formula and hope to minimise the damage.

Should I step aside? Or should I try to tough this out, and carry on?

Pete longed to fight. He saw the implications of Parvinder's casual statement that CAID's strategy could be discussed 'another time' – if Pete resigned, then the rest of the Board would be free to change how CAID operated. *It's my campaign,* he thought. *I founded it.* He felt deeply possessive.

Yet he wanted to preserve CAID, rather than tear it apart with a boardroom battle. And if he stepped aside voluntarily, then he might have more control over the circumstances, more influence in the interim, and more chance of a future return.

"Perhaps it would be best if I took a leave of absence," Pete said.

"I think that's a good idea," Hannah replied, with the air of someone trying not to sound too relieved. "And while you're away, you might want to think about how many patches you're using. Why not try reducing them? Then you could get off the hamster wheel, stop working so hard, and enjoy life a bit more."

Pete knew that Hannah's advice was well meant, but it annoyed him nonetheless. It wasn't her business how many patches he used. How would she like it if he commented on her weight?

"Working hard and enjoying life aren't mutually exclusive," said Pete.

"Neither are they identical," said Hannah.

Pete cleared his desk, shoving everything into carrier bags. He'd agreed with the Board that for the next month he wouldn't come into the office or speak to the media. Hannah would take charge. After a month they'd review the situation, and discuss whether Pete could return in some capacity. Pete knew that his departure might easily become permanent.

His throat tightened as he left CAID's headquarters. He turned and looked at the building: the gleaming fascia with CAID's logo of a crossed-out dunce's cap, the fresh white paint on the walls... Every few weeks, the latest mocking graffiti needed to be painted over.

The strong sunshine was disorientating. Pete never normally stood in the street in the middle of the day. He was either working, or eating in the canteen. Recently he'd even stopped going to the canteen, in favour of eating sandwiches at his desk while scrolling through news and stats.

Might as well go home, he thought. At home, he could monitor the media reaction to the *Sentinel* story and his withdrawal from CAID.

Yet when he arrived at his fifth-floor apartment in Edinburgh's Old Town, he found himself reluctant to check for updates. It would be too frustrating to see events unfold without being able to react to them. Of course, he could respond in a personal capacity, rather than on behalf of CAID. But that might prolong the life of the story, in a cycle of claim and counter-claim. Best to leave it entirely, as he'd agreed, and hope that the fuss would die down.

Pete's fingers twitched. They wanted to be busy at something. He picked up his guitar, and switched on the amplifier. He strummed a few chords in a fast, choppy rhythm. Only when he heard these staccato chords did he realise how tense he was after the morning's events. After a few seconds, the auto-accompaniment kicked in, providing a bassline and a simple 4/4 drum pattern.

Pete had played guitar all his life. As a boy, he'd played by ear, helped by people showing him chord shapes or teaching him a particular song. Back then, he hadn't understood key signatures on anything other than an intuitive level. As the patches gradually boosted his intelligence, he learned to read tab notation, and then full scores. He started studying music theory, discovering different scales, and listening to the music of other cultures. He created his own compositions.

He'd customised the accompaniment algorithm that was harmonising with him now. After establishing a chord cycle, Pete stopped playing rhythm and switched to lead guitar, improvising a melody built from blocks of riffs.

As he played, his mind drifted back to the meeting, and Hannah's suggestion of reducing the patches he used. Instinctively, he rebelled against the notion. Yet he recognised the practical argument for it. He could flush out all the obsolete patches, along with some of the experimental ones that he suspected weren't adding much. He could cut down to a core of necessary boosts, and get a new brain-scan image to prove he'd done it.

Then he could return to CAID, with a narrative of having overcome his addiction. He would be like a celebrity coming out of rehab, all cleaned up. Everything would return to normal, and he could continue his work of campaigning against discrimination.

He was tempted. He wanted to return to CAID: there was still so much work to do, so many people who needed him.

Yet the thought of removing any patches filled him with dread. He couldn't be certain which patches were marginal or superfluous. The brain was a complex organ: everything interacted with everything else.

Pete only knew that if he removed too many patches, he would regress. He wouldn't be able to write complex music, or tinker with auto-accompaniment algorithms. He'd sink back to the old days of playing guitar by ear, barely understanding the chord patterns.

The thought made him shiver, as it brought back all his childhood memories of living in a fog of incomprehension, of being taunted and bullied... *I won't go back to that. I won't!*

Rationally, he knew that no one was telling him to pull out every single patch and revert to his old condition. He could selectively reduce them, leaving him enough comprehension to function in society and perform some kind of useful work.

Yet why should he have to remove any? What was wrong with his brain-scan? *It's all relative.*

In the early days of gene therapy, having even one patch was unusual. Moralists campaigned against them, romanticising the glorious natural states of stupidity and schizophrenia and all the rest. Writers appealed to vague notions of authenticity, constructing carefully contrived narratives in which the natural condition was noble and soulful, ignoring the vastly more common circumstances in which it was brutal and degrading. CAID retorted that this was like saying disabled people should boycott wheelchairs and learn to cherish immobility.

Eventually it became obvious that gene therapy delivered practical benefits. A new definition of normal arrived: a small number of patches for those who needed them.

Still, why stop there? As more patches arrived, more people could be helped in ever more ways.

I'm not abnormal, Pete told himself. *I'm the new normal, but people just don't know it yet.*

The thought reassured him. *I don't need to remove any of my patches. So I won't.*

He was still playing guitar, his fingers on autopilot while he cogitated. During his improvisation, the accompaniment algorithm had started incorporating his riffs into the harmonic structure, filling out the sound with piano and brass. Now Pete triggered a 'delay' effect to create a sustained chime. Each new note resounded above the echoes of the last. The collective sound grew louder and louder as the auto-accompaniment helped to swell the climactic crescendo. The music thundered in orchestral ecstasy.

Then silence.

Pete put down his guitar, switched off the equipment, and made himself a cup of peppermint tea. While the teabag infused, he wondered what to do next. Deciding not to remove his patches was all very well, but it meant that he probably couldn't return to CAID. What should he do instead?

No obvious answer occurred to him. CAID had been his life for the past ten years. Its absence left a void that Pete didn't want to contemplate.

His hands, eager to be busy, started emptying the carrier bags he'd brought home from the office. It was mostly the detritus of years working at the same desk: coffee mug, ergonomic wrist-rest, headache pills, and so on.

One bag held the padded envelopes that had been waiting in his in-tray. *New patches!* Pete felt the same sense of delight that had always accompanied childhood trips to the fair.

He spent an absorbing hour reading the specifications for the experimental patches, analysing the manufacturers' claims with a connoisseur's eye. Some of the patches duplicated ones that he already possessed, or were contra-indicated because they conflicted with his existing infrastructure. However, several appeared to be feasible additions. One in particular enticed him with the promise of noticeably incrementing his IQ.

Pete washed his hands, then opened the sterile package containing the pin-like delivery device. With practised ease, he opened the port at the base of his skull and guided the pin into it. A delicious tingle rushed through him.

The patch needed a little while to take effect. Tonight, he might have vivid dreams as it began readjusting his brain.

And then tomorrow, or the day after, he'd decide what to do next. Pete smiled, confident that soon he would think of something clever.

"Pincushion Pete" is another 'if this goes on' tale, sitting alongside "The Equalisers" and "The Shapes of Wrath". There's a historical tendency (at least in the West) for various forms of discrimination to become less acceptable over time: for instance, racism, sexism, and homophobia are now largely frowned upon. Yesterday's commonplace prejudice becomes today's unacceptable discrimination.

And in science fiction, today's commonplace prejudice can become tomorrow's unacceptable discrimination. Nowadays it's inappropriate to call someone a faggot or a cripple (or other words that I daren't even write here), but no one will complain if you call someone an idiot. Yet why is it acceptable to discriminate against the stupid? No one can help being born with low intelligence, any more than they can help being born black, female, homosexual, or disabled. So in the world of "Pincushion Pete", it has become illegal to discriminate against anyone on the grounds of their intelligence.

The satirical side of the story reframes stupidity as a medical condition: Sub-Median Intelligence Syndrome. A pressure group, the Campaign Against Intellectual Discrimination, tries to redefine insults (e.g. 'idiot', 'cretin', 'moron') as being hate speech. After all, one measure of the traction of anti-discrimination campaigns is their success at reshaping public discourse and making particular words unacceptable.

The story's serious side examines what it means to treat intelligence as an anti-discrimination issue. This thematic territory has been explored before, for instance in "Harrison Bergeron" by Kurt Vonnegut. However, that story used the method of 'levelling down': social equality is achieved by handicapping the more intelligent members of society.

In my story, I decided to go the opposite route of 'levelling up': less intelligent people can use gene-therapy patches to boost their intelligence, in the same way that disabled people can use wheelchairs to improve their mobility.

There is a well-known story about boosting intelligence – "Flowers for Algernon" by Daniel Keyes. But in that story, the intelligence boost doesn't work very well: it's only temporary.

For my purposes, I assumed that the intelligence boost would work properly. It delivers a permanent benefit by improving a subnormal intelligence to a normal level. It doesn't create geniuses, but it does alleviate stupidity.

This raises a moral issue: to what extent is stupidity an affliction that should be cured?

My answer was influenced by another writer's story, which treated a similar theme in a way that I disagreed with. I'm reluctant to name the specific story, because I'm sure the other writer had what seemed like valid reasons for their choice. And there's little point in arguing, because stories are fiction, and fictional situations aren't evidence. Part of an author's craft lies in shaping the details of a story to support the desired conclusion. When this is done skilfully, the reader barely even notices how the dice have been loaded. In the other writer's story, I thought the circumstances seemed carefully contrived, in a manner that failed to reflect the true context. So I responded with my own story, presenting the circumstances in a different way to support my own interpretation of the issues.

Finally, aside from the moral aspect, there are the practical consequences. If intelligence-boosting patches become available, how does that affect society? What are the knock-on effects? What is the new normal?

EROSION

Let me tell you about my last week on Earth...

Before those final days, I'd already said my farewells. My family gave me their blessing: my grandfather, who came to England from Jamaica as a young man, understood why I signed up for the colony programme. He warned me that a new world, however enticing, would have its own frustrations. We both knew I didn't need the warning, but he wanted to pass on what he'd learned in life, and I wanted to hear it. I still remember the clasp of his fingers on my new skin; I can replay the exo-skin's sensory log whenever I wish.

My girlfriend was less forgiving. She accused me of cowardice, of running away. I replied that when your house is on fire, running away is the sensible thing to do. The Earth is burning up, and so we set forth to find a new home elsewhere. She said – she shouted – that when our house is on fire, we should stay and fight the flames. She wanted to help the fire-fighters. I respected her for that, and I didn't try to persuade her to come with me. That only made her all the more angry.

The sea will douse the land, in time, but it rises slowly. Most of the coastline still resembled the old maps. I'd decided that I would spend my last few days walking along the coast, partly to say goodbye to Earth, and partly to settle into my fresh skin and hone my augments. I'd tested it all in the post-op suite, of course, and in the colony simulator, but I wanted to practise in a natural setting. Reality throws up challenges that a simulator would never devise.

And so I travelled north. People stared at me on the train. I'm accustomed to that – when they see a freakishly tall black man, even the British overcome their famed (and largely mythical) reserve, and stare like scientists assessing a new specimen. The stares had become more hostile in recent years, as waves of African refugees fled their burning lands. I was born in Newcastle, like my parents, but that isn't written on my face. When I spoke, people smiled to hear a black guy with a Geordie accent, and their hostility melted.

Now I was no longer black, but people still stared. My grey exo-skin, formed of myriad tiny nodules, was iridescent as a butterfly's wings. I'd been told I could create patterns on it, like a cuttlefish, but I hadn't yet learned the fine control required. There'd be plenty of shipboard time after departure for such sedentary trifles. I wanted to be active, to run and jump and swim, and test all the augments in the wild outdoors, under the winter sky.

Scarborough is, or was, a town on two levels. The old North Bay and South Bay beaches had long since drowned, but up on the cliffs the shops and quaint houses and the ruined castle stood firm. I hurried out of town and soon reached the coastal path – or rather, the latest incarnation of the coastal path, each a little further inland than the last. The Yorkshire coast had always been nibbled by erosion, even in more tranquil times. Now the process was accelerating. The rising sea level gouged its own scars from higher tides, and the warmer globe stirred up fiercer storms that lashed the cliffs and tore them down. Unstable slopes of clay alternated with fresh rock, exposed for the first time in millennia. Piles of jagged rubble shifted restlessly, the new stones not yet worn down into rounded pebbles.

After leaving the last house behind, I stopped to take off my shirt, jeans and shoes. I'd only worn them until now as a concession to blending in with the naturals (as we called the unaugmented). I hid the clothes under some gorse, for collection on my return. When naked, I stretched my arms wide, embracing the world and its weather and everything the future could throw at me.

The air was calm yet oppressive, in a brooding sulk between stormy tantrums. Grey clouds lay heavy on the sky, like celestial loft insulation. My augmented eyes detected polarised light from the sun behind the clouds, beyond the castle standing starkly on its promontory. I tried to remember why I could see polarised light, and failed. Perhaps there was no reason, and the designers had simply installed the ability because they could. Like software, I suffered feature bloat. But when we arrived at our new planet, who could guess what hazards lay in store? One day, seeing polarised light might save my life.

I smelled the mud of the path, the salt of the waves, and a slight whiff of raw sewage. Experimentally, I filtered out the sewage, leaving a smell more like my memories from childhood walks. Then I returned to defaults. I didn't want to make a habit of ignoring reality and receiving only the sense impressions I found aesthetic.

Picking up speed, I marched beside the barbed wire fences that enclosed the farmers' shrinking fields. At this season the fields contained only stubble and weeds, the wheat long since harvested. Crows pecked desultorily at the sodden ground. I barged through patches of gorse; the sharp spines tickled my exo-skin, but didn't harm it. With my botanist's eye, I noted all the inhabitants of the little cliff-edge habitat. Bracken and clover and thistles and horsetail – the names rattled through my head, an incantation of farewell. The starship's seedbanks included many species, on the precautionary principle. But initially we'd concentrate on growing food crops, aiming to breed strains that would flourish on the colony world. The other plants... this might be the last time I'd ever see them.

It was once said that the prospect of being hanged in the morning concentrated a man's mind wonderfully. Leaving Earth might be almost as drastic, and it had the same effect of making me feel euphorically alive. I registered every detail of the environment: the glistening spiders' webs in the dead bracken, the harsh calls of squabbling crows, the distant roar of the ever-present sea below. When I reached a gully with a storm-fed river at the bottom, I didn't bother following the path inland to a bridge; I charged down the slope, sliding on mud but keeping my balance, then splashed through the water and up the other side.

I found myself on a headland, crunching along a gravelled path. An ancient noticeboard asked me to clean up after my dog. Ahead lay a row of benches, on the seaward side of the path, much closer to the cliff edge than perhaps they once had been. They all bore commemorative plaques, with lettering mostly faded or rubbed away. I came upon a legible one that read:

In memory of Katriona Grady
2021 - 2098
She Loved This Coast

Grass had grown up through the slats of the bench, and the wood had weathered to a mottled beige. I brushed aside the detritus of twigs and hawthorn berries, then smiled at myself for the outdated gesture. I wore no clothes to be dirtied, and my exo-skin could hardly be harmed by a few spiky twigs. In time I would abandon the foibles of a fragile human body, and stride confidently into any environment.

I sat, and looked out to sea. The wind whipped the waves into white froth, urging them to the coast. Gulls scudded on the breeze, their cries as jagged as the rocks they nested on. A childhood memory shot through me – eating chips on the seafront, a gull swooping to snatch a morsel. Within me swelled an emotion I couldn't name.

After a moment I became aware of someone sitting next to me. Yet the bench hadn't creaked under any additional weight. A hologram, then. When I turned to look, I saw the characteristic bright edges of a cheap hologram from the previous century.

"Hello, I'm Katriona. Would you like to talk?" The question had a rote quality, and I guessed that all visitors were greeted the same way; a negative answer would dismiss the hologram so that people could sit in peace. But I had several days of solitude ahead of me, and I didn't mind pausing for a while. It seemed appropriate that my last conversation on a dying world would be with a dead person.

"Pleased to meet you," I said. "I'm Winston."

The hologram showed a middle-aged white woman, her hair as grey as riverbed stones, her clothes a tasteful expanse of soft-toned lavender skirt and low-heeled expensive shoes. I wondered if she'd chosen this conventional self-effacing look, or if some memorial designer had imposed a template projecting the dead as aged and faded, not upstaging the living. Perhaps she'd have preferred to be depicted as young and wild and beautiful, as she'd no doubt once been – or would like to have been.

"It's a cold day to be wandering around starkers," she said, smiling.

I explained that I no longer needed clothes. "I'm going to the stars!" I said, the excitement of it suddenly bursting out.

"What, all of them? Do they make copies of you, and send you all across the sky?"

"No, it's not like that." However, the suggestion caused me a moment of disorientation. I had walked into the hospital on my old human feet, been anaesthetised, then – quite some time later – had walked out in shiny new augmented form. Did only one of me leave, or had others emerged elsewhere, discarded for defects or optimised for different missions? *Don't be silly,* I told myself. *It's only an exo-skin. The same heart still beats underneath.* That heart, along with the rest of me, had yesterday passed the final pre-departure medical checks.

"We go to one planet first," I said, "which will be challenge enough. But later – who knows?" No one had any idea what the lifespan of an augmented human might prove to be; since all the mechanical components could be upgraded, the limit would be reached by any biological parts that couldn't be replaced. "It does depend on discovering other planets worth visiting. There are many worlds out there, but only a few even barely habitable."

I described our destination world, hugging a red-dwarf sun, its elliptical orbit creating temperature swings, fierce weather, and huge tides. "The colonists are a mixed bunch: naturals who'll mostly have to stay back at base; then the augmented, people like me who should be able to survive outside; and the gene-modders – they reckon they'll be best off in the long run, but it'll take them generations to get the gene-tweaks right." There'd already been tension between the groups, as we squabbled over the starship's finite cargo capacity, but I refrained from mentioning it. "I'm sorry – I've gone on long enough. Tell me about yourself. Did you live around here? Was this your favourite place?"

"Yorkshire lass born and bred, that's me," said Katriona's hologram. "Born in Whitby, spent a few years on a farm in Dentdale, but came back – *suck my flabby tits* – to the coast when I married my husband. He was a fisherman, God rest his soul. *Arsewipe!* When he was away, I used to walk along the coast and watch the North Sea, imagining him out there on the waves."

My face must have showed my surprise.

"Is it happening again?" asked Katriona. "I was hacked a long time ago, I think. I don't remember very much since I died – I'm more of a recording than a simulation. I only have a little memory, enough for short-term interaction." She spoke in a bitter tone, as though resenting her limitations. "What more does a memorial bench need? Ah, I loved this coast, but that doesn't mean I wanted to sit here forever... *Nose-picking tournament, prize for the biggest bogey!*"

"Would you like me to take you away?" I asked. It would be easy enough to pry loose the chip. The encoded personality could perhaps be installed on the starship's computer with the other uploaded colonists, yet I sensed that Katriona wouldn't pass the entrance tests. She was obsolete, and the dead were awfully snobbish about the company they kept. I'd worked with them in the simulator, and I could envisage what they'd say. "Why, Winston, I know you mean well, but she's not the right sort for a mission like this. She has no relevant expertise. Her encoding is coarse, her algorithms are outdated, and she's absolutely riddled with parasitic memes."

Just imagining this response made me all the more determined to fight it. But Katriona saved me the necessity. "That's all right, dear. I'm too old and set in my ways to go to the stars. I just want to rejoin my husband, and one day I will." She stared out to sea again, and I had a sudden intuition of what had happened to her husband.

"I'm sorry for your loss," I said. "I take it he was never" – I groped for an appropriate word – "memorialised."

"There's a marker in the *fuckflaps* graveyard," she said, "but he was never recorded like me. Drowning's a quick death, but it's not something you plan for. And we never recovered the body, so it couldn't be done afterward. He's still down there somewhere..."

It struck me that if Katriona's husband had been augmented, he need not have drowned. My limbs could tirelessly swim, and my exo-skin could filter oxygen from the water. As it would be tactless to proclaim my hardiness, I cast about for a neutral reply. "The North Sea was all land, once. Your ancestors hunted mammoths there, before the sea rose."

"And now the sea is rising again." She spoke with such finality that I knew our conversation was over.

"God speed you to your rest," I said. When I stood up, the hologram vanished.

I walked onward, and the rain began.

I relished the storm. It blew down from the northeast, with ice in its teeth. They call it the lazy wind, because it doesn't bother to go round you – it just goes straight through you.

The afternoon darkened, with winter twilight soon expiring. The rain thickened into hail, bouncing off me with an audible rattle. Cracks of thunder rang out, an ominous rumbling as though the raging sea had washed away the pillars of the sky, pulling the heavens down. Lightning flashed somewhere behind me.

I turned and looked along the coastal path, back to the necropolis of benches I had passed earlier. The holograms were all lit up. I wondered who would sit on the benches in this weather, until I realised that the lightning must have short-circuited the activation protocols.

The holograms were the only bright colours in a washed-out world of slate-grey cloud and gun-dark sea. Images of men and women flickered on the benches, an audience for Nature's show. I saw Katriona standing at the top of the cliff, raising her arms as if calling down the storm. Other figures sat frozen like reproachful ghosts, tethered to their wooden anchors, waiting for the storm to fade. Did they relish the brief moment of pseudo-life? Did they talk among themselves? Or did they resent their evanescent existence, at the mercy of any hikers and hackers wandering by?

I felt I should not intrude, so returned to my trek, slogging on as the day eroded into night. My augmented eyes harvested stray photons from lights in distant houses and the occasional car gliding along inland roads. To my right, the sea throbbed with the pale glitter of bioluminescent pollution. The waves sounded loud in the darkness, their crashes like a secret heartbeat of the world.

The pounding rain churned the path into mud. My mouth curved into a fierce grin. Of course, conditions were nowhere near as intense as the extremes of the simulator. But this was *real*. The sight of all the dead people behind me, chained to their memorials, made me feel sharply alive. Each raindrop on my face was another instant to be cherished. I wanted the night never to end. I wanted to be both here and gone, to stand on the colony world under its red, red sun.

I hurried, as if I could stride across the stars and get there sooner. I trod on an old tree branch that proved to be soggy and rotten. My foot slid off the path. I lurched violently, skidding a few yards sideways and down, until I arrested my fall by grabbing onto a nearby rock. The muscles in my left arm sent pangs of protest at the sharp wrench. Carefully I swung myself round, my feet groping for toe-holds. Soon I steadied myself. Hanging fifty feet above the sea, I must have only imagined that I felt spray whipping up from the waves. It must have been the rain, caught by the wind and sheeting from all angles.

The slip exhilarated me. I know that makes little sense, but I can only tell you how I felt.

Yet I couldn't cling there all night. I scrambled my way across the exposed crags, at first shuffling sideways by inches, then gaining confidence and swinging along, trusting my augmented muscles to keep me aloft.

My muscles gripped. My exo-skin held. The rock did not.

In mid-swing, I heard a *crack*. My anchoring left hand felt the rock shudder. Instinctively I scrabbled for another hold with my right hand.

I grasped one, but nevertheless found myself falling. For a moment I didn't understand what was happening. Then, as the cliff-face crumbled with a noise like the tearing of a sky-sized newspaper, I realised that when the bottom gives way, the top must follow.

As I fell, still clinging to the falling rock, I was drenched by the splashback from the lower boulders hitting the sea below me. Time passed slowly, frame by frame, the scene changing gradually like an exhibition of cels from an animated movie. The hefty rock that I grasped was rotating as it fell. Soon I'd be underneath it. If I still clung on, I would be crushed when it landed.

I leapt free, aiming out to sea. If the cliff had been higher, I'd have had enough time to get clear. But very soon I hit the water, and so did the boulder behind me, and so too – it seemed – did half of the Yorkshire coast.

It sounded like a duel between a volcano and an earthquake. I flailed frantically, trying to swim away, not understanding why I made no progress. Only when I stopped thrashing around did I realise the problem.

My right foot was trapped underwater, somewhere within the pile of rocks that came down from the cliff. At the time, I'd felt nothing. Now, belatedly, a dull pounding pain crept up my leg. I breathed deeply, gulping air between the waves crashing around my head. Then I began attempting to wriggle free, with no success.

I tried to lift up the heavy boulders, but it was impossible. My imprisoned foot kept me in place, constricting my position and preventing me from finding any leverage. After many useless heaves, and much splashing and cursing, I had to give up.

All this time, panic had been building within me. As soon as I stopped struggling, terror flooded my brain with the fear of drowning, the fear of freezing in the cold sea, the fear of more rocks falling on top of me. My thoughts were overwhelmed by the prospect of imminent death.

It took long minutes to regain any coherence. Gradually I asserted some self-command, telling myself that the panic was a relic of my old body, which wouldn't long have survived floating in the North Sea in winter. My new form was far more robust. I wouldn't drown, or freeze to death. If I could compose myself, I'd get through this.

I concentrated on my exo-skin. Normally its texture approximated natural skin's slight roughness and imperfections. Now my leg became utterly smooth, in the hope that a friction-free surface might allow me to slip free. I felt a tiny amount of give, which sent a surge of hope through me, but then I could pull my foot no further. The bulge of my ankle prevented any further progress. Even friction-free, you can't tug a knot through a needle's eye.

Impatient and frustrated, I let the exo-skin revert to default. I needed to get free, and I couldn't simply wait for the next storm to rattle the rocks around. My starship would soon leave Earth. If I missed it, I would have no other chance.

At this point I began wondering whether I subconsciously wanted to miss the boat. Had I courted disaster, just to prevent myself from going?

I couldn't deny that I'd in some sense brought this on myself. I'd been deliberately reckless, pushing myself until the inevitable accident occurred. Why?

Thinking about it, as the cold waves frothed around me, I realised that I'd wanted to push beyond the bounds of my old body, in order to prove to myself that I was worthy of going. We'd heard so much of the harsh rigours of the destination world, and so much had been said about the naturals' inability to survive there unaided, that I'd felt compelled to test the augments to their limit.

Unconsciously, I'd wanted to put myself in a situation that a natural body couldn't survive. Then, if I did survive, that would prove I'd been truly transformed, and I'd be confident of thriving on the colony world, among the tides and hurricanes.

Well, I'd accomplished the first stage of this plan. I'd got myself into trouble. Now I just had to get out of it.

But how?

I had an emergency radio-beacon in my skull. I could activate it, and no doubt someone would come along to scoop me out of the water. Yet that would be embarrassing. It would show that I couldn't handle my new body, even in the benign conditions of Earth. If I asked for rescue, then some excuse would be found to remove me from the starship roster. Colonists needed to be self-reliant and solve their own problems. There were plenty of reserves on the waiting list – plenty of people who hadn't fallen off a cliff and got themselves stuck under a pile of rocks.

The same applied if I waited until dawn and shouted up to the next person to walk along the coastal path. No, I couldn't ask for rescue. I had to save myself.

Yet asserting the need for a solution did not reveal its nature. At least, not at first. As the wind died down, and the rain softened into drizzle, I found myself thinking coldly and logically, squashing trepidation with the hard facts of the situation.

I needed to extract my leg from the rock. I couldn't move the rock. Therefore I had to move my leg.

I needed to move my leg, but the foot was stuck. Therefore I had to leave my foot behind.

Once I realised this, a calmness descended upon me. It was very simple. That was the price I must pay if I wanted to free myself. I thought back to the option of calling for help. I could keep my foot, and stay on Earth. Or I could lose my foot, and go to the stars.

Did I long to go so badly?

I'd already decided to leave my family behind and leave my girlfriend. If I jibbed at leaving a mere foot, a minor bodily extremity, then what did that say about my values? Surely there wasn't even a choice to make; I merely had to accept the consequences of the decision I'd already made.

And yet I delayed and delayed, hoping that some other option would present itself, hoping that I could evade the results of my choices.

I'm almost ashamed to admit what finally prompted me to action. It wasn't logic or strong-willed decisiveness. It was the pain from my squashed foot, a throbbing that had steadily intensified while I mulled the possibilities. And it was no fun floating in the cold sea, either. The sooner I acted, the sooner I could get away.

I concentrated upon my exo-skin, that marvel of programmable integument, and commanded it to flow up from my foot. Then I pinched it into my leg, just above my right ankle.

Ouch! Ouch, ouch, ouch, owwww!

Trying to ignore the pain, I steered the exo-skin further in. I wished I could perform the whole operation in an instant, slicing off my foot as if chopping a cucumber. But the exo-skin had limits, and it wasn't designed to do this. I was stretching the spec already.

Soon – sooner than I would have hoped – I had to halt. I needed to access my pain overrides. It had been constantly drilled into us that this was a last resort, that pain existed for a reason and we shouldn't casually turn it off. But if amputating one's own foot wasn't an emergency, I didn't ever want to encounter a true last resort. I turned off the pain signals.

The numbness intoxicated me. What a blessing, to be free from the hurts of the flesh! In the absence of pain, the remaining tasks seemed to proceed more swiftly. Soon the exo-skin had completely cut through the bone, severing my lower leg and sealing off the wound. Freed from the rock-fall, I swam away and dragged myself ashore. There I collapsed into sleep.

When I woke, the tide had receded, leaving behind a beach clogged with fallen clumps of grass, soggy dead bracken, and the ubiquitous plastic trash that was humanity's legacy to the world. The pain signals had returned – they could only be temporarily suspended, not permanently switched off. For about a minute I tried to live with my lower calf's agonised protestations; then I succumbed to temptation and suppressed them.

As I tried to stand up, I discovered that I was now lop-sided. At the bottom of my right leg I had some spare exo-skin, since it no longer covered a foot. I instructed the surplus material to extend a few inches into a peg-leg, so that I could balance. I shaped the peg to avoid pressing on my stump, with the force of my steps being borne by the exo-skin higher up my leg.

I tottered across the trash-strewn pebbles. I could walk! I shouted in triumph, and disturbed a magpie busy pecking at the new shoreline's freshly revealed soil. It chittered reprovingly as it flew away.

Then I must have blacked out for a while. Later, I woke with a weak sun shining in my face. My first thought was to return to the landslip and move the rocks to retrieve my missing foot.

My second thought was – *where is it?*

The whole coast was a jumble of fallen boulders. The cliff had been eroding for years, and last night's storm was only the most recent attrition. I couldn't tell where I'd fallen, or where I'd been trapped. Somewhere in there lay a chunk of flesh, of great sentimental value. But I had no idea where it might be.

I'd lost my foot.

Only at that moment did the loss hit home. I raged at myself for getting into such a stupid situation, and for going through with the amputation rather than summoning help, like a young boy too proud to call for his mother when he hurts himself.

And I felt a deep regret that I'd lost a piece of myself I'd never get back. Sure, the exo-skin could replace it. Sure, I could augment myself beyond what I ever was before.

But the line between man and machine seemed like the coastline around me: constantly being nibbled away. I'd lost a foot, just like the coast had lost a few more rocks. Yet no matter what it swallowed, the sea kept rising.

What would I lose next?

I turned south, back toward town, and walked along the shoreline, looking for a spot where I could easily climb from the beach to the path above the cliff. Perhaps I could have employed my augments and simply clawed my way up the sheer cliff-face, but I had become less keen on using them.

The irony did not escape me. I'd embarked on this expedition with the intent of pushing the augments to the full. Now I found myself shunning them. Yet the augments themselves hadn't failed.

Only I had failed. I'd exercised bad judgement, and ended up trapped and truncated. That was my entirely human brain, thinking stupidly.

Perhaps if my brain had been augmented, I would have acted more rationally.

My steps crunched on banks of pebbles, the peg-leg making a different sound than my remaining foot, so that my gait created an alternating rhythm like the bass-snare drumbeat of old-fashioned pop music. The beach smelled of sea-salt, and of the decaying vegetation that had fallen with the landslip. Chunks of driftwood lay everywhere.

The day was quiet; the wind had dropped and the tide was out, so the only sounds came from my own steps and the occasional cry of the gulls far out to sea. Otherwise I would never have heard the voice, barely more than a scratchy whisper.

"Soon, my darling. Soon we'll be together. Ah, how long has it been?"

I looked around and saw no one. Then I realised that the voice came from low down, from somewhere among the pebbles and the pervasive trash. I sifted through the debris and found a small square of plastic. When I lifted it to my ear, it swore at me.

"*Arsewipe! Fuckflaps!*"

The voice was so tinny and distorted that I couldn't be sure I recognised it. "Katriona?" I asked.

"How long, how long? Oh, the sea, the dear blessed sea. Speed the waves..."

I asked again, but the voice wouldn't respond to me. Maybe the broken chip, which no longer projected a hologram, had also lost its aural input. Or maybe it had stopped bothering to speak to other people.

Now I saw that some of the driftwood planks were slats of benches. The memorial benches, which over the years had inched closer to the eroding cliff-edge, had finally succumbed to the waves.

Yet perhaps they hadn't succumbed, but rather had finally *attained* their goal – or would do soon enough, when the next high tide carried the detritus away. I remembered the holograms lighting up last night, how they'd seemed to summon the storm. I remembered Katriona telling me about her husband who'd drowned. For all the years of her death, she must have longed to join him in the watery deeps.

I strode out toward the distant waves. My steps grew squelchy as I neared the waterline, and I had to pick my way between clumps of seaweed. As I walked, I crunched the plastic chip to shreds in my palm, my exo-skin easily strong enough to break it. When I reached the spume, I flung the fragments into the sea.

"Goodbye," I said, "and God rest you."

I shivered as I returned to the upper beach. I felt an irrational need to clamber up the rocks to the cliff-top path, further from the hungry sea.

I'd seen my own future. The exo-skin and the other augments would become more and more of me, and the flesh less and less. One day only the augments would be left, an electronic ghost of the person I used to be.

As I retrieved my clothes from where I'd cached them, I experienced a surge of relief at donning them to rejoin society. Putting on my shoes proved difficult, since I lacked a right foot. I had to reshape my exo-skin into a hollow shell, in order to fill the shoes of a human being.

Tomorrow I would return to the launch base. I'd seek medical attention after we lifted off, when they couldn't remove me from the colony roster for my foolishness. I smiled as I wondered what similar indiscretions my comrades might reveal, when it was too late for meaningful punishment. What would we all have left behind?

What flaws would we take with us? And what would remain of us, at the last?

Now we approach the end of my story, and there is little left. As I once helped a shadow fade, long ago and far away, I hope that someday you will do the same for me.

"Erosion" was sparked by a trip to the seaside. I walked on a cliff-top path by the coast. Beside the path stood a long row of benches, all facing out to sea, and all bearing memorial plaques. Each bench was dedicated to someone who had died, or sometimes two people — say, a husband and wife. Some of the plaques contained quotations, or short messages composed by the relatives of the deceased.

The path stretched out ahead, and likewise the benches went on and on. After a while, the effect became vaguely oppressive. It was like walking through a graveyard, with the commemorative plaques resembling the inscriptions on gravestones.

Memorial benches are common. After that seaside walk, I began noticing them all the time, and reading the plaques. And eventually it occurred to me that a commemorative plaque is severely limited in what it can say. (How do you summarise a life in a couple of sentences?) Surely technology could do a better job. I envisaged a memorial plaque augmented by a computer chip containing the encoded mind of the deceased, projecting a hologram so that anyone sitting on the bench could converse with the recorded personality.

A hologram of a dead person is like an electronic ghost. I imagined that when no one was around — when the weather was too stormy for walkers to sit on the benches — the holograms might activate themselves in order to further their own concerns. Maybe they would welcome the gales, calling in the wind and waves to erode the coast on which they stood... In my mind I had an image of a ghostly hologram standing on a cliff edge, summoning the storm.

I built the rest of the story around that image.

ABOUT THE AUTHOR

Ian Creasey was born in 1969 and lives in Yorkshire, England. He began writing when rock and roll stardom failed to return his calls. His first story appeared in 1999, and since then he has sold numerous stories to magazines and anthologies.

His spare time interests include hiking, gardening, and conservation volunteering: anything to get him outdoors and away from the computer screen.

If you've enjoyed *The Shapes of Strangers*, the author's earlier collections *Maps of the Edge* and *Escape Routes from Earth* are also available. Details of these and other publications are on his website: www.iancreasey.com, where you are also invited to download some audio recordings and sign up for the author's mailing list.

You can also follow Ian on Twitter: @ian_creasey.

New from NewCon Press

Rachel Armstrong – Invisible Ecologies

The story of Po, an ambiguously gendered boy who shares an intimate connection with a nascent sentience emerging within the Po delta: the bioregion upon which the city of Venice is founded. Carried by the world's oceans, the pair embark on a series of extraordinary adventures and, as Po starts school, stumble upon the Mayor's drastic plans to modernise the city and reshape the future of the lagoon and its people.

David Gullen – Shopocalypse

A Bonnie and Clyde for the Trump era, Josie and Novik embark on the ultimate roadtrip. In a near-future re-sculpted politically and geographically by climate change, they blaze a trail across the shopping malls of America in a printed intelligent car (stolen by accident), with a hundred and ninety million LSD-contaminated dollars in the trunk, buying shoes and cameras to change the world.

Kim Lakin-Smith – Rise

It's time to act. Now is the time to throw off the shackles of opression and RISE
People of Earth, too long have we lived in fear, too long have we suffered at the hands of our conquerors. Now is the time to strike back. Now is the time to seize our freedom. JOIN US!
Before it's too late.

Simon Morden – Bright Morning Star

A ground-breaking take on first contact from scientist and novelist Simon Morden. Sent to Earth to explore, survey, collect samples and report back to its makers, an alien probe arrives in the middle of a warzone. Exposed to both the best and worst of humanity, the AI probe faces challenges far beyond the parameters of its programming, and is forced to improvise in ways that will reshape the future of our world.

NewCon Press Novellas

Released in sets of four, each novella is an independent stand-alone story. Each set is linked by shared cover art, split between the books, providing separate covers that link to form a single image greater than the parts.

Set 1: Science Fiction
Novellas by Alastair Reynolds, Simon Morden, Anne Charnock, Neil Williamson.
Cover art by Chris Moore

Set 2: Dark Thrillers
Novellas by Simon Clark, Alison Littlewood, Sarah Lotz, Jay Caselberg.
Cover art by Vincent Sammy

Set 3: The Martian Quartet
Novellas by Jaine Fenn, Eric Brown, Liz Williams, Una McCormack.
Cover art by Jim Burns

Set 4: Strange Tales
Novellas by Gary Gibson, Adam Roberts, Ricardo Pinto, Hal Duncan.
Cover art by Ben Baldwin

Set 5: The Alien Among Us
Novellas by Dave Hutchinson, Philip Palmer, Adam Roberts, Simon Morden.
Cover art by Peter Hollinghurst

Each novella is available separately in paperback or as a limited numbered hardback edition, signed by the author. Each set is available as a strictly limited lettered slipcase set, containing all four of the books as signed dust-jacketed hardbacks and featuring the combined artwork as a wrap-around.

www.newconpress.co.uk

Immanion Press

Purveyors of Speculative Fiction

Venus Burning: Realms by Tanith Lee

Tanith Lee wrote 15 stories for the acclaimed *Realms of Fantasy* magazine. This book collects all the stories in one volume for the first time, some of which only ever appeared in the magazine so will be new to some of Tanith's fans. These tales are among her best work, in which she takes myth and fairy tale tropes and turns them on their heads. Lush and lyrical, deep and literary, Tanith Lee created fresh poignant tales from familiar archetypes. ISBN 978-1-907737-88-6, £11.99, $17.50 pbk

A Raven Bound with Lilies by Storm Constantine

The Wraeththu have captivated readers for three decades. This anthology of 15 tales collects all the published Wraeththu short stories into one volume, and also includes extra material, including the author's first explorations of the androgynous race. The tales range from the 'creation story' *Paragenesis*, through the bloody, brutal rise of the earliest tribes, and on into a future, where strange mutations are starting to emerge from hidden corners of the earth. ISBN: 978-1-907737-80-0 £11.99, $15.50 pbk

The Lightbearer by Alan Richardson

Michael Horsett parachutes into Occupied France before the D-Day Invasion. Dropped in the wrong place, badly injured, he falls prey to two Thelemist women who have awaited the Hawk God's coming, attracts a group of First World War veterans who rally to what they imagine is his cause, is hunted by a troop of German Field Police, and has a climactic encounter with a mutilated priest who believes that Lucifer Incarnate has arrived...*The Lightbearer* is a unique gnostic thriller, dealing with the themes of Light and Darkness, Good and Evil, Matter and Spirit. ISBN 9781907737763 £11.99 $18.99

http://www.immanion-press.com
info@immanion-press.com